R.I.S.E.

R.D. BRADY

BOOKS

BY R.D. BRADY

The A.L.I.V.E. Series
A.L.I.V.E.
D.E.A.D.
R.I.S.E.
S.A.V.E.
Into the Cage
Into the Dark

The Nola James Series
Surrender the Fear
Escape the Fear
Tackle the Fear
Return the Fear

The Belial Series
The Belial Stone
The Belial Library
The Belial Ring
The Belial Recruit
The Belial Children
The Belial Origins
The Belial Search
The Belial Guard
The Belial Warrior
The Belial Plan
The Belial Witches
The Belial War
The Belial Fall
The Belial Sacrifice

Vinci Books

vinci-books.com

Published by Vinci Books Ltd in 2024

1

Copyright © R.D. Brady 2019

The author has asserted their moral right to be identified as the author of this work in accordance with the Copyright, Designs and Patents Act 1988
This work is a work of fiction. Names, characters, places and incidents are the product of the author's imagination or are used fictitiously. Any resemblance to actual persons, living or dead, places and incidents is entirely coincidental.
All rights reserved. No part of this publication may be copied, reproduced, distributed, stored in any retrieval system, or transmitted in any form or by any means, including photocopying, recording, or other electronic or mechanical methods, nor used as a source for any form of machine learning including AI datasets, without the prior written permission of the publisher.
The publisher and the author have made every effort to obtain permissions for any third party material used in this book and to comply with copyright law. Any queries in this respect should be brought to the attention of the publisher and any omissions will be corrected in future editions.
A CIP catalogue record for this book is available from the British Library.
Paperback ISBN: 9781036700300

Printed and bound in Great Britain by Clays Ltd, Elcograf S.p.A.

CHAPTER 1

HUNTSVILLE, ALABAMA

1961

Janet Fairfax took the rollers out of her daughter's hair, arranging the curls around her face. Face to face, they sat at the makeup table, an almost identical pair in profile. "Now, just don't let them see how smart you are. And don't tell them when they're wrong."

Matilda Fairfax looked up from the book in her lap. It was Wernher von Braun's *Project MARS: A Technical Tale*. "Mother, they want me to work for them. I'm pretty sure they want to know I have a brain in my head."

Janet's lips tightened, a sight Matilda was all too familiar with. "Matilda, this may be your last chance to find a husband."

Matilda opened her mouth to respond, but her mother held up a hand, holding her off. "No, you listen to me. I know you're a smart girl. But you are going to be a lonely girl. You need to find yourself a man. And no man is going to marry a woman who reads books on rocketry for fun."

Then he's not the man for me, Matilda thought but wisely kept to herself. This was an old argument.

Not that Janet didn't love her daughter. Matilda knew her mother loved her. She just didn't understand her. For Matilda, though, being married was not the ultimate goal in life, which set her apart from most of the girls her age, and all of their mothers. She wasn't against marriage, necessarily. She just wanted to marry a man who viewed her intelligence as a benefit, not a character flaw.

For Janet Fairfax, however, a high IQ was the equivalent of having a scarlet letter branded across her chest. Matilda was her only daughter. It had been bad enough when, as a toddler, she'd started correcting her father when he explained how things worked. But then Matilda had skipped grades and never seemed interested in playing with any of the girls. She tinkered away in the basement, building little contraptions. Janet knew how much those little contraptions meant to her daughter. But she also knew how difficult life could be for a woman on her own.

Janet turned the chair around so that Matilda could see her reflection in the mirror. Soft curls framed her delicate face. Her blue eyes peeked out from underneath her fringe. A blue ribbon was tied up on the side of her head. The blue of her dress further accentuated the blue of her eyes.

Her mother smiled. "You look lovely. And I have no doubt that you will find a husband on that base."

Matilda rolled her eyes. A husband was not what she was looking for. But her mother looked happy. And Matilda had to admit that she did look pretty for a change. So she said nothing except, "Thank you, Mother."

There wasn't much that happened in Huntsville, Alabama. It was a small town in rural America. It had its share of problems and had been a military manufacturing hub in 1940. In 1941, however, it became a central research area for the U.S. rocket program. In 1950, Huntsville led the field in rocketry, leading to the development of the Redstone, Jupiter, and Pershing missiles.

But the residents liked to think that Huntsville, Alabama, was the smartest town in all of America. Why? Because Huntsville, Alabama, had the George C. Marshall Space Flight Center (MSFC), the U.S. government's civilian rocketry and spacecraft propulsion research center.

Von Braun had actually come to Huntsville two years before the Marshall Space Center was created. He and his team of scientists had worked at the Redstone Arsenal, where they successfully developed a modified Redstone rocket called a Jupiter-C to launch Explorer I, America's first orbiting satellite. It was at Marshall that the Saturn V launch vehicle, the super booster that would propel Americans to the Moon, was developed under the guidance of Wernher von Braun.

Huntsville was also as red-blooded and patriotic as any other city in the United States. There'd been some grumbling when the first of the German scientists had arrived. But as success built upon success, the grumbling slowly began to go quiet, especially when it came to beating the Russians into space. There wasn't an American alive who didn't want the U.S. to beat the Russians to the Moon.

And all of those hopes were pinned on the man who President Eisenhower had named to run NASA: Wernher von Braun.

And Matilda was about to meet him.

She smoothed down her blue dress, pressing down the edges of her white collar before running a quick hand over her hair. She'd chosen the blue dress with the white polka dots, but now she was rethinking her choice. Maybe she should've gone with something a little more somber. After all, at eighteen, she would be one of the youngest employees at NASA.

This dress probably makes me look like I'm on my way to an afternoon at the movies.

She took a breath, pushing away her doubts. She wasn't one who was normally bothered by self-doubt. Since the age of three, she'd been telling people what they were doing wrong whenever they did it wrong. It had not endeared her to her teachers ... or her parents, for that matter. But her chess teacher had been thrilled, and once it was understood that her brain worked at a much higher level than those around her, she'd been forgiven oversights of decorum ... for the most part.

At the age of seventeen, Matilda had already graduated from college. While she'd been written up in the paper and the town had proudly proclaimed her the new genius on the block, her mother had mourned the fact that she would never find a husband.

Matilda, though, worried she would never find a job. Women in the sciences were not common. A woman as young as she was in the field? Well, Matilda had never heard of any.

But both mother and daughter had been elated when Matilda had been invited to apply for a job at the Army base. Matilda because she couldn't believe that Wernher von Braun had actually extended the invitation to her personally. Her mother's excitement had a decidedly different angle: She had visions of handsome, muscular soldiers surrounding her daughter day and night. She overheard her mother talking to her father, saying that if Tilda couldn't find a husband on the Army base, then there was simply no helping her.

Tilda tried not to let the remarks sting, but being she was still thinking about it weeks later, she supposed she'd failed on that count. She shook her head. This was not the train of thought she should be thinking about right now. Reaching up, she pulled the bow out of her hair and shoved it into the pocket of her dress. Then she smoothed down her hair once again. That was better. Less like a girl out for an afternoon on the town and more of a woman ready to take on whatever task was set in front of her.

Or at least, that's what she hoped.

As she reached Room 217, she paused in front of the door. It was at the end of the hall and looked just like all the other doors on the floor. But Tilda knew this door was different. This door was the door to the future that she'd dreamed of. Taking a breath, she knocked.

"Come in." The voice was strong and masculine, with a very heavy Austrian accent.

She pulled open the door and stepped into the room. There was a desk sitting in front of her that was empty, the door beyond it open.

"Come on back."

Walking past the desk, she stood in the open doorway. The man behind the desk looked up with a smile. Blond hair and bright blue eyes looked back at her warmly. The man stood up and walked around the desk, towering over Tilda. "Miss Fairfax, it is a pleasure to meet you."

As she reached out her hand, she marveled at how at ease she felt in the man's presence. This was a man who was her intellectual superior. For once in her life, she would not be the smartest one in the room. And more than anything, she was looking forward to learning from him. "Dr. von Braun, it's a pleasure to meet you as well."

The scientist, who had just one month ago created the Mercury 3, the rocket that sent the first American astronaut, Alan Shepard, on a suborbital flight on May 5, 1961, the scientist who America had pinned its hopes on getting to the Moon before the Russians, smiled back at her. "Please call me Wernher."

He gestured to the corner of the room. She was so focused on von Braun that she hadn't realized there was someone else in here with them. Although as she got her first look at him, she wondered how that was possible.

He was the most beautiful man she'd ever seen.

Tall with a muscular build, his cheekbones were sharp under piercing blue eyes. They were so blue she wondered about the lighting or if she was turning into one of those women from the romance novels her mother read.

"Matilda Fairfax, I'd like to introduce you to Joseph Watson, my right-hand man. We three are going to accomplish great things together."

CHAPTER 2

PRESENT DAY

CANSO, NOVA SCOTIA

Nervousness ran along Dr. Maeve Leander's skin like an electrical current. She knew it was a delayed reaction to everything that had occurred in New Mexico. An image of the Kecksburg charging at her wafted through her mind.

She cringed, closing her eyes as if she could hide away from the image, but it was just replaced by others: Alvie in the containment unit, about to be loaded onto a train headed to who knew where by Martin Drummond; the large winged creature that attacked the chopper that had nearly taken Maeve, Chris, and a dozen others when they'd burst free from the Archuletta; and finally, Agaren, the large Gray whom Maeve had first seen at Area 51 when he'd caused a distraction allowing Maeve, the triplets, and Alvie to escape detection, and whom they'd liberated from Dulce as well.

Those hours leading up to that fight, and through it, had felt like the longest in Maeve's life. Afterwards, they had spent hours shifting from cars to planes and back to cars again before coming to a small camp that looked like a deserted summer camp rather than a safe house.

Dr. Greg Schorn, one of Maeve's closest friends and former colleague from Wright-Patterson Air Force Base, stepped out of one of the SUVs carrying Iggy, the Maldek who'd saved his and Norah Tidwell's life. Greg met her gaze, the moonlight flashing off his glasses. He gave Maeve a tight smile before carrying the wounded Iggy into one of the buildings. Norah walked quickly next to them and disappeared into one of the cabins.

Maeve had looked over the wound, and despite the amount of blood, it was actually pretty shallow. If they kept it clean, Iggy should be all right.

The triplets were chasing Hope, their black-and-white Labrador retriever mix, in the area in front of the cabins. They had too much energy after being cooped up for too long. Alvie was with them but not joining in. The triplets were Alvie's clones, created at Area 51 only a year ago. Alvie was twenty-nine years old, but his height of just under four feet made him seem so much younger. He had a disproportionately large head that came to a point at his chin. He had two large black eyes over two holes that served as his nose and a very small mouth.

And he was gray in color. The triplets looked identical to him except for Snap, the only girl, who had thin wispy white hair.

Alvie and Maeve had been raised together as brother and sister, although somewhere along the way, her role had shifted to a more maternal one. It was an unusual upbringing, but she could not imagine her life without him.

And now, she couldn't think of anything she could do to help him.

The triplets had been spared most of the danger, but Alvie had been held by Martin for days. And Maeve held no illusions that he was treated well during that time. The burns on his body were evidence of the cruelty he'd been exposed to. Maeve watched Alvie, but for the first time in their lives together, he was keeping his thoughts from her. He had been doing so ever since she'd removed him from the containment unit.

Maeve tried not to feel hurt, but it wasn't working. But she knew Alvie had been through a lot. He needed time to process. Alvie was not fully human. He was half human and half gray alien. And all good. Cruelty wasn't something he was used to.

And while he hadn't shared what had happened, she knew it was harsh. She wasn't sure what kind of lasting damage Martin Drummond had done to him. Although Maeve wasn't a violent woman, she promised herself that Martin would pay for what he had put her family through.

An arm slipped around her waist. She looked up into Chris Garrigan's blue eyes. A former Air Force captain, he had been in charge of Alvie's security at Wright-Patterson. And he was also the reason she, Alvie, and the triplets were still alive. "He'll be okay. We just need to give him time."

Maeve leaned in to Chris, soaking up his warmth. She nodded her head but couldn't speak past the ball of emotion that suddenly appeared in her throat.

A throat cleared behind them. Maeve glanced back at the round African American gentleman who stood there. Jasper Jenkins cleared his throat again. "Sorry to interrupt, but I thought you might want to get everyone settled."

Her gaze shifting to the triplets and Alvie, she squeezed Chris's arm. "Let them play a little longer. I'll go see what the situation is."

Chris kissed her cheek. "Okay."

Jasper led Maeve into one of the cabins. She braced herself, expecting spiderwebs, rat droppings, and dirt. She was pleasantly surprised. Someone had recently cleaned it. She could still smell the lemon cleaner. There were two bunk beds and two cots, along with a bathroom at the back. A small stack of clothes had been placed on the bunk at the front.

"This is great. Thanks." Maeve sank onto the nearest bunk, looking through the clothes. There were pajamas and new sweats for all of them, which was good because they were all desperately in need of a change of clothes.

"There's shampoo, soap, and everything else you'll need in the bathroom. If you need any—" Jasper's words cutting off, his eyes widening as he stared behind her.

Maeve looked over her shoulder.

Agaren stood in the doorway. He was six feet tall, with a large triangular-shaped skull and gray skin tone. His black eyes offered no clue to his thoughts. But the slightest movement of his small chin toward Jasper told Maeve he was communicating with him.

"Um, yeah, so I'll leave you two alone?" Jasper looked at Maeve for confirmation.

She stood. "It's fine."

Agaren stepped into the room and to the side to allow Jasper to pass. Jasper paused in the doorway before heading outside.

Nerves fluttered through Maeve's stomach. She gripped her hands tightly behind her back. "How are you?"

"Good. It is good to be free. Thank you."

It was shocking hearing the words coming out of his mouth. Maeve had assumed that his communication would be telepathic as well. "You speak?"

The large gray inclined his head. "It took a great deal of

time to figure out how to. It is a very rudimentary form of communication, but eventually I was able to master it. Although it is not entirely comfortable."

Maeve wanted to be insulted by his interpretation of speech, but the fact that he was correct stopped her. Although humans did believe that they communicated mainly through speech, nonverbal communication was more indicative and communicative of how humans actually felt and what they intended than the spoken word.

Plus, being Maeve now understood how Alvie and the triplets communicated, she had to admit it was a much more comprehensive way of getting one's thoughts across. She could feel how Alvie felt when he asked questions that conveyed so much more than just the question itself. She could tell when he asked why if he was curious, scared, excited, or all of the above. With humans, if you just went from the spoken word, all you knew was that they were curious. But really, could just one characteristic describe the motivation for a human's behavior or questions?

"I am all right with telepathic communication. I've had a great deal of practice," she said with a small smile.

Yes, you have. Alvie is a remarkable individual, he said switching to telepathic communication with a feeling of gratitude.

Although worried about Alvie, the first feeling she felt when thinking go him was love. He was her heart. "He is. I care a great deal about him."

And he you.

There was a link between Alvie and the alien in front of her. Unlike Alvie, Agaren was pure Gray. He'd been captured by Martin decades ago and held all that time. Yet he had approved when she had protected Alvie over him. She looked him right in the eyes. *"Who is he?"*

Agaren did not feign ignorance at what she was truly asking. *He is the key to humanity's peace or their destruction. I fear now that recent events have pushed your fate closer to annihilation.*

Mouth dropping open, it was a struggle to hold back the shiver his words elicited. "Why?"

I am part of a council. Our job is to monitor Earth and its development. You are a very young planet. Only a few billion years old. Yet your species has been invasive. You have overtaken all of your resources, using them to the brink of depletion. You have destroyed large swaths of your own population. Your aggressive ways concern the Council and have for centuries.

Once again she wanted to argue, but she knew what he said was true. When *Homo sapiens* became the dominant hominid on the planet, they had destroyed much along their way. Australia had been teeming with giant animals before humans stepped foot on its shores. Two thousand years later, all those large beautiful beasts had disappeared. The same phenomenon was observed in Madagascar.

In fact, there had been three waves of extinction tied to human behavior. The first wave of extinctions was caused by the spread of foragers. The second wave accompanied the spread of farmers. And the third wave has proven the deadliest to the planet, caused by pollution spewing into the environment at an unprecedented rate.

Experts estimated that at humankind's current rate of resource consumption, we'd kill off between 200 and 2,000 animal species annually and that climate change would result in between 10 and 20% reductions in global production of food in the next five to twenty-five years, not to mention the coastal areas that would become flooded and areas of the world that, due to the heat, would be completely uninhabitable for humans. So Maeve could not argue that the Council had no right to be concerned.

Agaren's voice once again appeared in her mind. *I must*

return to the Council and explain about my absence. They will know what I have experienced, what I have seen. There is no way to keep it from them, and I would not want to anyway. Truth is always the way forward, but I fear it will push them away from humanity.

"What happens then?" She asked.

They may decide that humans no longer deserve to be protected. That they are an invasive species that needs to be, at the very least, contained, at worst, removed.

A chill rolled over Maeve and this time she did shiver, wrapping her arms around her stomach. "Removed?"

He nodded. *It has happened before. But you and Alvie, the other humans who have risked much to protect him and his clones, you are the hope. I will stress this with the Council.*

"And if they don't take your word for it?" She asked.

There have been twenty-three hominids on this planet. Homo sapien sapiens will fall like the others.

Maeve sucked in a breath.

The door opened, and the triplets rushed into the room. They sprinted for the nearest bed, clambered on, and began to jump with happy squeals.

His head tilted to the side, Agaren watched them for a moment before walking over to them. The triplets all went still, looking up at him with their small mouths hanging open.

Raising his pointer finger, Agaren pressed it gently to the middle of each of their foreheads. Snap, Crackle, and Pop all smiled and closed their eyes. Pop opened his eyes first and reached up for Agaren. The slight widening of Agaren's eyes indicated his surprise at the motion. After a moment's hesitation, he reached out his arms.

That was all the encouragement Pop needed. He hopped into them. For a moment, Agaren stumbled back before his arms closed around the little alien hybrid. And then a smile formed on his face as well.

Alvie appeared in the doorway. Agaren stared at him, and

the hair on Maeve's arms stood on end. She knew they were having a conversation. Maeve said nothing, just watched in silence. Then Alvie broke the contact. He walked over to Maeve and took her hand, which gave Maeve the distinct impression that he had just picked a side.

Maeve prayed that for his own sake it was the right one.

CHAPTER 3

SEATTLE, WASHINGTON

A soft rain fell against the hood of Martin's white BMW X6. It had rained every day since he'd been back in Seattle. After that first night and the visit from Tatiana and Dietrich, he'd thought about leaving. But he knew that wherever he went, they would follow. There was no getting away from them.

There never had been.

He pulled into a parking spot in front of the old warehouse. It had been erected in 1973 as a furniture manufacturing building before it had finally gone bust in the late 1990s. It had sat empty and abandoned for nearly twenty years before Martin purchased it and had it refurbished. It was one of two dozen hubs he'd created across the country.

The one in New Mexico had been the largest. Losing that base stung, but they had all the data. He supposed that was the most important part. And the destruction of the base had also offered some new data. Creatures that they had had locked away for years had suddenly come to life. A few had escaped the facility, but most had been killed.

Martin sat in his car, drumming his fingers on the steering wheel. The creature he truly wanted had not been killed in the explosion. No, the one they called Alvie had been rescued. *Damn you, Tilda.*

He'd honestly thought she was dead. Matilda Watson was good. He would give her that much. And being he'd thought she was dead for years, his new goal was to make sure she lived up to that belief.

But it wasn't the sudden appearance of Tilda that weighed on his mind. No, it was the resurrection of Joseph. Seeing him at the train station had been like seeing a ghost. He hadn't aged a day. Which could mean only one thing …

Stepping out of the car, he hurried into the warehouse. He pulled open the old door, noting the cobwebs in the corner of it. He hurried through the old factory's reception area. Plastic chairs served as a waiting area for former clients while an old linoleum desk stood directly across from the main doors. The sign for Hanley's Furniture was still displayed behind it. Another door led into the old warehouse.

Martin pushed through and stepped into a different world. Steel reinforced walls surrounded him on four sides. An airlock door was directly in front of him. After an eye scan and entering a password, the door slid open. While from the outside the warehouse looked like a decrepit old building, the inside had every modern convenience. In fact, the outside was simply a shell. They had cleared out the entirety of the inside of the warehouse and built a new interior, complete with walls and ceiling.

And while the area around the warehouse may have looked abandoned, he had been under surveillance for two blocks. Every car and pedestrian within five miles of the warehouse was inspected. If the individuals continued on their way, they would never think the derelict warehouse was anything but abandoned. But if anyone dared to try to enter the warehouse or even its property, well, that would not end well for them.

Entering the main hub of the warehouse, the low hum of computers and work greeted him. On the far wall to his right were servers encased in refrigerated glass containers. In front of them were a dozen cubicles where his analysts worked. On his left was a long line of glass walls holding his office, and then in the back was his small apartment. On the other side was a small lounge area. It contained three leather couches, a couple of beat-up chairs, and a small kitchen area.

He ignored all of the analysts and headed for his office. He stepped into the room, tapping a button on the console on his desk that would darken the glass around him. No one would be able to see in, but he would be able to see everything happening outside the room. Shaking off his jacket, he hung it on the stand by the door.

Stacy Mal hustled in. She placed a coffee on the desk in front of him. At forty-two years of age, Stacy still dressed like the college kid she had been when Martin had recruited her. She wore her blonde hair in a ponytail, a Harvard sweatshirt, jeans, and Converse sneakers. From the back, she could easily be mistaken for a college kid. But from the front it was clear from the lines in her face that she had lived a life.

Placing two files on the desk in front of him, next to the coffee, she said, "I have something for you."

Martin took a seat behind the desk and pulled one of the files close. He scanned the filename: Sandra Gillibrand. It took him a moment to place it. The case out in Kansas. It had been a D.E.A.D. case. Two science experiments from Area 51, the Blue Boys had targeted the son at the home. It was the farthest east the creatures had traveled. Sandra Gillibrand was the mother and had taken down one of the Blue Boys, not an easy task.

But the second one had been taken down by a creature that had never been meant to escape Area 51. It should have died there.

I should have killed it years ago. Out loud he asked, "What did you find?"

"You know the basics: Sandra Gillibrand, single mother, former Marine, widow. Luke Gillibrand, age ten, autistic. Nothing for the last ten years sent up any red flags. They've been struggling financially, she has a strained relationship with her parents. And Luke has had some trouble at school due to behavioral issues."

"Aggression?" He asked.

"No. He's been targeted by bullies," she said.

Martin rubbed his eyes, trying to tamp down his annoyance.. "Why are you bringing this to me?"

She spoke quickly. "I did a search on Luke's father. He died in Iraq before Luke was born. Luke never met him."

A headache was building behind Martin's eyes. He scrounged in the desk drawer to his right for some ibuprofen. Latching on to the bottle, he said, "Yes, and?"

"And his career was pretty unremarkable except for one thing: He was part of a project called Antaeus," a small smile crossed her face as she watched him expectedly.

Popping two pills, he swallowed them down with some coffee. Antaeus was an interesting choice of names. In mythology, Antaeus was the son of Poseidon and Gaia. He was incredibly strong when physically connected to the earth. "I'm not familiar with the project."

"I thought as much. It was actually a project spearheaded and designed by Robert Buckley," she said, landing the name without realizing how much of an impact it would have on Martin.

But Stacy had all of his attention now. Robert Buckley, his former mentor, had taught Martin almost everything he knew.

But Martin had slowly outpaced him, developing his own base of knowledge and cache of secrets. And apparently, Buckley had kept his own secrets as well, including Project Antaeus.

She continued. "Antaeus involved trying to create a more advanced soldier. The soldiers were given shots under the guise of vitamin supplements, to enhance their abilities. Then they were studied over the course of a year."

He grunted. Another Captain America attempt. "And the results of the study?"

Stacy shook her head. "A complete failure. Most of the soldiers were killed in action by the end of the year. But even before that, they showed no greater ability, no higher kill rate, no improvement at all in their functioning."

Martin focused on one word in her statement: most. "What about the ones that didn't die?"

She spoke quietly. "They're all dead now. If they didn't die in Iraq, they did when they got home."

Martin met Stacy's eyes. Apparently Buckley made sure that all traces of the project had disappeared.

"But I believe they overlooked one piece of evidence: Luke." Stacy pointed to a line on the file he was reading.

It was the dates that the project had run and then been officially abandoned. Martin looked up and smiled. Sandra Gillibrand became pregnant while her husband was on leave, and while he was part of the project.

"What was in the supplements?" Martin asked as he sat back at his desk.

She nodded to the folder on the desk. "It's in the other file. Buckley created the supplement from some sort of sample they had at Wright-Patterson Air Force Base."

Martin went still. *No, that bastard. He wouldn't.*

Pulling the file to him, he quickly scanned through the data, his anger rising. If Buckley wasn't dead, Martin would take great joy in killing him all over again. He closed the file.

"I'm going to need a strike team. Tell them to bring me Luke Gillibrand. I want him unharmed."

Although Stacy nodded, she asked, "What about the mother? She'll defend him."

Martin waved her away. "She's unimportant. If she gets in the way, kill her."

CHAPTER 4

TRIBUNE, KANSAS

Sandra Gillibrand's eyes flew open, her heart pounding. The images of the blue creature reaching for Luke stayed in the forefront of her mind. *It's a nightmare. It's not real.*

The words didn't help, because she knew they *had* been real. The Blue Boys had been at her home. They had tried to kill her and her son. If not for Sammy …

She stopped that line of thinking. She didn't know what to make of the winged creature that had saved them. But she knew that contemplating who or what he was would go nowhere, especially in the early morning hours.

She took a few deep breaths, trying to calm her heart rate while her gaze raked the room for any sign that something was wrong. The bedroom looked as it always did these days. The blinds were drawn tight, but the night light in the corner provided enough of a glow to see the three beige walls and one dark green. At one point, the green wall had been beige as well. She and Noah had stenciled 'Always kiss me goodnight' on it the first week they had moved in. A month after he died in Iraq, she'd painted over it, unable to sleep in the room otherwise.

She hadn't shared her bed with another man in the ten years since. She'd had two casual relationships in that time, but she'd never brought them home. Home was her and Luke.

The only other person who'd slept in her bed had been her son, Luke. He'd slept there most of his toddler years and then on and off until age eight, when he'd stopped altogether. But after what had happened in the cornfield, he had not wanted to be more than a few feet from her, especially in sleep.

The gray blankets shifted as Luke rolled to his side. Sandra reached across the bed as the first moan began. "Luke, Luke. Wake up."

Sandra's ten-year-old son moaned again, his eyes still closed. But his chest rose and fell quickly, his breathing coming out in pants. The blankets and sheet had become entangled in his legs. She pulled them free, smoothing them around him. "Wake up, honey."

Luke's eyes flew open as he jolted upright. His brown eyes were huge as they scanned the room, his head shifting from side to side.

Sandra was careful not to touch him. Sometimes her touch made it worse when he was not fully awake. "It's all right, honey. It was just a dream."

Luke's head continued to swivel back and forth, his chest heaving before he seemed to be able to focus on Sandra. He stared at her, looking heartbreakingly young, his bottom lip trembling. "Mom?"

Sandra forced a small smile to her lips. "It's me, baby. Everything's fine. It was just a bad dream."

Luke slid back down to the bed. Sandra reached over and pulled the blankets back up to his chin, tucking them in around him again. "Go back to sleep. Mama's here."

Fear laced his words. "You won't let the bad men get me?"

Her heart aching, Sandra pushed the hair back from his forehead. "Never."

He nodded, closing his eyes. But Sandra didn't leave. She sat next to him, her back against the headboard as his breathing slowed and evened out.

You won't let the bad men get me? He'd asked her the same question every night since it had happened. He never mentioned the Blue Boys. They weren't what had scared him. No, for Luke it was the government people who'd shown up afterward that brought out his fear and no doubt crowded his nightmares.

She pushed back his hair once again and then traced the contour of his face. She loved him more than she could possibly explain. And each night he slipped into a world of nightmares that she could not protect him from.

After what they had been through, she knew it was normal. The government still hadn't explained how it was that blue apes had somehow appeared at their home. They hadn't explained where they had come from or how they'd escaped. And they certainly hadn't explained why they seemed to have targeted Luke.

And they definitely hadn't explained Sammy, the dark winged creature that had saved him from the same blue apes. Of course, Sandra had kept her mentions of Sammy short, practically nondescript. She wasn't sure why. Maybe it was because he saved Luke. And she had a feeling that whatever the government intended toward Sammy, it wouldn't be good for the creature.

At the same time, she was wracked with guilt. What if she had read the creature wrong? What if he actually was dangerous? He had saved Luke, but those wings of his were not soft, fluffy angel wings. They were dark, leathery, and came to a sharp point at the edges.

Those wings were built for battle or destruction.

Sandra ran a hand through her hair, knowing that once again she was tying her mind up in knots. She relived the events of that night, like she'd done a dozen times a day. Her memories slowed when she came to the follow-up after the incident. She hadn't liked the first D.E.A.D. agent that she had met. But the second one, Norah Tidwell, she had been different. Sandra had the feeling Norah knew that she had been holding back. But Norah hadn't called her on it.

Sandra reached over to the bedside table and pulled up the business card that Norah had given her. The card was now worn at the corners. Sandra must've looked at it twelve times a day lately. Once again, she wondered if maybe she should call her. If maybe the agent might be able to tell them something, anything, that might help Luke sleep.

That might help me *sleep.*

With a sigh, Sandra stood, slipping the card into the pocket of her sweatpants. She knew from experience that she wasn't going to sleep any more. A quick glance showed that it was four o'clock. She had to be at the diner at eight after she got Luke to school, assuming he would even go to school. Some days he refused, and she didn't have the heart to fight him on it.

But with him asleep, it was a good time to check the latest rental listings. Sandra had decided that she and Luke needed to move. The house had too many bad memories now. She hoped that maybe a new place without those memories might help Luke sleep a little bit easier. But she also knew mentioning it to him would just open a whole new can of worms. She planned on telling him about moving once she had everything set up.

Making her way downstairs, she set up the old coffee maker on the counter and pulled out a box of cereal. By the time she had her cereal set up, the coffee had started to brew.

Replacing the coffeepot with her mug, she waited while staring out the window above the sink for the mug to fill. Unnerved by the darkness outside, she quickly pulled the curtains shut.

Replacing the mug with the coffeepot, she took the bowl of cereal and the mug to the table and set them up next to her laptop. She sipped on the coffee while she waited for the laptop to boot up. It was ancient and had to weigh close to ten pounds, and it had Windows 95 as its operating system.

But a new laptop wasn't in the budget. She'd been hoping to go to college in the fall, but she wasn't sure if she would be able to afford it and a new laptop. She'd gotten money from the government for their "trouble." Some had gone to car repairs, she'd started a college fund for Luke, and she hoped the rest could help her get a master's degree at the local community college. A laptop was an extravagance at this point.

When the laptop was finally ready, she did another search for apartments and houses to rent. There was still nothing that would work for them. The ones in their school district were simply too expensive. And the ones outside of their school district were simply unthinkable. Luke struggled at school. Kids were simply not that understanding of a sensitive autistic boy like Luke. But she also knew that Luke would be even more terrified by a new school. That would set them back even further.

Damned if I do, damned if I don't.

Tears built against the back of her eyes. She reached up, rubbing her eyes hard, pushing against her eyelids and hopefully pushing away the tears. She didn't have time for tears. She didn't have time to give into that kind of weakness. She was all Luke had. She needed to stay strong. But some days, like right now, it was so overwhelming. She shoved the thoughts away and took a bite of her now soggy cereal. She ate on autopilot, her mind blessedly blank.

She stood up and placed her bowl in the kitchen sink, quickly rinsing it out and washing it and the spoon before placing them in the dish rack next to the sink. She started to refill her coffee when she heard movement upstairs. Her eyes darted to the clock. It was barely five. Luke was going to have a rough day if he got up this early.

Oh, who am I kidding? Every day's a rough day lately.

Luke barreled down the steps. Sandra placed the mug quickly on the counter and hurried over to him. "Luke? What's the matter, honey?"

He gripped her hand, pulling her toward the door. "They're coming. We need to go."

Sandra dug in her feet, holding herself where she was. What was this? Was he sleepwalking? He looked awake. "No one's coming, honey. We're fine. It was just a dream."

Reaching up to his head, he yanked on his hair. "No, they're coming. We have to go. Sammy says we have to go." Tears brimmed in his eyes, and the look on his face was full of terror.

The hair on the back of Sandra's neck rose. She glanced around their small kitchen. It was quiet. Nothing was wrong. And yet …

Taking his arm, she pulled him toward the door, grabbing her pocketbook from the hook by the door along with her keys, before she slipped her feet into her sneakers. "Okay, let's go."

CHAPTER 5

THE COAST OF NOVA SCOTIA

Iggy leapt for the branch five feet from the ground. Despite the fact he stood only slightly over two feet tall and had a stocky body with a small potbelly, he made the leap with no problem. Talons extended from each of his hands, reminding Norah of lobster claws. The sun filtered through the branches, highlighting the small patch of white hair on his head between his pointed ears.

His white bandage stood out against his green skin. According to Greg Schorn, he was healing incredibly fast. But with each acrobatic move he made, she tensed, expecting him to rip open the stitches Greg had placed. When he reached a few branches higher, former D.E.A.D. agent Norah Tidwell lost sight of him for a moment, his green skin blending into the leaves. But then she caught a glimpse of his red shorts as he leaped down, throwing a somersault before grabbing a branch to slow his fall and rolling to his feet on the ground.

In less than a breath, he swung himself into the next tree. In seconds, he'd made his way to the top of the tree as well.

Norah made her way to the trunk, her hands on her hips as she looked up at him. "You are seriously fast."

"Ig, Ig."

He leaped from the top of the tree, plunging six feet before grabbing a hold of a branch from the next tree over and slinging himself to the top of it.

Her heart pounding, Norah released the breath she'd been holding when he'd leaped. *Well, that decides it. I am never having kids.*

Iggy chattered away happily, not even noticing how terrified his antics made Norah. And why should he? He was just doing what came naturally to him. He wasn't human. He wasn't even from Earth. She needed to learn what he could do so that Iggy just being Iggy didn't shove her heart into the cardiac arrest range.

Norah shook her head at the thought. She had never been one to tie herself down. She'd had a few relationships over the years, but none had really stuck for the long term. She'd moved from place to place, and she'd liked the thrill of checking out a new location and finding spots to haunt. But when it was time to pack up, she'd happily done so, ready for the next adventure.

It was why working for D.E.A.D. after her military career was over had been such a good fit. She and her former D.E.A.D. partner, Bob Maxwell, had crisscrossed the country tracking down their targets. All had been escapees from Area 51.

The US government had been creating alien hybrid creatures in their labs. It was still hard to believe. But she had personally seen the database with over fifty different types. Threat level for the targets ranged from level 1–5, although Norah had only seen one creature ever labeled a level 5. All the cases she'd been given were level four: terminate on sight.

And now she knew that the threat level had been a smoke

screen. It was a termination mission she was being sent on. No creature was supposed to survive.

The feeling of guilt pushed down on her chest. Iggy was supposed to have been one of her targets. But Norah hadn't been able to bring herself to pull the trigger. They'd been told everyone on the hit list was dangerous. But there had been something innocent about Iggy, something that made her unable to kill him or to even let anyone know she had found him.

She wasn't sure if it was just because he was Iggy or the doubts that she'd secretly been developing that had caused her to react differently that day. But she was glad she had. While she'd never wanted to be tied down, not even to a dog, she simply could not imagine her life without Iggy. They belonged together. She knew it in her bones.

And now she needed to figure out a way for them to live without the world finding out about him. Or without D.E.A.D. trying to kill them. And right now the only safe place was with Tilda's group. And she wasn't even sure how safe that was. She'd never heard of the agency. And Tilda, the woman in charge, wasn't exactly forthcoming with a lot of information.

She looked around, not sure where the heck they even were but keenly aware of the guards surrounding them. They were said to be there for their own protection, but Norah wasn't convinced of that yet.

Not that she currently had a lot of options.

She thought they were somewhere along the coast of Canada, but she couldn't swear to it. This was their last burst of freedom before they headed to the airfield. Norah didn't know where they were heading, but she prayed it was somewhere that Iggy could at least swing from some trees.

She glanced at her watch. *Time to go.* "Come on, Ig. We need to head back." She scanned the treetops but had lost sight of him. "Ig?"

A shadow flew over her, and she managed to get her hands up as he flew at her. "Ig!" He exclaimed.

Laughing as she caught him, she hugged him to her chest. She released him, and he scrambled up to her shoulders. Taking a seat, he rested his arms on the top of her head. "Ig," he sighed happily.

With a smile, Norah patted his legs as she headed back to the building. But the happy feeling drifted farther and farther away the closer she got to the buildings. She gripped Iggy's legs a little tighter.

"Ig?"

"It's okay, buddy," she said softly. "I've got you."

And she did. Because protecting Iggy was her new life goal. And she would do it until there was no breath left in her body. He had her, and she had him. Keeping him safe was now her primary motivation.

And God help anyone who tried to harm either of them.

CHAPTER 6

TRIBUNE, KANSAS

Before leaving the house, Sandra grabbed them each a sweatshirt and Luke's shoes. He'd run outside without putting them on. She hurried to join Luke in the car. He sat trembling in his seat as she tossed his sneakers at the floor in front of him before sitting.

Luke grabbed the shoes, hugging them to his chest. "Hurry up, Mom. Hurry up."

His terror was contagious. Sandra found herself shaking as she inserted the keys into the ignition. She had the car in drive and was moving quickly down the driveway and onto the street before she reached over and yanked on her seatbelt.

In the passenger seat, Luke continued to shake, rocking back and forth emitting a soft hum. Sandra white-knuckled the steering wheel to keep from punching down on the accelerator.

This is crazy. He had a dream. That's all. He hadn't mentioned Sammy since the incident. She watched him from the corner of her eyes. "Did you see Sammy, honey?"

Her son shook his head. Sandra studied him, not sure what to make of his behavior. Her attention shifted from the road to the sky, and she realized she was looking for a large set of wings. She took a breath. *Okay, pull it in. He had a nightmare. That's all. Time to calm things down.* "Well, since we're up, how about we go to the diner? Mitch will make us some pancakes. Doesn't that sound good?"

He didn't answer, but Sandra knew that she could do with some pancakes herself. Mitch, the owner of the diner, had been trying to force-feed both her and Luke ever since the incident at the farmhouse. And there was something comforting about having someone else cook for you.

Sandra glanced down at the worn sweatpants and old T-shirt she was wearing. She wasn't exactly dressed for going into town. But luckily no one but a few regulars would be around this early in the morning. And they had definitely seen her looking worse.

Her heart calming, she felt a little better. Maybe she just needed to get out of the house. Break the routine of nightmare, morning rush, work all day, evening fear of the night's nightmares, followed by the actual nightmares, and repeat.

She breathed in deep, rolling down the window. Fresh air, tinged with the scent of fresh dirt, drifted through the open window. It smelled like home. She smiled. There was no one out on the road yet. The sun hadn't even broken the horizon, although the telltale pink showed that it wasn't far off.

Luke continued his humming and rocking.

The momentary peace slowly disappeared. She couldn't pretend this was some sort of progress. Sandra didn't know what had spurred Luke's need to get out of the house. Normally the house was his safe zone. But the attack had ripped all that away. She wasn't sure how to recreate a safe zone for him. And kids like Luke needed that. They needed one place that was consistent, a place that they felt no one or nothing could touch them.

Luke's humming stopped.

Sandra watched him from the corner of her eyes as he stared straight ahead, his lips moving but no sound coming out. She frowned, trying to figure out what he was doing. For a moment she worried that maybe it was the beginning of a seizure. He'd had them when he was younger, but then he seemed to have grown out of them.

Thank God.

But maybe the stress of what had happened was somehow going to bring them back on. The doctors she had taken Luke to see had warned her to look out for them. *Please, God, not that. We have enough to deal with.*

She kept one eye on Luke and one eye on the road, grateful for the lack of traffic that allowed her to split her attention.

"Turn! Turn! They're here!" He yelled, his eyes flared wide as he scrambled for the wheel.

"Luke!" Sandra struggled to keep the car in the road as Luke yanked on the side of the wheel. "Luke, no!"

He backed away, cringing. Shaking, she pulled off the road onto Kelly Drive. Putting the car in park, she took her foot off the brake. The car idled as her whole body shook, images of a fiery crash rushing through her mind.

Luke had never done anything like that before. If she had been going faster or if they had been on a busy road … "Luke, you cannot do that. It's not safe. It's not—"

His head whipped around. He stared out the back window.

Eyes locked on the back windshield, she turned slowly just as the first car appeared. It was a black SUV. Even in the dark light, she could tell its make. Cars were the one thing she knew well. And she knew it was a Tahoe, just like the government ones that had shown up after the incident. Four more SUVs followed, a quiet parade heading toward her farmhouse.

She turned slowly to Luke. He met her gaze. "They're here," he said softly.

Frozen in place, she stared at him in shock. Cars like that didn't just drive around Tribune. She couldn't risk going back to the farmhouse if it was in fact the government. But she also couldn't assume that Luke was right.

She reached across Luke and opened up the glove compartment. She fished around and pulled out the binoculars before she looked at Luke. "Stay here. I'm going to watch them."

He shook his head. "No."

"They won't see me, but you can. I'll be right up there," Sandra assured him as she pointed to the observation post of the corn maze. It was a wooden structure two stories high in the middle of the field.

Years ago, the fields all around them had been full of corn that had been organized into a maze. When you made it to the observation tower, you had successfully completed the maze. The maze was long gone now. The Bradleys, who'd run the maze for sixty years, had gone out of business five years before. Now the only sign of the maze was the lonely wooden platform.

"I'll be right back," she said as she stepped outside quickly, closing the door to extinguish the light. She glanced around but didn't see anyone, then took off at a fast jog for the platform and quickly scaled the stairs. She moved to the edge of it, already pulling the binoculars to her eyes. She adjusted the focus, and it took her only a few seconds to find her home.

The four SUVs were just pulling into her driveway, but if she hadn't been looking for them she wouldn't have seen them. Their lights were off.

She watched as the cars emptied of their occupants, all dressed in black. There were twelve of them, and they spread out, with half covering the back and half the front.

Her mouth went dry. They were not coming to ask more

questions, not at five a.m. They were surrounding the house, making sure she and Luke couldn't escape. That was not how you treated the victim of crime.

That was how you treated a suspect.

With a spark of light, a small object flew through the air from one of the individual's guns. It cracked through the window of her living room, and then a small flash of light burst from inside.

Her mouth fell open. It was a flash bang. For a split second, she imagined what would've happened if she'd awoken to one. She'd been around them in the service, and they always disoriented whoever the target was. But for Luke it would have been beyond terror inducing.

You bastards. She gripped the binoculars more tightly as one of the men gave the signal and all of the individuals burst into the house.

Rage and fear warred inside of her, but she couldn't allow either of them to take hold. She hurried back down the stairs and sprinted for the car. She tossed the binoculars onto the back seat and was driving before she'd wrestled her seatbelt on.

Flicking a glance at him, she struggled to hold the panic from her voice. "You were right, Luke. The bad men are there."

He didn't answer her right away and when he did his voice was quiet, scared. "Where are we going?"

She flicked another quick glance at him and then looked back at the road. She pressed down on the accelerator, knowing she needed to move quickly.

"Where are we going?" He repeated.

Sandra shook her head, not answering him. Because she didn't have an answer. She had no idea where they were going to go. She just knew she had to get Luke as far away from them as possible.

All the while worrying if she'd ever be able to go far enough.

CHAPTER 7

SEATTLE, WASHINGTON

"Where are you?" Martin scanned the map in front of him, but it offered no clues. He had been looking for Tilda's base for decades. Even after he believed her to be dead, he knew her work carried on. He didn't expect to find it magically this afternoon, but he knew that's where Tilda had absconded with Subject One and Agaren.

Over the years, he'd found one or two of their safe houses but never the main base. If he could find it, well, then things would definitely change. But years of searching had resulted in no leads.

He punched his fist into the desk. *God damn Tilda, always wrecking my plans. Where did you take them?*

He looked up as Stacy crossed the hallway out in front of his glass wall. She held up a file. He waved her in. "I take it the Gillibrands are in custody?"

"No, sir. The farmhouse was empty when we arrived," she said.

"Empty?" He asked softly.

Stacy nodded, speaking quickly. "Clothes were still there. But her car was gone, as was her pocketbook. There was a withdrawal from an ATM in town at about the same time the team was at the farmhouse. After that, all electronic traces went dark."

She knew. Somehow she'd known they were coming. How? He pictured the being that Luke called Sammy. Was it possible he was somehow responsible for their escape?

"Were there any unusual aerial sightings?" He asked.

Pausing, she said, "No. Should they have been looking for something?"

"No. This something would have deftly made himself known," Martin mumbled.

Once again Stacy's words came out in a rush. "I have the footage from all the cameras in the area being sent to us. It's only a matter of time before we find their car."

He wasn't so sure about that. Sandra and Luke should've been home tucked in their beds. They should have been easy to pick up. The fact that they weren't meant that they were not the easy targets they appeared to be.

Of course, if "Sammy" was in the mix, he wasn't the only one who would be interested in him.

"There is some good news, however," she added.

He looked up at her, saying nothing.

She shifted nervously from foot to foot. "I may have found a source inside Matilda Watson's operation."

Martin's eyebrows rose. Now that could be worthwhile. "How?"

She snorted. "A fake Facebook account. But it's tied to someone named Ethan McCallum."

He'd heard the McCallum name before. Hope built inside him. Promising indeed. "Keep at it. Let me know if you find anything more concrete."

"Will do." Stacy quickly left the office.

He turned his gaze back to the map. *Where are you, Tilda?* He turned his gaze from the map and pulled up the file on Tatiana Brecknoff. He stared at the photo that accompanied the file. Tatiana had been caught lunching at Spago in Beverly Hills. Her head was thrown back in laughter. Sunlight shone off her stunning blonde hair. Her eyes were covered by dark sunglasses.

Even from the still shot, her confidence and entitlement shone through. She looked like any one of the hundreds of wealthy women that frequented the exclusive restaurant.

But you're not like all the others, are you, Tatiana?

He debated for a few moments more before he picked up the phone and dialed quickly.

"Yes?" The deep voice that answered was not friendly.

"This is Martin Drummond. I need to speak with Tatiana."

CHAPTER 8

BALLANTRAE, SCOTLAND

With a look of complete disappointment on his face, Greg stared out the window of the aircraft. "I am underwhelmed," he declared.

Maeve had to agree. They had been traveling for hours. The first leg of the trip had been three hours, followed by a four-hour layover for mechanical repairs in a small, freezing garage in Greenland. The second leg had been six.

What had kept them going was the promise that they were heading somewhere completely safe. Somewhere well out of Martin's reach.

The plane that had taken them to their current location had not inspired confidence. A holdover from the Cold War, it had rattled the entire trip. It was so loud, Maeve wasn't sure if her hearing would ever return. No one had slept well. The kids because of the noise, the adults because they feared they were about to plunge to the ground when a wing fell off.

As soon as they stopped, Jasper had bounced out of his seat with a grin. "Made it!" He threw his hands in the air.

His words earned him a plane full of glares. But Jasper explained the plane was a necessary security precaution and that the next mode of transport would be much more comfortable.

Maeve stared daggers at the man. Her whole body was still vibrating, the same way the plane had for the entire ride.

"I'd punch him if I could stand," Greg muttered from the row behind her.

"I'd be happy to shoot him if someone would hand me a gun and help me keep my arm straight," Norah said from next to Greg.

Standing, Chris winced as he stretched his back. "Let's save shooting him until we see where we're heading."

"Now can I shoot him?" Norah mumbled ten minutes later as she stood next to Maeve on the shore of some beach.

"I vote yes," Greg said.

Maeve just grunted, not sure what to say. She had to admit she was disappointed as well. Tilda had let drop that she was affiliated with a secondary space program, one that predated NASA. When you heard something like that, there was a certain expectation that came to mind. She had imagined a super sleek aircraft that would take them to the base. Or maybe even an incredibly technologically advanced underwater craft that would help them avoid being seen.

Instead she was staring at two old fishing boats, and by old she meant *old*. The paint was flaking off. They looked like they were from the turn of the century. The *previous* century.

"*This* is how you get to your ultra-secure base?" Maeve asked as she looked at Tilda.

The enigmatic woman nodded. "One of the ways. The McCallum family has been ferrying people to the base for decades. They are highly trusted and our first line of defense."

Without another word, she strode toward the boat that was pulling up to the dock. Adam was already waiting and caught the rope thrown from the back of the boat.

Walking up with Crackle hanging from his shoulders, Greg watched Tilda stride away with raised eyebrows. "So are we sure Tilda isn't just crazy?" He murmured.

Maeve watched the woman who'd managed to gather a small army to help them free Alvie and Agaren from the Dulce base but who now wanted them to believe that two decrepit fishing boats were any form of security for a beyond top-secret base. "Oh, I have no idea."

A tall woman with strong cheekbones stepped off of the boat, wearing canvas pants and a peacoat to protect her against the cold. Her wavy red hair was pulled up in a messy bun on top of her head. She looked over at Maeve, nodding before flicking a glance at everyone on the shore. Her eyes widened for a moment as she caught sight of the aliens, but then she simply nodded and stepped back on board.

Tilda waved them all over.

"Well, we've come this far," Greg muttered.

And we have no other choice, Maeve thought. She turned and called for Alvie, Snap, and Pop, who hurried over. They'd been running around with Chris to vent some energy. Chris, with Hope by his side and Iggy perched on his shoulders, followed them. They all clambered into one boat. The redheaded woman was standing, waiting for them, Tilda by her side.

As Maeve, Norah, and Chris stepped on board, Tilda nodded to her. "This is Tara McCallum. She is in charge of transportation to and from the base. Her brother, Ethan, is captaining the other ship. This is Dr. Maeve Leander, Dr. Greg Schorn, Captain Chris Garrigan, and Agent Norah Tidwell."

Tara smiled, an Irish lilt in her voice when she spoke. "It's nice to meet you all. No title for me. Just call me Tara. It would be best if you all took refuge below. The winds can get pretty rough up here."

Tilda headed into the little cabin. "I'll show you the way."

With Snap in her arms, Maeve followed behind her. There was a set of stairs inside the cabin, leading down. Tilda moved down them quickly, and after a moment's hesitation, Maeve followed.

Now this was more of what she was expecting. The ship under the waterline was about three times the size of the ship above the waterline. And it was decked out with comfortable couches bolted to the wall. There were even some cots in the back. A small kitchenette had been set up on the other side.

Holding Crackle once again, Greg stepped down. He looked up with a nod. "Now this is more like it."

Maeve smiled at him. "I was just thinking the same thing."

Tilda waited until everyone was secured and they were on their way before she spoke. "We found it best to give the appearance of unimportance. The façade of this vessel doesn't attract attention. And that is exactly what we want."

"But still, wouldn't it make more sense to fly people out to the base?" Norah asked.

"Occasionally we do," Tilda admitted. "But currently the base is on lockdown. Also a necessary precaution. And until we are sure that we have not been followed, we will stay in lockdown. When we are in lockdown mode, nothing computerized can reach the island. All electrical signals are blocked."

"You've made it a Faraday cage," Greg said.

"Yes. It extends almost five miles outside of the island," Tilda explained.

Maeve was stunned. She'd heard of what a Faraday cage was, of course—it was essentially a barrier to protect against electromagnetic fields. But she had never heard of one that large. "How are you able to do that?"

Tilda gave a small smile. "Our technology is more advanced than what you have seen pretty much anywhere. There's a lot we are capable of that you would not expect. Now, why don't you all get a little sleep? It will be two hours until we reach the island. I'll be on the other boat. Tara will be able to contact me if you need anything." With that, she headed back up the stairs.

Alvie had already taken the triplets to the back of the room and got them all settled into a cot. Snap let out a big yawn as Hope curled at their feet. Maeve followed with her own yawn almost immediately. Apparently she was more tired than she thought.

Chris rubbed her arm. "Go ahead. Get some sleep. I'll stay up."

He knew she wasn't comfortable falling asleep and was just hoping that everything turned out well. He'd keep an eye out for all of them so she could rest a little easier. She kissed him lightly on the lips. "Thank you."

She made her way to the back of the room. "Any space for me?"

The triplets grinned widely, scooting over for Maeve.

Maeve smiled as she slipped off her shoes and curled up with them. Crackle crawled onto her chest, and Snap curled to one side while Pop crawled over her and curled into the other side. Maeve turned her head, looking at Alvie, and reached out a hand. He held on to it as his eyes closed.

With tired eyes, Maeve looked out over the room. In the corner, Chris was sitting with Greg. Norah lay on one of the couches with Iggy curled up in her arms, both of them looking like they were about to fall asleep.

And before Maeve did the same, she sent up a prayer. *Dear God, please let this be the right choice.*

CHAPTER 9

ROCK SPRINGS, WYOMING

The motel parking lot was quiet. Sandra sat at the small table by the window, the curtain slightly pulled back so she had a view of the whole parking lot and part of the street.

She was getting worried. Actually, no, she was quickly becoming terrified. After seeing the black SUVs at her home, she had gone into town and taken all the money from her ATM that she could manage: 272 dollars. It was a risk. She knew that. But she also knew they were not going to get anywhere with the seven dollars she had in her wallet.

Then she had driven. No destination, no plan, just going. She'd stayed off the highways and stuck to long back roads. If she saw a sign for something she was familiar with, she went in the opposite direction. She didn't want to go anywhere near something that might lead the government to her.

The government is after us. Her mind still struggled to accept that. Part of her hoped it was some rebel branch of the government and not the government she, as a staff sergeant, had been willing to die for. But even if it was a rebel branch, they certainly had a lot more power than a single mom on the run with her autistic son with about two hundred dollars to her name.

She struggled to come up with a plan. She couldn't cross any borders that required ID, or she'd send up flags. Planes were out for the same reason, although she didn't have enough money for flights anyway. She couldn't draw the attention of any police. They really needed to stay away from cameras as well. She had a little leeway there. She'd had an extra pair of license plates in her trunk that she had switched out. She'd meant to give them to Noah. They read LUVB3R. She thought he'd get a kick out of them.

And then he'd died. She hadn't been able to get rid of them, but she couldn't look at them either, so she'd left them in the trunk.

She couldn't go to anyone they knew because the government would no doubt be looking for them there. She had a vague idea about maybe trying one of her friends from high school who'd moved to Pennsylvania. But that was a really long trip, and she wasn't sure she'd have the money for gas to get there.

Luke stirred on the bed behind her. She turned around, ready to intercede if the nightmares returned, but he rolled onto his side and settled back down. The first night, they'd slept in the car. Well, stayed in the car overnight at least. Luke had been unable to keep his eyes closed. He'd jumped at every sound, every movement outside the vehicle.

She'd had to dip into their limited funds to risk a motel room for last night. He needed to sleep. Yesterday, he'd been so tired he'd barely been coherent.

But as soon as he woke, they needed to get on the move again. And yet she still didn't have much of a plan. Right now it consisted entirely of not staying in one place too long.

She ran a hand through her hair, trying to ignore the terror crawling up her throat. She could not keep running forever. The government would find them eventually. But what did they even want?

Luke mumbled in his sleep, his arm reaching for something before it fell back on the bed. In her gut, she knew it had to do with Luke and his friend "Sammy." When he'd first told her about his new friend, she'd worried about him being too old for imaginary friends. But that imaginary friend had saved Luke from those blue creatures.

And saved both of us from the government, she thought. She still didn't know how Sammy had told Luke they were in trouble. Luke insisted he hadn't seen Sammy. Sandra didn't like to think about what other means the strange creature might have used to contact her son.

Reaching into the pocket of her sweatpants, she fingered the business card. It was a fluke that she had it in her pocket when they left the house. She had debated whether or not to reach out to the agent. She didn't know if she could trust the woman, but she hadn't seemed like the other feds who'd shown up. But she wasn't quite ready to take that step yet.

Soon, though, she had to make a decision. The room had cost them sixty dollars, which meant if she was lucky, she could manage three more nights in similar ones, but that also meant they didn't have much money for food.

She could call her parents and ask them to wire money, but that would automatically tip off anyone who was looking for her. And besides, she hadn't spoken with her parents in years.

At the same time, she couldn't believe this was what her life had come to. She had served her country. Her husband had as well. Shouldn't that count for something? Shouldn't it at the very least mean they weren't tracked down by that same country?

She buried the anger warring with terror inside of her. She

didn't have time for that either. Keeping Luke safe was all she had time for.

But how do I do that? She pulled out the business card and stared at it. It was a gamble. But she was at the end of her rope. Truth was, if it was just her and Luke versus the U.S. government, the government was going to win. Debating, she looked down at the card.

At least maybe this way I'll have an idea of why this is all happening.

Luke sat up in bed, rubbing at his eyes. "Mom?"

She placed the card back in her pocket. She turned from the window and smiled at him. "Hey, honey. I was just about to wake you."

CHAPTER 10

THE NORTH CHANNEL

BETWEEN IRELAND AND SCOTLAND

An hour later, Maeve was wide awake. Alvie and the triplets were breathing softly in their sleep. Hope yipped softly, her feet moving as she dreamed. Across from them, Norah was curled up with Iggy. Chris also slept nearby, his head back. Only Greg was missing.

Maeve moved up to the deck, needing some fresh air. The sun approached the horizon, leaving the sky a brilliant mix of greens and pinks. Ahead, she could make out the island. It was covered in fog, but she could make out a few peaks and a very rocky shoreline.

Greg gave her a rueful smile as she stepped next to him at the railing. "Couldn't sleep either?"

"Guess not," she said.

"You two are very lucky. Very few people get to see this island," Tara said as she joined them.

"You mean because you keep them away?" Greg asked.

Tara shook her head, some of her red curls coming undone and blowing in the wind. She tucked them behind her ear. "No. Hy-Brasil has always been picky about who it allows to see its form."

Hy-Brasil. The name triggered a memory somewhere in the back of Maeve's mind, but she couldn't tease it out.

Next to her, Greg's jaw dropped, forcing him to push his glasses back up his nose. "Hy-Brasil? *The* Hy-Brasil?"

"I see you've heard of our little isle." Tara smiled.

"I'm afraid I'm drawing a blank, though," Maeve said.

Nodding toward the fog-enclosed coast, Tara said, "According to legend, Hy-Brasil is only seen every seven years. It's a vanishing island. It would sometimes appear for sailors, and then the next year they would come back to the same spot, and it would be gone."

"That's not possible," Maeve said looking between Tara and Greg.

Tara let out a little laugh. "I find that amusing coming from someone with the family you have."

Maeve conceded the point with a smile of her own.

Tara continued. "It appeared on maps between 1325 and the 1800s. Even when it was visible, it was incredibly difficult to reach. Some say that it was the home of an ancient advanced civilization. Others say that it was a paradise created by priests to lure sinners to the Church."

Maeve knew that over the centuries there had been numerous arguments for the existence of previous advanced civilizations, from Atlantis to Shangri-La, so she supposed it only made sense that Ireland had their own legend of an advanced civilization.

"There's only one recorded account of a visit to the island. A Scottish sea captain on his way from France to Ireland is said to have spotted it and sent four of his people on board. The searchers were said to have found a castle with a lone magician living there. But the island itself was uninhabited. Except for, of course, the giant black rabbits," Tara said, her eyes twinkling.

"Giant black rabbits?" Maeve asked. She knew that there were giant rabbits. Flemish Giant rabbits grew to two and half feet long, about the length of a good-sized Labrador. They originated in Belgium but in reality it wasn't very far from Ireland, and it was possible an offshoot of the breed was found on the mysterious island. Although she'd never seen a black one. Not that the fur shades of Flemish Giant rabbits had been a research subject she had delved into.

Greg, who'd been shifting from foot to foot during Tara's explanation, burst out with, "But there's also a UFO connection. The Rendlesham Forest incident."

That one, at least, Maeve was familiar with—Britain's Roswell. The incident actually was a series of sightings that occurred over three days in England between two NATO Air Force bases RAF Bentwaters and RAF Woodbridge. Both bases were being leased to the United States Air Force. Strange lights were reported over both bases from December 26 to 28 in 1980. The strange lights were even pinged by radar.

But the most scintillating part of the report happened on December 26, when lights were seen through the trees adjacent to the base. A patrol was sent out to investigate. U.S. Air Force Sgt. James Penniston was one of the individuals in the patrol group. He reported a metallic object about two to three meters with pulsing lights of red and blue underneath.

Penniston observed the craft for forty-five minutes, mentioning in his descriptions what looked like hieroglyphs along the craft's side. At one point, Penniston even touched the craft. From that contact, he said he pictured a series of zeros and ones, a binary code.

"Years later, the binary code was translated into longitude

and latitude," Greg said. "The location indicated was Hy-Brasil."

Tara nodded. "We had a lot of lookie-loos out here after his code was translated. But none of them made landfall. None of them even saw the island. The weather helped. It blew pretty fierce for a few months, until all of the traffic died down."

"Are you suggesting the island was protecting itself?" Maeve asked.

Tara shrugged. "There are stranger things that have happened."

A shiver rolled through Maeve as the wind tugged at her jacket. An island that was alive. Tara was right. It wasn't the strangest thing she'd heard lately.

CHAPTER 11

HOGANSFIELD, MONTANA

The car was acting up. The Subaru was thirteen years old. The mechanic had warned her that the transmission would need to be replaced soon. But Sandra had really hoped she had at least another year before she had to splurge on that kind of fix.

She gently eased the car over to the side of the road. They'd been on the highway. She'd taken the first ramp off when the engine started chugging. She had no intention of leaving them relying on the kindness of strangers or the attention of the highway patrol.

They were in a little town called Hogansfield. It looked like dozens of other towns that they had driven through. There was a McDonald's, a Home Depot, and a Target farther down the road, but here there were some older mom-and-pop stores that had seen better days and a diner that had definitely needed a fresh coat of paint.

Luke dozed in the passenger seat. Sandra turned off the

engine and rested her head on the steering wheel. *Oh, come on. I just need a little break.*

No magical winged being appeared to restore her car to its showroom condition. She blew out a breath and looked up, trying to figure out what the new game plan was. She was almost out of money. The car was on its last legs. And she didn't even really know where she was. She knew she was in Montana, but that was all.

She pulled out the cell phone she had bought at a convenience store two states ago. She still wasn't sure who to call, but she felt better having one on her. Once again, she fingered the business card from the D.E.A.D. agent. She knew she was at the end of her rope, but she hated the idea of making a call when she was in dire straits. There had to be another option.

Terror simmered at the edge of her thoughts as she scanned the road, *I need money. I need a place for us to stay. I need to stay off the grid.* Those were the three priorities right now.

At the same time, she'd been second-guessing herself for the last twenty-four hours. Maybe she had misread the situation at the farmhouse. Maybe those agents thought they were in danger and were actually coming to help them.

But she knew she was grasping at straws. If by some stretch of the imagination they thought there was a hostage situation in the farmhouse, they certainly wouldn't have begun the process of extracting the hostages with flash bangs. No, the government had come for her and Luke. Which meant until she could figure out what exactly was going on, she couldn't trust the government.

She wanted to cry. She wanted to scream. She wanted to hit something. But she did none of that because it would upset Luke. She blew out a breath and counted to ten. *I can handle this. Whatever happens, I can handle this.*

Her stomach growled. She'd barely eaten in the last few days. She would order food for Luke and take a bite or two, but that was about it. She knew she couldn't keep going that way. She needed to keep her energy up. Already her thinking felt slow.

She was down to her last 150 dollars. The golden arches of McDonald's beckoned in the distance. The idea of some fries stirred up the first sense of excitement she'd felt in the last couple of days. She reached over and tugged on Luke's shirt. "Hey, sleepyhead. Let's go get something to eat."

Luke's eyes shot open quickly, and he jolted up.

Sandra put up her hands. "Hey, hey. It's okay. Everything's fine. There's a McDonald's up there. Let's go get something to eat."

"A chocolate shake?" He asked.

She ruffled his hair. "Yes, but a small one."

He smiled at her, the first smile she'd seen since they'd left the farmhouse.

Thirty minutes later, they were walking back to the car, and Sandra's stomach felt, if not full, at least not completely empty. Luke was happily slurping on his shake next to her. He tilted it toward her. "Want some?"

She shook her head, even though she really, really wanted some. "No, I'm full. You enjoy it."

Another smile was aimed in her direction before his lips once again closed around the straw. Sandra studied the storefronts as they passed. At the diner, she stopped, noticing a sign in the window: Help Wanted.

She debated for only a moment before tugging Luke toward the diner door.

"Are we going to eat again?" Luke asked.

Sandra shook her head. "Nope. Mama's going to get a job."

CHAPTER 12

HY-BRASIL

They arrived at the base late at night. Maeve had wanted to get some explanations from Tilda about where they were and what the plan was, but last night all any of them could think of was getting some sleep.

Now, Maeve squinted her eyes open. Finally, the sense of vibrating had passed. This time there was a white metal roof high above her, and she was lying on a solid bed, although it still felt like it was moving. Chris lay quietly in the bed next to her, his eyes still closed. Maeve sat up slowly. Twelve cots lined the room, seven of them occupied. Medical equipment sat at the far side of the room, but there were no monitors attached to any of the "patients" in the beds. Maeve's gaze roamed over each of them, checking to see the careful rise and fall of each of their chests.

Voices broke through her thoughts, and she turned her head, seeing Tara squared off with Tilda at the end of the room. "You can't keep going this way," Tara said, breaking off when she caught sight of Maeve. Without another word to Tilda, she strode over to Maeve's bed. She slowed as she approached, the anger she'd had on her face shifting to concern. "Are you all right?"

Maeve nodded slowly. "I think so. What happened?"

"You were each given a sedative last night after you fell asleep," Tara said.

"What?" Maeve exclaimed.

Tara put up her hands. "I know. But Tilda wanted to make sure you all got a good night's sleep."

Gritting her teeth, Maeve looked passed Tara to glare at Tilda. "She can't just drug people."

"No, she *shouldn't* drug people. Apparently she can." Tara moved to the table next to the bed and poured a glass of water from the pitcher sitting here. She handed it to Maeve. "It's all right. It's safe."

For some strange reason, Maeve believed her. She took the cup and drank slowly, the water quenching her dry throat. She nodded. "Thank you."

Taking the cup back, Tara replaced it on the side table before taking a seat on the bed. "Your family will wake soon. It was a simple sedative. There will be no recurring issues." She pulled a small device from her pocket. It was a small rectangular box only about three inches by two. A single button sat in the middle of its face. She handed it to Maeve. "If at any point you don't feel safe and want to leave, press this button, and I will come for you, no questions asked."

Maeve stared into the woman's eyes. In the light, she realized her hair was a deep auburn. Freckles dotted her pale face, and her bright blue eyes were closer to gray. "Are we safe here?"

Tara hesitated. "Tilda means you no harm. Her methods, however, sometimes leave a great deal to be desired."

"And my family?" Maeve asked.

As Tara's gaze strayed across the beds, a smile of wonder

crossed her face. "They are especially in no danger. They are the culmination of everything that has been done until this point."

"Then why would I need this?" Maeve nodded to the small box.

"Tilda means you no harm, but no defenses are perfect. If you need help, you call, okay?" Tara asked.

The warning was clear in the woman's gaze. And yet again, Maeve trusted her, even though she had no reason other than her gut instinct to go on. "Okay. Thank you."

Nodding, Tara stood then slid her hands down her jacket to straighten it out. "It was a pleasure to meet you, Dr. Leander. I hope we can speak again under better circumstances."

"Call me Maeve, and I do as well." Maeve extended her hand.

Tara shook it with a smile. "I need to get back to the boat before Ethan decides to take it for a joyride. I swear, he has the emotional capacity of a thirteen-year-old."

Flicking a gaze toward Greg, who lay sprawled on his back now, one arm flung over his face, Maeve smiled. "I know the type."

Tara laughed. "Ah, men, they never truly stop being boys, do they?"

This time, Maeve looked at Chris. "Some do."

"Aye, some do indeed. Take care of yourself, Maeve."

"You too, Tara," Maeve said softly before she watched the woman leave. She gave Tilda an abrupt, cold nod as she passed.

Chris stirred. Maeve slung her legs over the side of the bed and sat on the floor next to his cot, brushing the hair back from his eyes. "Chris?"

His eyes blinked open a few times before they focused on Maeve. "Maeve." He smiled and then jolted upright, his head swinging from side to side.

Rearing back for a moment, Maeve placed a hand on his chest. "It's okay. It's okay. We're all here. We're fine."

Beneath her hand, Chris's heart pounded away. His gaze searched each of the cots. "Are you sure?"

Maeve met Tilda's gaze from across the room. Tilda held her eyes but made no move toward her. After a moment, Tilda turned her attention back to the tablet in her hand.

"No, but I hope so," Maeve said quietly.

CHAPTER 13

The cool breeze slipped through the slight opening in the window. Maeve relished it and the scent it brought with it. It was crisp and cool, like the end of fall. Outside, she could see tall blue spruces but not much else. From the front door, she could see a path leading to another building. She could just make out the top of the building, although with its green rounded roof, it was difficult to discern from the green surrounding it.

Chris sat with the triplets, playing some sort of game that was keeping them distracted. Alvie sat near them, an expression Maeve couldn't read on his face. He'd woken up shortly after Chris had. Maeve had sat with Alvie curled up in her lap, and he'd shaken for a good twenty minutes. But he still kept his thoughts from her. She knew he was doing it to spare her the pain, but it hurt to know that Martin had for one moment driven a wedge between them.

Norah had Iggy curled up in her lap at the other end of the room. Maeve had checked his wound when he'd woken up. It had shrunk, so she'd cleaned it and placed a smaller bandage on it. She was amazed at his healing capacity and desperately wanted to get a look at his blood under a microscope.

She'd taken a brief walk with Norah and Iggy after they'd woken up. As far as they could tell, the "base" consisted of only four buildings, bearing a closer resemblance to a camp from the TV show *M*A*S*H* than from any high-tech sci-fi movie. Doubts crawled through her. What were they doing here?

The only one still sleeping was Greg. He mumbled and shifted on his cot, an arm over his eyes.

Maeve turned her attention back to the scene outside the window. A sparrow flew to a tree opposite her. It looked so carefree, and she felt so hemmed in. Tilda had left right after Chris had awoken, saying that she would speak with them once everyone was awake. Maeve didn't know what to think about the woman. She knew she was in charge. But so far she had been very close lipped about everything, including where they were.

She felt him before she saw him. She turned as Alvie slipped his hand into hers. "Are you all right?"

He looked up at her, and she knew he wasn't quite sure how to respond. And what did she expect? He had been held captive in that horrible place. To say the idea of him being hurt broke her heart was a radical understatement. It sliced her in two. Alvie above everything else was a gentle soul. She'd never seen him do something even slightly unkind in her entire life. She wasn't sure how he was processing what had happened to him at Martin's hands.

She supposed she should be thankful for the events at Area 51. Before them, he hadn't ever been exposed to cruelty. But Area 51 and Martin once again had made sure that he knew just how cruel humans could be. And the monsters that Martin had created were beyond what even the human imagination could rustle up in the worst of nightmares. She shuddered, imagining the blob-like creature following her and Chris across the lobby of the administration building.

Kneeling down, Maeve pulled Alvie into her arms. "I'm sorry for what happened to you. You did not deserve any of it."

Why? He asked.

She shook her head. "I don't know. For some people, when they see something different they need to find out why it is different. But they do it in a way that is hurtful."

A vision of Martin flitted through Maeve's mind, along with a questioning thought.

She tried to keep the anger out of her voice as she spoke with him. Anger wouldn't help Alvie, and he was so sensitive that it would only hurt him. "I don't know what is wrong with him. Humans have a capacity to be cruel, to be evil. But I've never truly understood why. There must be something that explains why he has become the man he is."

Family? He asked.

"I doubt he has one. I don't think a man like that could ever truly love anyone."

"Rats in burgers!" Greg yelled, jolting himself awake as he fell out of the cot. Chris walked over and offered him a hand. Greg grasped it, letting himself be pulled up, and then sat heavily on the cot, his head in his hands. "Oh, I feel awful."

Alvie hurried over to Greg's side and put one of his hands over one of Greg's. Greg looked up, forcing a smile to his face. "It's good to see you too, Alvie."

Maeve sat on the cot across from him, speaking softly. "Hey."

"No need to shout." Greg muttered wincing as he looked around. "So what did I miss?"

Chris took a seat next to her, taking her hand while Alvie climbed up on Maeve's other side. "Nothing. Tilda said she was waiting until we were all awake."

Greg nodded to the door. "Well, I guess I'm the last one."

Tilda walked into the room with Adam right behind her and a small, slim woman with dark hair and dark eyes on her other side. Tilda walked toward Maeve and the others, standing at the edge of the break between the two beds. Norah with Iggy in her arms strode over as well, standing along the back of the bed that Greg sat on.

Making her way over to them, Tilda said, "Good. You're all awake. And looking no worse for wear. I'd like to introduce you to Pearl Huen. She is my second-in-command."

The serious woman nodded at the group. "If you have any problems or needs, please bring them to me."

Not waiting for anyone to respond, Tilda continued. "First, I want to apologize for the way that we needed to bring you to the base. But this base is beyond top secret. There are only five people in all of the world that know where it is located."

Greg shook his head. "Tilda, has anyone ever told you that you are seriously paranoid?"

"It has been mentioned," she said dryly. "But there is a reason for such extreme security. This base has been in existence for nearly sixty years. The only reason it has survived that long is because of that paranoia."

"Okay, so you're not going to tell us where we are," Chris said. "Because you seem to be suggesting we're at some sort of government base. So whose base is it? The DOD? The CIA? The ISA?"

"The ABCs? The DFGs? The XYZs?" Greg mumbled under his breath.

Ignoring Greg, Tilda said, "None of the above. You are among the only handful of civilians who have ever been introduced to this federal agency. I mentioned before that there was a secondary space program within the United States government. You are at the hub for the main base of that program. Welcome to R.I.S.E."

CHAPTER 14

Tilda's announcement was met with silence before Norah broke it. "I think I speak for everyone when I say: what?"

"It is a rather long story and quite involved. I thought perhaps we could discuss it over a meal. I'm sure all of you are famished," Tilda said.

As if her words had made it so, Maeve's stomach grumbled. She realized she hadn't eaten in over twenty-four hours. With everything happening, it hadn't exactly been a priority. But now, as she looked over to the triplets, she knew they needed to eat. "Yes, I think that's a good idea," she said.

Once outside, Maeve got her second look at where they were. It didn't help. There was a small hill in the foreground and dozens of trees. Beyond that, all she could make out was a building to their left. It was green with a round roof and reminded her of the Quonset huts she'd seen at Area 51.

She glanced back at the barracks where they had all woken up. It was the same type of building. The green and brown coloring on the buildings helped them blend into the trees.

From the air, she doubted you would be able to even discern that they were there.

Which is probably the point, she realized. But nothing about it screamed secret space agency, which was also probably the point.

A small wind blew across the open space, scattering a few leaves. Maeve shivered. Her gaze immediately darted to the triplets. They were very sensitive to the cold. "Tilda?"

Eyebrow raised, Tilda glanced back over her shoulder.

"The triplets and Alvie are going to need warmer clothes. It's too cold for them here," Maeve said.

"I'll see that it's taken care of immediately," Tilda replied. At the same time, Pearl pulled a radio from her belt and issued an order for fleeces and sweatpants to be brought to the cafeteria in children and adult sizes.

Leaning toward her, Chris whispered quietly. "Well, at least it looks like they're going to be taking care of us."

"Do you really think they will?" She murmured.

Chris shook his head. "Honestly, there's no way to know. All of this is so far out of any of our comfort zones, I don't even know what to expect."

"Have you ever heard of R.I.S.E.?" Maeve asked.

"No," he said keeping his voice low.

Greg whispered loudly on her other side. "Me either. And let me tell you, I have researched all of the good conspiracy sites ... And most of the bad ones."

Ahead, Tilda opened the doors to another Quonset hut. She smiled as the triplets skipped past her.

Maeve took a breath. "Well, it looks like it's time to get some answers."

CHAPTER 15

The answers didn't arrive immediately. In fact, when they walked in and everyone saw the food lined up buffet style along the back of the room, answers were no longer everyone's priority. The entire building was set up like a cafeteria. To the far left of the doors was a long steel counter lined with food. Behind it was a pass-through almost the length of it that looked into a large industrial kitchen. The rest of the room was lined with long tables, benches on either side. It could easily seat three hundred people.

Greg, Chris, and Maeve all set about loading up plates for Alvie and the triplets. Norah saw to getting herself and Iggy fed as well.

They all hunkered down at one table with overloaded plates. And no one really spoke or asked questions while they ate. Maeve was happy to see the triplets digging in without any ill effects. Alvie still had some of his thoughts closed away from her, but he seemed a lot more content.

Her gaze strayed to where Norah and Iggy sat quietly eating. Iggy was practically humming as he bounced in his seat, happily taking in everything on his plate. Maeve couldn't help but smile watching him. He was like a Disney character come to life.

"Does he eat everything?" Greg asked from where he sat across from Maeve, his attention also locked in on Iggy.

Norah shrugged. "I'm not sure. But he seems to like just about everything. I'm really hoping there're no allergies I'm not aware of." Her gaze caught Maeve's, and she gave her a tentative smile.

Maeve returned it, asking, "How are you doing?"

"Oh, well, you know, secret military base, surrounded by aliens, on the run from people I used to work for, and not sure where the hell I am, all par for the course," Norah said.

Maeve appreciated the lightheartedness of the response, knowing that she too was reeling inside at everything that had happened over a very short time period. But for Norah, that time was even shorter. She might have known about aliens, but she certainly hadn't known about everything else. She seemed to be adjusting pretty well. And Maeve was pretty sure that Iggy was a large part of that.

Patting his flat stomach, Chris sat back. "I don't think I can fit in another bite."

Greg pushed back from the table as well. "Me either. Unless, of course, maybe there's dessert ... Is there dessert?" he asked hopefully.

Tilda shook her head. "I'm afraid not yet. I thought everyone might need a little time to digest before we moved on to the next course."

"No problem. I was just asking for the triplets and Iggy. You know how kids love dessert," Greg said quickly.

"That's very considerate of you," Norah said pointedly.

He grinned as he put his hand to his chest. "That's me, always considerate."

The triplets started drumming their fingers on the table,

looking between Maeve and Chris expectantly. Tilda glanced over at them and then at Maeve. "What's going on?"

Maeve smiled. "They want to go play. They have some energy to burn. I don't suppose you have a playground around here somewhere?"

"Hm," Tilda murmured, "not for kids. We do have an obstacle course that our soldiers train on."

"Actually, that would be perfect," Maeve said.

"It's out back, behind the barracks. We can take them down there and then maybe talk when they're done," Tilda said.

Chris shook his head. "I'll take them down there. You guys start talking, and Maeve will fill me in later."

Adam stood up. "I'll show you where it is."

"Ig, ig, ig!" Iggy bounced up and down in Norah's lap. She frowned down at him. "I think Iggy wants to go, but I'm not sure if he should with his injury."

"He should be fine. Maldeks heal very quickly," Pearl said.

Everyone turned to Pearl. Greg and Maeve exchanged a surprised look.

"I'll keep an eye on him," Chris said.

Norah looked doubtfully down at Iggy, but he happily hopped across the table and leaped into Chris's arms. Chris stumbled back with a laugh. "Well, I guess that settles that."

Maeve looked over at Alvie. *Do you want to go or stay here?*

She could tell he was torn. He didn't like being away from the triplets, but he also knew that the conversation would be important.

I will tell you everything that she tells me, Maeve promised.

Alvie nodded and climbed down from his seat, going over to the triplets. Maeve got up and went to the stack of clothes that had been delivered shortly after they had started to eat. She sorted through sizes and then wrapped the triplets up in fleece-lined sweatpants and fleece jackets. Everything was green so that they would also blend into the surroundings.

Despite the singular coloring, she had to admit they looked adorable. Like a group of little elves. She kissed each one on the cheek. "Listen to Chris and Adam, okay?"

The triplets each nodded back at her before sprinting for the door. Maeve tossed a fleece at Chris. "You stay warm too."

"Yes, ma'am." He smiled at her before holding the door open for the triplets, Alvie, and Iggy to zip outside. Adam followed as well, giving Tilda a glance before disappearing through the doorway.

Once again, Maeve wondered about their relationship. Tilda said that Adam was her grandson, but they seemed awfully close. And even though he was her grandson, how had he ended up getting mixed up in all of this? But that was a small mystery for another day. Today the bigger mystery was what exactly was going on and how her family had ended up in the middle of it.

While Maeve was getting everyone suited up for the outside, Tilda had brought over a pot of coffee and a bunch of mugs to the table. Maeve took a seat, thanking Greg as he handed her one. Norah sat across from the two of them and met their gaze before the three of them turned and looked at Tilda, who sat at the head of the table. Pearl took a seat next to Norah.

Norah leaned forward. "I believe you said it was time for answers."

Tilda rested her hands on the tabletop in front of her, her fingers intertwined. "Yes, I believe those are long overdue."

CHAPTER 16

The door slid closed behind Chris and the others. Maeve kept her gaze on them through the glass until they disappeared from view. A chill crawled over her. She hated them being split up. Too much had gone wrong when they had been split up for her to feel anything but discomfort at the idea.

They are only a short distance away. And Chris won't let any harm come to them. She repeated the phrases in her mind over and over again, trying to convince herself that it was true. She wanted to run after them and demand that they all stay together. But to stay together, they needed answers. And that started with finding out where they were and what this secret program was all about.

She turned her attention back to Tilda, who sat quietly waiting for her to finish her inner discussion. When she met the older woman's gaze, she gave her a nod.

Tilda placed her mug back on the table. "You are the first civilians to ever step foot on the R.I.S.E. base. Everyone else who has been brought here has been slowly exposed to agency's goals over the course of their career. You, I'm afraid, will be given a crash course in the role the United States government has played in the development of this program ... and its role in communicating with intelligent life from other planets."

"I don't think that's an entirely accurate statement," Maeve said. "Each one of us has been exposed to intelligent life from other planets a great deal more than the average citizen."

Inclining her head in acknowledgment, Tilda said, "That is true. Your work with Alvie and the triplets is tremendous." She turned to Norah. "And no one can deny the bond that you have established with the young Maldek."

Greg cleared his throat. "And I worked with ... well, Hank."

"Hank?" Norah frowned.

"A Kecksburg-AG2. You know those incredibly terrifying alligatorlike aliens that nearly killed all of us in New Mexico?" Greg said lightly.

"Yes?" Norah drew out the word.

Meeting her gaze, for only a moment, Greg winced. "Well, I kind of sort of helped create him, or at least the first of him, and then I observed and cataloged his behaviors and traits."

Norah gave him a look of disgust.

He cleared his throat again. "Well, let's just move on to what you were talking about there, Tilda. You were explaining about R.I.S.E.?"

Blowing out a frustrated breath, Tilda shook her head slightly at him before composing her expression. "R.I.S.E. stands for Research in Intelligent Space Exploration. The program was established in 1956."

Maeve frowned. That couldn't be right. "But NASA wasn't established until 1960."

"Yes. We predate NASA," Tilda said.

"1956," Greg murmured. "An interesting year. It happens

to be the year after President Eisenhower allegedly met with the UFO at Camp Holloman."

Tilda nodded. "R.I.S.E. was created in response to that meeting. Eisenhower was a military man. He had been a five-star general in the United States Army and had also served as Supreme Commander of the Allied Expeditionary Forces in Europe. So when he learned that there was life outside of this planet, he automatically started thinking of it in terms of self-defense. But he also knew a great deal could be achieved through alliances."

"We have an alliance with Agaren's race," Maeve said.

"Yes, in a way," Tilda replied. "But when R.I.S.E. first began, the intent truly was exploration. And with Dr. von Braun as the head, the agenda for that exploration was most challenging."

Greg sat up. "Wait, von Braun? As in Wernher von Braun?"

A small smile slipped across Tilda's face. "He was a brilliant man."

Maeve had no doubt about that statement. Allegedly von Braun had shown an affinity for math and science as a child. Growing up in Austria, his parents had been at a bit of a loss as to what to do with their brilliant son. He was passionate about rockets from a young age, even getting arrested at the age of twelve for setting off fireworks attached to a cart. His lifelong focus on rocketry attracted the interest of the Third Reich. And as the Third Reich began its rise to power, von Braun's work was taken over, and he was subsumed under the Nazi banner.

Von Braun was credited with leading the team that developed the Nazis' devastating V-2 rockets. As the war drew to a close, von Braun was captured. He arranged for himself and 500 other Nazi scientists to immigrate to the United States through Operation Paperclip. They were taken to the White

Sands Proving Ground in New Mexico, and they began working on the U.S. rocket efforts.

When John F. Kennedy announced that the U.S. would be on the Moon by the end of the decade, he was relying on von Braun to get them there. When the first Apollo rocket reached the Moon, von Braun was given a parade in Huntsville, Alabama, his home at the time.

"Von Braun had been interested in space exploration from an early age," Tilda said. "He even wrote a science fiction novel back in 1952 called *Project Mars*, about a human expedition to the red planet. Some of his calculations, of course, were off, but many of them were right on point."

Maeve didn't know anything about his fiction writing, but she had seen one of his three movies made in coordination with Disney about space exploration. *Man in Space* had been released in 1955 and had Wernher von Braun explaining the potential for humans' exploration in the stars.

"Did von Braun know about Eisenhower's meeting at Holloman?" Norah asked.

Tilda nodded. "In 1956, when Eisenhower met with him to discuss the creation of R.I.S.E., von Braun was informed about the events."

Already Maeve's head was spinning. It was truly amazing when you thought about it. Just over a decade earlier, von Braun had been making rockets for Nazis. And then fifteen years later, he was trusted with one of the greatest secrets of the U.S. government.

"Von Braun became the first head of NASA when it was created in 1960. Who took over as the head of R.I.S.E.?" Greg asked.

A small smile slipped across Tilda's face. "Von Braun was the head of R.I.S.E. until his death in 1977. R.I.S.E., since its inception, has had two primary goals: to maintain an alliance with friendly alien species and to act as a defensive barrier for aggressive species. NASA was essentially R.I.S.E.'s public relations arm. No one in NASA besides von Braun knew that R.I.S.E. even existed. They thought they were on the cutting edge of space travel. But R.I.S.E. was years ahead of them in technology."

"Why bother with the subterfuge?" Norah asked. "If what you are saying is true, the space race with Russia could've been entirely avoided."

Tilda nodded. "It could have. But it served its purpose. It allowed the world to think that we were no more advanced than they were when it came to space travel. It helped keep R.I.S.E. a secret."

Frowning, Maeve shook her head. "That's the part I don't understand. *Why* keep it a secret? I mean, I know all about the belief that humanity would lose its mind if they learned that aliens existed. But humanity wouldn't be alarmed that we were more technologically developed. So why all the secrecy?"

When Tilda paused, Maeve had the sense that she was searching for her words.

"When we talk about finding alien life, we speak about it as if it is something we will do out there." Tilda pointed to the ceiling. "As if we will come across evidence of alien life through our space travels. The truth is, aliens have been living on planet Earth for centuries. And R.I.S.E. was created to make sure that they are never able to endanger humanity, beyond, of course, what they did to help create us."

CHAPTER 17

Greg's eyes were wide. "Beyond what they did to *create* us? You mean it's true? We're an alien ant colony?"

"Well, I wouldn't put it *that* way," Tilda said smiling. "But humanity's development has been encouraged by outside forces."

Her conversation with Agaren crossed Maeve's mind. "Agaren said that our aggressive nature concerns the Council."

Tilda nodded. "The Council is a group of intelligent beings that oversee life and our part of the galaxy. They have watched humanity's growth through millions of years of development. *Homo sapiens* were, in part, created with their intervention."

"But Mommy and Daddy aren't very happy now?" Greg asked.

"They are concerned," Tilda said. "Humanity has a capacity for doing good. But they have an almost equal capacity for evil. Destruction."

"How does R.I.S.E. fit into this?" Norah asked.

"We make sure that the world stays on an even keel, to the best of our abilities. The meeting at Holloman Air Force Base with President Eisenhower was a warning. The Council had seen the wars we had engaged in. They had seen the damage that had been done. They warned that the world could not go to war like that again. Since that time, we have aided in making sure there was never another world war."

"How?" Norah asked.

"We have operatives across the globe, from all different nations. R.I.S.E. is a U.S. agency, but we have pulled in talent from wherever we have needed it. There have been atrocities, but they have not spiraled out of control to the point that the Council felt the need to intervene. And we intend to keep it that way," Tilda said her gaze locking on each of them in turn.

"But you said that R.I.S.E. is a secondary space agency," Greg said. "Have you ever been to space?"

Tilda smiled. "I'm afraid that's need-to-know, and currently you do not need to know. What you do need to know is that our job and primary purpose is to keep all of you safe."

"Especially Alvie and the triplets," Maeve said.

"Yes," Tilda said with a nod. "They are an important aspect of the Council's plan for the planet."

Greg glanced around the room. "No offense, but if this is the secondary space agency, you're not very impressive."

Amusement twinkled in Tilda's eyes. "Oh, we hold our own. It is safer right now for you to stay here at our staging base. The hybrids are not known to the rest of R.I.S.E. I know the secrecy seems extreme, but it has kept us protected all these years."

"So what's the plan for all of us?" Greg asked.

Tilda took a deep breath. "For the time being, you will remain here at the staging base until we have assessed and neutralized any threats to the hybrids."

Studying Tilda, Norah spoke quietly. "You don't trust your own people."

"I trust *most* of my people," Tilda said. "Until I can say that

100%, you will have to stay here where you will be hidden from the majority of the base."

"How long will that take?" Maeve asked.

As Tilda stood up, Pearl did the same. "Hopefully not too long. But if it does continue beyond a reasonable timeframe, we will create different housing structures to allow you a more normal daily routine. Now, I need to head back to the base. Pearl will remain here in my stead, and again, if you have any problems, bring them to her."

Without another word, Tilda and Pearl strode toward the exit. Neither Greg nor Maeve nor Norah spoke until the two of them had stepped out of the building.

"You realize what that means, right?" Norah asked.

"Yeah, we're here for a little while, and then we'll move over to the super high-tech base," Greg said.

Maeve shook her head, feeling as if a cell door had slammed shut in front of her. "No. We are going to be living here for a very long time."

CHAPTER 18

Twenty-four hours after their "welcome to R.I.S.E." conversation, Norah's head was spinning from everything they'd learned, and she desperately needed something to distract her from what she now felt was a life sentence that had just been handed down by Tilda the Secretive.

She caught up with Adam outside the cafeteria. "Adam?"

He turned slowly. "Yes?" He didn't smile at Norah but immediately smiled at Iggy, who Greg was carrying to the obstacle course. It was an attribute she had noticed. He rarely smiled at adults, but he always had a smile for Iggy, the triplets, Alvie, and Penny.

She wondered what went on behind those glasses of his. He was the most controlled and reserved individual she had ever met. Emotions seemed to be an almost a foreign concept to him. He was incredibly loyal to his grandmother. He was a very strange man, and yet she felt a kinship with him. Maybe it was because they were both soldiers, but there was a straightforwardness to him that she liked.

"I, um, was hoping I could ask a favor," Norah said.

He waited, not responding. His facial expression didn't change.

Well, that's not encouraging, she thought. But she barreled ahead anyway. "I'm going a little stir crazy, and I was hoping maybe I could just surf the net a little, maybe check my email—"

He was shaking his head before she'd even finished. "Security protocol requires that you stay away from all electronic traces. Someone would know you'd checked your email."

"Look, my mom sends me email when she can't reach me by phone. I know I can't call her or write back, but I'd really like to read her emails. Isn't there any way?" She asked.

Adam didn't move, just continued staring at her, or at least she thought that's what he was doing. His dark glasses added an extra layer of inscrutability to the already undecipherable man. Norah was beginning to think that maybe she'd broken him with her request. He hadn't moved in what felt like a long time. "Um, well, never—"

"Follow me." Adam turned on his heel and headed toward the barracks. Norah hustled to keep up with him. Was he agreeing to help? Or was he about to turn her in? She simply couldn't read the man. Ahead, the main offices stood. Norah's concerns increased as the main administrative office came into view. That bastard. He *was* turning her in. If he thought for one minute she was going to stand around and be chastised like some errant schoolgirl, then he had another thing …

Her angry thoughts cut off as he turned away from the admin building. Instead, he headed up the hill toward a small building, only slightly larger than a shed.

Norah had never been inside. She'd assumed it was a shed. But Adam slid open the door and stepped inside. Norah followed him. The room was completely packed with computer equipment. Tall servers lined the walls, behind panes of glass. Norah touched one as she stepped past. The glass was cold to the touch. Monitors, consoles, and equipment she had never seen before lined three and a half sides of the room. It was a hacker's dream setup.

And sitting in the middle of it was Penny.

Norah hadn't seen Penny since before the infiltration of the base at Dulce. By the time she'd met back up with the group, Penny and her mother had been whisked away by Tilda's people. Now, as Norah saw Penny surrounded by towers of electronics, she wondered if that had been at Penny's request or Tilda's.

Penny glanced up when they'd stepped in but immediately returned her attention to the monitors in front of her.

Adam stopped at the edge of the ring of equipment. "Wait here." He walked toward Penny, crouching down so he was eye level with her.

His voice was too low, so she couldn't make out what he was saying. Norah stepped closer to the towers of servers. Cold air blew in from a vent along the top of the towers. The shed was much larger than she'd first thought. Penny was crammed up front. Tower upon tower was arrayed behind her. It must have stretched back another fifty feet. She recognized the name on it: Summit.

Her mouth dropped open. *Oh my God.* This was a supercomputer. She didn't know much about them except that they were lightning fast. Normal computers worked on millions of instructions per second. Supercomputers instead performed a hundred quadrillion floating point operations per second, or FLOPS. The system had to have cost millions, no, hundreds of millions of dollars.

And they gave Penny access to it? Norah stared at the young girl incredulously. It wasn't that Penny didn't know how to use it. Norah was absolutely certain she knew what she was doing. It was just what she would do with such power that was the question. Penny was beyond intelligent, but her moral judgment was questionable at best. And as a result, Norah questioned *Tilda's* moral decision-making ability in allowing Penny to access such a machine.

Adam stood and walked over to one of the monitors. He hit a few buttons on the keyboard in front of it before rolling a chair from the back of the room and positioning it in front of the monitor. He looked up and waved Norah over.

She moved over to him, darting a glance at Penny, who did not look away from her screen.

Adam nodded to the screen. "Penny will cover your tracks. You cannot respond to any of the emails. But you can read them."

She let out a sigh. "Thanks, Adam."

As Norah scrolled through her email, she finally felt connected to the normal world. Her mother had written her as expected. Norah's chest tightened, imagining her sitting at her computer picking away at the keyboard with one finger. Apparently the rescue dog she'd taken in had a fondness for her slippers. They were never next to her bed when she woke up in the morning. Last time, she'd found them in the bathtub.

Norah smiled. Her mom never complained about Norah and all of her travels. She'd just been thrilled when she'd been able to spend some time at the family home. She still had a room there for Norah, as well as her brothers.

Two of her brothers had sent her emails as well. One was in Afghanistan, the other one was in Germany. Her fingers itched to respond to both of them, knowing how much it meant to her when they had written to her when she was overseas. But right now she was in a different kind of war.

She spent a little time scrolling through the internet, catching up on news. There was nothing about the incident in

New Mexico. She shouldn't have been surprised. After all, it was a pretty isolated location. But still, she'd thought there might be something.

Her thoughts drifted to the tall winged creature that Luke Gillibrand had called Sammy. Where had he come from? And why had the creature helped them?

It must have been the same creature that had helped them in New Mexico. But what was it? And why had it chosen to help a little boy on a farm in Kansas? For that matter, what had drawn the Blue Boys there?

But more importantly, how had no one else noticed him? He must have flown over towns and cars. Did people just ignore it or write it off as a figment of their imagination?

Of course, before she started at D.E.A.D., she probably would've done the same. No one liked to stand out for being the one who called in a monster. Or a UFO. But both were real. And the U.S. government knew about both of them. And they had done a great job of making sure no one reported anything.

Her mental wanderings turned back to Sandra and Luke, a nagging worry forming in the back of her mind. Sandra had mentioned that Sammy had been communicating with her son. If anyone else at D.E.A.D. learned that, they would want to know why.

And she'd seen how they brought people in. She and Iggy had only avoided that fate thanks to Penny. Luke and Sandra wouldn't have anyone.

It's probably nothing. They're fine, she told herself. But Norah couldn't quite convince herself of that. She turned in her chair. Penny was still fixated on the monitors in front of her. "Penny, I need you to check on someone."

Penny didn't respond. Her fingers flew over the keyboard underneath her hands, her eyes scanning different monitors.

"Penny, did you hear me?" Norah prodded.

The girl's gaze darted to Norah before shifting back to the

monitors. Norah stood up and walked so that she was standing right behind one of the monitors. "I need you to check on someone. Sandra Gillibrand. She lives in—"

"Tribune, Kansas," Penny said without looking up.

"How do you know that?" Norah moved to stand to the side of Penny with the view of the monitors.

Sandra's military file flashed on the screen. Leaning forward, Norah scanned it and noted the commendations. Sandra had been a good soldier. Next to it, another military file was displayed. Noah Gillibrand, Sandra's husband and, Norah assumed, Luke's father.

Scanning it as well, Norah's gaze stopped at the blacked-out redacted portion at the bottom. She pointed to it. "Can you find out what's underneath this?"

The young girl's hands were a flurry of movement. The screens shifted from image to image. Norah turned her head against the onslaught, but Penny took it all in, her gaze moving from monitor to monitor, image to image, barely blinking. Lights from the monitors flashed across Penny's face, lighting up her glasses, giving her an otherworldly look. Finally, she nodded at the screen.

Norah leaned forward once again. Project Antaeus. Sandra's husband and Luke's father had been a subject of the project when he'd served in Iraq. But there were no further details.

Frowning, Norah started to ask. "Penny, can you—"

"There," the girl said.

Norah turned her gaze to where Penny pointed. A new file had opened up, this one from the Department of Defense. Project Antaeus's goal had been to create a stronger, more efficient soldier. It had been done in conjunction with the CIA.

A chill crawled over Norah. None of the CIA agents she had met while deployed had given her a sense of decency. If the CIA was involved, that didn't bode well.

A spreadsheet appeared on the screen. Norah scanned it quickly, finding Noah's name. She realized it was a list of all the soldiers who'd been involved in Project Antaeus. The first column listed the soldier's project ID number, the second their first and last name, the third their rank, the fourth the branch of the military, followed by columns indicating their age and medical issues. But it was the last column that drew Norah's attention. It displayed their day of death.

Every single one of them had died.

Norah stared at the screen, trying to make sense of it. It was highly unusual that all had passed, but if they were in the same platoon, it sadly wasn't out of the realm of possibilities.

She stared at the name Antaeus. It sounded Greek. "Penny, can you—"

The girl pointed at another monitor. It was a website on Greek mythology. Apparently Antaeus was the son of Poseidon and Gaia. He drew his strength from touching the ground. He was invincible when he was touching the earth. He was defeated only when he was lifted from the ground.

Norah frowned. It seemed an odd choice for a project name. But what exactly did it mean?

It was curious, but it probably had nothing to do with the incident on Sandra's farm. It could be a completely unrelated situation.

But it was also possible this was somehow connected. According to the dates, Luke's father had been killed shortly before Luke had been born. And Sammy had befriended Luke and saved him.

Rubbing her eyes, Norah pulled her thoughts back. No, she was reaching. The two were unconnected. Project Antaeus had been shut down over ten years ago. It wasn't connected to what had happened to Sandra and Luke recently.

But still ... "Is there a way for you to check up on Sandra

and Luke? Just, I don't know, check if there've been any police reports or activity reported around their house?"

Her hands once again flying over the monitor and keyboard, Penny nodded. Norah watched her in awe. In some ways, Penny was as foreign to her as Iggy, maybe even more so. In fact, Iggy was easier to understand. He simply wanted to belong, wanted to be cared for. And in return, he was loyal to those who he cared for and who cared for him.

But Penny ... Norah couldn't even begin to imagine how her brain worked. Norah could barely take in the images on the screen before Penny had whisked them away, replacing them with different one. Yet Penny was taking in all of the information, soaking it up like a sponge. Norah could barely look at the screens for more than five minutes before she started to get a headache. She had no idea how Penny managed it.

That wasn't the greatest difference between Penny and Iggy, though: Penny, unlike Iggy, didn't seem to need human connection. But she *did* need some connection. She had risked a great deal to protect Agaren. She considered him a friend, even though she had never met him or even talked to him. Norah wasn't sure if she was envious of Penny's intelligence or felt bad for how it seemed to keep her from being connected to those around her.

Penny's hands stopped moving.

Norah redirected her attention back to the monitor. She frowned, trying to understand what she was looking at. It was night-vision footage. It started in an SUV, and then whoever was recording the footage moved toward a house. A tingle of recognition ran over her. "Is that Sandra's house?" Norah asked.

Still not looking at Norah, Penny nodded. "Yes."

Leaning forward, Norah's gut tightened as a flash bang sailed through the front window. Her heart in her throat, she watched as a group of three soldiers stormed in ahead, and then they were in the house, but a quick search revealed that it was empty.

"Who is that?" Norah demanded.

"CIA black ops," Penny said before she frowned. "But I can't find the name of the supervisor who okayed it."

In her gut, Norah knew it was related to the events at New Mexico. "Did something happen to Sandra and Luke? Are they okay? Are they hurt?"

Penny shook her head. "No, they're still searching for them."

"Wait, why were they there?" Norah asked.

There was no emotion in Penny's voice when she spoke. "To take the Gillibrands into custody."

That made no sense. Norah frowned. "Was there a warrant out for them?"

"The order came through D.E.A.D," Penny said.

Dread rolled through Norah. *Oh no.* "Find everything you can on Sandra and Luke's last movements."

She didn't wait for a reply before she strode out of the shed. She needed to help them. She needed to find them. But first she needed to get off this damn base.

CHAPTER 19

Norah marched down the path toward the main administration building. She needed to get off the island. If Sandra and Luke were being hunted, they needed help. She didn't think Tilda would find that to be a priority. Maeve and Chris would help, but they had no authority here.

So who does that leave me with?

"Ig."

Despite her worries, Norah smiled at the sight as Iggy propelled himself toward her. When he was four feet away, he crouched low and leapt. Norah caught him, and he quickly scrambled up to her shoulders. She patted his legs. "Hey, buddy."

"Ig, ig, ig, ig, ig," he chattered away seemingly perfectly happy.

"Iggy, where are you—" Greg appeared, a harassed looked on his face. His shoulders drooped as he caught sight of Norah. "Of course. I should have known."

He made his way over to them, shaking his head. "Iggy, my

friend, I would appreciate it if you didn't just run off. You're making me look like the world's most irresponsible babysitter."

Iggy reached out a claw and patted Greg on the head. "Ig," he said solemnly.

Greg laughed. "I think he just said I *am* the world's worst babysitter."

"Seems like," Norah agreed.

Frowning, Greg tilted his head, studying her. "What's going on?"

"What? Nothing," she said quickly.

He grunted. "Yeah ... seriously, I know that look. It's the 'something is seriously wrong, and I am about to do something crazy' look."

She glared at him. "That is not what my face is saying."

He put up both hands. "Hey, don't yell at *me*. Your face is the one doing all the talking. So what's going on?"

Now it was Norah's turn to study the scientist. When she'd first met him, she'd put him firmly in the "not good in a fight" category. But Chris had told her that Greg would surprise her, and he had. In New Mexico, he'd been tough and smart. And not at all the nerdy scientist she had pegged him for when she'd first met him.

Well, actually, he was completely a nerdy scientist, but he also could be pretty useful in a fight. And right now, she could use someone pretty useful. "I'm worried about someone."

She quickly explained about Luke and Sandra. Greg stayed silent as she explained, his look growing more and more thoughtful. "I wonder ..."

When he didn't answer for a while, Norah prodded. "Wonder what?"

Giving her a bit of a sheepish smile, Greg spoke slowly. "Maeve told you about the winged creature that basically saved them when they were leaving their first hideout and then when they were leaving Dulce, right?"

Norah nodded.

"I wonder if it's the same guy. Or at least, one of the same species," he said.

She frowned. "So you think he might be one of the good ones?"

He shook his head. "Oh I'm not quite ready to go there yet. We don't know his motivations. But he definitely doesn't seem like the 'kill, kill, kill' ones I know and hate. Do you have any idea where Sandra might have gone?"

Picturing the mom and son, Norah felt a sense of responsibility to them. "No, but I figure with Tilda's resources, they've got to be able to track them down. But I need to figure out a way off this island. And I don't think commandeering a plane will be too easy."

Greg grinned. "Well, I've got an idea about that."

"About commandeering a plane?" She asked.

He linked arms with her, pulling her toward the main camp area. "Nope. About getting us an ally."

Norah let Greg pull her toward the main camp. They didn't pass anyone along the way. And once again, she wondered how this was an all-powerful military base. It looked like it wasn't much better equipped than some of the forward bases in Afghanistan. Nothing about it screamed unlimited resources. In fact, it seemed like a place where they rationed the toilet paper.

"There's our guy." Greg's voice interrupted her thoughts, and she looked up to see Adam step out of the administration building, speaking quietly to Jasper and Mike Bileris, the former Secret Service agent who was also on Tilda's payroll. The woman certainly had resources.

Norah waited until Jasper and Mike walked away before moving to intercept Adam.

His sunglasses firmly in place, Adam watched them go before heading toward the dormitory. He always wore them, even when there was no sun, even when he was inside. Maeve had explained how Adam had taken on two of the Hank creatures. Norah struggled to figure out how that was possible. She, Greg, and Iggy, along with a few of Tilda's men, had been required to take down one of them. So how did Adam do it on his own? He was like a one-man SWAT team.

Which is exactly what I need.

She grinned at Greg. "Thanks. Can you watch Iggy for a few minutes?"

"I can try." He held out his arms, and Iggy leapt into them. "Come on, dude, let's go get a snack."

"Ig, Ig."

Norah started to jog. "Adam."

He paused, his shoulders tensing before he turned. Once again, he did not say a word. He and Penny were actually a lot alike.

"I need some help." Norah quickly ran down the situation with Sandra and Luke. She added in the father's involvement in Project Antaeus, and it was the first time she saw a reaction from Adam. If she hadn't been studying him so closely, she wouldn't have noticed it, but his jaw ticked. And then it was gone, and he was back to his impassive self.

"Penny is trying to find out where they are now. But Sandra is former military. She'll have ditched her phone and any way of tracking her. She won't go to anyone that we would think of. But she needs help," she stared at the man trying to read him.

Adam didn't say anything. He turned his head and looked

at the administration building, but Norah had the distinct feeling he wasn't really seeing it, that his mind was running through possibilities.

Finally, he turned back to her. "Be ready to go in fifteen minutes."

CHAPTER 20

HOGANSFIELD, MONTANA

It had been two days since Sandra had pulled into Hogansfield. She'd gotten the job at the diner, although so far she'd only worked two shifts. The tips were pretty lousy, but at least it was something. She and Luke had had to sleep in the car for the last two nights. She'd taken the car to a mechanic who was also a former Marine. He told her the transmission was shot. It was still running, but the gears were slipping. Soon it would stop switching gears altogether, which she'd figured. But replacing it would cost a minimum of 2,000 dollars, and she simply didn't have it right now.

She was beginning to feel a little desperate. How had it come to this? She'd done well in school. She had gone on to serve her country. She'd been an officer. Her husband had been one as well. And yet here she was, living in her car with her autistic son, surviving on scraps from the diner.

If this is the American dream, it leaves a great deal to be desired.

Light sprayed through the front windshield. Sandra's heart raced as she waited. She wasn't sure who she was more worried about—the men who'd come to her home or the local cops. Either way, she'd be in trouble. She was parked on the edge of a field she'd found that was full of old abandoned cars. Sadly, her car fit right in.

She held her breath as the car slowly rolled past. She peeked her head out. Police. *Please just keep going,* she prayed.

The lights were off in the interior of her car, so it should look just like all the others. She didn't know what she would do if they got arrested. If Luke was taken from her ... She shook her head. She couldn't even think about how he would react. Or where they would put him.

Tears pressed against the back of her eyes. She bit her lip, trying to hold them back. *I can't keep doing this.* Staying in this little town was not a solution. It was a postponement. She needed to make a choice. She needed to ask for help. She just needed to decide exactly whom she was going to ask for it from.

Family was out. Estranged was a nice word for her and her parents' relationship status. The local cops were out. They wouldn't be prepared for any of this and would simply hand her and Luke over to those feds.

Which left only one option. She pulled the business card from her pocket. It was fragile now, closer to tissue paper than cardstock at this point because she'd pulled it out and looked at it so many times.

She sat watching the police car's taillights disappear down the road. She counted to thirty and then stepped silently from the car, easing the door closed behind her. Luke didn't even move. He was sprawled out on the back seat.

With trembling hands, she pulled out her cell phone. She took a deep breath and dialed.

CHAPTER 21

SEATTLE, WASHINGTON

The image of Joseph Watson filled the screen of Martin's monitor. Strong cheekbones, eyes hidden by dark sunglasses, blond hair that even in the black-and-white photo looked startlingly white. He wore a white T-shirt and green camo pants. An American flag was in the background. The site was Huntsville, Alabama, in 1961.

Martin had zoomed in to the background to get a closer look at Joseph because there were so few pictures of him available. But when he zoomed out, he got the complete shot: the meeting of JFK and Wernher von Braun. The photo was taken at Cape Canaveral in Florida, on November 16, 1963. The most famous image from the meeting was of JFK and von Braun looking to the sky, one arm of each raised next to a model rocket as they discussed the U.S.'s potential in space.

But this shot was taken as the men walked. The easy camaraderie between the two was evident in the photo. In fact, they'd gotten along so well, JFK invited Braun and his wife to the White House for dinner. It was scheduled for November 25, 1963, three days after JFK was assassinated.

But Martin wasn't interested in the famous men in the picture. He was interested in the man who had chosen to stay on the sidelines of America's space program. In this shot, Joseph was on the side and behind von Braun. Martin narrowed his eyes. There was a great deal of mystery surrounding Tilda's husband—too much mystery. Martin had been unable to find any information on him. He didn't even know the man's country of birth. And now that Tilda was back on the scene, Martin knew he needed to take a closer look at her significant other.

Stacy knocked at the door, interrupting his line of thought. He swallowed down his annoyance and waved her in. The woman never sent a text when she could talk. If she weren't so qualified in every other way, he'd fire her for that alone.

Or kill her.

"What is it?" he growled.

"We had a hit on Norah Tidwell's cell phone."

Surprise flashed through Martin. He thought she was smarter than that. "She used it?"

Stacy shook her head. "No. But she received a call from Sandra Gillibrand. We've traced it to Montana. She called from a place called Hogansfield."

Good. A location. "How long until you can have a team on site?" He asked.

"Two hours," Stacy said.

Martin glanced at his watch. "Good. Let me know when they have them." With a flick of his wrist, he dismissed Sandra and returned to the issue in front of him.

For the next hour, he reviewed information on both Matilda and Joseph Watson. But then when the hour was up, he reached for his phone. He dialed the number, waiting impatiently for the call to be answered. Finally, a rough voice answered. "What?"

Taking a breath despite his racing heart, Martin spoke calmly. "This is Drummond. I have some information for Tatiana."

CHAPTER 22

HOGANSFIELD, MONTANA

There was a small rush at the diner at lunchtime. Sandra had never worked the lunch shift, and she was happy to see the influx of customers. Evan, the owner, explained that a lot of the long-haul truckers liked to stop through. This was one of the only diners on the way to Hardin.

Sandra flitted from table to table, refilling coffee cups, taking orders, enjoying the familiarity of the routine. It didn't matter where you went, waitressing was waitressing. Some of the stress that had been weighing her down fell away as she filled orders and lost herself in small talk.

Luke sat at a small table in the kitchen, reading a book. Every time she went to the kitchen window to pick up an order or put one in, she glanced in at him. He looked fine. Evan had taken a liking to him and hadn't minded allowing him to stay nearby when Sandra worked.

Reaching down, Luke picked up a French fry from the plate next to him. He ate it without removing his eyes from the book. Then he took a sip from the chocolate shake next to him, his eyes still glued to the pages in front of him. The book was a *Minecraft* novel. Evan had explained that someone had left it at the diner months ago. It'd been sitting underneath the counter in the lost and found since then, along with a few other books. Evan had told Luke to grab whatever ones he wanted.

Sandra knew that Evan wanted to ask about Luke. Why he wasn't in school and what was going on with him. But she was thankful he didn't. He just quietly made him some food and let him have his space.

"Orders up," Evan called through the kitchen pass-through.

Winding her way through the tables, Sandra slipped behind the counter. She grabbed the four plates, carefully balancing them on both hands, and then made her way back toward the group sitting in the corner. After handing out their orders, she went back and refilled coffee mugs around the diner. Replacing the coffeepot on the burner, she set up the next one to brew.

Through the pass-through, Evan caught her eye. "Why don't you go take five minutes? It's been a pretty busy lunch."

"You sure?" She asked although she desperately wanted some time. Her legs ached as soon as the idea of getting off them for a few minutes entered her mind.

He nodded. "I'll take care of anybody that stops in. Just go get yourself a drink or something."

"Thanks." She hurried back into the kitchen, poured herself a water, and squeezed some lemon into it. Gripping the drink, she then headed back to the main room to sit with Luke. a

Sitting across from him, she snatched a fry from his plate, before resting her feet on the trestle underneath the table. Letting out a sigh, she smiled. Oh, that was nice.

Luke didn't even look up from his book.

But that was all right. Sandra didn't need the conversation. And she was used to just listening to him breathe. Sometimes that was all she needed. She took a deep breath and took a drink while munching on the fry.

She'd been keeping track of her tips throughout the morning and lunch. Today would be a good day. They might even be able to afford a motel room tonight.

She wasn't sure whether or not she should spend the money on it, because she really needed to figure something out with the car. But she was beginning to think that maybe she needed to get rid of the car and just start over from scratch. She'd probably get some money from the junkyard for parts at least. And maybe she could get an old beater that would get them from A to B.

Because they needed to get on the road again soon. Staying in one spot was a guarantee that they would get caught. She just needed a couple more days to get a little bit more money together, and then maybe she could do something.

She hadn't heard back from Norah, but she'd left her phone in the car this morning. She'd been so tired that she'd woken up only just before she needed to report to the diner. Then she'd had to wake Luke from a deep sleep and get him moving. The phone must have slipped from her pocket when she'd been sleeping.

But making that phone call had helped. She decided if Norah hadn't gotten back to her by the time they got back to the car, she'd contact one of her old Army buddies. Have him wire her some money. Sean was about to ship out again, which meant he'd be out of the reach of the D.E.A.D.

And she was desperate and needed to do something. She'd contact him tomorrow, and hopefully they'd be on the road again within a few days. She decided she was going to try and sneak them into Canada. The U.S. government was the problem right now, so Canada seemed like it would be a better bet.

She wasn't sure exactly how she was going to manage to

get over the Canadian border, but she had to think that it wouldn't be as tough as the Mexican border. After all, she'd never really heard a lot about people sneaking into Canada, and Canadians were nice people, right?

After polishing off another three fries, she downed the rest of her water, and then took a quick stop in the ladies' room. Splashing some water on her face, she tried to ignore her reflection in the mirror. The woman staring back at her looked tired. She looked like Sandra's mom.

And Sandra really didn't want to see her.

Leaving the bathroom, she grabbed her apron off the hook by the back. She tied it around her waist as she stepped through the kitchen doors and back into the dining room.

"Heads up. Looks like we got a big group coming in. They must be on their way to the Army base." Evan nudged his chin toward the parking lot as he arranged a plate.

Sandra's head jolted up, her gaze locking on the four dark SUVs pulling into spots at the end of the parking lot. *Oh God, no.*

CHAPTER 23

The bed was shaking. Norah rolled onto her side, trying to figure out why. Her eyes blinked open, and she struggled to make sense of the scene in front of her.

There was a pressure holding her back around her waist. Blinking, she tried to clear her eyes, her head feeling fuzzy. She was in a plane. A private plane, or at least it was what she thought a private plane looked like. She'd never actually been in one.

The bed she was on was actually a long cream-colored leather couch. Across from her was another leather couch. Four executive chairs were arranged behind her, another set on the aisle across from them. One was reclined all the way down, Greg sprawled in it, one hand flung over the side, his mouth open.

She pushed up the window shade. Fluffy white clouds and bright blue sky greeted her.

A soft snore reached her from one of the other executive chairs. She quickly unbuckled herself and on wobbly legs made her way to the chair. Iggy lay curled up, a seatbelt across him and a blanket tucked around him. She knelt down, running a hand over his head. "Hey there, little buddy."

Iggy's eyes slowly opened, a small tired smile crossing his face. "Ig," he sighed softly as he reached for her.

Smiling, Norah undid his seatbelt and cuddled him to her, pulling up the blanket to wrap it around him. As soon as he was snuggled tight, he fell back asleep.

With Iggy carefully ensconced into her arms, she headed for the front of the plane. Holding Iggy with one hand, she opened the door to the cockpit.

Adam glanced back at her from the controls. "Good. You're awake."

"Barely. Greg's still asleep." Norah slunk into the copilot's chair, careful not to touch the array of instruments in front of her.

Her stomach dipped a little bit at the view out of the cockpit window. She wasn't necessarily afraid of heights. She just wasn't a huge fan of them. Images of her accidentally hitting a lever and them plunging to the earth filled her mind. She hugged Iggy a little tighter to make sure no stray arms or legs caught on anything.

Adam's head was turned toward her, waiting.

"Funny thing about being asleep. I don't actually remember going to sleep on a plane," Norah said giving him a pointed look.

There was no apology in Adam's voice as he spoke. "I moved you and Greg while you were sleeping."

"And Iggy?" She asked.

There was a small smile on his face as he turned his attention back to the instruments. He fiddled with one and then adjusted another. "He wasn't asleep. He became agitated. I was afraid he would alert too many people to our departure, so I brought him too."

"Wait, you didn't tell anybody we were leaving?" Norah asked.

Adam shrugged. "It seemed wiser to wait until we returned."

She smiled. Apparently Adam wasn't entirely a "follow the rules" kind of guy after all.

The cockpit door opened. Greg stumbled in. He slumped into the jump seat, his head in his hands. "I think my head gained an extra ten pounds," he said before he gave Iggy, who had popped his head over Norah's shoulder, a little wave.

Iggy waved back. "Ig."

"You said it, buddy. Anything new on Sandra or Luke?" Greg asked.

Nodding, Adam hit a button on the console. "Penny called about twenty minutes ago. She said that Sandra called your old cell phone. She patched through the message."

There was a click before a recording started through the plane's speakers. "Um, Agent Tidwell, this is Sandra, Sandra Gillibrand."

The nerves in Sandra's voice were obvious. Her speech was hesitant with deep pauses. And Norah could hear the faint tremor underneath. Norah pictured her scanning her surroundings, looking over her shoulder as she spoke. Her chest tightened in response.

Sandra's voice hurried on. "Um, you came to our home after those things attacked my son. Three days ago, a group of SUVs came to my home. They were looking for me and Luke. We got away and have been on the run ever since."

The woman's deep breath was audible over the plane speakers. Her voice broke. "I don't know what to do. I have Luke with me, and … I'm scared. I don't know if I can trust you. I don't know if you're working with the people that came to our home. But we're in trouble, and we could really use some help."

The fear of the woman was coming through loud and clear. Norah could picture her trying to get control of her emotions.

Her voice shaking even more now, Sandra said, "I don't know if you're still even using this phone. But if you are, I really need you to call me back. And I really need you to be one of the good guys."

The message ended.

Traces of Sandra's terror and desperation were a tangible thing in the cockpit. Norah knew that Luke had some form of autism. It wasn't as extreme as Penny's, but it would still make going on the run extremely difficult. The fact that Sandra had managed to keep them out of Martin's grip until this point was pretty impressive. But she also sounded like she was reaching the end of her rope. She knew what resources the D.E.A.D. would bring to bear against a target.

"We have to assume that the D.E.A.D. has also heard this recording," Norah said.

Adam nodded. "It came from Montana. We're going to land in a small airport outside of the town where that call was made, called Hogansfield. We'll be there in an hour."

Leaning his head back, Greg closed his eyes. "Awesome. Small-town America. Iggy, get ready for some seriously boring scenery."

Although Norah knew Greg was right, she couldn't be quite so cavalier about it. An hour was a lifetime when you were on the run. Especially now that Sandra had made contact. And if the D.E.A.D. were closer than they were, they would reach Sandra first.

Scanning the horizon, she leaned forward in her chair. She pictured Luke with his messy brown hair and those big eyes. Sammy had saved him once, but she didn't think they could count on him saving them again.

"We need to get there faster," she murmured.

Adam didn't say anything, but Norah could feel the

slightest change in the plane. She nodded and flicked another glance at him. "Weapons?"

He nudged his head toward the back of the cockpit, where a large black trunk sat. "In there."

Norah stood up. Greg cracked an eye open, apparently still not quite awake. Norah handed him Iggy.

"Come on, little buddy. Let's go close our eyes for another few minutes." Greg disappeared into the cabin with him.

Kneeling down in front of the trunk, Norah flipped it open and smiled. Adam had come prepared. She pulled out a P90. It was a strange-looking weapon. It looked like something from some sci-fi movie with its short barrel and almost rectangular appearance. There was a thumb-hole grip, giving it the feel of holding a pistol with the power of a machine gun.

Strange looking though it may be, it was favored by the Secret Service, along with military and police services across the globe. Its magazine held twenty 28mm rounds, and the casings discharged down instead of up, where they couldn't block a shooter's view. Plus, they had a speed of 900 rounds per minute, and the whole thing weighed less than seven pounds.

Norah smiled. *This will do. This will do nicely.*

CHAPTER 24

HOGANSFIELD, MONTANA

For a few precious seconds, Sandra was frozen in place. She didn't know what to do. Should she run? She immediately discounted the idea. She could not outrun those cars. And right now, she didn't have a car. Her car was around the back of the junkyard. She hadn't wanted to waste the gas.

She slipped back into the kitchen, her mind racing. How had they found her? And then the realization hit her. Norah had told them. *Which means I told them.*

Stupid, stupid, stupid. Sandra kicked herself up one side of her brain and down the other. Why did she think she could trust the agent?

She thrust those thoughts out of her head. She didn't have time for them.

"Sandra?" Evan looked at her, concern on his face.

"Uh, my stomach is feeling off. I just need a minute." She hurried toward the bathroom, not waiting for Evan's response. She slipped into his office and grabbed his keys off his desk.

Turning around, she nearly screamed. Luke stood in the doorway, his eyes wide. "They're here."

Heart racing, Sandra had to keep herself from grabbing his arm and pulling him toward the door. "Yes, they are. We need to go." She grabbed her bag off the hook by the back door. Slowly, she pushed the door open and peered out. There was no one out back.

Looking down at her son, she prayed that she could keep him safe. "We need to go fast."

Luke slipped his hand into Sandra's. She looked back at him in surprise, but he was staring at the door. Squeezing his hand gently, she opened the door and slipped out, pulling Luke with her and hurrying over to Evan's old brown Ford Explorer.

Quickly she opened the driver's door using the key. She was afraid if she used the key fob, it would draw attention. She pushed Luke forward. He scrambled into the driver's seat and over into the passenger seat.

She climbed in after him, saying a quick prayer. "Luke, put on your seatbelt and duck down."

Pulling on her own seatbelt, Sandra put the key into the ignition. The engine flared to life just as a figure covered head to toe in black combat gear appeared around the side of the diner. The man let out a yell. Sandra threw the car into reverse and stomped on the accelerator.

The man started running after them. And then he opened fire. Sandra reversed out of the parking lot and down the street. She yanked the steering wheel to the left, her stomach shifting with the force, and two wheels came up. She held her breath, praying the car didn't roll. For a few tense seconds, she was convinced it would. But the car slammed back down with a bone-rattling jolt. She put the car into drive and punched down on the accelerator again.

The back windshield exploded. Glass flew through the interior of the car. Luke cried out.

Gripping the steering wheel, Sandra pushed the accelerator down as far as it would go, flying down the road. She darted a glance to the rearview mirror. Three men in combat gear stood watching her disappear.

And behind them, three SUVs screeched onto the road and gave chase.

Her mind racing, Sandra ducked her head down, trying to figure out where they could go. But Montana was all open ground and few roads. She wasn't going to be able to lose them in Evan's old Ford.

She tore down the road and then got onto the highway, heading toward Hardin. Her only shot was reaching it and losing them somewhere in the city. But even as she thought it, she knew that was a long shot. Montana was one of the least populated states in the United States. Hardin might be bigger than Hogansfield, but that didn't mean she'd see a huge city.

So losing herself there was definitely a long shot. But right now, a long shot was all they had.

CHAPTER 25

In Norah's mind, she had always pictured Montana as flat, with little vegetation and some mountains in the distance. It was the landscape of dozens of old country westerns. Touching down outside Hardin, the reality for once equaled the imagination. There was little around the "airport" that Adam brought them to. It wasn't actually an airport. It was a private field that for some reason had a very long driveway.

As soon as the plane stopped, Norah had her seatbelt off and Iggy's as well. She grabbed the P90 and strapped on the vest that she'd already loaded up with extra magazines, a few grenades, and one very sharp knife.

Greg had also grabbed a vest, a rifle, and a berretta in a holster at his side. Norah eyed the handgun. "You know how to use it?"

"Use it? Yes," he said. "Hit anything with any sort of reliability? No. But it seems stupid to walk in unarmed."

Adam stepped in from the cockpit. His gaze scanned each of them, and he gave a simple nod as he grabbed a series of guns and knives and a vest for himself.

A few minutes ago, Penny had contacted them to let them

know that there were reports of gunfire in Hogansfield. A woman matching Sandra's description had driven away, being chased by three dark SUVs.

"Time to go." Norah grabbed Iggy.

Greg had already released the stairs and was heading down them. Norah peeked her head out. A man waited next to a Range Rover.

"Wait here." Adam walked past her, carrying the trunk of weapons like it weighed nothing.

The man straightened as soon as Adam appeared. His eyes went wide at the sight of all the weaponry. He stepped away from the Rover, a nervous tremor in his voice. "It's all gassed up. The keys are in the ignition. Do you need anything else?"

"No. Thank you, Roger." Adam made his way to the back of the Range Rover.

The man waited for a moment before turning and getting into a waiting pickup, the engine idling. He put the car into gear and started to drive away.

Grabbing a blanket, Norah threw it over Iggy before hurrying down the stairs. She pulled open the driver's door. "Inside, Iggy."

Iggy vaulted into the driver's seat and then scurried into the back. Norah lost no time hopping in behind the wheel and turning the ignition as Adam closed the tailgate.

"Um, so, I guess Iggy and I will try and stay in the car?" Greg asked as he climbed into the back seat with Iggy.

"Yes," Norah said in a clipped voice.

Adam had barely gotten a foot in the door before Norah had the car moving. He dropped into the seat, just managing to pull his hand from the doorframe before it swung shut with the motion of the car.

He didn't say anything, and Norah didn't apologize. They both knew they had to get moving as quickly as possible. Norah turned the car in a U-turn and hit the gas. She'd studied the map while they'd been airborne. According to the reports, the SUV was headed north toward Hardin. Sandra was probably hoping to lose them in the traffic of the city, because with a population of around five hundred, Hogansfield wouldn't offer her much cover.

From the corner of her eye, she noticed the large weapon in Adam's hands. She frowned. "Where was that?"

He gave her a rare smile. "This one's mine."

She shook her head, but Adam's smile made her feel better. Not because it suggested they were becoming friends. But because it suggested he was about to go on the hunt. And she had a feeling Adam was a very, very good hunter.

CHAPTER 26

Sandra didn't know what to do. The SUVs had closed the distance, so now the closest one was only about three car lengths behind her. They hadn't shot at her again, but she knew it was only a matter of time. She also knew there was no chance she was going to be able to make it to Hardin before they were on top of her.

She cursed herself for not going to a larger city or more populated area when they'd first set out. She'd worried that a more populated area would have more cameras, making them easier to be found.

But then I went and made a phone call and led them right to us. Stupid, stupid, stupid, she silently berated herself.

She still didn't know what any of this was about. She and Luke had led the most normal of lives. Truth be told, her life was incredibly boring. How the hell did she go from sitting by herself at her kitchen table in old sweats to being chased down a highway by armed federal officers?

It had to do with those blue apes and with Sammy, but for the life of her, she couldn't figure out why. She had no idea why those apes had shown up on their property or why

Sammy had befriended Luke. According to Luke, Sammy had been talking to him for weeks before the apes had shown up. The apes must have somehow been tracking Sammy. Luke and Sandra had nothing to do with any of it.

An image of the black-clad team breaking into her home flashed through her mind. But someone definitely thought they had something to do with it. Those men hadn't shown up just to have a quick chat or to further question them. They came in with force.

Panic clawed up Sandra's throat. She forced it back down. She would panic later. In fact, if they got through this, she could curl up for a week in the fetal position if she wanted to, but right now she needed to figure out a way to protect Luke. Because if those guys got a hold of them, she knew the least they would do would be to separate her and Luke. And Luke would not handle that well.

Come on, Sandra, think. Think.

She swerved around a slower-moving Toyota Sienna. Through the back window, three kids stared out at her. The mom quickly moved over to the side of the road to stay farther away from her and her pursuers.

Sandra desperately wanted to trade places with that mom. But apparently her life was on a much more adventurous course. Up ahead, the next exit ramp was coming up fast. She couldn't stay on the highway. She had to pray that maybe there was something at the exit that would give her an opportunity. She stayed in the farthest left lane, waiting until the very last minute before she swerved over to the exit.

She cut off an Acura MDX that yanked itself out of the way and did a complete 180 to avoid hitting her. The SUV now blocked the exit. She hadn't intended for that to happen, but she would take all the help she could get.

Flying down the ramp, Sandra ignored the stop sign as she swerved to the right. The back of the car fishtailed out, and three cars slammed on their brakes. She just missed clipping a car sitting at the light.

Her heart pounded as sweat broke out along her entire body. But she didn't slow. If the military had taught her one thing, it was that your body was going to react whether you wanted it to or not. But you decided how much of that reaction was going to affect you.

The street was lined with small businesses and one strip mall on her left. But there was nothing that offered much coverage. She kept going, even as she heard the squeal of tires behind her, letting her know that her pursuers were after her again. She turned down a side street and slammed on the gas, praying that something, somewhere would give her a little help.

And then she saw an opportunity: a junkyard. Wrenching the wheel to the right, she crashed through the junkyard's gate. She tore down an aisle that towered with old cars stacked on top of one another like discarded toys.

As she reached the end of the aisle, she wrenched on the wheel, stomping on the brake at the same time. The back of the Ford still slammed into a tower of tires, and they tumbled down like dominoes, crashing into the back of the Explorer.

Luke let out a cry, his hands over his ears.

"It's okay, baby. It's okay," Sandra said quickly as she shot forward again, going down another aisle, although at a slower rate of speed. There was an opening up ahead between two stacks of four crumpled cars. She pulled in and quickly turned off the car. She flung open her door and reached down for Luke. "Luke, we have to go."

She could hear the SUVs one row over. Luke cringed away from her.

"Luke!" She ripped one of his hands from his ears. He let out a scream, tears running down his cheeks. Her heart split in two at the terror on his face, but there was nothing she could do about it at this moment.

Even as her heart raced and the hairs across her whole body stood at attention, she quieted her tone. "Luke, honey, I know you're scared, but we need to go. We need to go *now*."

Luke scrambled out of his seat. Pulling on his arm, she practically dragged him from the car and through a gap in the stack of cars. A ragged bumper caught on her pants and tore into the skin below. She sucked in a breath but didn't slow.

The SUVs had pulled to a halt near her abandoned car. She led Luke deeper into the junkyard, winding their way through heaps of metal trash and tires. Car doors opened and slammed shut behind them.

She moved more quickly, keeping Luke's hand firmly clasped in her own, saying a little prayer of thanks at how large the junkyard was. A dog barked somewhere in the distance.

Please don't let him be loose, she prayed.

She rounded another corner, then stopped. She reached up and pulled open the back door of an old sedan that was sitting on the remains of a station wagon. Inside, the car was just a skeleton of a car. There were no seats, no dashboard, no paneling of any kind. The top of the sedan was flattened, and the windows were gone, but otherwise it looked stable. It looked like an old cop car from the seventies.

The door squeaked as she urged it open. Wincing, she waited for someone to let out a yell. But no one did, and she didn't hear anyone in the immediate vicinity. She looked back at Luke, keeping her voice low. "I need you to climb up quietly, okay?"

He nodded and reached up. She clasped her hands together, bracing her legs as he placed his foot on them. She gave him a little boost. His chest fell into the car, and he squirmed forward before he finally disappeared inside.

Using the car underneath, Sandra hauled herself up through the same door. Once inside, she crouched low, slowly pulling the door closed softly behind her.

Luke was huddled in the back corner. Sandra put a finger to her lips.

But Luke didn't look at her. He just rocked back and forth slowly. Sandra peered out the window, careful to keep her movements slow, not sure how stable a resting place the station wagon was. A man all in black walked down the path between the towers of junk, his gaze scanning back and forth.

A hand over her mouth as her breathing came out in pants, Sandra ducked back down, In her mind, she imagined what she would do if he got closer. She knew she could take at least one, especially if she had surprise on her side.

But there was no chance she was going to be able to take out all of them. She glanced back at Luke, who was still rocking quietly in the corner. *Oh God, please help.*

The seconds ticked by at an agonizing pace. Each sound in the junkyard, each scuffle of a shoe, each creak of metal set Sandra's heart racing, knowing they were about to be discovered. She knew that their best chance of not being caught was to keep moving, to keep shifting from hiding place to hiding place, even doubling back to where the men had already searched. But Luke wouldn't be able to do that, at least not quietly.

Desperation clawed at the edges of Sandra's mind, slowly turning her thoughts to panic. But she couldn't panic. She needed to come up with something. Slowly, she moved toward Luke, trying to keep her movements silent. "Luke, honey, we need to run, sweetheart. Do you think you can run?"

Luke didn't meet her gaze, just continued to rock, a soft hum escaping his lips. Sandra stared around her desperately, trying to come up with any plan. How was she going to do this? There were at least three SUVs, which probably meant twelve individuals. In the military, they had practiced multiple-attacker drills. She'd defeated as many as six. But twelve who were heavily armed while she had nothing was beyond the scope of believability.

But not if you get one of their weapons. It was her and Luke's only chance, and it was a slim one at that. If she got ahold of one of their weapons, she could try and take them out one by one, and silently. If one of them called in or opened fire, the game was over.

No, she couldn't risk it. They would wait, and hopefully the men simply wouldn't find them. Luke's humming grew louder.

"Luke, I need you to be quiet, honey. Please, Luke, I need you to be quiet," Sandra whispered.

He only rocked faster, his mewling getting a little louder. "No, Luke, you need to be quiet. Please, Luke, please."

The creek of metal was the only warning she had. Sandra whirled around as the driver's door opened fully. A man in black, his weapon aimed at her, stood with his arms braced against the floor of the car. A second man in black appeared above the passenger-side window. "Lookie what we found. Out. Both of you."

Sandra put her hands up while her mind raced. But there were no good answers here. All she could do now was hope that she could pave the way to make this less painful for Luke. She reached her hand toward him, wanting to touch him one last time, but he let out a small cry, and she pulled her hand back. "Okay, baby. It's going to be okay."

The second one barked. "Out. Now."

As Sandra looked into his eyes, she knew he would pull the trigger. "Okay. Okay. I'm coming. Just give me a second."

She was forced to duck crawl because she couldn't stand up all the way. She reached the driver's door. She was about to turn around to lower herself out when the gunman grabbed the front of her shirt and yanked her face first through the opening.

A cry burst from her lips as her knees slammed painfully into the edge of the car. She was unceremoniously dumped on the ground. The second gunman stepped down from his perch and stood with his M4 aimed at her. "Don't move."

The first one stepped back. "I'll get the kid."

He swung the strap of his M4 around him and started to climb the station wagon. As soon as his head appeared in the opening of the sedan door, Luke's cries erupted.

The gunman standing above her turned his head to watch his partner. Sandra bolted from her position. She wrapped her hands around his ankle, jamming her shoulder right into his knee. He let out a scream as he fell back.

Sandra didn't give him even a second to gather himself. She slid up between his leg and slammed her knee into his crotch. She flung his left leg over and then crawled up his torso, slamming her elbow into his chin. He cried out, then his eyes rolled back in his head.

Snatching the gun, she raised it and pulled the trigger, catching the other man in the stomach as he turned.

Rolling off of him, she got to her feet. She needed to get to the other gunman. She needed to—

A third gunman stood balanced on the station wagon, his weapon aimed at Sandra. "Nice move. Stupid move, but nice move."

There was four feet between them. Too large a distance to cover before he could get a shot off. Plus there was another gunman to his left.

Luke's cries had grown quiet.

"They want the boy alive. You're optional," he growled.

Sandra tensed. *Oh God. Luke, I'm sorry.* She dropped the gun. "Don't shoot."

One of the men charged, grabbing her by the front of the

shirt and throwing her to the ground. He grabbed her left arm and yanked it behind her back, and a zip tie was cinched around her wrists before she could even breathe.

She was whirled around yet again and pushed toward the third man. "Take her back to the cars. Get the boy."

Sandra dug in her feet. "No, wait. He's autistic. You can't just grab him."

The man holding her didn't say anything, just yanked her forward, practically pulling her shoulder out of its socket.

"No, wait. Let me—"

Screaming erupted from the car. Sandra yanked herself free, whirling around. While she'd been distracted by the three men on the side of the car, another three had approached from the other side. One of them had Luke by the shoulders, pulling him from the car.

Sandra bolted forward. "No, no! He doesn't like to be touched! Leave him—"

Pain crashed through the back of her skull. Stars blinked across her vision as she fell to her knees. The man who'd been holding her gripped her roughly by the arm. "I said let's go."

Her vision blurring in and out, Sandra swayed. But there was nothing wrong with her hearing. Luke's cries sounded over and over again. She struggled against the man holding her.

The man's grip loosened. "What the—"

Without the man's support, Sandra fell once again to her knees. Without her hands to break her fall, she crashed forward onto her chest. Luke's cries had slowed. Sandra could hear fighting up ahead. She struggled back to her knees, knowing she needed to get to Luke.

Crawling, she reached for the car near her, using it to help her get to her feet. Screams rang out from the other side of the car. A spray of blood splashed against the car near her. She gasped. Her mouth fell open as two large wings appeared on the other side of the car. The men with her opened fire.

Dashing around the car, Sandra ducked her head. Luke sat against the car, his hands wrapped around his knees. Sammy flew over the car, moving faster than Sandra's eyes could track.

Sandra placed her hands over a piece of ragged metal and slowly started to cut away the zip ties around her wrists. "Luke? Luke, are you okay?"

This time, Luke did look up at her. "Sammy's here."

CHAPTER 27

The Range Rover had a little pep in it. Norah used all of it, coaxing out even more as she barreled down the I-90, heading toward Hardin.

Leaning forward, Greg looked over Norah's shoulder. "Triple digits. Maybe we could keep the speed to double digits, huh?"

Norah ignored him. There had been reports of erratic driving and three large black SUVs going at high rates of speed down I-90 not that long ago. They had gotten off at an exit, and then there were no further details.

Cops had been dispatched but had been held up by a car accident on the highway caused by one of the SUVs. Norah took the exit before the accident to avoid getting caught up in the traffic.

In the passenger seat, Adam scanned a map of the surrounding area, trying to figure out where Sandra might have gone to hide. Even though it was a logical approach, Norah didn't think it would be much help. Sandra wouldn't have been looking at a map. She would've been driving by instinct. Taking turns, shooting down roads, she would've just been moving on adrenaline.

Norah rolled down the window as they drove down Main Street. Scanning the street, she looked for any sign that Sandra had come this way. Anything that might—

Pausing, she turned her head, noting that Adam had done the same. It sounded like firecrackers somewhere in the distance. "Which way?" She asked.

"Ahead to the right," Adam said.

Norah didn't question him, just took the first right. Adam was an unusual man, but he was definitely skilled. If he said it was coming from this direction, then it was coming from this direction.

She met Greg's gaze in the rearview mirror. He gave her a nod. Greg had told her about when he'd first met Adam. How he'd come in as some sort of Rambo/assassin/hero and saved him from two unknowns. At the time, Norah had thought he was exaggerating. But after seeing Adam in New Mexico, she had a feeling that if anything, he'd undersold the man's abilities.

A man and a woman who were about to cross the road as Norah tore down the street. The couple dove back for the sidewalk. She winced, glancing at them through the rearview, but they seemed unharmed.

Even above the sound of the engine, she could make out the firecracker sounds. They were M4s. She was sadly familiar with the noise the semiautomatic machine gun made. She patted the P-90 in her lap.

"There." Adam nudged his chin down the road. But Norah's eyes had already focused in on the junkyard entrance. A semicircle sign above the wide truck entrance proclaimed it to be Pete's Metal and Scrap. A scrap-metal fence surrounded the large yard. The two chain-link fence gates that covered the entrance had been blown wide open, one hanging from only a single hinge.

"Ready?" Adam asked.

But Norah knew it wasn't really a question. It was a statement. "Yes."

CHAPTER 28

The car squealed around the corner. Greg held on to the back of Adam's chair to keep from being flung on top of Iggy. His stomach shifted ominously. He rolled his window down a crack to get some fresh air before he spewed.

Note to self: never get in a car with Norah ever again.

He'd been relieved when Norah had taken the wheel instead of Adam. He didn't know why, but he'd thought she was more reserved, a little more reluctant to jump into action. Apparently he was very, very bad at reading people. The car trip from the airport had been hair-raising. He could swear she missed at least seven cars by mere inches. And she didn't even blink. She merely kept going. She was like Adam's other half.

Greg's head jerked up at the sound of gunfire from up ahead. Some people might think it sounded like fireworks, but Greg knew better.

He strained to see something out of the window. He leaned forward between the seats to get a better view. That was when he saw the angel rise up from a junkyard, a man squirming in his arms before he was released. Greg cringed, knowing that from that height he was going to be in for a world of pain, if not a world of dead.

"You guys see him?" Greg asked, leaning between the seats.

"We see him." Norah flicked a glance above the junkyard before returning her gaze to the road. "I'm going to pull up by the entrance. Adam and I are going to go in. You are going to keep Iggy in the car."

"Excellent plan. I will stay in the car," Greg agreed quickly.

There wasn't time to say any more than that. Without warning, Norah pulled over to the side of the road, slamming the brakes hard enough to send up a huge dust cloud and cause whiplash. She and Adam bolted from the car, sprinting for the junkyard entrance. They stopped at the side of the entrance, peering through the gates before they disappeared inside.

Greg looked over at Iggy. "Well, that was fast."

More gunfire sounded from inside. Greg scanned the area, but all of the activity seemed to be inside the junkyard. "Not cowards for staying outside, right? I mean, they can handle a few guys. They should be fine."

Iggy tilted his head. "Ig?"

Drumming his fingers on the side of the door, Greg debated. Before Area 51, he never would've been the type to rush into the middle of a gunfight. He was firmly in the camp of "if you hear gunfire, call someone better equipped to handle it." And Adam and Norah were definitely better equipped to handle it than he was. But he also knew that things didn't always go as planned. And this junkyard looked huge, which left a lot of ground to be covered and a lot of ambush spots.

Climbing up onto the back of the driver's seat, Iggy peered through the windshield. "Ig?"

"She's okay. She's good at this, right?" Greg asked.

Gunfire rattled from inside. Greg ran a hand over the Beretta in his holster. "Well, I suppose I did get all dressed up. Okay, we'll take a look. But we're not going in. We're just going to stay by the gates, and if they need any help, then we'll be there to help them, okay?"

Iggy nodded repeatedly. "Ig."

CHAPTER 29

The sound of gunfire followed Sammy as he rose into the air. Sandra grabbed Luke's arm, ignoring his cry of alarm. They needed to move, and they needed to move now.

She yanked Luke to his feet and down a small break in the towering lines of cars. A man let out a scream behind her. She looked back in time to see him as he plunged from twenty feet up in the air, landing on top of the car that she and Luke had been hiding in. Her gaze darted to Sammy, who hovered above the car, his wings beating back and forth.

Once again, he looked to her like a demon summoned from a witch's book. He was over six feet tall, broad and muscular through the shoulders, with wings that seemed to span at least eight or nine feet. In the sunlight, they were even more terrifying than in the dark. They were leathery and crisp. They snapped when he moved them quickly. And each point came to a razor edge that shone when the light hit them.

In her imagination, he had been black, but in reality he was more of a dark maroon. She was surprised to see that he looked like he was wearing pants, although why he would be was beyond her. Sammy met her gaze. Terror tore through her. Ripping her gaze away, she tightened her grip on Luke and picked up her pace.

As a child, her parents had taken her to church every Sunday. And she had attended Bible study twice a week. Her parents' religious demands were part of the reason that she no longer spoke with them.

That and the beatings they doled out in response to any interpreted transgression of God's will.

A large part of her early religious education involved discussions about the devil. Her church impressed upon her that the devil was alive and well and waiting for her to show vulnerability. Waiting for her to slip up so that he could slip into her mind and use her as a weapon, pulling her from God.

When she'd escaped her parents and the Church, she'd shoved all of that to the back of her mind. And the more she learned and the more she read, the less of a role the devil played in any of her thoughts. He was a construct created to keep weak-minded individuals in line as far she was concerned.

She swallowed hard. *Maybe I was too hasty in that decision.*

CHAPTER 30

Norah didn't understand junkyards. Everything that surrounded her looked like garbage. Cars were piled on top of one another with their roofs caved in. Old washing machines and car parts were packed six feet high. And there were tires everywhere. Some were stacked on top of one another, but most were just haphazardly thrown on top of mountains of other mixed metals. How did anybody make money out of this stuff? Even if you were looking for a specific part, how would you find it in all of this?

But that wasn't the reason she disliked junkyards today. Today she hated them because they provided plenty of hiding spots and cover for anyone who wanted to snipe at them.

Given the landscape, though, it had been Sandra's best option. She couldn't outrun all the SUVs, and it wasn't like the area was teeming with people. There was no train station, mall, or city where Sandra and Luke could lose themselves in a crowd. From what little Norah had seen of this part of the state, she wasn't sure they even had enough people to make a crowd.

With the group chasing Sandra, they'd probably just doubled the local population.

Adam walked five feet in front of Norah and to her right. His head acted like it was on a swivel, moving from side to side. He held up a hand when they reached the end of the aisle and pointed two fingers to the left.

Norah tucked the P90 a little more firmly into her shoulder. With a glance behind them to make sure no one was creeping along their rear, she followed him. A scream echoed through the junkyard, followed by a crash of metal.

Swallowing hard, Norah hoped that Sammy realized that they were the good guys. If, of course, there was such a thing as good guys and bad guys in his mind. Maybe if you weren't a kid or an alien hybrid, you were all bad. If he'd been locked up at Area 51, she couldn't exactly blame him for that mentality.

A crunch of gravel sounded behind them. Norah turned, dropping to her knee as a shot rang out. It pinged off the metal a foot to her right at head level. She drew a bead on the offender, quickly noting his vest and took aim for his knee, then pulled the trigger.

He screamed, dropping down to one knee. He looked up.

Sorry. Norah pulled the trigger again, and the next bullet entered his forehead. A spray of blood coated the ground, soaking quickly into the dry earth. She swallowed, a sweat breaking over her. It wasn't the first time she'd killed someone, but she'd hoped she'd left those days behind.

Gunfire broke out behind her. She whirled again as Adam took out two black-clad individuals and lunged at a third.

Turning back to make sure they were still in the clear, movement pulled her attention to the left. She dove for the ground as gunfire broke out. A ricochet sent a shard of metal across her cheek. She could feel the blood dripping down.

Okay. You guys want to play. She gripped her gun with narrowed eyes. *Let's play.*

CHAPTER 31

Greg moved to the side of the junkyard doors. Iggy was crouched on Greg's back, making Greg feel little bit like Luke Skywalker with Yoda. "Okay, I don't see anybody. So I guess that's good?"

Gunfire burst from somewhere deeper in the junkyard.

"Ig?"

Grunting, Greg nodded. "Right, okay, granted, gunfire is not a good sign. But I'm sure that—"

"Ig!" Iggy clambered down from Greg and darted through the opening.

"Iggy, no," Greg stage-whispered. But Iggy was moving too fast to hear him or completely ignoring him. Greg debated for only a second before sprinting after him. *Please don't get me shot. Please don't get me shot.*

The little alien sprinted down the main pathway, moving incredibly fast for a guy incredibly short. Greg couldn't even think of keeping up. Iggy reached the end of the path and then turned, disappearing from view.

Lengthening his stride, Greg picked up his pace, but slowed as he reached the end of the aisle. He stopped next to an old burned-out van. He peered around the corner. There was no Iggy in sight. He groaned. *I am so dead.*

A scream sounded from above him. His gaze shot to the sky just as the winged creature from Dulce dropped someone to the ground. He slammed into a car with a loud thump. The winged creature was already speeding off after someone else.

Dust billowed up around the man, but through the dust, Greg saw movement. A woman was running. He could see her long hair.

Oh, this is so stupid, Greg thought before he took off after her. Greg kept a parallel track to where he'd seen the woman. There were at least two men giving chase. As far as Greg could tell, they didn't know he was there. Gunfire and return fire sounded from somewhere behind him. Apparently Norah and Adam were hard at work.

Focusing on the situation at hand, Greg leapt over an old tire that had become dislodged from a stack of metal and rubber to his left. Up ahead, he could see that his aisle ended at a cross path. The cross path was big enough for a car, which meant that the aisle next to him also ended.

He swallowed, not sure exactly what he was going to do at that point, but he kept moving. Ahead, the woman and a boy burst out of their row, turning and heading to the right, which brought them across Greg's path. The two gunmen sprinted after them. Greg slammed to a stop, pushing himself between two piles of rusted cars to avoid being seen.

As Greg stepped forward to give chase, a dark shadow covered the ground in front of him. He didn't even think. Diving for the ground, he rolled as the winged creature soared over him, crashing into the two men. The winged creature grabbed one of the men, rising up with him into the air. The other one got to his knees.

Bursting forward, Greg tackled the man around his waist as he stood up. The two of them hit the ground, the man underneath Greg. Greg grabbed the back of the man's head and slammed it into the ground with a wince.

The man groaned and then rolled onto his side, dislodging Greg. He crashed to the side, his hand coming to rest on a pile of discarded pipes. He gripped one as he vaulted to his feet and slammed it into the man's jaw. He winced again as blood sprayed across the ground. The man's knees buckled, and then he dropped, landing face first into the ground.

Sandra and her son had stopped to watch. Wind blew Greg's hair across his face. He wiped it away as he looked up, his whole body tensing. Sammy hovered only a few feet away, his wings keeping him aloft. Greg dropped the pipe and put his hands up. "Not one of the bad guys," he said.

The creature hovered there for a few seconds more before flying low and disappearing around the path. Greg's knees buckled causing him to sway. His breath came out in a whoosh as he patted himself down. *Not dead. I am not dead.*

He turned to where Sandra and Luke stood. Sandra stood protectively in front of him. Greg raised his hands. "I'm here with the good guys. I'm not with those guys."

Luke appeared around Sandra's back. "Sammy said you would help us."

Sandra looked down at her son in alarm.

But Greg nodded. "Yes. That is the plan."

CHAPTER 32

Norah had crept quietly into a car stacked upon two others to use it as sort of a sniper's nest. Adam kept watch to make sure she could get up there safely and then disappeared to do his own hunting.

She could see four men one row over still scanning the area, which was good. It meant Sandra and Luke hadn't been found yet. Farther back in the junkyard, she could see the winged creature flying low before he tore into two black-clad figures. Norah assumed that Sandra and Luke were somewhere over there and that he was helping them. At least she hoped they were over there and that he was helping them. And that they had not misread its motivations.

The four men from one row over headed toward her. Norah took a deep breath, calming her breathing. *Okay. Here we go.* She placed the P90 on what was left of the dashboard of the hollowed-out Ford. Her hands didn't shake. Her breathing remained consistent. It was both amazing and horrible how quickly one could fall back into old habits.

Wanting to wait until they were close enough that they

wouldn't be able to get out of range easily, She lined up her shot. *Just a little closer. Just a little closer,* she urged silently.

She pulled the trigger. The first man went down. She quickly sighted the second, but her shot went wide, catching him in the vest. He still dropped from the impact of the bullet. The other two sprinted back, looking for a hiding spot in between the metal. She caught one in the back of the thigh before he could reach it, but the fourth slipped through.

Well, better than I would've done on the ground. Speaking of which …

Norah scrambled from her position, knowing that the men would be up and looking for her. She just stepped onto the frame of the second car when gunfire burst out around her. She dropped to the ground, hitting hard and rolling as gunfire dotted the ground next to her.

She crawled underneath a beat-up Volkswagen van across the small passage from her hiding spot. A glance at the other three sides told her she'd chosen badly. There was only one escape route, and it was currently littered with bullets.

Way to go, Norah. So much for it all coming back to you.

One of her instructors back in Basic had stressed that you never got yourself into a position that you couldn't get yourself out of.

He would not be happy.

She backed as far away from the opening as she could, but it was an awkward angle to get a shot off from, so she had to choose between either putting herself closer to the opening in order to lie down and get a shot or pull all the way back and shoot badly.

She chose shooting badly, at least for this situation. She switched the P90 to automatic. She was just going to spray anything that came within her view. It wouldn't matter if she could sight something from this position. She wouldn't get much more than a look at the people's feet.

Scrunching down low, she gripped the handle with her right hand. A crunch of gravel nearby told her she was about to have company. She said a quick prayer before a set of boots appeared in the pathway. She pulled the trigger, spraying gunfire across the opening.

The man screamed and dropped to the ground. Norah sprayed the rest of him and then let out a breath.

"Sandra Gillibrand, come out from the car with your hands up. If you don't, I'm just going to lob this grenade under there. We're supposed to take you alive, if possible. But if you don't cooperate, then I guess it's not possible."

They think I'm Sandra. If she could maybe pass herself off as Sandra, maybe that would buy her some time. It wasn't like she really had any other options.

Shrugging out of her bulletproof vest, she dropped all her weapons except for the P90 and the knife hidden in her boot. She grabbed the knife and slid it into her sleeve. Sandra wouldn't have any of those on her, and she needed to sell her identity or else this guy was going to shoot her as soon as he caught sight of her. At least she and Sandra had about the same build, even though their skin tone was a little different and Sandra's hair was a little bit darker. But she was hoping this guy didn't really have a firm idea of what Sandra looked like. After all, how many women would be running around a junkyard trying to avoid them?

"I'm coming out. Don't shoot." Norah pulled her hair out from the ponytail, letting it fall around her face as she moved forward. The man stood somewhere to her left. She couldn't get a bead on him, which was a smart move on his part. She left the P90 underneath the car at the edge. She stuck her hand out first, her fingers splayed wide. "I'm unarmed."

"Get out here."

Keeping her head bowed, Norah's hair covered her face as

she crawled out from underneath the car. And that's when she realized her mistake. It wasn't one man.

It was two.

One of the men stepped forward while the other one stayed six feet back. Norah slipped the knife from her sleeve into her palm.

The man stepped right in front of her, only a few inches away. "Okay. Let's— Hey, you're not Gillibrand."

"No, I'm not." Norah plunged the blade underneath his chin. The man's eyes widened. He grabbed for the knife, but it was too deeply embedded.

His partner, recognizing the danger, opened fire. Norah grabbed the man she'd stabbed and used him as a shield, keeping him between her and the gunman. He had an M4 strapped around his body, but the gun was behind his back. She'd have to let go with one hand to pull it toward her, but then she had no chance of keeping her shield upright.

Damn it.

The gunfire cut off. It took Norah's ears a moment or two to register it. They were still ringing from the close-range gunfire. She took a breath and glanced out from behind her shield. The other gunman was face down. And sitting on his back, his talons wet with blood, was Iggy.

CHAPTER 33

The dark-haired guy with the glasses certainly didn't look like the other commandos. He was wearing jeans and a gray T-shirt for one. Plus, he'd used a pipe to take out the men who'd been following them.

Eyeing the weapon at his waist, Sandra wondered why he hadn't just shot the guy. But from the way he was looking around, she had a feeling he wasn't a soldier.

"So, um, I think maybe we should get out of here," the man said.

She wasn't exactly sold on that idea. Getting out of here, yes, getting out of here with this guy, not so much.

Luke started to walk around her. Sandra grabbed his arm. "Luke."

"It's okay. Sammy said he's okay." Luke walked up to the man while Sandra watched him, dumbfounded. Luke was not a fan of strangers. Any strangers. But apparently if Sammy said it was all right, then he had no problem walking up to a guy standing twenty feet away who'd just taken out a guy with a pipe and still had a gun.

At the same time, Sandra had to admit she didn't exactly

feel threatened by the guy, despite the gun at his waist. *Well, if Sammy says it's okay ..., she thought. I can't believe I'm trusting the word of a winged demon.*

But nevertheless, she found herself following Luke. If she had to choose between the commandos and this guy, she definitely chose this guy.

"Who are you with? The police?" Sandra asked.

He shook his head. "Uh, no, Norah. I mean, Agent Tidwell and Adam."

Sandra backed up. "Norah? She told them where we were. She's with them."

He shook his head again. "No. She didn't. We heard that you were under attack when we were on our way to get you. Norah had no idea. They probably were keeping an eye on her phone. It wasn't her. She would never do that."

"Keeping an eye on her phone?" Sandra asked.

"Norah's not with the D.E.A.D. anymore. They had a disagreement over policy."

Sandra bit her lip. What the hell did that mean? They'd been standing here for too long. They needed to get moving. But should they go with this guy or should they strike off on their own? And if Norah wasn't with the D.E.A.D., then how would she be able to help keep Luke safe? Sandra didn't know what the right call was here. But she knew standing around wasn't going to work.

She knelt down next to the guy who was lying unconscious a few feet away. She unstrapped the M4 and pulled it to her chest. She quickly detached the magazine to check if there were any rounds left. She grabbed another magazine from the front pocket of the man's vest and then stood up.

Glasses Guy didn't seem bothered by her action. In fact, he nodded. "Good call. The car's out at the front of the junkyard. This way." The guy started down the path and then cut in between two towers of metal. Luke didn't hesitate to follow.

Shaking her head, Sandra did not like anything about this situation. But she quickly picked up the pace so she didn't lose sight of Luke. She glanced up at the sky but saw no sign of Sammy.

Okay, Sammy, looks like I'm trusting your judgment. Please don't let that be a mistake.

CHAPTER 34

Having a gun at your back was not a comforting position to be in. Greg scanned the area, looking for any trouble, but it had gone quiet. He checked Sandra behind him, and she, too, was scanning the area, the M4 snuggled very confidently in her arms.

She met his gaze for a moment before continuing her search. Greg swallowed hard. He knew she did not trust him. He couldn't blame her. He just really hoped she didn't decide to use that weapon against him.

Checking the sky again, he saw no sign of Sammy, as Luke called him. Luke, meanwhile, was walking in between Greg and his mom, looking completely unbothered by the situation, which was ... weird. Shouldn't he be freaked out? Greg was freaked out, and all the life-threatening situations he'd been in lately had started to blend together.

"Sammy says it's safe," Luke said.

Greg started, looking at the kid. "What was that?"

"You were wondering why I'm not scared. Sammy said it's safe," Luke said.

Greg frowned. "How did you—"

"Luke, get down!" Sandra reached up, yanking Luke behind her and bringing her M4 up. Greg's head whipped from side to side as he tried to spot the danger. A small movement on top of a tower of tires caught his attention before the movement appeared closer to the ground.

Smiling, Greg carefully reached out and lowered the barrel of Sandra's weapon. "It's okay. He's with us."

Iggy vaulted into view. Reaching up with one of his claws, he swung himself up and landed on the hood of an old Chrysler only three feet away from Greg. "Ig!"

"Hey, buddy." Greg noted the dried blood on the end of Iggy's claws as he stepped toward him. "You okay?"

"Ig, ig."

Sandra stepped forward. "Luke, don't—"

But Luke appeared by Greg's side. His mouth hung open as he stared in fascination at Iggy.

Looking between Luke and Iggy, Greg said, "This is Iggy. He's a friend of mine and Norah's."

Luke reached a hand out slowly. But Sandra grabbed his shoulder.

"It's okay. He won't hurt him," Greg said.

"He won't, Mom," Luke said.

Sandra met Greg's gaze, holding it for a long moment before she released her son. Luke reached out again. He lightly touched the white hair on Iggy's head. Iggy closed his eyes, leaning into Luke's hand. Luke smiled and ran a hand over Iggy's head. Iggy let out a small purr.

"He really likes that," Greg said.

"What is he?" Sandra asked.

"He's called a Maldek," Norah said as she walked up, Adam right behind her.

Greg felt relief flow through him. He walked over and threw his arms around Norah. "Thank God. I was worried about you guys."

She surprised him by hugging him back. "I thought you two were supposed to stay in the car."

Greg gave a nervous laugh. "Did you say that? I couldn't remember if it was stay in the car or stay in the yard."

"Ha-ha." Norah looked past Greg. "Hey, Sandra, Luke. You two all right?"

"I, uh, think so. The guys in black?" Sandra asked.

"Down. But we should get moving just the same. This here is Adam." Norah gestured to Adam, who was still watching the area.

"Oh, and I'm Greg. With all the bullets flying, I didn't exactly get to introduce myself.".

Sandra nodded at him but immediately returned her gaze to Norah. "Norah, what's going on?"

Scanning the area, Norah said, "That's a very good question. But maybe we could answer it once we've put a few miles between us and this place."

"Yeah, that's a good idea," Sandra said.

Iggy jumped into Norah's arms and then scampered up to her shoulders. Sandra watched in what Greg assumed was absolute disbelief. He could relate. Stepping into this world was like visiting Wonderland on acid. Everything was strange.

And sadly, he knew Sandra's trip had just begun.

CHAPTER 35

The small town had been no less crowded on the way out of town as it had been on the way in. Closer to the junkyard, there'd been a few people on the street glancing in its direction, but no one looked overly concerned. From where they were located, it probably just sounded like fireworks or the junkyard crushing something.

Norah scanned the street and the sky above. She hadn't seen the winged creature that Luke called Sammy again. She wasn't sure what to make of him. He'd shown up and helped Sandra and Luke according to Sandra's recounting. And he'd let Greg go.

So who was he? And what exactly was his role in all of this? Like Sandra, Norah had a lot of questions. But none of those questions were a priority right now. Right now the priority was getting Luke and Sandra on the plane and out of town. And the sooner they were up in the air, the safer they would all feel.

"Still nobody behind us," Greg said, shifting to look forward again.

"Let's hope it stays that way." Norah glanced in the back

where Luke sat in between Greg and Sandra. Iggy had crawled into his lap and was resting his head against Luke's chest. Luke had a giant smile on his face, his arms around Iggy and his chin resting on Iggy's head.

Norah was glad that Iggy was helping keep the boy calm. But she had to admit a little piece of her felt jealous, and she hoped it didn't mean that Iggy had switched loyalties.

He cracked open an eye and looked at her. "Ig," he said softly before closing his eyes again.

She smiled. Nope, he was still hers. She turned back and recognized the sign ahead. The airfield was only about another mile down the road. She let out a breath, some of the tension seeping from her shoulders.

"Hey, we made it!" Greg exclaimed from the back.

She turned to look back at him her attention was pulled to the two SUVs that had pulled onto the road behind them. They were moving at a fast clip toward them. There wasn't a lot out this way. In fact, they hadn't passed any cars in the last five minutes.

"Not quite yet." Norah picked up the P90 from the floor, gripping it in her hand.

Greg's head whipped toward the back of the car, and he groaned. "I jinxed us. I totally jinxed us." But Norah was glad to see that he'd picked up his Beretta.

Norah met Sandra's gaze and got a confident nod in return as she gripped the M4. *All right, then. Here we go again.*

"Hold on." Two wheels lifted up in the air as Adam took the turn at a breakneck pace. Norah was convinced they were going to flip over. She gripped the door handle and then gritted her teeth as the SUV slammed back down to the ground. Luke let out a cry behind them.

Norah glanced out the rearview mirror. The two SUVs were still back there and gaining on them. Norah stared at one of the SUVs. It was big, but it wasn't an Escalade. She squinted, trying to figure out the make. It definitely wasn't a Ford or Chevy.

"Is that a Rolls-Royce?" Norah asked, her eyes wide.

Flicking a glance at the rearview mirror, Adam nodded. "It's a Cullinan."

"What's a Cullinan?" Greg asked.

"A Rolls-Royce SUV," Sandra said.

"You mean like a luxury SUV?" Greg asked.

"No, I mean an *actual* SUV made by Rolls-Royce," Sandra replied.

Dumbstruck, Norah stared at it. She didn't know Rolls-Royce even made an SUV. And who the hell would take one to a gunfight? She didn't know much about the brand, but she did know that their interiors were handmade and that they started somewhere in the six-figure range. "How much does that cost?"

"Upwards of 300k," Sandra said.

The number blew Norah's mind. "Well, then, that's definitely not the feds."

Adam's only response was to push down harder on the accelerator. But their Range Rover was absolutely no match for the Rolls. It was slowly closing the distance between them.

"Luke, I need you to get on the floor, please," Sandra said before she leaned forward between the seats. "Got any extra magazines?"

Norah shook her head. "Not for the—"

Adam handed a magazine over his shoulder.

Sandra took it. "Thanks."

Norah grabbed her P90. She was running low on ammo as well. She also had a Beretta, but it wasn't great for distance. Of course, she hadn't been planning on shooting from a car. *Next time, I really need to plan ahead.*

She leaned out the window, getting a bead on the car that was closing the distance incredibly fast. A snap from the air caused her head to jerk up. Sammy flew over the top of the car, heading straight for the Rolls.

Gunfire burst from the luxury SUV, but it was all aimed at Sammy above them. Sammy dipped into a dive, avoiding the gunfire or at least not seeming to be bothered by it if it actually hit. A massive wing swiped across the windshield of the car, shattering it.

The squeal of brakes sounded through the air as smoke rose from the front of the car. Two dark shapes appeared in the sky—one a helicopter and the other a projectile aimed straight for Sammy. He lowered until he was just above the second car and then burst straight up just before the projectile caught him. It exploded across the car, sparks shooting up from it.

Norah watched it all in amazement. But who the hell were these guys? And why was Sammy so interested in protecting Luke?

She had no time to think about it, as Adam took yet another death-defying turn, this time into the field of the airport. "Sandra, you need to start up the plane," Adam ordered.

Sandra's gaze turned to the small Embraer executive jet sitting in the field. "I've flown crop dusters. *That* is *not* a crop duster."

"We tend to learn fast in this outfit. I'm sure you'll figure it out," Greg said.

Adam didn't reply. He slammed on the brakes when they were only fifty feet from the plane and hopped out.

"Go, go!" Norah yelled as she scrambled out of the car.

Greg rushed out the door behind her. He turned to Luke with a wince. "Sorry about this." He grabbed Luke and flung him over his shoulder, sprinting for the plane. The stairs were down, and the door gaped open. Norah bolted ahead, saying a silent prayer that there was nobody inside.

She tore up the steps, her Beretta in her hand as she

scanned the cockpit and fuselage, but everything appeared empty. Sandra ran up the stairs right behind her.

"Start it up. We'll get Luke into a seat," Norah said.

With a terrified glance, Sandra hurried into the cockpit. Greg lowered Luke into a seat. "I'm going to see if I can help Sandra." He hurried into the front of the plane.

Iggy hopped up on the seat next to Luke. "Ig."

Norah knelt down in front of Luke. "It'll be okay. Let's just get you strapped in."

Luke looked up at her with his big blue eyes. "I know. Sammy won't let the bad people harm us."

She wasn't sure what to say to that, so she just snapped the seatbelt on him and hurried back to the door.

The first Rolls-Royce SUV was barreling down the road toward them, sans a windshield. Norah shook her head. Why would anyone choose those kinds of cars for this kind of situation? They stood out like a sore thumb. Whoever it was obviously had money to burn.

Her gaze focused on the sky. The unmistakable sight of a chopper appeared over a hill. The chopper turned just then, so she had a perfect view of the open door and the gunman sitting there.

Oh God.

Adam knelt at the end of the runway, a grenade launcher over his shoulder. With a puff of smoke, the grenade sailed through the air and landed inside the chopper. A muffled explosion, followed by smoke and flames, burst from the interior of the chopper. It tilted to the side and then crashed into the ground, sending shards of metal everywhere.

The plane started up underneath her. When she glanced back, Adam was already halfway from where he'd been just a second ago. She jolted, watching the speed with which he ran. Above them, Sammy flew toward the remaining SUV.

As Adam charged up the stairs, Norah hustled out of the

way. He disappeared into the cockpit without a word. Norah pulled up the steps as Sammy sideswiped the SUV before plunging his wing through the open windshield frame. Norah secured the door, confident the SUV's occupants would not be a problem.

Seconds later, they were taxiing down the runway. Norah buckled herself in next to Luke, but her mind whirled. There had been two different sets of attackers. One had been the government—they had been the ones at the junkyard.

But the ones after the junkyard had not been government flunkies. Somebody else was after Luke. Somebody with very deep pockets.

CHAPTER 36

The plane was quiet. Once Adam took over the controls, Sandra hurried back to be with Luke. Norah stood up and took a different seat when Sandra arrived. As soon as they leveled out, Norah went to the back of the plane and pulled out two blankets. She handed them to Sandra, who looked up at her with wide glassy eyes. "Thank you."

Norah nodded, taking a seat across from them as Sandra tucked a blanket around Luke and then one around herself. Norah didn't say anything. They both looked like they needed a little time to adjust. So she sat quietly, waiting. Iggy curled into her lap and closed his eyes.

Finally, Sandra turned to her. "Where are we going?"

Norah had known that would be the first question, and she had also debated how she would answer it. Normally in this type of situation, she would say something like "somewhere safe." But she wasn't sure yet whether or not the R.I.S.E. base was actually safe. Although she supposed it was safe from the people who were chasing Sandra and her son.

"It's a very secure government base." At Sandra's alarmed

expression, she hurriedly continued. "No one knows about this place. The people who are chasing you definitely don't know about this place. To be honest, I can't even tell you where it is because I don't know."

Sandra looked into Norah's eyes, refusing to let her look away. "Will Luke be safe there?"

"He will be safer there than anywhere else."

Sandra held Norah's gaze for a long moment. She understood what Norah hadn't said. That Sandra was now in the middle of something where they had very little control. But for the moment, they would be safe.

"How long until we get there?"

"It will take a few hours." Norah paused, thinking of Iggy, Alvie, the triplets, and Agaren. "And it's an unusual place. You're going to need to prepare yourself."

"Unusual? How?"

Norah studied the woman across from her. She'd kept her son safe for days with little to no resources. She'd been in the service. She was not a shrinking violet. She could handle what was coming. And if she couldn't, she would force herself to handle it for her son's sake.

"What do you know about aliens?"

CHAPTER 37

MALIBU, CALIFORNIA

The Pacific Ocean was quiet today. Tatiana lay on a chaise lounge on the deck of her three-story beach house. The back was composed almost entirely of glass. It offered incredible views of the water. She loved waking up and being able to look out her window and see the power of the waves. Being close to powerful things always made her feel more alive.

Her home was located on the exclusive "Billionaire's Beach," legally known as Carbon Beach. Her neighbors consisted of billionaire tech entrepreneurs who often lent their houses to celebrities. Currently, the beach was home to an Oscar winner, two record label execs, three hedge-fund billionaires, and a few actors Tatiana couldn't be bothered to learn about.

They'd be forgotten by next year anyway.

Her house was located in between a rising starlet and an NFL player who had won two Super Bowls. Tatiana stretched, loving the feel of the sun on her skin. For some people, the sun was too strong today. But Tatiana loved days like this. She loved to revel in the sun.

Her phone beeped on the small table next to her. She scanned the screen, her lip curling as she read the message. With a growl, she grabbed the phone and headed indoors. Dietrich stood just inside the main room of the house, holding a robe. She slipped into it, patting his hand once she had her arms in the sleeves. She tied the belt firmly around her. "Thank you, darling. Now what the hell went wrong?"

"There was interference," Dietrich said in his deep voice that was closer to a growl than an actual human voice.

Tatiana made her way to the kitchen island. The kitchen was a designer's dream. The island was granite with a cascading countertop in soothing whites and pale grays. The cabinets were modern with no appliances visible, hidden behind false façades. Not a handle in sight. Everything was pure, unbroken white.

Tatiana poured herself a glass of water with lemon from the crystal pitcher waiting for her. "R.I.S.E.?"

Dietrich shook his head as he followed her, taking a seat at one of the stools so he didn't tower over her. "Yes, but that was not the problem. The Sentinel appeared."

Tatiana stopped with her glass halfway to her mouth and then placed it back on the counter. "He followed them to Montana?"

Dietrich nodded.

Tatiana resumed her drinking, absorbing this new information. When she'd learned about Project Antaeus from Martin, she'd been curious. But all of the subjects had been killed in action, or at least killed. But then she'd learned of the existence of an offspring. One whom the Sentinel had already shown an interest in.

Going for the boy had been a lark. Tatiana wanted to see what made him tick, she wanted to see what had drawn the

Sentinel. In all honesty, she had expected to find nothing, just a normal human child.

And then she'd planned to dispose of him.

But now this human child was much more interesting.

"The cars were destroyed. And five of our people were injured."

Tatiana waved away the damages. Cars didn't matter. She had more money than some countries. But the injured were a problem. "Will they be all right?"

Dietrich nodded. "They have been taken home. It will take them a few weeks, but they will all fully recover."

Tatiana's mind shuffled around the latest pieces on the board as she stared out the glass windows toward the ocean. The waves rose and fell, leaving a white foam on the beach as they broke. The waves were constant. She had never been here when they had not been continuing their incessant movement.

She knew the Moon was responsible for that little piece of beauty. The gravitational effect of the large celestial body on the oceans resulted in a bulge in the ocean that in turn caused the ebb and flow of the tides. During full moons, the effect was greater. It was an awesome impact, worthy of awe.

But the Moon was also part of her problem.

Dietrich said nothing while Tatiana thought. He knew his opinion was unimportant. It was hers that mattered. He would sit there for hours without a word if she required it. It was why he was her favorite of all her guards. The rest would attempt to do the same, but they were younger and had less control over themselves.

A Sentinel. What a wonderful pet he would make.

Tatiana turned her attention back to Dietrich. "Tell me about R.I.S.E. How did they avoid us? How many did Matilda send?"

"Only three."

"Three? They sent three? You expect me to believe that our

people were thwarted by the Sentinel and only three—" She went silent, realization dawning. "He was there, wasn't he?"

Dietrich nodded. "Yes."

Tatiana drummed her bright red fingernails on the countertop. She pictured the blond hair, the strong build. "Who was he with?"

"The D.E.A.D. agent, Norah Tidwell."

"She was the one the mother contacted, correct?"

"Yes."

Tatiana growled. These humans were so frustrating. In all her years, her people had never been able to find the R.I.S.E. base. But that needed to change. They were at a critical point. They could not allow R.I.S.E. to stick their heads into their business. They needed to remove them from the equation once and for all. "Find the base. Find a way in. I will not have them interfering."

"I already have people working on it."

Tatiana leaned across the counter, running a nail down the side of Dietrich's face, a line of blood following her path. He turned toward her hand, his eyes closing. "Don't disappoint me."

"Never, my queen."

Tatiana once again headed outside. She slipped her robe off at the door, letting it fall to the ground. She resumed her seat on the chaise lounge, which had warmed in her absence. She sighed as the warmth seeped into her back. But even as her body basked in the warmth, her mind railed against the debacle in Montana. The blonde man had been a thorn in their side for too long.

She needed to get that thorn removed.

CHAPTER 38

What do you know about aliens? The question was insane. And Norah hadn't been able to expand upon it. Almost as soon as she'd asked it, the other guy had come out of the cockpit and said Norah was needed.

Sandra wasn't sure what to think. Ever since the junkyard, she'd been running on adrenaline. When the adrenaline had worn off on the plane ride, she'd wanted to close her eyes and give herself a few moments. But she hadn't been able to.

Because she needed answers. And until she had some, she could not close her eyes. Luke didn't seem to have the same problem. He'd fallen asleep almost as soon as the plane had leveled out.

Across from her, the man who'd appeared in the junkyard with the agent sat. What was his name again? Derek? He drummed his fingers on the edge of the seat rest.

She studied him now that she had a chance. He obviously was not military. Even though he did have a strong build, he was too scattered. His eyes shifted around the fuselage, the nervous energy drumming from him. No, he definitely was not former military.

Now the other two, they were definitely former military, if not current military. She'd noticed it with Norah when she'd first met her. The confidence, the strength, there was something about former military where you just could kind of recognize one another. And Norah's other friend. Sandra wasn't sure what to think about him. He seemed to be a one-man army all on his own.

The cockpit door opened. Norah stepped out, closing the door behind her. She took a seat across from Sandra and held out two water bottles. "I thought you guys might be thirsty."

Sandra reached out for the bottles and then hesitated. The man reached across the aisle and grabbed one. He unscrewed it and drank about half its contents before handing it back to Sandra. "It's not drugged."

Norah looked over at him, her eyes wide. "Why would she think it was drugged?"

The man shrugged. "I would."

Sandra took the bottle and drained the remaining half. She *had* wondered if it had been tampered with. "Thanks."

Norah sat back in her chair. "I'm guessing you have a lot of questions. I'll answer what I can. So you know that I used to work with the D.E.A.D."

"Used to?"

Norah nodded. "We had a differing of visions."

Iggy murmured something from the seat next to Greg.

Sandra nodded toward him. "Was he the differing of visions?"

Norah gave a small smile as she watched him. "He was a big part of it. This here is Dr. Greg Schorn, formerly of Wright-Patterson. He's been working with the A.L.I.V.E. projects for years."

"A.L.I.V.E.?" Sandra asked.

Greg put up a hand as Norah opened her mouth. She frowned, looking at him. "Look, before you go into all that, you better make sure she wants to be in on all of it. I realize that the D.E.A.D. is after her and that strange winged guy seems to be milling about, but that doesn't mean that she needs to know everything, at least, not if she doesn't want to. Because once you step into this world, there doesn't seem like there's any way to step back out."

Norah turned back to Sandra. "He's right. If you want, we can try to find you a place to hide. Maybe somewhere out of the country. Somewhere that D.E.A.D. doesn't have any reach."

"And where exactly would that be?" Sandra asked.

"Honestly? I have no idea. But the woman who runs the organization that we're currently affiliated with, she does have a lot of connections. It's possible she could find a place for you."

Sandra studied the two people in front of her. Both seemed earnest in their desire to help her and Luke. And she appreciated that. And to be perfectly honest, she did want to stick her head in the sand and not hear anything more about aliens or secret government agencies or anything along those lines. She wanted to go back to a quiet life, just her and Luke.

But down deep, she knew that wasn't possible. Sammy had somehow found them hundreds of miles away. He was drawn to Luke. There was a reason for that. And as much as she hated the idea of getting further embroiled in all of this, the truth was she was already up to her neck. The only difference was she was up to her neck without any answers. So maybe some answers would make it a little bit easier.

She rested her hand on Luke's back, pulling the blanket a little tighter around him. "If you tell me what's going on, will we still be able to go somewhere, to start over?"

Norah nodded. "Yes."

At the same time, Greg shrugged. "Maybe."

Sandra took a breath. "Tell me."

Ten minutes later, Sandra wasn't sure what to think. The United States government had created alien hybrids. It was like something out of a sci-fi movie. But then, of course, she'd seen Sammy. And she was currently looking at what could only be an alien. She nodded toward Iggy. "He's one of the hybrids?"

Norah shook her head. "No. We think Iggy's a pure breed. He something called a Maldek."

"Basically he's a Martian dog," Greg said.

Her teeth gritted, Norah glared at him. "He is *not* a Martian dog."

Greg put up both hands. "Hey, no offense. I think Iggy is awesome. But Tilda said that he is the equivalent of a Martian pet."

Listening to the two of them, Sandra's mind reeled. So the U.S.'s little pet projects had escaped, which was why D.E.A.D. was created. But apparently Norah had left the D.E.A.D. because she realized that not all of the creatures that they were going after were dangerous, like Iggy. But the D.E.A.D. wasn't differentiating. It was just a "kill first, ask questions never" kind of policy. But that still didn't explain everything.

"Why did the Blue Boys come after Luke and me? I mean, they escaped from Area 51, right?"

Greg nodded.

"That's hundreds of miles from Kansas. Why would they travel all that way? And what about Sammy? He was an experiment that was released as well, right?"

"The Blue Boys were definitely part of the Area 51 projects," Norah said.

"You can say that again," Greg grumbled.

Norah ignored him and continued. "But we don't understand why they would have traveled all that way. It seems odd."

"Odd? Odd?" Sandra felt the hysteria rising up inside of her. It took a supreme effort of will to get it to tamp down. "Yeah, giant Martian blue ape things traveling hundreds of miles to try and kill me and my son, that's *odd*."

Greg leaned forward. "Look, I know this is all insane. I know you feel like you just got dumped into the middle of a really bad acid trip. But here's what I do know: The Blue Boys traveled all that way for a reason. Yes, they're animals. But animals do things out of instinct, not randomly. There is a reason the Blue Boys were trying to find you." He shot a glance at Norah. "Were there any other sightings of the Blue Boys or attacks anywhere near her farm?"

Norah shook her head. "I don't think so. In fact, Kansas was the farthest out from Area 51 that we had a report."

"There's a reason they targeted you," he repeated as he turned back to Sandra. "I don't know what that is. But I do know that a reason exists. And if you want some help figuring out what it is, I can do that. I can't promise I can give you an answer, but I can promise I will try."

For some reason, Sandra believed him. She could see that he understood what it was like to be hunted. There was something in his background that had terrified him and at the same time given him strength. "Thank you."

Greg nodded, sitting back in his chair again.

"What about Sammy? He didn't try to hurt us. He tried to help us," Sandra said.

"I honestly don't know anything about him." Norah glanced over at Greg, who shrugged. "I never read anything on his file. But Maeve has seen him. He helped her and the triplets escape when Martin's men were moving in. And he helped Greg here back at 51. I don't know, maybe he's just some sort of guardian angel."

"Huh," Greg said, his hand on his chin. "I wonder."

"Wonder what?" Norah demanded.

"All the creatures from Area 51 were created from some form of alien DNA and animal DNA," Greg said slowly.

"But Sammy doesn't look like an animal," Sandra said.

"No, he definitely doesn't," Greg said. "I think he was mixed with human DNA. But that still leaves the question of the original alien DNA. There's only one report of an alien sighting that I can recall that involves wings. In 1984, three Russian cosmonauts reported a strange orange smoke filling their space capsule when they were in low orbit around the earth. When they looked out the capsule windows, they reported these large humanoid creatures floating there. All of them had wings. They called them space angels."

Norah scoffed. "Space angels? It was probably some sort of reaction to whatever the orange smoke was."

Greg nodded. "That's what everybody thought, that or some sort of shared delusion. But a few days later, three more astronauts joined them on the station. And these new individuals also saw the winged creatures. They were there one moment, and then they simply disappeared."

"So are you saying that's what Sammy is?"

Greg shrugged. "Or that's who he's related to. I don't pretend to know where they got all of their samples. But he came from somewhere. And for a giant winged creature, he sure is good at staying out of sight."

Sandra shivered, picturing the seven-foot-tall creature. There was something human about him, but there was so much more about him that wasn't. "But he's in the files or something, right?"

"He is now," Norah said. "When I first heard about him, though, I looked him up, and he wasn't in the files. But then a few days later, he was. Normally the creatures in the file all had the same order attached to them: kill on sight. He was the only one that had something different."

"What was the order for him?" Greg asked.

"If he was sighted, you were supposed to call a number and then just keep him in sight, making no move to interfere."

"Well, that sounds like Martin," Greg muttered.

"Who's this Martin guy? You guys keep mentioning him. Is he someone with D.E.A.D.?" Sandra asked.

Greg shook his head. "To put it bluntly, Martin is the bad guy. He's a spook who seems to be behind everything awful that has happened. He was also part of a torture prison camp for aliens. And he's just an all-around really horrible human being … who is employed by the U.S. government."

Sandra looked between the two of them. "You're kidding, right?"

Norah shook her head. "I wish we were. Unfortunately, Martin is one of the deep dark ugly stains that the U.S. government likes to keep in the shadows. He does the things that the U.S. government doesn't want people to know about."

"So where is this Martin guy now?"

Greg shrugged. "Last time anyone saw him, he was escaping a secret government base where he conducted experiments on aliens and alien hybrids through an underground train through underground secret tunnels developed by the U.S. government to connect the military bases on the western half of the United States."

Staring at him, Sandra waited for the punch line. It never came. "Oh."

"I didn't have as much interaction with Martin as Greg did, but we do know that he is behind the scenes, pulling strings like a puppet master. And it's safe to say that whatever he's up to, it's not good for the rest of us."

CHAPTER 39

SEATTLE, WASHINGTON

Martin slammed his phone down on his desk. They had failed to capture the Gillibrands again. He flung himself back in his chair. Most of his men required hospitalization. And who was reported among the group that had absconded with the Gillibrands?

A winged creature and an extremely blond man with dark sunglasses.

Damn you, Joseph.

Martin wasn't sure who he was angrier at: the creature or Joseph. But then he realized it was neither of them, nor any of the others who'd joined the little ragtag rescue mission. It was Tilda. It was always Tilda.

A cold sweat broke out along his body when he thought of "Sammy" showing up in Montana. There'd been no reports of him in any areas nearby. Which left only one other way of traveling.

He gripped the edge of the desk. *But it couldn't be. He never demonstrated those abilities while in captivity.*

Then again, many of the other creatures that escaped Area 51 had demonstrated unknown abilities once they were free. Apparently the behaviors of the creatures observed while in captivity were only the tip of the iceberg.

Martin's phone rang, and he growled at it before he yanked it up. The number on the screen sent another shiver through him. He took a deep breath and answered. "Hello?"

Tatiana's voice was quiet with suppressed rage. "Your *son* has been causing us some problems."

Ice cold fear flashed through Martin. "He's not my son. I don't understand why you would—"

Tatiana cut him off. "You and your government are responsible for his creation, therefore you are his father."

The tension that had coiled up in Martin eased at her words. "I assure you, he is not a creation I am proud of. He was never supposed to be released. I am not responsible for that."

"Yes, I know. Your little hacker girl let him out," Tatiana said, her tone set the hairs at the back of Martin's neck to stand straight up.

His mind raced. Tatiana should not have that intel. She had someone inside, someone who was feeding her information. He'd have to flush out the rat but do it in a way that didn't tip Tatiana off.

Tatiana continued. "But apparently your information panned out. The Sentinel is attached to the boy."

Keeping his tone even, he said, "I thought you would find that of interest."

"He was of interest, but another member of the rescue team proved even more intriguing," Tatiana said.

Martin didn't need to ask of whom she was speaking.

"What can you tell me about him?" She asked.

"He goes by the name Adam. He has been with R.I.S.E. for decades. He is very … close … to the leader. He has been aiding R.I.S.E. in the protection of the abominations and their support team."

"He always was a do-gooder," Tatiana growled. "I am not happy with you, Martin. But the revelation of 'Adam' has taken some of the sting from that anger. But I would strongly suggest you do not disappoint me again." Tatiana disconnected the call.

Martin glared at the phone before tossing it on his desk. He needed to be rid of Tatiana and her followers.

But soon, he would have help in that endeavor. His anger dwindled as he imagined how Tilda was going to respond to the information about Tatiana's presence in Montana. In fact, if he played his cards right, soon Tilda would make sure Tatiana never bothered Martin again.

CHAPTER 40

HY-BRASIL

Time felt like it was standing still. Maeve had been climbing the walls all day. Now she'd stopped inside the barracks to stare out the window. The sun had dipped below the horizon. Greg had told her about the trip to find the Gillibrands before he left. Maeve had of course plead ignorance when Jasper had asked where everyone was.

But now as the hours wore on, she was rethinking that approach. What if they were in trouble? What if they needed help? Should she tell Tilda what the rest of them were up to?

"Stop worrying," Chris said as he joined her, slipping his arm around her waist.

"Should we tell someone? It's been hours," Maeve said.

"Let's give them a little more time, and then we can raise the alarm. Norah and Adam know what they're doing," Chris said.

Maeve raised her eyebrows at him. "You didn't mention Greg."

Chris grinned at her. "Greg is incredibly intelligent. But not exactly Rambo."

Although Maeve chuckled, she felt out of loyalty to Greg, she should try to defend him. "Hey, he can hold his own when he has to."

He kissed her on the forehead, and his eyes lit up. He nodded beyond her. "Yes, he can. And here come the conquering heroes now."

Maeve's head whipped back to the window. Iggy loped along the path with Adam and Greg right behind him. Maeve looked up at Chris, who nodded. "Go on."

Maeve needed no further urging. She hustled out of the barracks. Greg caught sight of her and jogged over. Maeve threw her arms around him. "You guys had me worried."

"What? Worried? Nah," Greg said as he returned the hug.

"We're good," Norah said.

Maeve noted the new bandage on her cheek. "I'm guessing it wasn't a simple pickup."

"Not exactly. I'm going to get Sandra and Luke settled. Greg can tell you about it," Norah replied.

Maeve met the gaze of Sandra, who was standing a short distance away, her son next to her but not touching. "Hi."

Sandra gave her a small nod, her gaze straying to the barracks. Luke just stared at the ground. Norah led them away.

Maeve watched them go, waiting until they were out of earshot. "So what happened?"

Greg spoke quietly. "D.E.A.D. was there. And so was Sammy."

Maeve jolted. "Really?"

He nodded. "He's the reason we made it. A second group tried to stop us on the way to the plane."

Frowning, she asked. "A second group? Who were they?"

Greg gave Maeve a quick rundown of the junkyard and the attack afterward.

Trying to picture it, she couldn't. "Rolls-Royce SUVs? Who would bring that to a gunfight?"

"I don't know, but I bet Tilda does," he said.

Maeve grunted. "I think Tilda's keeping a lot of things from us."

Greg's voice was grim. "So let's go get some answers."

CHAPTER 41

Answers had to wait until the next morning, however. According to Pearl, Tilda was unavailable until then. She showed up when everyone was finishing up breakfast. Sandra and Luke had already stepped away from the cafeteria with Norah. Chris had taken the triplets and Alvie for a walk, so it was only Greg and Maeve left.

Tilda walked in and headed straight over. She paused halfway to them and switched directions, pouring herself a cup of coffee before sitting down across from them. "I believe we need to talk."

"Adam filled you in?" Maeve asked.

Tilda nodded.

"So who the heck were those other guys? Why didn't you tell us about them?" Greg asked.

Tilda sighed. "I had foolishly hoped that you would not have to deal with them. But apparently Luke Gillibrand and his connection to the Sentinel has pulled them out of the shadows."

Maeve tried to tamp down her frustration. *"Who* are they?"

There was a pause before Tilda answered. "The Draco."

Greg faltered, nearly spilling his coffee as he replaced the mug back on the table. "The Draco? You can't be serious."

Maeve looked between the two of them. "Who are the Draco?"

"There have been two groups who have been responsible for the majority of human UFO abductions. The first are referred to as the Grays. They tended to take humans, much like animals are tagged in the wild. Their goal is to understand the physiology, to record changes, and then to release them," Tilda said.

"And the Draco?" Maeve asked

"They aren't looking to study them. The Draco are looking for ways to involve themselves in human society. To that effort, they try to impregnate human females to allow for hybrids that could be a way in."

Maeve gasped. "That's barbaric."

Tilda gripped her mug a little more tightly. "And so are they. I mentioned them when we discussed the creation of humanity. I mentioned there were different groups, more aggressive groups, that were included in your DNA. That was the Draco."

"They're on the planet?" Maeve asked.

Greg shook his head. "No, no. I mean, I didn't get a good look at them with all the gunfire and fear and all, but they were human looking."

"It has taken them a long time to achieve that." Tilda took a sip of coffee as if to steel herself and then began to speak. "The Solar system, as we know it today, is not how it always was. Not even our position is the same as it once was. Earth, at one point, was the second planet from the sun."

Maeve frowned. She knew about planetary movement, of course, that the order of the planets in the galaxy was not how it had always been. But she also knew that movement would have happened an incredibly long time ago. Why would that be relevant now?

"The Draco were a race of aliens whose only goal was destruction and submission of worlds." Tilda took a breath. "They're a reptilian race that ran over life across the galaxy. A group of refugees escaped from the Draco to our galaxy and took refuge on two planets: Mars and Maldek. They were called the Lyrans."

"Maldek? Like Iggy?" Greg asked.

Tilda nodded. "He's from the planet of Maldek. It no longer exists. It is now the asteroid belt between Jupiter and Mars."

Maeve was familiar with the arguments that the asteroid belt had once been a planet. Individuals had maintained that there was a symmetry to the Solar system and the planets located within it. And it was true that there was a huge asteroid belt instead of a planet between Jupiter and Mars. But she was also equally familiar with the arguments against it. The most compelling being that the mass of the asteroid belt would make the planet less than half the size of Mars, although that argument often relied on the spurious argument that Mars was a moon of the destroyed planet.

"What happened?" Maeve asked.

"The Draco followed the Lyran refugees. They were a race skilled in the art of war. They hollowed out asteroids to use as ships, even some as large as planets. They sent one of these planet-sized asteroids through our system. It destroyed Maldek. As it passed close to Mars, it siphoned off Mars's environment and shifted its axis."

"Did anyone survive?" Greg asked.

"Some Martians, and even a few Maldekians, managed to retreat underground on Mars. They sustained themselves there for generations." She nodded toward the doors. "Your young friend Iggy was one of their species. The comet eventually reached Earth, pulling Earth into its orbit and siphoning some of its water. Eventually Earth was sent shooting out, launching it farther from the sun."

"And the comet?" Maeve asked, although she had a feeling she knew.

A small smile slipped onto Tilda's face as she nodded to the sky. "It established an orbit around the sun. We call it Venus."

Greg looked at Tilda. "You can't be serious."

Maeve looked into Tilda's eyes. The woman met her gaze unflinchingly. Every time they learned something new about the universe, it threw other things they knew into question. In 2018, NASA had discovered that the moons of both Saturn and Jupiter may actually contain small organic molecules. Organic matter and methane were also found on Mars by the Red Planet rovers. Harvard researchers even suggested there was a chance that the cigar-shaped asteroid named Oumuamua may be an alien probe from an ancient civilization. So was it possible? Maeve supposed it was.

"And then humanity developed on Earth?" Maeve asked.

"Not exactly," Tilda said slowly. "The Draco were stranded here. They were isolated from the rest of their empire. And the empire was not known for coming to its people's aid. The refugees from both civilizations claimed parts of the earth for themselves."

Chris frowned. "Why? If the Draco were there …"

"They were also looking for payback for what the Draco had done. The two civilizations fought the Draco and sent them underground," Tilda explained.

"They won," Greg said.

"In a way," Tilda said. "A peace council was convened, and it was determined that the only way to ensure peace was to allow a new species, a species with a mix of all species DNA, to flourish on Earth. It took many iterations to get the mix right. There were twenty-two versions, but eventually *Homo sapiens* were created."

Greg frowned. "If the Draco were so warlike, why would they agree to that? Why would they stop fighting?"

"Because they could not risk their people. They were cut off and reproducing, but it was becoming beyond their ability," Tilda said.

"Why?" Maeve asked.

"Without the benefit of their home environment, they struggled to reproduce. They needed intervention oftentimes. So they agreed, believing that the reptilian DNA would allow them to control the newly created species. They believed they would eventually conquer us."

"Why didn't they?" Greg asked.

"Apparently we humans are a bit stubborn and not fans of being controlled by others. But allowing their DNA into humanity's was a mistake. It doomed humans to be warlike and perpetually fighting. But that was the deal the Council agreed to, and as long as they continued to abide by it, no one could interfere."

"But then they didn't abide by it," Maeve said.

Meeting Maeve's gaze, Tilda nodded. "Correct. The Council did not realize that they were continuing their genetic manipulations. Over time, they created human-reptilian hybrids. They looked human, but they were reptilian in their mindset. The reptilians seeded them throughout the world. When the Council learned what they were up to, they knew that once again they needed to intercede." Her gaze strayed to the doors where Maeve's gang had disappeared a few minutes earlier.

And it clicked. Maeve's breath froze in her lungs for a moment before she could speak. "They created Alvie. He doesn't have any reptilian DNA."

"None. He is pure human and Gray. He is the answer," Tilda said meeting her gaze again.

Greg frowned. "But he's fought. He's defended himself."

Tilda nodded. "When the Lyrans flourished, they did not have a military or an army. But they did not have the instinct to protect themselves. It was why they were so easily defeated. We could not create a species who would suffer the same fate. So yes, he will defend himself and those he loves when necessary. But he will not let aggression rule him. He does not possess that capability."

Maeve had always wondered why certain people were more aggressive than others. Environment played a role, but the same environment could result in two different responses. And even peaceful environments could create an aggressive individual. Yet there were others who were the antithesis of the aggressive individual. What made two of the same species so very different?

Greg interrupted her line of thought. "But what is he the answer to?"

"The problem of humans," Tilda said softly. "Without the aid of greedy humans, the Draco would never have flourished. They would not have even survived to this point. The Council created Alvie as the next step in human evolution, should *Homo sapiens* fail to combat the Draco threat, or worse, be influenced to work against their species' best interest."

"We were created as a weapon, though," Greg said.

Tilda inclined her head. "It's true. They did hope we would defeat them. But they soon realized how wrong their approach was. They had hoped that by interceding, they could help the primitive species of this planet realize its true potential. And at the same time, they have made sure that Earth is not touched by other alien species."

"But that's not everything, is it?" Maeve asked, thinking of all the other human species that had once existed. "Because if the Council has created a new hybrid of alien-human DNA without Draco, then they would need to remove the other version from the planet, wouldn't they?"

Tilda met her gaze for a long moment before speaking. "Our ability to keep the Draco in check has stayed the Council's hand. As long as the Draco are not seen as a full-fledged threat to human rule, the Council will not act. And having the hybrids here, it allows the Council to observe our interaction with them. They have been heartened by the lengths you, Maeve, in particular, have taken to keep them safe."

"Way to go, champ." Greg punched Maeve lightly on the shoulder.

Maeve didn't take her gaze from Tilda. "But if the Draco rise up ..."

"If it looks like the Draco could succeed, that they could take over even a corner of this planet, then the Council will have to determine if their experiment on Earth has been a failure, in which case it would be time to start anew ... without us."

CHAPTER 42

MALIBU, CALIFORNIA

The smell of the Pacific Ocean drifted in through the open glass doors. Tatiana smiled and stretched her fingers, touching the leather headboard, her toes nearly reaching the end of the king-sized mattress. She sat up and pressed a button on her side table, then picked up her robe from the floor, slipped it over her naked form and then tucked her feet into her slippers.

Yesterday had been a disappointment, but she had had a wonderful night. And now she was filled with optimism.

She walked out to the balcony and watched as some early morning surfers got in a few runs. She didn't turn as she heard the maids bringing in breakfast. When she heard them depart, she turned and took her seat at the small bistro set.

She never ate breakfast with anyone. This was her time to enjoy the world. She pulled the silver lid off of her tray. Her eyes scanned the eggs and toast before falling on the raw bacon. Tasting the eggs, she poured herself a cup of coffee.

She unfurled the newspaper, scanning the headlines before

turning to the financial pages. She smiled, noting her stocks were up, and the stock she'd just shorted had dropped. It would be another successful day.

She ate her breakfast as she made her way through the newspaper. It was one of the only old-fashioned habits she liked. She adored technology, but there was something about sifting through a paper newspaper that just brought her joy. And as Marie Kondo recommended, she kept the things in her life that brought her joy.

Thirty minutes later, she was finished with both her breakfast and the newspaper. She tapped on her cell phone. *Come.*

The door to her bedroom opened. Dietrich's strong, heavy steps made their way toward her. He stood in the doorway, a scowl on his face as he blinked against the bright sunlight and then pulled out his sunglasses.

Tatiana waved him toward the other chair. "What have you found?"

Moving into the room, he said, "A link. We should be able to use him to find the location."

"How certain are you?" She asked as he stood behind the chair, his large hands grasping the back of it.

"Very. I have people on the ground already making contact."

Tatiana narrowed her eyes. "Who?"

"Sebastian and Samantha."

Tatiana nodded approvingly. They were good choices. Both were strong, attractive, smart, but also likable. And both were complete and utter sluts. Depending upon which way the target fell, that could also come in very handy. "Excellent. When will they be making contact?"

"Within the hour," he said.

Calculating all the angles, she asked, "And how long after that until we are ready to go?"

There was a anticipatory gleam in Dietrich's eyes when he

answered. "Ovid is already on site. He will be ready to go as soon as we have a location."

Finally, after all these years, they would have the base's location. R.I.S.E. had been a thorn in her people's side for generations. But now they could take care of that problem once and for all. And then there would be nothing and no one standing in their way. The secrecy of R.I.S.E. would be its own downfall. The world would not even know that they had disappeared. And the world would be less safe because of it.

Tatiana smiled, her gaze straying once again to the surfers who were now carrying their boards onto the beach. The boys couldn't be more than twenty years old. They had that lean swimmer's body that Tatiana strongly approved of. One had short-cropped blond hair and the other slightly longer brown hair. She nodded toward them. "Find out who the boys are and if they're available."

Dietrich nodded. "Of course, my queen." He nodded back toward the bedroom. "Would you like me to have the maids take care of that as well?"

The two men who had occupied Tatiana's evening lay on the bed. One was face down, blood dripping down his arm and onto the floor. The other lay on his back, his arms spread wide, his chest ripped open. His eyes stared at the ceiling, his mouth gaping open.

So focused on a beautiful morning and the news about R.I.S.E., she had completely forgotten about them. She waved her hand dismissively. "Yes, yes. Make them go away."

Dietrich bowed and took his leave. Tatiana once again dismissed the bodies from her mind as she began organizing all that she needed to do if Dietrich's information panned out. The end of R.I.S.E. And the acquisition of the hybrid.

She smiled. This really was going to be a wonderful day.

CHAPTER 43

HY-BRASIL

The wind blew a little stronger today than yesterday. Maeve pulled her jacket tighter around her. Sandra and Luke appeared on the hill, heading toward the group. Sandra paused when she caught sight of them. Her gaze strayed over the group, focusing slightly longer on Alvie and the triplets. Then she squared her shoulders and headed to meet them.

The two of them had arrived just over twenty-four hours ago. Maeve gave Sandra credit for taking everything as well as she had. Alvie and the triplets scared her. Maeve could see that in her response, but she covered it pretty well.

Luke, however, was fascinated by them. A huge smile on his face, he broke into a run as soon as he caught sight of them. "Hi, guys!"

The triplets let out a squeal and ran for him, dancing around him as they led him back to where they had been playing. Maeve smiled at their easy taking to one another. If only people could always be so accepting.

Another wind blew, this time a little stronger. With a jolt, she realized it was the end of October. It wouldn't be too long before much cooler weather was upon them. She pictured Hy-Brasil covered in snow. Was this where they would spend Christmas? Would they even celebrate this year?

The triplets had never celebrated a Christmas. She wanted them to have that. She wanted them to have a normal childhood, because in their hearts, they were still just children, no matter what they looked like on the outside.

She darted a glance at Alvie and the triplets, but the four of them looked completely unbothered by the drop in temperature. She'd have to talk to Tilda about getting them some real winter gear. Just the idea of it made her heart heavy. Was this going to be their life from this point on?

She'd grown up at Wright-Patterson, but her mom had always given her a sense of home, a sense of family, unusual as it had been. There'd been soccer games, picnics, movies. How was she going to create that same sense of normalcy here? It was as if they were on a deserted island with only about a dozen people.

Iggy swung in from a tree above, rolling once he hit the ground and then bouncing to his feet. Snap hurried over to him. Iggy chattered at him happily.

Luke sat on the ground, playing some sort of game involving a small ball and rocks with Pop. Hope circled the area, happily flitting from group to group before curling up next to Alvie. Alvie reached out a hand to gently pet Hope, who gave a lazy tail wag in response. Alvie and Crackle were lying down on the ground, investigating a small bug making its way across the grass.

"It's amazing how normal they all are," Sandra said as she joined Maeve.

"That's funny. Because I was just wondering how I was

going to give them a normal life if this is all they would experience for a while."

Sandra shook her head. "There's no such thing as normal. Each kid's life is a little bit different. I mean, Luke was never going to have a 'normal' childhood, even before all this. Penny was never going to have a 'normal' childhood. I definitely didn't have a normal childhood. I think normal is overrated."

"I've got to agree with you there," Norah said as she joined them. "I loved my childhood. It was my parents, me, and my five brothers. My parents were both in the service, and we moved from military base to military base all throughout my life, sometimes twice in the same year. I was always starting a new school, meeting new people. Some people would have hated it. I loved it. But I know it wasn't normal."

Maeve didn't say anything, just turned and studied the group of young people in front of her, removing her own biases. None of them looked unhappy. None of them looked as if they were missing out. Maybe normal *was* overrated. As long as they were happy, what did it matter? And really, with the reports she'd heard on the stress placed on kids growing up these days, maybe her gang was better off not being part of that "normal" world.

"Maybe you're right. But I still hate the idea of them spending their first Christmas here," Maeve said even as she knew her idea of a tree, her gang and the house in the suburbs with the white picket fence was unrealistic.

"Are you kidding?" Norah asked. "R.I.S.E. has a ridiculous budget. They are all going to have the best Christmas ever. There's going to be decorations, presents, food. Oh my God, the food. I'm going to demand that we have turkey, gravy, stuffing, all the fixings and desserts, lots and lots of desserts."

Watching Norah's excited face, Maeve smiled. Maybe Christmas here wouldn't exactly be the worst thing ever. Norah's face went from exuberant smiling to a frown of concern. Maeve followed her gaze to where Iggy stood. He'd been crouched down with Snap just a second ago.

But now he stood straight, his head turned toward the water. A small growl erupted from deep in his throat. The hairs on the back of Maeve's neck stood straight up.

Gasping, Sandra stumbled back.

But Norah ran toward Iggy, yelling over her shoulder. "Get everyone back inside!"

Maeve was already striding forward. "Alvie, we need to go now."

Iggy lunged, his growls growing louder. Alvie hustled Snap and Crackle toward Maeve. Pop sprinted for her, leaping into her arms. Luke followed them quickly, and Sandra grabbed his arm.

With a vicious snarl, Iggy took off like a shot, sprinting toward the beach. Norah was right on his heels. But Maeve and Sandra grabbed the kids and ran as fast as they could in the opposite direction.

CHAPTER 44

There were four wooden picnic benches that lined the beach, about twenty feet from where the water came in at high tide. A cool wind blew in from the ocean, but with the fleece on, Greg didn't mind it. In fact, he liked it. There was something that screamed "freedom!" when you sat outside in the air.

And right now, he needed something that suggested he was free, because the island was beginning to feel more like a prison than paradise. The allure of Hy-Brasil had worn off. And more disappointing, he hadn't seen a single giant rabbit. This whole mythological island thing was a complete bust.

Plus, Maeve and his conversation with Tilda wasn't going down very well. A reptilian alien race targeting them. And the only solution was never to join the world ever again. They might not have a life, but they'd be safe.

He just wasn't sure if the trade-off was worth it.

The junkyard had been terrifying, but he'd felt alive, even as he'd worried about dying. But here, here he was just twiddling his thumbs, without a purpose. This morning, he'd had Pearl get him in touch with Tilda, and he'd practically begged her to give him a job, any job. She said she'd think about it, but she hadn't come up with anything. So he made his own.

He turned his head from his search of the landscape, which he'd been doing in hopes of catching a glimpse of a giant cottontail disappearing into the trees, back to his laptop. A report of the latest results from Iggy's testing was open on the screen in front of him. He'd gotten Tilda to at least run a few tests on Iggy's blood. Iggy was such an incredible specimen, besides the obvious intrigue of him looking a lot like Yoda. Had George Lucas heard about the Maldek? Were they the inspiration for Luke's mentor?

Greg shook his head, focusing back on the report. As far as he and Maeve could tell, Iggy's claws were made of an unknown substance, much stronger than bone. His claws could cut through steel. And although compact, he was incredibly strong.

But that's not what interested Greg. What he was really interested in was his connection with Norah. After his conversation with Tilda, Pearl had taken him to a separate building a few dozen yards back from the others. And low and behold, there'd been an MRI machine. It was like coming over a sand dune in the desert and seeing an oasis.

With Norah's permission, he'd been able to run Iggy through it. It had been amazing. Iggy's entire brain had been mapped out. Whenever he heard Norah's voice, an entire region lit up. The sound of Greg's voice lit up the same region but at a much-reduced power. It was fascinating.

He had to admit, he was a little jealous. He wouldn't mind having a little alien buddy who was always by his side. Maeve had four, for God's sake. Was it so much to ask for maybe just one?

He closed the laptop as his stomach growled for the second time. He really needed to get something to eat. He'd been sitting at the beach for a while, hoping that maybe one of the ships would come in. He thought he'd overheard Tara say she would be coming by today. But that could be hours from now.

He tucked the laptop underneath his arm, a chill inching down his back. Man, it was really starting to get cold. He'd have to see if he could get a jacket and maybe some gloves if he was going to continue working outside.

He headed up the path toward the cafeteria. The kitchen was fully stocked, and although for dinner there was a staff that came in and cooked, for breakfast and lunch, everyone fended for themselves. Greg actually preferred that. It made him feel like he was more at home rather than a visitor. And he had a sad feeling this was going to be his home for a while.

The sound of a boat caused him to pause. He turned, hope growing and then dashing as he saw Tara's brother, Ethan, jump onto the dock and tie the boat off. It never ceased to amaze Greg that they had this entire hidden base, and yet the primary way on and off it were old fishing boats.

A man in green camo hopped off the boat after Ethan had it tied off. Greg frowned, not recognizing him. It was unusual for them to have a new visitor. There were maybe five staff members from R.I.S.E. that he'd met, but everything was generally handled by Tilda, Pearl, Jasper, and Mike.

So who are you? Greg wondered.

He waited on the path, figuring he could be one of the first to meet the new guy. Ethan caught his gaze and looked away quickly. The man's usual ego seemed to be missing. That was strange. Or maybe whoever this new guy was, he was high up on the food chain, and Ethan was on his best behavior.

Ethan hurried up the path, the man walking behind him, scanning the area from side to side. The closer they got, the more something seemed off. Greg didn't know why, but there was something about the guy with Ethan that just, well, scared him.

Greg took a step off the path and then a few more. He

turned and headed into the trees, knowing he probably looked like an idiot. But fear had taken hold of him, and he simply did not want to cross paths with this new guy.

And his life experiences over the last few months had told him to listen to that little voice that warned him to run.

Cutting through the trees, he headed for the administration building. He moved at a fast clip, wanting to get there before Ethan and his new friend. Something was wrong. And he wanted to be with everyone else when they found out what it was.

His breath coming out in pants, Greg burst through the tree line at the top of the hill. Chris and Adam looked up from where they were looking at the engine of one of the solar-powered jeeps. Greg hurried over to them, trying to get his breathing under control.

Chris narrowed his eyes. "Everything all right, Greg?"

He shot a glance back at the beach and then at Adam. "Is somebody new coming to the island?"

Adam shook his head.

His stomach bottoming out, Greg spoke quickly. "Yeah, hmm, well, Ethan's walking up the path with somebody new, and I don't know, something just felt—"

A snarl erupted from the path. Seconds later, Iggy bolted past. Norah was right behind him. "Something's wrong!" she shouted.

Chris and Adam didn't waste any time. They took off after Norah and Iggy. Greg waited for just a moment and then placed his laptop on the hood of the Jeep and sprinted after them as well.

One for all and all for one.

CHAPTER 45

Norah didn't know what was wrong with Iggy. But he'd caught the scent of something, something that had him on full alert. Norah tore down the path after him, glad to hear the sound of Chris and Adam giving chase behind her.

Iggy burst from the ground, grabbed a tree branch, and swung himself ahead twenty feet just as two shapes appeared over the rise in the path. Ethan let out a yell as he ducked out of the way. But the man with Ethan dove for the ground, rolling to his feet impossibly fast. Iggy landed, turning around with a snarl at the man.

Ethan crab-crawled backward, his eyes wide as he watched Iggy and the man. The man, dressed in the green uniform of the R.I.S.E. soldiers, stood with his arms out wide, his shoulders hunched. He hissed at Iggy.

The hair on the back of Norah's neck rose.

Iggy launched himself at the man, his claw aimed right for the man's face, before he switched direction midair and dove in between the man's legs. His left claw sliced along the inside of the man's thigh.

The man wheeled around, catching Iggy in the side of the head with a brutal kick.

"Iggy!" Norah dashed forward, but Adam sprinted ahead of her, tackling the man at the waist.

Norah rushed to Iggy's side, curling him into her chest as she pulled him away from Adam and the man. Iggy's eyelids fluttered.

Chris appeared at her side. Flicking a glance at Iggy, Chris kept his attention on the two combatants only a dozen feet away.

Neither of them said anything. There was nothing to say. Watching Adam and the new man fight was like something out of a sci-fi movie. The hits that each of them took were insane. And the speed with which they moved …

The man slipped a knife from a sheath hidden in his pocket. He slashed out at Adam, who bent backward at the waist, avoiding the attack before grabbing the man's arm and twisting it. He pressed the back of his forearm against the flat of the knife, and it went flying off into the trees. He twisted the man's wrist, and the man tumbled to the ground before rolling to his feet.

The two men circled one another. The sun came out from the clouds, and for just a second, it flashed on the man's eyes.

Norah reared back as Chris sucked in a breath. "You saw that too, didn't you?" Chris asked.

Backing away from Adam and the stranger, Norah nodded mutely. The two men circled one another. A shot rang out from behind her. It crashed into the man's thigh. He dropped to one knee with a screech. Adam slipped behind the man, putting him in a choke hold and holding him there even as the man batted at his arms, trying to loosen Adam's grip. But Adam didn't let go.

The man's eyes slowly closed, but Adam held on a few seconds longer to make sure he was out and not playing possum. As soon as he dropped, Chris hurried over, pulling zip ties from his back pocket.

Norah turned to find the shooter, surprised to see Greg standing there. He raised an eyebrow at her. "Y'all need to stop thinking this always has to be some sort of martial arts throwdown. Bad guys should be shot, okay? That's going to be our new motto. Bad guy shows up, we shoot them."

Still shaken by how fast the man had moved and how violent Iggy's response had been, Norah nodded. A "I agree."

Eyes narrowing, Greg raised his gun again. "And where do you think you're going, Ethan?"

Ethan, who'd started to crawl away, hunched his shoulders before looking over his shoulder and standing slowly with his hands up. "I-I didn't know anything was wrong with him."

The lie was splashed across the man's face. "You believe any of that?" she asked Greg.

"Not a word," he said not pulling his gaze from the man.

Iggy's eyes flickered open before he scrambled up to her shoulders. Norah narrowed her eyes at Tara's brother as the man's gaze shifted between the gun in Greg's hand and Norah. This time she bared her teeth. "Don't even think it. You're coming back with us. It's time for a little chat."

CHAPTER 46

Maeve and Sandra had hustled all of the kids back to the barracks. Maeve kept glancing over her shoulder, waiting for a shout or a yell. She didn't know what was going on. But she knew her priority: keeping her gang safe.

Keeping pace, Sandra ran next to her, her hand tightly clasped around Luke's. She could tell Sandra had the exact same plan.

Sprinting ahead of the pack, Alvie pulled open the barracks door. Maeve ushered everyone through, taking Alvie's place. Once inside, Sandra pushed all of them to the back of the barracks while Maeve made a beeline for her storage locker. She pulled out the weapon that she'd asked Tilda for the day after they arrived. She grabbed the holster and slipped it over her shoulders, locking it in place. Then she slid the Beretta into the holster after checking to make sure that one round was in the chamber.

Sandra noted the weapon and gave her a nod.

Alvie stood by the door, glancing out.

"Alvie, get away from there," Maeve ordered.

Alvie stayed where he was. The triplets huddled on the bed behind Maeve. She knelt down to each of them, running a hand over each of their heads. "It's all right. Everything will be all right."

Snap, Crackle, and Pop all leaned into one another. She sat on the bed next to them. Pop climbed over her to lean in on one side. She wrapped her arms around all three of them at once.

A shot sounded from down near the beach.

Terror in her gaze, Sandra glanced down at Maeve's gun. Leaping to her feet, Maeve hurried next to Alvie to look out, although she was careful to stay to the side of the window.

Jasper and Mike appeared, powerful machine guns in their arms as they took point in front of the barracks. On the hill, she could see more soldiers, although none came near.

Alvie tried to peer around her but Maeve pulled him back. "It's not safe."

It's all right now. The immediate danger has passed.

Looking down at him and then the trembling triplets, Maeve forced a smile to her face. "You see that? Everything's fine. All safe."

She felt Alvie's gaze on her and turned to look at him. *No. One danger is over. But it is not safe. Not anymore.*

CHAPTER 47

Greg kept his weapon trained on Ethan as they made their way up the path, trying to hide the tremble in his arms. He didn't like guns. The power they contained was too much. But his new reality made keeping a weapon on him a part of his daily existence.

But R.I.S.E. is supposed to be safe. It's the safest base on the planet, he thought.

"Why don't I take that from you?" Norah asked, holding out her hand.

He was more than happy to hand the weapon over. "Thanks."

Behind him, Adam and Chris had the other man between them. His leg was bleeding badly. That was another new thing. Normally when he shot a gun, he was running away from something. He'd never actually seen the effects of his handiwork. And to be perfectly honest, it was making him a little sick.

Speaking of sick ... Greg thought, frowning as he stared at the man. His jaw moved back and forth as if he was eating something or maybe checking to see if his teeth were all there?

The man jolted upright, his head flinging back, his neck muscles straining.

"What the hell?" Chris gripped the man's arm to keep him from being flung backward to the ground.

White foam appeared at the man's mouth and dribbled down his chin.

"He took something!" Greg darted back toward the man. Adam and Chris were already laying him out on the ground. He had been trembling when Greg started toward him, but now he'd gone perfectly still. His eyes stared straight up.

Already knowing what he was going to find, Greg reached down and put his fingers to the guy's neck. No pulse. He reached forward to check the man's pupils and then reared back. The man's pupils weren't round. They were elongated, like a lizard's. "Holy crap."

Adam gripped him under the arm while Chris grabbed the man's other arm. "Let's get him out of here," Chris said. Between the two of them, they dragged him forward, the man's feet leaving a trail in the dirt.

His mouth hanging open, Greg stared after them, before he got to his feet and hurried to catch up with Norah, who had moved Ethan aside to allow them to pass.

Norah raised her eyebrows in question.

"He's dead," Greg said, still struggling to believe what had just happened.

Ethan whirled around to look at them. "What?"

"Keep walking," Norah said, pushing Ethan forward. Ethan stumbled but then righted himself, continuing up the path.

Flicking a glance ahead, Greg kept his voice low. The wind was pushing against them, which would also help keep the conversation from Ethan. "It must've been some sort of poison, fast acting. But his eyes, Norah, they weren't human."

"So what is he?" Norah asked.

"I think he was probably a Draco," Greg said swallowing hard. He hadn't wanted to believe the idea of human-passing aliens, but if he was right, this man was proof of exactly that.

They reached the rise, and Greg noted that more soldiers had appeared. There were now two soldiers at the entrance of each building and another eight in the common area, patrolling around each building. He caught sight of Chris and Adam as they put the body on the back of a truck with Jasper's help. Mike got behind the wheel, and Adam leaped into the back as Chris tapped on the side of the truck. The truck took off at a quick clip, heading toward a part of the island that none of them had seen yet.

Norah and Greg escorted Ethan to the administration building, where Tilda was waiting. The look on Tilda's face would have terrified anyone. Two MPs strode forward, grabbed Ethan's arms, and yanked him none too gently into the building.

Greg let out the breath he was holding only when he knew Ethan was firmly in Tilda's custody.

"I see your shooting's getting better." Norah lowered her weapon at the same time.

Greg winced. "I was actually aiming for the man's chest."

"You still hit him. That's what counts," she said.

Iggy shifted back down to Norah's arms and gave Greg a small smile. "Ig?"

He smiled. "Yeah, buddy. Ig. Now come on, let's get you checked out."

Inside the medical ward, Greg examined Iggy. He didn't think there was anything seriously wrong with him. He seemed to be back to his old self. But he warned Norah to keep an eye on him. If he was acting at all strange, he'd contact Tilda about getting a CT scan.

Norah tucked Iggy into his bed as Sandra and Luke came in.

"You guys all okay?" Norah asked.

Sandra nodded. "We got the kids back to the barracks. Maeve's there with her gang."

Norah nodded at Iggy. "You mind keeping an eye on him?"

"Of course. Is he all right?" Sandra asked studying the little alien.

"He took one for the team." Greg ran a hand over Iggy's head. Iggy leaned into Greg's hand with a soft little purr. "Who's the best Maldek ever?" Greg cooed.

"What happened?" Sandra asked.

"We had an intruder. Iggy managed to intercept him but got a kick to the head for his trouble."

"Oh no. I hope—" Sandra broke off as Luke hurried across the room, sitting on the bed next to Iggy. Iggy rolled over so his back was resting against the side of Luke's leg.

"Well, I can see when I'm not needed." Greg stepped away from the bed. "Keep an eye on him, kid, okay?"

Luke nodded, slowly reaching out to rest his hand on Iggy's side.

"We'll watch him. But where are you two going?" Sandra asked.

Norah looked at Greg, who nodded back at her. "To get some answers," she said.

CHAPTER 48

Chris found his family in the barracks and quickly explained to Maeve about the unknown man on the island. Neither of them wanted to leave the triplets and Alvie, but both of them also wanted to know what exactly was going on. Finally it was decided that Maeve would head to the administration building to get answers while Chris stayed with their family.

As Maeve strode toward the administration building, the argument she was going to use to get Tilda to allow her in on whatever conversations they were having ran through her mind. She slipped in the door of the administration building. Tilda stood waiting. She nodded at Maeve. "About time. We've been waiting for you."

Tilda disappeared inside, and Maeve quickly followed. Ethan sat in the middle of the room tied to a chair. Two guards stood by the doors. Greg and Norah stood on the left-hand side of the room. Maeve joined them, glancing around. "Where's Adam?"

"With the other guy," Greg said. "And you should know, we think he's a Draco."

Her mouth falling open, Maeve's head jerked toward him. "What?"

Keeping her voice low, Norah said, "He's dead. Apparently there was some sort of failsafe involved if he was caught. I saw his eyes for a second during the fight. They weren't human."

Maeve turned back to stare at Ethan. Had he known? He couldn't have. It wouldn't just be betraying R.I.S.E. He'd be betraying his species, his planet.

There was no chance for further conversation, though, as Tilda strode toward Ethan. "Why did you bring him to the island?"

Ethan glared at her. "I got orders. I was told to bring him to the island. It was just like any other—"

Tilda slapped him across the face. "Do *not* lie to me, Ethan."

A large red handprint was clearly visible on the left side of Ethan's face. His mouth fell open in shock.

"How did they get to you?" Tilda demanded.

"I don't know what you mean." Ethan looked around desperately, his gaze falling on Maeve. "I didn't do anything. This is all a misunderstanding. Help me. Please."

Maeve's gut tightened as she looked at Tilda. There was no compassion on the woman's face. Was it possible that Ethan had been used? That somehow he really was a patsy in all of this?

Tilda's voice held no doubt. "There was an account opened in your name. $500,000 was deposited there two hours ago. Tell me, Ethan, were they going to pay you another $500,000 once the job was done?"

Sweat dripped down the side of Ethan's face. "I don't know what you're talking about. I swear."

Before Maeve could react, Tilda slipped a baton from her pocket and whipped it across the side of Ethan's knee. He screamed, lurching forward, but the ropes held him tight. "I do not believe you."

Tears streamed down Ethan's face. "I didn't! I didn't do anything!"

Stepping forward, Tilda raised the baton again. Maeve bit her lip to keep herself from yelling out. But as Tilda raised the baton higher, Maeve opened her mouth. She couldn't let this happen. Before she could say a word, though, Ethan spoke. "Okay, okay. Just stop."

"Explain," Tilda ordered as she lowered her hand and took a step back.

Ethan's head dropped forward. For a moment, Maeve thought he was crying. But when he looked back up, it wasn't guilt or desperation on his face.

It was anger.

"Explain? How come you don't already know? Matilda Watson, the all-knowing head of R.I.S.E.," Ethan sneered, his face ugly with hate.

Maeve reared back from the vitriol in the man's voice. He wasn't some innocent patsy. He was a full-fledged supporter of the actions he'd taken.

The anger didn't seem to ruffle Tilda, however. She took a seat on the chair one of her soldiers placed in front of Ethan—out of kicking range. "I'm not all knowing, apparently. So why don't you explain to me where I went wrong?"

Ethan's lips became a thin line. They moved back and forth as if he was trying to swallow back the words that wanted to escape. His eyes narrowed to slits. "My family has ferried members of R.I.S.E. to this godforsaken island for generations. Only the McCallums have been allowed to know the location of Hy-Brasil. But with that knowledge came ties. We were never allowed to go anywhere outside of this island. We are Americans living in Ireland. But I've never been to America. Do you know where we live?"

"Your family homestead," Tilda said her arms crossed over

her chest. "McCallums have lived there for two hundred years."

Ethan scoffed. "Homestead. It's a drafty, broken-down ruin. But we are required to live there because it guards the entrance to here. So we are bound to the land like slaves. Did you ever think that maybe we wanted a different life?"

"You could've had a different life!" Tara yelled as she stormed across the floor toward her brother.

Maeve's head whipped around, watching the enraged woman. For once, Maeve saw the resemblance between brother and sister. Tara's anger looked to match her brother's. But unlike Ethan, whose anger was directed at R.I.S.E. and Tilda in particular, Tara's anger seemed to be aimed entirely at Ethan.

She came to a stop four feet from her brother, her hands on her hips as she glared down at him. "You ungrateful bastard. In the McCallums' entire legacy, there has never been a traitor amongst us until you."

"Traitor? I'm not the traitor. I'm getting what I'm owed. What *we're* owed," Ethan argued.

"Money? You did this for *money*?" Tara demanded.

Tilda put up a hand, and Tara quieted, taking a step back.

"What did you tell them?" Tilda asked.

A cruel smiled slipped onto Ethan's face. "Everything. They know where you are. They know how to get through your security. They know how many people you have here and where they're located. They know everything."

"You fool," Tilda murmured.

"*I'm* the fool? At least I'm finally getting paid what I'm owed!" Ethan snarled.

Tilda leaned closer to him, her voice driving dangerously low. "You think you were going to get paid? The Draco don't leave any witnesses. Your payment would have been found at the bottom of the ocean. Once they were done with you, they would have been completely done with you."

Ethan shook his head. "No. They paid me. I already have the money."

"Do you?" Tilda asked. "There was a backdoor on the account. They had access to it. They could take that money back as quickly as they gave it to you. Did you know that?"

"That's not true. I ... I would have had to sign for that," Ethan stammered.

Tilda laughed. "You really are a fool. Who set up the account, Ethan? Did you set it up? Or did they do it for you?"

The man paled. "But, but—"

"You really are stupid," Tara spit out. "I knew you never should've been given this position. I told our parents. But they insisted that you would grow into it. They insisted that you were a McCallum and that you would rise to the occasion. But you didn't rise. You sank. And now you might've sunk us all."

Tilda nodded to the two guards, who grabbed Ethan roughly by the arms and pulled him from the room. Ethan screamed, squirming against the men. "Let me go! What are you going to do with me? Tara, help me!"

But Tara only turned her back on her brother. Yet Maeve saw the woman close her eyes, her chin trembling. No matter Tara's anger, this was not an easy moment for her. Once Ethan was outside the building, Tara turned to Tilda. "What are you going to do with him?"

"He'll get what he deserves," Tilda said as she watched the doorway where Ethan had disappeared. There was no compassion in her tone.

Maeve swallowed at the finality in her words. "Goodbye, Ethan," Greg said softly.

Her tone still serious, Tilda turned to the three of them. "There are some arrangements I need to make. I'll return shortly. We still have more to discuss."

As Tilda headed for the door, Tara followed her. Greg turned to Norah and Maeve. "Holy crap. That was tense."

Norah kept her gaze on the empty doorway. "I have a feeling things are going to stay tense for a while. Our safe haven just blew up."

CHAPTER 49

It was only fifteen minutes later when Jasper and Mike arrived. Everyone was in the barracks together as they stepped in the door. Jasper looked around. "I'm going to need everyone to gather all their stuff. We're going to take you over to the main base."

"This isn't the main base?" Greg asked.

Jasper grinned, but it was missing some of his usual humor. "No. This is where we keep people who we don't want to see the regular base."

"But current events have changed all of that. We need everyone to be together. Tilda is evacuating the base," Mike said.

"Where to?" Norah asked.

"Still working on that," Mike said. "Penny and her mother have already been taken off the island. Your gang's destination requires a little more planning, however. As soon as I have a firm answer, I'll let you know. But for right now, we need to get everybody over to your new digs."

Jasper held his arms wide. "So, who needs help packing a bag?"

Ten minutes later, they were piled up into the back of a truck. Maeve sat with Snap on her lap, Alvie next to her. Crackle and Pop were in Chris and Greg's laps respectively. Norah had Iggy, and Sandra had Luke. As Maeve looked around, she realized that every adult had at least one individual they would need to look out for. They had a common bond: protecting the ones they loved.

The truck rattled as it made its way down the dirt road. They drove through the woods for about fifteen minutes before they reached a paved road. Maeve let out a sigh of relief at the transition to a smoother ride.

Greg twisted, stretching out his back. "That's better."

The hair on Maeve's whole body stood up for a second. It felt as if energy had just passed over her.

"Holy cow," Norah exclaimed, looking toward the front of the truck.

Maeve craned her neck, trying to see what Norah was looking at. And then she stared in shock. A half mile down the road stood a small city. But it was a city unlike any she had ever seen. The buildings seemed to shimmer in the light. And they were made of the material that she didn't recognize. It wasn't concrete. It wasn't wood. The closest she could guess was steel, but it seemed shinier than that. There was almost like an iridescent glow underneath the metal.

The buildings that they could see rose up only about four stories. But there was one that was six stories high. And a strange craft sat at the top of that building.

The window separating the cab of the truck from the back slid open. Jasper's face appeared. "Now you are really seeing R.I.S.E."

CHAPTER 50

The base was small. It contained only about ten blocks. Each building gave off a pearly iridescent glow. There were dozens upon dozens of soldiers, scientists, and personnel on the streets. Most drove solar-powered jeeps, but there were a few solar-powered Hummers as well.

Mike pulled up in front of a three-story building, and they all clambered out of the back. Greg stared up at the building, trying to figure out what kind of material it was.

Joining him, Mike followed Greg's gaze. "It's a polymer-based material. It's incredibly strong but also incredibly flexible. Once set, it can withstand a great deal. But it's also incredibly light. You could pick up that entire wall and put it in place if you needed to."

"Where did you get it?" Greg asked.

Mike grinned. "Where do you think?"

Greg shook his head. "Why exactly were we stuck over in Camp Nowheresville when this was right here?"

"No one is brought to the main campus unless absolutely necessary," Mike explained,

"And we're not absolutely necessary?" Greg asked in disbelief.

Mike just shrugged.

Jasper clapped his hands together, drawing everyone's attention to the front of the building. "Okay, folks. You are all going to be assigned apartments in this building behind me. It will just be for the night. First thing in the morning, we will all be getting on transports. I will have more information on that probably in the morning. Right now, if you'll follow me, I'll give you your room assignments, and you can all get settled."

They all headed toward the building. But Mike tapped Greg's shoulder, shaking his head. "Actually, Tilda needs you and Maeve for a little bit. She needs your help with something."

"What?" Greg asked.

"An autopsy."

CHAPTER 51

The autopsy lab was located in the six-story building, and it was state of the art. But Maeve expected no less after seeing the actual R.I.S.E. buildings. State of the art was actually an understatement. It was more like state of the universe.

The same iridescent walls lined all of the spaces. The floors were also made from the same material. It muffled footsteps, which gave it an unreal quality as she walked down the hall toward the lab where they would be conducting the autopsy.

Everything about the building felt light and yet incredibly strong. There were no door handles or even keypads. Every panel could be used as an information center, and doors just opened as they approached them.

And while she was still reeling from the attack and from the revelations of the actual R.I.S.E. base, she couldn't deny that there was a kernel of excitement growing inside of her at the idea of examining a Draco specimen.

The soldiers had delivered the body to the autopsy suite. The lab itself was small, baring a striking resemblance to an operating room. One soldier stood outside the door while the other two who had been guarding the body moved over to the door.

Maeve and Greg wasted no time gowning up and getting to work. The body now lay on the steel table. She and Greg cut away the clothes and bagged them, handing them off to a waiting soldier for analysis.

Now they had just the Draco lying in front of them. At first glance, the Draco appeared completely human. His skin tone marked him as Caucasian, his hair color was brown, his lips a pale pink.

"Well, he's got all the correct appendages." Greg lifted up the towel covering his private parts. "And apparently they were graced with a little extra in certain areas."

Maeve moved slowly from the man's head down to his feet, just doing a visual examination. She stopped at his hands, examining his fingers more closely. "Greg, come look at this."

Greg hurried around to her side, taking the hand from her. There was skin stretched between the fingers. "Webbing."

Maeve nodded. Webbing wasn't unheard of amongst humans, although it was rare. She moved quickly down to his feet. "Same thing."

"Do you think this is standard, or he's just not quite fully evolved?" Greg asked.

"There's no way to know without a second specimen." Maeve said.

Standing back, Greg's gaze roamed over the body. "This is really unfair. I mean, you see Agaren, you know he's an alien. You see Iggy, and you think, hey, there's another one. This guy looks like he could shop at Trader Joe's and no one would even blink."

"Speaking of which." Maeve moved to the man's eyes as Greg started jotting down measurements. She was jumping all over the place, but she wasn't sure how much time they had to do the autopsy, and she wanted to gather as much information as possible.

She pulled back an eyelid, the skin offering more resistance than she expected. But a very normal human-looking eye stared back at her. White sclera, dark brown iris, black pupil. She flashed the light into the eye and then paused, squinting. There was an outline slightly darker than the pupil running from the top to the bottom of the eye.

Working on a hunch, she moved to the side of the eye, pulling back the skin there. She was rewarded with another layer of skin. "Greg."

He carried the chalkboard over, setting it on the man's stomach as he peered down where Maeve pointed. "Holy crap. He's got a second set of eyelids."

"And check this out." She flashed the light on his pupil. "Do you see this darker outline? The pupils *do* change shape."

"Now that would make someone stand out at Trader Joe's." Greg grinned at her. "Let's see what else we can find."

And despite everything that was swirling around them, she understood and felt the same sense of curiosity. Curiosity was what had led them both into science. And neither of them had been able to feed that curiosity much in the last few months. She found herself excited for the first time in a long time. She was back in a lab. She grinned. "Can't wait."

They studied the body for over two hours. It had been an illuminating investigation. The Draco's body was amazing. From its skin to its internal organs, everything was designed for battle, for efficiency.

From a purely biological standpoint, they were an absolute marvel. As an enemy, they were absolutely terrifying. The first most obvious problem was their skin. It wasn't human skin, despite what it looked like. It was tougher, much more resistant. In fact, Maeve had a sneaking suspicion that because of the density with which the molecules were packed, it would repel sharp instruments and potentially even bullets.

Which made them awfully hard to kill.

The second problem was their internal organs. First off, their hearts were located on the opposite side of the chest as a human's. And they were much smaller. Neither she nor Greg thought that was an aberration with this particular Draco. She was pretty sure that was by design. Their bodies just pumped blood much more efficiently. Their blood itself was much less dense than human blood. In fact, their bodies in general were less dense except for the skin. It made everything more efficient, which explained how they could be so fast and so muscular at the same time.

They also had a second set of teeth. There were actually humans that had a second set of teeth too, but the second row within the Draco was much sharper, and although they couldn't confirm it, Greg had a feeling they could actually replace the first row in a fight.

"These things are beasts." Greg dropped the clipboard onto the desk behind him with a clatter. "Okay, so we've got creatures that have nearly impenetrable skin, highly efficient circulatory systems, strong musculature, and a basic badassness to them. We are so screwed."

Maeve ignored the last part of his comment. "It's true they do have some amazing natural defenses. But their eyes are weak points, and so are their mouths." The interior of their mouths was made of a much less dense material. As a result, it could be harmed with a bullet and maybe even with a knife.

"Great, we'll just hope that they all run toward us while screaming so that we can actually hit them in their mouths. I've been shooting for a couple of months now at stationary targets while giving myself plenty of time to line up my shot, so sure, no problem," Greg muttered.

Maeve rolled her eyes. "I know it's not the best news, but at least it's something."

"Yeah, a very little something," Greg muttered.

Maeve gave him a baleful look. He put up his hands. "Sorry, sorry. Just feeling a little bit overwhelmed."

Maeve walked over and threw an arm around his shoulders. "Hey, we escaped a military installation that was completely teeming with hundreds of aliens that wanted to kill us. Those were impossible odds too, and yet here we are."

"True. But I was kind of hoping that impossible odds were a one-time thing and that now we would move on to more reasonable odds, or better yet, ones that favored us for a change," Greg said.

"Well, maybe the next life-threatening situation will be more in our favor."

He sighed. "Dare to dream."

CHAPTER 52

Maeve and Greg wrote up the results of their initial evaluation. They handed off blood and tissue samples, along with a list of analyses that needed to be done, to Mike, who replaced the soldiers who'd originally been stationed inside the lab. Mike promised to have the results back to them as soon as possible.

Then there was nothing for Maeve and Greg to do but get settled back in the apartments before they left first thing in the morning. Mike offered to drive them back to their building, but both Maeve and Greg wanted to walk.

The evacuation seemed to be in full swing. The streets were packed with trucks, jeeps, and even a few motorcycles. They'd also had to step out of the way of more than one individual carrying a large box or pushing an overloaded dolly. Everyone was definitely getting ready to leave.

Maeve said goodbye to Greg in the hallway outside her apartment and let herself in.

She sighed at the quiet in the apartment. For the first time in a long time, it was just her, Chris, and the kids. She welcomed it, along with the accommodations. They were much nicer than the ones at the smaller camp. It felt like they were living in high-end Silicon Valley campus housing rather than the front lines in a fight against an alien presence on Earth and above.

Tilda had given them an apartment on the first floor of a three-story building. Their apartment was the largest, with three bedrooms, two bathrooms, a full kitchen, dining room, living room, and even a small fenced-in area out back.

Greg had a smaller apartment at the end of the hall. Norah and Sandra each had apartments on the second floor. And Adam and Tilda lived on the third floor.

Guards were stationed out front, and Maeve liked to think that they were there to keep them safe and not to keep them in. But it felt like everything was shifting under her feet and it was hard to know exactly what was going on and exactly who was on their side.

Maeve's entire goal was simply to keep her family safe. And now her family extended to Greg, Norah, Iggy, Luke, and Sandra. But being in the middle of an intergalactic war—that was never part of her plan.

But once again, no one seemed to care what Maeve wanted. *Oh, Mom, I wish you realized what a can of worms you opened up.* She didn't regret Alvie. She didn't really blame her mother either. The military was going to go ahead with their project with or without her mother's cooperation. And after seeing Area 51, she knew that Alvie had been in a much better situation with them than he ever would've been with anyone else.

She just hated the feeling that they were pawns in the middle of a giant chess game that was well beyond their skill level.

Hope stepped out of one of the bedrooms and padded over to her, rubbing up against her. Maeve leaned down and rubbed her coat, receiving a few licks in return. "Good to see you too, girl."

Maeve straightened and headed to the room Hope had just exited. Chris sat on the bed reading a book to the triplets, all of them hanging on him. Alvie was cuddled into his side. Maeve smiled at the normalcy of the moment.

She stepped into the room. Five sets of eyes darted toward her. The triplets sprang off the bed, sprinting for her and wrapping their arms around her legs and nearly tipping her over. She laughed as she patted their backs. "I missed you too, guys."

Maeve climbed back onto the bed with all of them as Chris finished the story and then tucked them all in. They all wanted to sleep in the queen bed in there, and Maeve liked the idea of them being together. Personally, she thought she might try to squeeze in there with them later when she went to sleep herself. She would just feel better if they were all together.

She pulled the navy-blue comforter up to Alvie's chin. The triplets were already closing their eyes. The day had been a lot for them. They had sensed the stress and angst. And Iggy's response to the intruder had scared them all.

But thank God for Iggy. If he hadn't recognized that there was an intruder, who knew what damage the man could've done? Tilda thought he was just a scout trying to get the lay of the land, and Maeve knew that was probably correct. But if he'd come across one of the triplets or Alvie, maybe he would've decided that information wasn't all he was going to bring back.

Maeve still struggled with the idea that Ethan had betrayed them. Tara looked beyond devastated. Maeve hadn't had a chance to speak with her, but she'd seen her again at the main camp. Tara had walked by with Tilda, her eyes rimmed red. Maeve hadn't had the courage to ask what had happened to Ethan.

Iggy?

Smoothing the blankets along Alvie's chest, she answered, "He's all right. He's right upstairs with Norah."

Brave.

"Yes, he is. We are very lucky to have him."

Friend.

She started at the word. It was true. Iggy was Alvie's friend. He was his first friend he'd made without Maeve's help. All the other people who Alvie had ever met had always been very carefully introduced to him through Maeve.

Smiling, she kissed his forehead. "Yes, he is your friend."

Alvie smiled, snuggling next to Crackle and closing his eyes. Maeve stayed with them until she was sure they were asleep, and then she went in search of Chris. She stopped at the front door and made sure all of the locks were on. Realistically, she knew if someone tried to get in, it wasn't going to be much of a deterrent. But she felt better knowing that at least it would be a small hindrance.

The door to the patio was open. She wended her way around the large dining table and stepped outside. Chris sat in one of the Adirondack chairs, a beer open next to him. He looked over at her and then pointed at the table. "Brought you one too."

Maeve pulled the beer from the container filled with ice. She unscrewed the cap and took a long swig. The bubbles tickled her throat, and she sighed in response. "I needed that."

She took a seat in the Adirondack chair next to Chris. He held out his hand, and she put hers in it. He squeezed gently. "Everyone asleep?"

Picturing their gang, she nodded. "Somehow, miraculously yes. Personally I don't think I'm going to be getting much sleep tonight."

"Me either. It's been a hell of a day," Chris said with a sigh.

Maeve looked at him and giggled. A stronger laugh

worked its way up her throat. She placed the beer bottle on the ground before she dropped it as laughter spilled out of her.

Chris stared at her like she'd lost her mind and then slowly he smiled, a laugh erupting from him. The two of them sat together, laughing hysterically until Maeve doubled over, holding her stomach. "No more. No more."

Chris reached over and rubbed her back, chuckles still running through him.

Maeve sat up, taking in some deep breaths and wiping the tears from her eyes. "We find out there's an alien race that has been living on the planet Earth for centuries and is now out to get us, and your summation is it's been a hell of a day."

Chris grinned. "Well, it has, hasn't it?"

She nodded, taking Chris's hand again. "I don't think I could do this without you."

"You could. And you would. But you don't have to," he promised.

Maeve looked into his eyes, trying to imagine how she would've gotten through this last year without Chris. She simply couldn't imagine it. He'd been her rock. The one safe place she had whenever everything else became overwhelming. "I love you."

"I love you too." Chris nodded back toward the apartment. "You sure everybody's asleep?"

A small thrill, this one the good kind, rolled through Maeve as she nodded. "Yes."

Chris leaned toward her. "Then I say we take advantage of the quiet while we have it."

CHAPTER 53

The Draco knew where the base was. After all these years, they had finally found it. Tilda had spent the last couple of hours fortifying their security measures. At the same time, she was aware it was only a matter of time before the Draco arrived.

I should have known.

There'd been more and more intelligence reports about the Draco inserting themselves into society. They'd been buying up land, placing their people within various world governments. Tilda had read the reports with growing alarm, knowing that something would happen eventually. She had a meeting planned for next week with Agaren to discuss the possible ramifications and whether the Council would intervene or if it would be left entirely in human hands. But she feared the time for those conversations was well past.

The priority right now was getting everyone and everything that they could off the R.I.S.E. base. But that was not going to be an easy job.

They had been here for decades. And the security protocols

in place that kept them hidden from satellites and human view could not be easily switched to a new location.

They did have other locations that they could fall back to, but Tilda wasn't sure if she was ready to make that move yet. After all, if the Draco could find them here, they would no doubt find them at a less secure location.

So the question became: Should she cancel the evac and have them stay and fight here or leave to fight at another location?

The larger problem was where to hide the hybrids and Iggy. None of them would blend in no matter where they sent them.

Tilda scanned the sheets on the desk in front of her: All of the security protocols they put in place. All the technology that they used to keep them safe. But technology was never enough. It was always human error, or human greed in this case, that allowed the enemy to slip through their defenses.

She remembered reading something about plane crashes and human error. People often thought that as the planes aged, their technology broke down, and that was the reason for the plane crashes. But a study in 2004 found that three quarters of all fatal plane crashes could be attributed to human error.

She'd always known that humanity was the one factor she could not account for. She had technicians and statisticians and analysts who could tell her what components of her security system could fail. They could identify the pitfalls and then back them up. But no one could pinpoint which human would similarly fall, or when.

Over the years, she'd contemplated who it would be. She had her people on the lookout for anyone that was going through a divorce or an uptick in gambling or some other risky behavior. Any sort of financial difficulty was enough to get someone red flagged, their file reviewed, and in most cases, they were placed on a different assignment until the situation resolved itself. But all of those people would always be under a microscope until they were ruled a non-threat.

But Ethan McCallum had never made that list. He was paid well, had no living expenses, was given free rein to and from the base. There were no red flags with him. And yet the Draco had somehow realized that he was the one weak link in their security chain.

It was a devastating turn of events, especially for Tara. Tara had first come to the base when she was only a girl of twelve. She'd been fascinated by the location and the goals of R.I.S.E. She'd been a true believer from the first day. Her parents had looked upon it as a sacred duty to protect the Earth. Tara had the same mentality.

But apparently for Ethan it was merely a job, one that did not pay him well enough.

Tilda rubbed her forehead, as if somehow she could rub away the memory of Ethan's face. His parents would roll over in their graves if they knew.

But Ethan's motivation was merely a distraction from the larger problem. The Draco had tried to get to R.I.S.E. multiple times over the decades. They had never gotten anywhere close. In the 1970s, she'd lost six of her people. The Draco had grabbed them and demanded they reveal the location. Not a single one of them broke.

And not a single one of them survived.

But that was the mentality that was necessary to be a member of R.I.S.E. When Tilda had been younger, when Wernher von Braun had first introduced her to the parallel space program, she'd automatically grasped its importance.

And that had been before she'd been made aware of the Draco's existence.

She could still remember von Braun's face when he explained about the race of creatures that lived underground. Tilda remembered the absolute terror that had shot through her at the description of them. It had been, bar none, the most terrifying day of her life.

It had also been the greatest day of her life. For that was the day she met Joseph Watson, the man who would become her husband.

Stifling a yawn, the words on the sheet blurred in front of Tilda. She rubbed her eyes and reached for her coffee mug, but it was empty. Two hours ago, she'd brought the materials back to her apartment. She thought if she was here and a little more comfortable, it would help her stay more focused.

Unfortunately that didn't seem to be the case. She pushed away from the desk, grabbed her mug, and headed to the kitchen. The front door opened. Adam stepped in, his gaze automatically shooting to her. "You should be in bed. You need your sleep."

Pouring more coffee into the mug, Tilda shook her head. "There's too much to do."

He crossed the room, placing his sunglasses on the counter and taking the mug from her hands. "You've done all you can do tonight. You need to get some sleep. Just get a few hours, okay?"

Tilda looked up into the face that she knew so well, a face that she'd known for nearly sixty years. "All right, Joseph. I'll sleep for just a little while."

He leaned down and kissed her gently on the lips. "Good."

CHAPTER 54

Maeve and Chris had spent the last few hours reminding each other just how important the other one was. Chris had fallen off to sleep. Maeve had fallen asleep for a short while but then had jerked awake, visions of Hank running through the base flying through her mind.

Careful not to wake Chris, she slipped from the bed. Pulling on some clothes, she made her way into the kids' room. They were all nestled close together.

Hope lifted her head and wagged her tail slowly. Maeve walked over and ruffled her fur. "Good girl."

Hope closed her eyes again after giving Maeve's hand a lick. Her tail still doing a lazy wag, the pup dropped her head back down again. Snap, Crackle, and Pop were all curled up together. Crackle was in the middle with the other two snuggled up tight. Alvie was next to them, lying on his side, turned toward them.

Maeve crawled up in the chair in the corner of the room. Her gaze roamed over the triplets and Alvie. They all look so peaceful, so innocent.

And the Draco wanted them dead.

Just the idea of it terrified Maeve. How was it possible that anyone could look at her four children and think of harming them?

When she and Alvie had lived together at Wright-Patterson, she'd been worried because she felt as if he was hemmed in and not allowed to live his life. But at least then she never worried about him being physically harmed. She never worried that his life was in danger. She had simply worried that he was missing out on life experiences.

Right now she would take the security of Wright-Pat over the mind-numbing terror of not knowing where she could possibly go with her kids if push came to shove. There was no safe port for them. Without government protection, they would be killed by the Draco. It wasn't as if they could slip into some town and just set up house. One look at the triplets or Alvie would send people running.

Maeve ran a hand through her hair, tugging on it as she got to the ends. It was all completely overwhelming.

Her gaze drifted over to where the triplets slept. They were Alvie's clones. It was surreal, and yet at the same time, it was her reality. She didn't have the lengthy history with them that she had with Alvie, and yet her feelings for them were no less strong. She would risk life and limb to protect them too.

Even with that resolve, she knew her life and limb might not be enough to keep them safe. The last few months had shown them that. Martin had made it clear that he would do anything to get Alvie. His focus on the triplets was no less intense.

What was wrong with that man? What had happened to him in his life to make him so cold? Was he always like this? Or had something created him just like all of those creatures created on military bases across the United States?

And now he wasn't even their biggest worry. The Draco,

creatures Maeve hadn't even heard of until yesterday, were after all of them as well. They wanted to destroy Alvie and the triplets because other creatures had created them as the next step in human evolution.

Maeve didn't completely understand that, although Tilda seemed concerned. And being she wasn't someone who often went off in wild fits of panic, she knew she should be incredibly concerned.

Massaging her temples, Maeve felt the doubts, fears and worries pound away at her. God, why did this all have to be so difficult? Why couldn't people just accept Alvie and the triplets? Why couldn't they simply go out to a movie, live in a neighborhood, play with other kids? Why did different always have to equal scary?

Maybe she shouldn't be asking what was wrong with Martin. Humans in general tended to act with fear toward the unknown. She paused, realizing that wasn't entirely true. It was *adults* who acted with fear toward the unknown. Children acted with curiosity but not malice. Malice was taught.

Hope's head jerked up from the bed, and she tilted her head toward the door. Maeve turned to look and heard a soft knocking. Hope scrambled off the bed. Maeve followed her to the front door. Hope was excitedly jumping around the front door.

Apparently not a Draco. Maeve ushered her back before opening it.

Hope bolted past Maeve and jumped on Greg. "Oh, hey. Good to see you too, Hope," Greg whispered.

Maeve stepped back to let Greg in. "Everything all right?"

Greg nodded. "I couldn't sleep. I thought maybe you might be up too."

"Sadly I am. You want something to drink?"

"I wouldn't say no."

Hope followed the two of them over to the kitchen area,

accepting a few more pats from Greg before disappearing back into the room with the kids. Maeve made some tea, setting out the mugs on the small kitchenette counter. She took a sip, embracing the warmth.

Greg dumped about five teaspoons of sugar into his before taking his first sip. And then he dumped two more spoonfuls.

Maeve stared at him. "You want a little more tea with your sugar there?"

Greg flushed. "I only have tea when I'm sick. My grandmother used to make it for me. She loaded it up with sugar. It's the only way I can take it."

Maeve started to stand. "You want me to get you—"

"No, no. It's good. Reminds me of Grandma. I could use that kind of reminder right now," he said quickly.

Maeve knew what he meant. Anything that could distract them from the current situation and remind them of what life could be was a welcome distraction.

"So, what are you thinking about all this?" Greg asked.

Maeve took a deep breath, trying to assemble her thoughts. "Any particular aspect?"

He gave a soft chuckle. "Oh, just pick one: the Draco anatomy, our chances for survival, the mere existence of R.I.S.E., any other craziness that has happened over the last year?"

Maeve thought for a moment. "The Draco's anatomy is kind of intriguing, isn't it?"

Greg leaned forward. "I know. I mean, completely and totally terrifying, and I would be perfectly happy if the world was completely removed of their presence, but they are fascinating."

"Did you hear anything about the test we asked to be run?" Maeve asked.

Blowing out a breath, Greg shook his head. "Nothing helpful. The DNA tests didn't match up with anything, which was expected. I've got some ideas for further testing, but of course, who knows when we'll be able to get around to that."

Although Maeve knew that it was important to understand the Draco's anatomy, right now she just couldn't focus on it. She needed a break from all that. "Any chance we could talk about something else? Maybe something a little lighthearted?"

Greg nodded to the corner of the living room. "Actually, I kind of feel like vegging in front of the TV. What do you think?"

Maeve smiled. She could not remember the last time she'd vegged out. There was nothing they could do right now to help any of their situations. Which meant all she would do was focus on worrying, but TV might provide the ideal distraction.

"That sounds perfect."

CHAPTER 55

The room was dark. It was two hours before dawn, but Tilda couldn't sleep. The truth was, she'd barely slept all night, even though she had tried. Adam had insisted.

He lay quietly next to her, his face soft in sleep. It was rare for him to sleep so soundly. Ever since the two of them had gone to the ranch in Colorado and picked up Maeve and the hybrids, he had been sleeping for only an hour or two a night. But finally his body had demanded that he sleep. It was not giving him a choice.

Tilda lay on her side and stared at the man she'd first met sixty years ago. That first day in von Braun's office, she'd thought he was the most beautiful man she had ever seen. Sixty years later, he had barely changed. He was still the most gorgeous creature she had ever seen. Time had left him untouched. But she'd suffered over the years. Her hair had grayed, her wrinkles had gathered, and she'd seen age take its toll year after year. She'd tried to set him free a few decades ago. She'd insisted that he needed to find someone younger, someone who looked more like him.

His words drifted through her mind again. *I don't care about any of that. I love you for who you are. As long as you stay you, then nothing else matters.*

He was a good man. No, that wasn't right. He was the most amazing man she'd ever met, and she'd met some of the greats. Wernher von Braun, JFK, intellectuals, formidable soldiers—none of them held a candle to Adam.

But she'd seen a new side of him these last few weeks. The hybrids had brought out a paternal nature in him that she hadn't known was there. He'd connected with Penny, understanding what she needed and providing it before she even had to ask. They had never had children. Tilda wasn't sure if the fault lay with him or with her, or maybe they just were never meant to reproduce together. But as she watched him with the young ones, she realized what a loss it was that he never had the chance to be a father.

But I suppose when I'm gone one day, he may. Because the truth was, he would be here long after she was laid in the ground to rest.

She shook her head, trying to wipe away the maudlin thoughts. It wasn't like her to dwell on the past or to think about what could be or what should be. Since she'd started working with R.I.S.E., she'd been focused on protecting this planet. That had been her one and only goal. Everything she'd done up until this point had been for that goal.

R.I.S.E. was the last bulwark against a foe that most of the world couldn't even conceive of. She knew if R.I.S.E. fell, the floodgates would open, and the world would never be the same again. The Draco welcomed that carnage. They wanted the world to change because they believed it meant they would rule. They had been slowly, patiently, building their strength, waiting for the moment when they could rise up.

And in her heart, Tilda knew they thought that moment was here.

Grabbing her tablet from the side table, she slipped silently from the bed, not wanting to disturb Adam. She walked to the bathroom and quickly got changed before heading down the stairs. She checked the status of the evacuation progress as she made her way to the kitchen. Everything looked to be in place. Transportation would arrive at dawn, and they would start offloading the staff.

Tilda had debated where to send everyone. They had multiple bases strewn throughout the world, but this was supposed to be the most secure. If the Draco had found them here, there was a good chance they knew of the other bases as well. Given what Ethan had said, she had to assume they did. So Tilda was going to have to separate their forces. She couldn't let all of R.I.S.E. be grouped in one location.

They would have to separate across the globe. Once the Draco threat had been neutralized, then she would bring R.I.S.E. back together.

Neutralizing that threat was the other problem. She knew what would be required. But she hoped she would have more time to make that decision. Because once that can was opened, there was no going back.

Her thoughts drifted to Maeve Leander and her incredible relationship with the hybrids. They were the hope, the hope for the future, the hope for peace, and a warning of the dangers of failing. They had to be protected at all costs.

Tilda had known about Alvie's existence for years. But rather than worry about what he could be the harbinger for, she'd been amazed that Alice Leander had managed to pull off the cloning. She was decades ahead of anyone else in the field. Her daughter had proved no less intelligent. But both women had also made Alvie's emotional well-being a priority. They had nurtured his compassion along with his intelligence.

He'd sacrificed himself to save the others when Martin's men had found them. He'd done it without hesitation. He was an amazing soul. Agaren was right—he was the best among them.

But then so too were the humans surrounding him. Each of them had sacrificed a great deal for a different species. Maeve, Chris, Greg, Norah—they all had risked life and limb. Tilda prayed Agaren was able to show the Council the good that still existed in humans like them.

The coffeepot beeped on the counter. Tilda grabbed a mug from the cabinet and poured herself a cup. She eschewed any milk or sugar. It was going to be a tough day. Tough days called for black coffee.

Footsteps sounded on the stairs. Seconds later, Adam was striding across the kitchen toward her. He stood in front of her, looking down, and then pushed her hair back from her face. "Couldn't sleep?"

"I got a little. But there's much to do."

Her tablet beeped. She walked over to the kitchen table and glanced down at it. That was strange. A sensor at the edge of their boundary had gone down. A single sensor. That shouldn't be a problem but still …

She grabbed her phone and quickly dialed. Jasper answered almost immediately. "I saw it. I have a team on the way to check it out. Hold the line. I'll have an answer for you in two minutes."

The line went quiet. Adam took a sip of Tilda's coffee and then placed it on the table in front of her while they waited. Jasper was back in less than two minutes. "I've lost contact with my men."

All thoughts of introspection and philosophizing disappeared from Tilda's mind. The commander of R.I.S.E. took over. "Send out the alarms. All guards are to be in their emergency positions now. I'll be there in five."

Tilda put down the phone and looked at Adam. "They're here. Get to the hybrids."

CHAPTER 56

The R.I.S.E. base had all the accoutrements, including access to a complete catalog of TV shows and movies. Maeve and Greg settled on *Chuck*, the TV show from the 1990s starring Zachary Levi. It was silly, it was fun, and it helped them forget at least for a little while.

But even as Maeve watched Chuck attempt to be a spy, she couldn't completely forget what was surrounding them. She glanced at her watch. It was coming up on 5 a.m. She wanted to let everyone sleep as long as possible. The longer they slept, the less stress they would be under. Hopefully sleep would keep them from realizing how dangerous their world had just become.

Of course, the constant movement of the last couple of days had surely reinforced the danger of their situation. But today, Maeve would swallow down her own fear, help them pack up, and help them move again. But from the look on Tilda's face, she knew that even Tilda was worried about their safety. This base was supposed to be the safest base on the planet. Where could they possibly go now that was safer?

Maybe I need to go off the planet with them, she thought, thinking of Agaren. How amazing would that be to see the base on the Moon? Even thinking it made her feel ridiculous. People who talked about things like a base on the Moon or UFOs were ridiculed in current society. The disinformation campaign had worked simply too well. Now even Maeve, who grew up with an alien hybrid, felt foolish at thinking such thoughts.

And that was after meeting Agaren, an actual visitor from another world. She wondered when he would return and if he was successful in his mission. Did they know about the Draco's incursion? Had the movement of the Draco pushed them to make a decision that all of them would regret?

Did the other species, whatever they were, even experience emotions like regret? Or were they so advanced that logic ruled everything, like Vulcans?

She hated not knowing how she was being judged. She hated not knowing what the judges were like. She felt like a primitive human stumbling around in the dark, trying to find the answers to mathematical physics using a slide rule while others were allowed to use a computer. It all felt so unbalanced.

Greg elbowed her arm gently. "Hey, none of that. No serious thoughts. We've had enough of those. This is a no-serious-thoughts zone."

"Okay," she said.

He patted her hand. "You're lying, but I appreciate the effort."

She grabbed their mugs from the table as Greg turned off the TV. They'd switched from tea to coffee about an hour ago. Her stomach rumbled. "I think I'll get breakfast started. You joining us?"

"Are you actually asking me that? You've had my cooking, right?" He asked.

Maeve shuddered. "I never knew eggs could be crunchy before."

"Well, that's because you've never put the egg shells into them. It adds a whole new texture. I was trying something. It didn't go well." Greg followed her to the kitchen.

"You want to grab some plates and cups and set them out?" Maeve opened the refrigerator door, hoping there was food there. She was rewarded with the sight of eggs, milk, butter, and bread. It was enough.

Hope padded out of the kids' room, her tail wagging, Chris right behind her. He walked over and kissed Maeve on the cheek. "You were supposed to be sleeping."

"I got a little," she said not meeting his eyes.

"Why don't I believe that? I'm going to take Hope out. Hey, Greg." Chris headed for the patio doors, where Hope was anxiously pacing back and forth. He slid the door open, and Hope zipped outside.

Maeve watched her go with a smile. At least the kids still had Hope. And Hope was completely loyal to them. They needed that kind of loyalty.

Chris crossed to the kitchen area. "What can I do to—"

The front door flew open. Maeve whirled around, her heart pounding. Chris planted himself in front of Maeve, his arms wide, as if to protect her from whatever was coming.

Adam sprinted into the room. "They're here. We need to go."

CHAPTER 57

A series of loud bangs sounded from somewhere in the distance. The noise spurred Maeve into action. She burst into the kids' bedroom. Alvie was already up, his eyes impossibly large. *They're here.*

"Yes," Maeve said, her heart racing.

Alvie grabbed Snap, who was right next to him, shaking her awake. Chris was right behind Maeve. He walked in and scooped up Crackle and Pop. Alvie hopped off the bed, and Maeve took Snap from him. They hurried to the door.

The front door was thrown wide open. Hope was barking up a storm in the outdoor area. Alvie zipped over to the patio doors and slid them open. Hope bounded in. Alvie put his hands on either side of her head and looked into her eyes. Hope's frantic barking stopped, and she walked next to him, her body thrumming with energy.

They stepped out into the hallway. Adam stood by the front doors, his gaze locked outside. Down the hall, Norah stepped into the hallway, Iggy perched on her shoulder, followed by Greg, then Luke and Sandra. Luke looked like he was still half asleep. Sandra and Norah looked wide awake, as if they knew exactly what was going on. Both had M4s strapped around their chests.

Chris stopped next to Adam. "What's the plan?"

"We're going to the hangar. My priority is getting you all out of here," Adam said.

"I like that priority," Greg announced, shifting from foot to foot as his gaze darted around.

Through the glass doors, the hangar looked like it was a mile away. A dozen guards rushed toward the front of the building. Eight of them stayed outside the front entrance, scanning the area, heavy weapons in their arms. Adam held the door open for the other four. They nodded at him before hurrying past the rest of them and heading for the stairs.

"Tilda's still here?" Maeve asked.

Adam gave an abrupt nod. And for the first time, Maeve saw a crack of emotion on his face. It was taking a lot for him to not protect Tilda in the middle of all of this.

"Stay together. Stay close. No one breaks off." Adam strode out through the doors.

With an intense look at Maeve, Chris followed with Pop and Crackle in his arms. Greg gave Maeve a nervous smile before he ducked out the door as well, Alvie's hand in his.

Then it was Maeve's turn. Holding Snap, she hustled outside, keeping close to Greg and Chris as Norah and Sandra with Luke and Iggy followed.

The city that she'd thought was so captivating just hours before looked sinister in the dim light. In the darkness, the buildings had lost their shimmer. And now they were just shadowed hulks.

As if the base was responding to her thoughts, spotlights blared on, focused on the hill. Maeve frowned. Why would they put on lights?

Shadows moved over the hill, dozens of them. They were fast. They were tall. And thanks to the light, she could see what they truly were: Draco.

And they were heading right for them.

CHAPTER 58

Greg had never been so scared in his entire life. He stared in horror as wave after wave of Draco rolled over the hill. The lights accentuated the scaly crocodilelike nature of their skin. The skin that was practically impenetrable. Their faces were flattened, their mouths more rounded than humans'.

And although he couldn't see them from this distance, he knew that within their mouths was a second row of extremely sharp teeth.

Explosions rang out. The buildings on the periphery of the camp went up in flames. Then buildings farther in started to burst into flame as well, shards of metal flying through the air.

Their quiet, contained walk had turned into a frantic sprint. Greg's legs pumped as he kept up with the group. At the front of the group, Adam was leading the charge, eight guards surrounding them.

But Greg knew that those guards wouldn't be enough. The weapons in their hands wouldn't be enough. From the corner of his eye, he saw something fly over his head and hit the building next to him.

He opened his mouth to shout out a warning, but the building exploded, flinging him into the air before he could even utter a sound.

CHAPTER 59

"Ig!" Iggy flung his weight back, digging his heels into Norah's chest. She stumbled back, trying to keep her balance. But Iggy pulled on the back of her shirt, yanking her to the ground as he vaulted off her and onto Sandra and Luke behind them, forcing them to the ground as well.

Sandra screamed, but the scream was cut off with the sound of the explosion as the building they were about to walk in front of blew apart. Norah rolled onto her stomach, covering her head with her hands as debris scattered around her.

A sliver of metal impaled itself in the ground right next to her elbow. She looked up, her ears ringing. If Iggy hadn't pulled her back …

Best not to think about that. Norah scrambled to her feet. Iggy lay sprawled across Sandra and Luke. He lifted his head, turning to look at Norah, a scratch above his eye. "Ig?"

Behind them, she saw a group of Draco appear from around the corner of their apartment building. She ran to Sandra and Luke and grabbed each of them by the elbow and yanked them to their feet as Iggy started barreling down the road.

Luke let out a cry, but Norah ignored him, urging him to his feet. Sandra figured it out quicker than Luke did and was already moving forward. She reached for Luke. "I've got him."

Norah nodded, releasing the boy. She grabbed her M4, scanning it quickly to make sure it hadn't been damaged in the fall. It looked all right. She turned around and let off a spray of gunfire. She might as well have shot cotton balls at them for the damage it did. But it did make them hesitate.

"This way!" Sandra turned into an alleyway between two buildings.

Iggy stood crouched on top of a dumpster, bouncing anxiously. Norah let loose another round of fire as she entered the alleyway.

This time it didn't even slow them down.

"Iggy, let's go!" Norah yelled as she sprinted down the alley. Iggy galloped next to her. Sandra reached the end of the alley and jerked Luke to the left. Norah and Iggy were right behind them.

A Draco sprinted up around the corner, skidding to a stop in front of them. Its mouth open, saliva dripped from its lips. Sandra pulled Luke to a halt and then thrust him behind her as she brought her own weapon up, aiming for its face.

The Draco dodged and shifted, then sprinted forward. It shoved the weapon out of the way and then slammed a giant palm into Sandra's chest. With a scream, she went flying through the air and slammed into a Hummer nearly twenty feet away. She crumpled to the ground.

Four Draco bolted up behind them. With a shriek, Iggy flung himself at them, his talons ripping into the Draco skin.

The Draco that had attacked Sandra reached for Luke. Norah tossed the M4 aside, realizing the magazine was empty, and pulled her knife from its sheath. With a yell, she tackled the Draco reaching for Luke. It grunted as the two of them hit the ground.

Norah slammed her knife into the creature's neck.

It broke.

Her heart raced as the Draco let out a screech. She took the broken knife blade and plunged it into the creature's mouth and into its throat.

Blood gushed over her hand as she yanked her hand and the knife out before taking the remnants of the knife and stabbing it into the Draco's eye. The creature convulsed and then went still.

Norah got to her feet. "Luke, run!"

Norah whirled around as Iggy let out a scream. A Draco was right behind her. It backhanded her across the face. She flew into the air and slammed into the building. Stars danced in front of her vision for a moment before everything went black.

CHAPTER 60

Maeve's head rang like a bell. She'd flown through the air a good twenty feet before slamming back down to the earth. By some miracle, she'd managed to keep Snap curled in her arms and safe from the impact. But she felt her fear.

A throbbing pain pulsed through Maeve's back, but she knew nothing was broken. Small miracle. She stood up slowly.

Okay? Snap asked.

She rubbed Snap's back. "I'm okay."

She looked around but couldn't spy anyone else from her group. She'd been blown in between two buildings. Keeping Snap's head tucked into her, she started to jog to where she'd last seen everyone, but a twinge in her ankle turned it from a jog into a fast walk.

Movement from the left pulled her attention. Three Draco sprinted into view. Maeve ducked back into the shadows, trying to calm her breathing enough to not give herself away. The Draco threw themselves at the guards who'd been escorting Maeve and the others to the hangar.

Maeve knew she should turn and run, but she couldn't

look away from the spectacle. The Draco's power was incredible. They had no weapons because they needed none. Sharp nails on the end of their hands made quick work of the chests of the guards, even through their vests. One Draco wrenched the head of a guard clean off.

Terror stole over Maeve. *We're never going to be able to defeat these things.*

A new thought, this one, not hers but Snap's flew into her mind. *Go. Go now.*

Snap's fear pushed Maeve into action. She sprinted to the end of the alley, ignoring the twinge in her ankle. A sore ankle would be the least of her worries if the Draco caught up with them.

She reached the end of the alley and peered out. A small contingent of guards had created a small barricade at the end of the lane. From it, they were shooting at the oncoming Draco. Their weapons weren't doing much. But then one lobbed a grenade. Perhaps the Draco didn't realize what it was, because they ran straight for it.

One Draco's leg blew off, and he crashed to the ground. But there was no time to celebrate, as three more sprinted at the guards, overrunning the barricade in a matter of seconds.

Maeve didn't know where to go. There were Draco behind her. There were Draco to her right. If she ran to the left, her movement would undeniably attract them. She had no good options.

Beyond the Draco, she saw more soldiers. She felt a moment of optimism that maybe they would be able to do what the other ones hadn't. But then she noted their uniforms were different.

The soldiers weren't theirs. They were the human-looking Draco. Maeve slipped back down the alley to a side door she had seen. She pulled on it, but it was locked. *Oh, come on.*

She hurried to the other side of the alley. There was no one around. She could see movement at the crossroad. She turned left and hurried down the sidewalk before ducking into the doorway. She tried the door and was rewarded with it giving way. She quickly slipped inside with Snap.

Running wasn't an option, so she was going to try hiding instead.

CHAPTER 61

Someone was pulling at Greg's arm. He felt rough ground underneath his face. He slowly opened his eyes, trying to figure out how he'd ended up lying facedown in grass.

Greg okay?

Alvie's question floated through his mind. Greg turned his head, seeing Alvie frantically pulling at his arm. Beyond Alvie, he could see shadows shifting as the base's soldiers fought the Draco. But there was no contest between the two. The Draco were the far superior fighters, and the government soldiers were going down faster than they could be replenished.

Greg fought the dizziness trying to keep him down to get to his feet. He gripped Alvie's hand and pulled him away from the worst of the fighting. But it wasn't like there was any spot that was particularly safe. It seemed like every direction he turned, there were more Draco.

He sprinted along the path, dodging fighting groups, keeping Alvie right next to him, his hand clasped firmly in his. He kept his eyes peeled for anyone in their group, but that blast had separated all of them. More than a few buildings had collapsed, and he prayed that none of their people were underneath them.

His mind scrambled to figure out a way to get them out of this. The hangar was somewhere to their left, but he couldn't fly. And he didn't think right now was a good time to give it the old college try. But maybe he could grab one of the boats down by the dock. It was a slim chance, but he really didn't have any other ideas.

He aimed toward the water as he ducked between two buildings, one that was just half of its former glory. He reached the pathway and saw two soldiers with their backs to him. Thank God.

He sprinted up to them. "Hey. Where should we—"

The soldiers turned, their mouths opened in the facsimile of a smile. Two rows of teeth smiled back at him.

Backing away, Greg pulled Alvie behind him. The soldier pulled out a black wand. Two prongs sprung from the end of it, lodging into Greg's chest. Pain coursed through him as he dropped to his knees, his whole body feeling like it was on fire before he pitched forward.

CHAPTER 62

Maeve knew they couldn't stay hidden forever. She stayed near the doors, knowing that if one of those blasts hit the building, she would have to sprint out quickly. The building across the street had just come down in an avalanche of metal and debris. Dust covered the street for a moment, blocking her vision.

She gripped Snap to her, her whole body shaking. She didn't know what to do. She didn't know where to take Snap. She had no idea where any of the others were. Terror threatened to overwhelm her.

No, no. Focus. One thing at a time. Get yourself and Snap safe. That's what Chris would tell you to do.

But she didn't know how to do that. It was a war zone outside the door. And she knew it was only a matter of time before they were found. A figure walked through the fog of debris. Dust clung to his body.

Maeve pushed open the door. "Adam!"

Adam's head turned before he ran over to her. "Are you all right?"

"Not hurt. Where's everybody else?" She asked.

"I'm not sure. Let's get you two out of here."

On closer inspection, she noted that Adam's clothes had been ripped and singed, but the skin underneath looked untouched. She had no time to think on it, though, because Adam pulled her out into the street, keeping himself in front of her.

They made their way quietly through the fighting, and Maeve realized they were heading toward the coast.

A scream rang through the air behind them. Maeve whirled around in time to see a soldier flying across the sky before slamming into a building.

When she turned back around, she nearly ran straight into Adam, who'd stopped still. She peeked around him at the group of six Draco that snarled at them from only ten feet away.

"Head to the water. Don't stop for anything or anyone," Adam ordered.

"But—"

"No, Maeve. They want the hybrids. You can't let them have them." Adam launched himself at the group before Maeve could even respond.

CHAPTER 63

Blood dripped into Chris's eyes as he shook his head. He was buried under part of a building. His ribs ached, and his left hand wasn't working quite properly. But he ignored all of that. "Pop? Crackle?"

They had been in his arms when the explosions had hit. Where were they?

Carefully, he shifted the debris above him, making sure that he wasn't pushing it toward either of them. They were nowhere in sight. He pushed the last of the debris off and stood, frantically scanning the area, looking for any sign of them.

A bark had him whirling around. Hope, her coat slick with blood, dug frantically at the debris. Chris scrambled over the remains of the building to her side. He reached her, and she let out a deep growl, showing her teeth.

Chris reared back. "Hope."

Hope launched past him as a Draco hurled itself through the air at Chris.

CHAPTER 64

Maeve had seen Adam fight before, but she'd never seen anything like this. He moved between the Draco like they were standing still. Had it only been two or three, she had no doubt he would be victorious, but six was more than even he could handle. Before long, he was on the ground, the Draco on top of him.

Feeling like a complete coward for not helping him, Maeve gripped Snap as she sprinted away. At the same time, she knew there was nothing she could do, and her responsibility was to keep Snap safe.

They want the hybrids.

Ahead, a group of Draco was making quick work of a group of soldiers. Maeve ducked down an alley in between the hangar and a maintenance shed. She burst out onto the street on the other side and then stopped short.

One of the human Draco stood with a group of five behind him. Snarls sounded from behind her. A quick glance showed that another five Draco had slipped into the alley behind her.

Pain lanced through her chest. She looked down. Two prongs extended from her chest, emitting electricity from some sort of wand the human-looking Draco held. Her blood felt like it was on fire. Her knees felt like water, and she crashed to the ground.

Snap let out a little cry. Unbidden, Maeve's arms uncurled. Snap rolled to the ground.

No! Maeve tried to cry out, but her lips didn't seem to want to work. Her body was no longer under her control as she fell to the ground, spasms racking her body before everything went dark.

CHAPTER 65

Pain lanced through Chris's side as the Draco's nails penetrated his skin. He screamed as he crashed to the ground, the Draco on top of him.

Growling erupted from somewhere near his feet. The Draco lifted its weight to peer down at Hope, who had taken the back of its leg in her mouth. She held on, digging her teeth in. The Draco lifted up his foot to slam it into Hope, but Chris managed to shift his weight and fling the Draco to the side.

"Back, Hope," Chris yelled as he got to his feet.

The Draco rolled quickly to it's feet as well and let out a scream. Through its open mouth, Chris could see two rows of sharp teeth. Chris pulled his sidearm and pulled the trigger over and over and over again. The Draco grunted, but none of the bullets even damaged it skin.

Eyes and mouth, he reminded himself, remembering the conversation with Maeve. He shifted his aim higher and let loose again. But the Draco shifted to the side and barreled straight at him.

Chris waited to the last second as the Draco dropped his shoulders to go for the takedown. Twisting to the side, he grabbed the back of the Draco's head and flung it to the ground. It skidded three feet before coming to a stop with a snarl.

It rolled back to its feet, turning toward Chris incredibly fast. But Chris was ready. As soon as it opened its mouth to scream, Chris pulled the trigger. Three shots hit the back of its mouth. It stuttered, its mouth hanging open, staring in wide-eyed disbelief at Chris before it crashed to the ground.

Chris's heart pounded as he stared at the Draco, making sure that it was down for good. But the shots through its mouth had come out the back of its head. It would not be getting up again.

Hope limped over to him. Chris reached down and pet her. "Good girl."

Two more Draco sprinted between two buildings toward him. Chris straightened. He released the magazine before slamming in a new one and taking aim, knowing that there were undeniably more coming behind these two.

And all the while, in the back of his mind, he worried about his little family. *Be safe, Maeve.*

But that was all the time he had to think, because the Draco were on him, and now it was time to fight.

CHAPTER 66

Explosions and gunfire sounded in the distance. Sandra lay facedown in the street. Her cheek throbbed, as did her back and hands. Even recognizing the danger, it took her a minute to gather her senses. And when she did, she stumbled to her feet. "Luke?"

She leaned heavily to the side and grabbed a jeep turned on its side for support. She scanned the area. A body lay behind her against the building. She made her way over, dropping heavily to her knees. "Norah?" She reached out, grabbing Norah's shoulder.

Norah groaned and rolled to her side. "Ouch."

Sandra examined Norah. She had a ton of scrapes and bruises. Her clothes were ripped and torn in places, but she didn't see any obvious life-threatening injuries. "What hurts?"

Norah sat up slowly. "I think it would be easier to catalog what doesn't. And right now that seems to be my small left toe."

She struggled to stand and Sandra helped her to her feet.

"I need to find Luke," Sandra said as soon as Norah was on her feet.

"Iggy!" Norah yelled. But there was no response.

A Draco appeared at the end of the lane. Sandra tensed, scanning for anything she could use as a weapon, even while knowing how useless it would be to fight this thing.

The Draco stopped, tilted its head as it inspected the two women. Then it turned and ran toward the coast.

More creatures appeared, following the first. They were all heading in the same direction—away from the buildings.

Norah stared after the creature. "I think they're leaving."

Norah and Sandra exchanged a glance before hurrying toward the end of the road. A group of soldiers was following behind the Draco, weapons at the ready but not firing. Norah grabbed one of the men. "What's going on?"

"They're leaving. They're all leaving," the man said looking just as confused by the behavior as she was.

"Did we win?" Sandra asked.

The man shook his head. "No. We were losing. I don't get it."

"They left because they got what they came for."

Norah looked up as a man walked toward them. She recognized him as the Secret Service agent, Mike. "What do you mean they got what they came for? What did they want?"

Mike turned to the group of soldiers. "Make sure they all leave the island and then help look for survivors."

The soldier nodded before following the Draco who were already out of sight, heading toward the coast.

Mike turned to Sandra and Norah. Something in his face caused Sandra to reach out and grab Norah's hand.

He spoke quietly, his gaze shifting between the two women. "The Draco, they didn't come just for destruction. We think that was just a side effect. They were looking for certain individuals. They took them with them."

Sandra swallowed, her mouth suddenly dry. "Who? Who did they take?"

Mike's eyes and voice were full of sympathy. "I'm sorry. Luke was one of the ones they took, and so was Iggy."

CHAPTER 67

One second, Chris was fighting for his life, and the next, the Draco raised its head as if hearing some sort of signal, and it took off. Chris sat up, blood leaking from where the first Draco had impaled him with its nails. More scratches and cuts were across his torso and his upper shoulder.

Dawn was just cresting across the sky, providing enough light to see the Draco disappearing over the hill. What was going on? Why were they leaving?

He got slowly to his feet. To his right, Hope lay panting on her side, blood covering her fur. Chris moved toward her. She gave a lazy wag of her tail but didn't move otherwise.

Chris slipped his arms underneath her and pulled her to his chest, stumbling a little under her weight and wincing as her body came in contact with some of his own cuts. He walked to where he'd first seen her when this had all began and gently set her down.

Then he started to clear the debris from where Hope had been digging. He moved as quickly as he could manage without dislodging the debris and sending more cascading inside. After three minutes, he saw a small foot. His heart nearly jumped out of his chest, and he had to keep from flinging everything to the side and potentially damaging them more. Another few pieces removed, and he saw Pop.

He had large gashes in his chest. His eyes were closed, red marks along his skull. His hand was still buried, and Chris pulled it out, realizing it was clasping Crackle's hand. He quickly removed more of the debris to unveil Crackle. Crackle had a deep cut on his head. And his knee was at an unnatural angle. Both were breathing, but Crackle's breathing was coming out like a wheeze.

"No, no, no, no." Gently, Chris pulled Pop from the rubble, his heart breaking as he unclenched Pop's hand from Crackle's. He laid Pop down next to Hope and then picked up Crackle.

Movement flickered near the corner of his eye. He whirled around, but it was only Norah and Sandra stumbling into view. Chris looked behind them, but there was no one else.

From their faces, he could tell that something horrible had happened to both Iggy and Luke, but it didn't stop him from speaking. "Help me. Please help me."

CHAPTER 68

The small creature felt so light in Sandra's arms. This one was called Crackle. The large gash on his head was still bleeding, soaking the makeshift bandage they had wrapped around it's skull. She was surprised to see the blood was red.

She had expected green.

Its little chest rose and fell, but she could hear the wheezing. If he were pure human, she would've thought he had a collapsed lung. Perhaps their anatomy was the same.

She hadn't spent much time with the triplets, as they were called, but she knew how much Maeve and Chris cared for them. They were their children in every sense of the word. And Luke really liked them as well. He considered them friends.

Pain, this time emotional and therefore more searing, punched her in the chest. Luke. She pictured his terrified face, heard his scream again in her mind.

She hadn't been able to protect him. She hadn't been able to save him. Those things had him now. She shoved the thoughts aside, knowing that once she fully embraced the reality, she was going to completely lose it.

But this little guy in her arms needed her to keep it together until they reached the medical ward. Chris was ahead of her, blood dripping down his side. He ignored it, focused entirely on getting his kids help.

Next to her, Norah held Hope. The poor dog's breaths were stuttered, her coat slick with blood. Sandra didn't know if she would make it. She didn't know if any of them would make it.

A soldier held open the door to the medical unit, which was blessedly still intact. Apparently the attacks by the Draco had been random, with no strategy in mind. Or else they would have taken out the medical unit to make sure that the damage was complete.

Stepping past the soldier and into the building, Sandra's footfalls were lost in the noise of all of the other people crushed into the space. The place was packed. Soldiers and staff lined the hall, all with different injuries. Other less wounded soldiers tended to them, moving from person to person. A scream sounded from down the hall and then was cut off.

Sandra shivered, not sure if it was from what was in front of her or a ghost of times past. The whole situation reminded her of Afghanistan.

It was not a good reminder.

Chris ignored all of it. He wasn't waiting in line to help his kids. He stepped into the door of the room with it's light spilling into the hallway. Sandra stepped through a few seconds later, unsurprised to see it was the main medical unit.

Jasper looked up from where he was helping a soldier onto a bed. His face paled as he took in the hybrids in Chris's and Sandra's arms. He grabbed the doctor at the next bunk, who was leaning over an unconscious patient, and dragged him over to the door.

The woman glared at him. "Jasper, I have patients who need—"

He cut the doctor off. "These two come first."

The doctor turned and finally got a look at who Jasper was referring to. She went still, and then she was barking out orders. In a flash, stretchers rolled toward them. Chris gently placed Pop on one as Sandra carefully placed Crackle on the other.

They looked so small in the middle of those large stretchers, so fragile. They were wheeled to the end of the ward. Three people surrounded each stretcher, working quickly to attach lines, assess, and peel back makeshift bandages to determine the damage.

Unsure what to do, unsure where to go, Sandra stood still.

"Help me." Norah walked past Sandra, bumping her shoulder to get her moving.

Norah found an empty bed and placed Hope upon it. A soldier walked up, shaking his head. "You can't put her there. She needs to—"

Norah snarled at the soldier. The man backed up, his hands raised. "Okay, okay."

Norah grabbed a stack of bandages that were next to the bed. She handed them to Sandra. "Place these on her wounds."

Grabbing them quickly, Sandra placed them on the dog's chest. They were quickly soaked with blood, and she replaced them. Norah rifled through the tray next to the bed and then underneath it, coming back with a scalpel and a tube.

Sandra watched in fascination as Norah made a small incision along Hope's chest. Then she reached in with her finger, feeling around. Nodding her head, she inserted the tube before packing the incision with more gauze.

The dog's breathing seemed to become more even. "How did you know how to do that?" Sandra asked.

"I saw a lot in Afghanistan. The canine units were incredible. When one of them was injured, it was all hands on deck." Norah stepped back and wiped her hands on the bottom of her shirt, not caring about the blood. "Let's see if we can help anywhere else."

Sandra nodded her agreement. She needed to do something. If she was left alone with her thoughts right now, she was going to break down. It was too much in too short a time period.

The medical ward went silent. Sandra stared at Norah, who was looking toward the entrance, her mouth hanging open. Sandra turned around slowly.

Adam stood at the entryway, Tilda in his arms, covered in blood.

CHAPTER 69

Chris felt completely helpless. A team of doctors and nurses worked on Crackle and Pop furiously. But from the way they were talking and gesturing, he could tell that things were not going well.

Someone had come along and placed a pressure bandage on his own wound. He barely felt it, his focus completely on the two little ones struggling for life in front of him.

Tilda lay in the bed across from Pop and Crackle. Another team worked just as ferociously on her. Adam stood silently off to the side, not moving. No one asked him to get out of the way. No one dared. The look on his face made it very clear that he wasn't going anywhere.

Chris wiped his forehead and then looked down at his hand, which was covered in blood. He wasn't sure whose it was. It could've been his for all he knew.

Jasper walked over and handed him a towel. "Thought you might want to clean yourself up a little bit."

Taking the offering with a nod of thanks, Chris wiped his hands and then his face. "I need to get back out there. I need to find Maeve and Alvie. I haven't seen them since we got split up."

Jasper glanced over at where Pop and Crackle were before nodding to a chair behind Chris. "Maybe you should take a seat."

Cold took root in Chris's chest. "Tell me."

Jasper flicked another glance at the chair, looking like he was going to insist before he focused back on Chris. "You won't find them. They're not on the island anymore. We had reports that the Draco took some of our people. Maeve and Alvie were two of the ones that were sighted being carried away."

"Who else? Who else did they take?" Chris asked feeling lightheaded and wishing he'd taken that seat. Instead he locked his knees.

"If that's Pop and Crackle, then they also have Snap as well as Iggy, Greg, and Luke."

Chris's gaze flew to Sandra, who was holding pressure on a woman's wound at the end of the ward while Norah administered a shot to the soldier's arm. "Oh my God." He took a breath, shoving the fear and terror down. "Do you know where they've gone? Do you have eyes on them?"

"We had satellites tracking them. But then we lost them. They were heading across the Atlantic. That's all we know," Jasper explained.

Anger kindled under Chris's skin. "That's all you know? I thought this was supposed to be the most technologically advanced base in the world? How the hell can that be all you know?"

"We *are* the most technologically advanced base," Jasper said both his gaze and tone turning hard. "But the Draco caught us with our pants down. They knocked out our communications. They left people behind who took out the satellite link. They sacrificed themselves to destroy it. As far as we know, your people are all still alive. They took them for a reason. The same can't be said for all of our people."

Chris winced as he took in the carnage around him. Jasper was right. This wasn't his fault, but Chris was so damn angry right now he wanted someone to yell at.

And that's when the perfect target arrived: Agaren stepped into the room.

CHAPTER 70

A loud droning noise sounded in Maeve's ear. The ground beneath her vibrated as well. Visions of the attack on the base swam through her mind. Her eyes flew open, pain lancing through her head with the action.

A metal ceiling was above her. Small windows lined the room she was in.

Her thoughts were muddy, and it took her a moment to recognize where she was. *A plane. I'm on a plane.* For a moment, her hopes rose. Adam had gotten them out.

But then her gaze fell on the others in the cargo hold with her. Alvie and Snap were sprawled out next to Greg, Iggy, and Luke. They had not been placed in seats. Their comfort had not been seen to. They were left on the ground in a heap.

She tried not to give away any movement to let anyone know she was awake as she scanned the rest of the plane. Six reptilian Draco were seated along the walls of the fuselage. Another three human-looking Draco sat toward the front as well.

Snap let out a small whimper. Maeve's eyes flew to her as Snap moved. One of the human-looking Draco's heads snapped up as well. He unbuckled himself and strode toward her, the wand with the metal prongs in his hand.

"No." Maeve scampered over to Snap, covering her. "No, leave her alone."

The Draco smiled, a smile filled with malice as he raised the wand. The prongs plunged into Maeve's side. Pain once again lanced through her, and her blood once again boiled. Her body gave up control, the synapses feeling like they were firing all at the same time before the darkness took her again.

CHAPTER 71

The medical suite was full of people, but Chris didn't see any of them. He moved in a straight line, heading right for Agaren. Agaren stood waiting for him as if he knew why he was the target of Chris's rage.

Chris stopped right in front of him. "Where the hell have you been?"

"I was speaking with the Council. I returned as soon as I heard about the attack," Agaren said.

Trying to keep a leash on his anger, Chris rolled his hands into fists. "And what exactly has this Council been doing while people here have been dying? You guys let the Draco stay on this planet, and now people are paying the price for that decision. Maeve, Alvie, Snap, Greg, Luke, and Iggy are all paying the price right now."

Agaren tilted his head. "They are dead?"

Chris nearly spit out the word. "No. The Draco *took* them."

The large gray met his gaze for a long moment, and Chris had the feeling that he was rifling through his memories to see what Chris had seen during the attack. Agaren's gaze snapped to where Crackle and Pop lay at the end of the ward. "How bad are their injuries?"

"Bad." Chris didn't trust himself to say any more than that.

"They cannot die." Agaren said.

"Well, I don't get to decide that," Chris spit out the words. "And neither do you. But the Draco did their best to make sure that they do. Tilda is in the other bed. She's not doing well, either."

Agaren's gaze strayed to where Adam stood against the wall, his focus completely on Tilda as the medical staff worked on her.

Agaren closed his eyes. Chris opened his mouth to ask what he was doing and then stopped. He could almost feel the energy coming off Agaren. He wasn't closing his eyes to the disaster in front of him. He was doing something else, and Chris had the distinct impression that he needed to allow him to do it.

So he waited. Agaren kept his eyes closed for a full three minutes. When he opened them, he looked more tired than when he'd begun. "I have been given permission to bring the hybrids with me."

"With you? What do you mean *with* you?" Chris demanded.

"I will take them to the Council. Our technology far exceeds yours. We will be able to save them," Agaren said.

Chris stared at him. "You want to take Pop and Crackle with you?"

Agaren nodded. "I give you my word that I will save their lives."

Pausing, Chris frowned. Something about Agaren's choice of words bothered him. "And then what? Will you bring them back? Or will you keep them?"

Agaren hesitated, and that told Chris everything he needed to know.

"That decision isn't up to you, is it? That will be up to the Council," Chris said softly.

Agaren nodded. "The Council knows that keeping the hybrids alive is critical. But if they deem that it is safer for the hybrids to stay with them, they could rule that is what must be done."

"Is there any way you could bring the technology needed to save them down here?" Chris asked.

Agaren shook his head. "Not in time. I am reading their vitals, and they do not have much time left."

Fear and hope colliding in him, Chris stared at Agaren and then at Pop and Crackle, who looked so tiny in the beds at the end of the ward. If he let them go, there was a chance he would never see them again. There was a chance that the Council would keep them. But if he didn't let them go, there was a very good chance that they would die. He didn't think he could live with either outcome.

But he needed them to live. "Take them."

Agaren disappeared as soon as the decision was made, after telling Chris to take the hybrids outside. Chris wasn't sure why. Was he going to beam them up? Land a ship? No one had mentioned how Agaren traveled. But Chris didn't waste any time. He hustled to the back of the ward and explained the plan to the doctor as quickly as possible. The doctor stared at him like he was crazy. But Chris didn't have time to explain more than what he already had.

Jasper commandeered Pop's stretcher. "Okay, people, we're taking this trauma on the road. Let's move."

The medical staff jumped into action, hurrying along Pop's stretcher, securing lines and tightening bandages. Chris followed behind, pushing Crackle's stretcher, Crackle's medical team going through the same process.

The doctor hurried beside Chris. "I can't guarantee that they will survive the trip. They are in a very fragile state. I'm not sure—"

"Can you guarantee that you can save them if I keep them here?" Chris demanded

The doctor opened her mouth, then shut it, shaking her head.

Chris didn't stop moving. "Then get them as stable as you can."

Soldiers made a hole in the hall so that they could hurry past all of the other injured. More soldiers held open the doors.

Pushing through the door, Jasper paused for a moment before tucking in his shoulders and heading outside. Chris stepped through the doors, pushing Crackle, and he saw what had made Jasper hesitate.

A cigar-shaped ship twenty feet long illuminated from inside by a bright white light with red and blue lights along the bottom hovered just outside the building.

Chris pulled up his stretcher next to Jasper. Jasper kept his gaze on the saucer. "I've never seen one of those before," the agent said, a slight tremor in his voice.

Chris didn't say anything because he heard a voice in his head. *Bring the stretchers underneath the ship and then step away.*

"Come on." He pushed Crackle under the ship, pausing when he was in the center of it. Jasper did the same with Pop. All the medical professionals backed away until they were out from under the ship. Jasper paused next to the head of Pop's stretcher.

Leaning down, Chris placed his forehead against Crackle's. "You heal. And then you come back to us." He kissed Crackle's forehead, wiping away the tear that cascaded down his cheek. "I love you."

He turned to Pop and said the same thing. Then he placed a hand on each of them. "You are loved. Never forget that."

He backed away from the stretchers with Jasper at his side. Chris wiped the tears from his eyes as a light engulfed both stretchers. It was blinding, and he had to look away. By the time he looked back, all that remained were the stretchers. Pop and Crackle were gone.

The ship shot straight up, moving faster than Chris could track. But he still stared up at the sky, praying that Agaren could save their lives.

And praying that Agaren could bring them back.

CHAPTER 72

Standing outside, Chris stared up into the sky while everyone else went back to their duties. He felt empty. His whole family was now out of his reach. Pop and Crackle were somewhere in space above them. Alvie and Maeve were God knew where with those horrible creatures. All that was left was poor Hope.

Jasper clapped him on the shoulder. "You made the right choice. Now let's go help out where we can, and I'll see what we know and get you a report as soon as I have one."

Chris nodded, knowing that his help was needed. Everyone's help was needed. But he couldn't go back into the medical ward. He couldn't face that right now. So he joined a group that was searching from building to building, looking for people who were trapped under the debris.

For hours, he helped scour the base. They found twelve people, who they rushed to the medical ward. And they found another twenty-two who didn't need to be rushed anywhere. It was difficult, back breaking, and emotionally draining work.

And Chris appreciated it. It didn't let him dwell on things

he couldn't control. It gave him a focus, and right now he needed that more than anything.

But finally everyone was accounted for. They had lost fifty-seven people. Another hundred and twelve had been injured. Helos had been arriving, taking the injured over to the mainland. Now, the less injured would be taken over. Hope had been flown to a vet hospital. She would be all right after some rest. Only a skeleton crew would be left at the base, to wipe out the systems and secure it as best they could.

Chris crashed into a seat on the Airbus. Norah and Sandra sat in the two seats next to him. Both of their eyes were rimmed red. Chris didn't ask how they were doing. They were doing as well as he was, which wasn't good at all.

Jasper walked down the aisle behind Pearl, who was checking people's names off on a manifest. Pearl checked off Chris, Norah, and Sandra before moving on without a word. But Jasper stopped and knelt down. "We caught sight of the Draco's transport as it approached North America. We know it didn't exit on the other side. We believe it's landed somewhere in North America."

"North America is kind of big. Do you have anything more specific?" Norah asked.

Jasper shook his head. "I'm afraid not. Right now that's all the information we have. But our people are still looking. I'm sure we'll have something soon."

Standing up, Jasper continued down the aisle. Tears silently ran down Sandra's cheeks. She dropped her face into her hands. Chris met Norah's gaze, who just shook her head, despair covering her features.

"Somewhere over North America" was as good as saying they had no idea. Chris turned his head toward the window, bringing his fist to his mouth.

I've lost them all.

CHAPTER 73

The flight to RAF Bentwaters didn't take long. Norah felt like they'd just gotten in the air when the announcement came over the PA to prepare for landing. She didn't really remember anything in between. She tightened her seatbelt, noting Sandra sitting next to her and staring straight ahead. A quick glance told her that Sandra's seatbelt was in place, so Norah didn't disturb her.

On her other side, Chris was staring out the window as if he could somehow find Pop and Crackle out there. They were a row of loss—living in a world where the most important people to them were out of their reach.

Tilda had spoken about how Maldeks bonded with their person. But what they didn't seem to understand was how strong that bond was from the person to their Maldek. He was a part of her. She would lay her life on the line for him in a split second, just as he would do for her. Just as he *had* done for her.

After the plane touched down, they were all taken over to the NATO base. It was a quiet group that was on Norah's bus. Most were sporting bandages and bruises of some kind. And all had a haunted look in their eyes. Some because of loss but also because of what they had seen.

The Draco were right out of a nightmare. They were a Hollywood horror movie run amok. In the movie, there would be some plucky hero who figured out the creatures' vulnerability. It would be something simple that had been overlooked, like water or sand.

Greg and Maeve had studied the human-looking Draco, the one who should be easier to kill. But their skin didn't get hurt by bullets, not the way human skin did. And Greg and Maeve had only come up with two slim possibilities: eyes and the back of their throat.

All in all, they were completely terrifying. A stronger, faster, invulnerable opponent. And Norah knew this was only the first salvo. The Draco had taken their people alive. There was a reason for that. And Norah was clinging to the hope that they would keep them alive for a while.

And their ultimate goal was to take over the world. They wanted to set the world on a collision course between Draco and humans. A collision course that would remove the Council's protection of humanity and leave the Earth under Draco control.

And if that happened, Norah had no doubt that humanity would lose. The Council allegedly would replace *Homo sapiens* with new creations like Alvie and the triplets. But who knew how long that would take? And the Draco could make hell on Earth a reality in that time.

As they stepped off the bus, they were each assigned a different bunk. The bunks were temporary until they got everyone situated and figured out whatever the next steps were. Although Norah wasn't sure exactly who was currently making those decisions.

Norah had seen Tilda. She was still alive, but she wasn't sure how Tilda was going to bounce back from her injuries.

Tilda was a force of nature who defied her age. But Norah also knew that when bodies experienced trauma, no matter how resilient the personality, the body still responded according to their age.

Which meant someone else was in charge now. Pearl didn't seem to have the vision. She struck Norah as a bureaucrat, not a leader. Jasper seemed to fly by the seat of his pants. She wasn't sure how helpful that would be for running an organization the size of R.I.S.E. And Adam? Adam didn't talk enough or interact enough to possibly be in charge.

Norah stepped into the barracks that she'd been assigned. She had a bottom bunk by the door. Sandra had been assigned the bunk next to hers. Norah sat down for a minute, realizing she had nothing to put away. She had no clothes, no personal effects. She had nothing.

Norah looked around the bunk. There were a dozen or so people milling about, all looking equally lost. And suddenly Norah could not be inside. She needed fresh air. She needed *out*.

She strode from the room and stepped outside. The RAF was a working base. Two jeeps filled with individuals in camo drove past. In the distance, she could see a plane landing while another one taxied down a separate runway.

She turned away from the buildings and headed for the open field. She just needed a minute. She had been with people every single second since everything had happened. She hadn't been able to take a single minute to process losing Iggy. And right now she felt that loss creeping over her.

She started at a walk and then moved up to a fast jog, and before she knew it, she was sprinting across the field. Her time with Iggy flew through her mind. They might have only had a short acquaintance, but it had been filled with moments.

Reaching a tree at the edge of the camp's perimeter, she slunk down to its base. Her shoulders heaved as she sobbed, her breath coming out in pants. *I'm sorry, Iggy. I should have protected you better.*

Across the field, the sun was beginning to sink toward the horizon. She watched the sky shift in color. Footsteps caused her to turn her head. She was unsurprised to see Sandra. Silently, Sandra sat next to her, her shoulder brushing against Norah's. Sandra slipped her hand into Norah's, and together they watched the sunset as tears ran down their faces.

CHAPTER 74

Chris didn't know what to do. He'd lost about half the skin on the upper half of his left arm. He had more bruises and scrapes than he could count, but no broken bones or penetrating injuries, which was just dumb luck as far as he was concerned.

He'd been checked over by a doctor and told to rest. They'd given him a hospital room down the hall. But how the hell was he supposed to rest? Part of his family was out there somewhere. Those things had them. There was no chance he was going to rest.

There was also no chance that anyone was going to let him in on the plans for going after them. Chris had walked the hospital floors, searching for something. He didn't know what to do with himself. He turned the corner, flinching as his hip knocked into a food trolley left in the hall. He swallowed down a curse, his eyes straining to the window of the door in front of him. Adam sat next to a hospital bed. Chris quietly opened the door.

A giant white bandage covered the top half of Tilda's skull. For once, she actually looked old. It was as if with one fell swoop, the Draco had aged her. Her pale skin blended into the white bandages and sheets below her.

Adam looked up from the chair next to the bed, his sunglasses still in place. Chris walked over to the edge of the bed. He nodded down toward Tilda, keeping his voice low. "How's she doing?"

Adam cleared his throat. "The doctor says she should recover. But it would be better if she regained consciousness soon."

Chris studied the unusual man. The veins of Adam's arms stood out as his hands gripped the side of the chair. He looked like he was on the edge of throwing himself from the chair and doing some damage. Chris had the feeling the damage wasn't aimed at him or Tilda. And for just a moment, he felt sorry for whoever it was aimed at.

"Do you mind if I ..." Chris gestured to a chair next to Adam. "I'm going a little crazy. No one will tell me anything about Maeve, Greg, the kids, and I just don't want to ..." He shrugged, not wanting to finish the statement.

Adam nodded to the chair next to him. Without a word, Chris took a seat. He and Adam sat there, neither speaking, just listening to the machines next to Tilda. Chris dozed off eventually. The door opening behind him jarred him awake. He glanced up as Pearl stepped into the room.

Pearl frowned as she caught sight of Chris. "Captain Garrigan, you should be in your room. I can have a soldier escort you—"

"He stays." Adam's voice held no room for argument.

For a second, Chris wondered if Pearl would argue. After all, Pearl was second-in-command of R.I.S.E. And with Tilda out of commission, Pearl was in charge. Pearl stared at Adam for a long moment before nodding. "Fine. I was coming to check on Tilda. Has there been any change?"

Shaking his head, Adam angled himself slightly toward the

bed, then he jolted. Chris looked at the bed as well, surprised to see Tilda's eyes open, looking at Adam.

Adam jumped out of his chair. He took Tilda's hand and held it carefully. An unspoken conversation occurred between the two of them as they stared into each other's eyes. Chris felt uncomfortable being in the room. Even without words, it was incredibly intimate.

Finally, Tilda turned to Chris, giving him a nod before giving Pearl her attention. Her voice was raspy and weak, but the command was still there. "Sit rep."

With a quick flash of relief on her face, Pearl stepped forward. "The island's defenses were completely destroyed. Damage was sustained by eighty percent of the buildings on Hy-Brasil, including transportation and development."

Pearl paused, staring at Tilda before Tilda nodded. "Understood. Continue."

Pearl's gaze returned to her tablet. "Approximately sixty percent of R.I.S.E. was injured in some way, shape, or form during the attack. Fifty-seven individuals were killed, an additional ten are still in critical condition. The rest of the injured are expected to make a full recovery."

Tilda closed her eyes for a moment and took a deep breath. "What about our guests?"

Pausing, Pearl shot a look at Chris before she spoke. "Doctors Maeve Leander and Greg Schorn were taken hostage. Along with Alvie, one of the triplets, the Maldek, and Luke Gillibrand."

Tilda's eyes shot open, and she looked at Chris, then her gaze returned to Pearl. "Government response?"

"The government is aware of the incident. The media has been blacked out. There is no reporting of it on any major or minor television station," Pearl said.

Frowning, Chris tried to figure out how that was possible.

Someone must've heard the explosions or noticed the choppers that had been sent in to carry out the wounded.

But then again, these people had been keeping Hy-Brasil secret for decades. He supposed they had their methods in place.

Pearl rattled off a bunch of other information about the attack.

Chris listened to half of it, not really understanding the words that were being used. He'd been around the military long enough to know it probably was code. He let their words drone over him as he pictured Maeve when he'd first started at Wright-Patterson. He'd thought she was beautiful and completely untouchable. Smart, sexy, and kind. Then when he'd seen her with Alvie, he been absolutely amazed. But that had been nothing compared to what he'd seen since the attack at Area 51.

And now she was in danger again. And he was in no position to help her. He cut into Pearl's running dialogue. "What are the plans to get Maeve and the others back? Do you have a location?"

Pearl glanced at Tilda, who nodded. "We believe that they are somewhere on the West Coast of the U.S. We are still waiting on confirmation."

"Initiate MAURC," Tilda ordered.

Pearl's hands stilled over the tablet, her gaze shooting to Tilda's face. She paled noticeably before she nodded. "Initiating MAURC."

Tilda turned to Adam. "Take the captain to the first floor and have him suited up. I'm sure he will want to be involved in the next step of the process."

Sensing something that wasn't being said, Chris looked between the two of them. "Who's Mark?"

Tilda closed her eyes wearily. "Adam will explain."

Standing, Adam kissed Tilda's cheek, before he headed

from the room. Chris followed. Once in the hall, he stopped Adam. "Who's Mark?"

Adam paused, looking up and down the hall before turning to Chris. "Not who, but what. MAURC stands for Military Arsenal Under R.I.S.E. Control. It's the failsafe for when the Draco finally make their move. Once initiated, the entire arsenal of the United States military is under Tilda's control." Adam headed down the hall.

Chris was rooted to the spot before he shook himself into motion. He hurried after Adam, not sure if he should be grateful that they had reached that stage or terrified.

CHAPTER 75

Hurry up and wait. After years of being in the military, Chris thought he was used to it. He'd spent countless hours just waiting after orders had been issued. The military, like any bureaucracy, moved slow, painfully slow at times. But right now, with Maeve and everyone else in danger, the wait was downright unbearable.

After Adam and Chris left Tilda's room, Adam had escorted Chris to the first floor. He'd been outfitted with new clothes as well as a sidearm. Then he'd been taken to the barracks. Adam had disappeared then. But Sandra and Norah had been there. Sandra's eyes had been rimmed in red. Chris knew exactly how she felt. She was a mirror to his own feelings. But they hadn't stayed in the barracks long. Less than an hour later, they had been escorted to a truck and taken to an airfield. They had been loaded onto an Atlas.

This plane was smaller than the Airbus. Only a few dozen people were on it, including Tilda. Her hospital bed had been wheeled into the back room. Adam and Jasper disappeared into it with her.

Barely a minute after they had their seatbelts on, they

were taxiing down the runway. Pearl appeared from the cockpit after they'd leveled off to explain that they were heading back to the States and that everyone on board would remain under the protection of R.I.S.E. until the situation normalized.

Pearl did not explain what exactly would normalize this particular situation.

When they arrived in the States, they were taken to Maxwell Air Force Base in Alabama. It was a training ground for entry-level airmen and housed Air University, a key part of Air Education and Training Command and the Air Force's center for professional military education. It had over 12,000 active duty, civilian, and contracted personnel and covered over 4,100 acres.

Not that they had been given the tour. Chris knew about the base because he'd been stationed here for two months during officer candidate school.

No, instead of a tour, Chris, Sandra, and Norah had been taken to yet another set of barracks. When they'd stepped out of the truck, there hadn't been a soul around. That had been three hours ago. Now Chris paced up and down the barracks room, not sure what to do with himself. Sandra had collapsed into one of the bunks at the end. She wasn't sleeping, just staring off into space.

Norah sat on the floor near Sandra, her back up against the wall. Her eyes shifted from person to person, window to window. Chris wasn't sure what was going through her mind, but none of them felt like talking.

Chris's arm itched as the skin began to regrow and dry out. A medic had replaced the bandage on the plane. Chris stretched his arms, feeling the skin stretch. God, he hated this. He was doing nothing.

The door to the back of the barracks opened. Adam strode in, nodding at Norah and Sandra before heading toward Chris.

Norah got up from her seated position and followed Adam toward him. Sandra didn't even move.

Adam stopped right in front of Chris. "You need to come with me."

Chris put his arms over his chest. "Why?"

"I don't have time to explain. If you want answers, you need to move quickly," Adam said.

Chris exchanged a look with Norah, who nodded back at him. "Go. Find out what's going on."

Chris studied the man in front of him. Adam was strange, but there was something about him that Chris trusted. "Okay, let's go."

Adam took off at a quick pace, and Chris had to hurry to keep up with him. They climbed into a jeep already running, and Adam quickly drove through the base. Chris frowned, not recognizing the section of the base they were entering.

Adam pulled the jeep into a small overhang next to an old hangar. Chris put a hand on the door handle, but Adam stopped him. "Wait."

Climbing out of the car, Adam scanned the area before nodding back at Chris. "Okay. With me."

He led Chris farther into the hangar and to a door in the back. Chris was surprised when the door led to a staircase heading down. He hustled after Adam in the dark, amazed at how quickly the man could move. Chris kept a strong grip on the railing so he didn't topple forward. They reached the bottom level, three levels below the surface. Adam pulled open an old metal door, revealing a dim hallway. The hallway stretched left and right. Without hesitation, Adam headed left.

Following behind him, Chris broke into a jog to keep up. They made four more turns until Chris had absolutely no idea where on the base they would pop up. He'd heard rumors about the tunnels underneath the base, but he'd never actually been in them. Finally, Adam reached another metal door similar to the dozen or so they had already passed. There was no marking on this one to distinguish it from any of the rest. Adam pulled it open and hurried inside, jogging up a flight of stairs.

Once again, Chris followed. He cursed silently on the second flight of stairs when he missed a step and banged his knee on the landing.

Instead of going to the surface, Adam stopped one level below it. He opened a door and all but sprinted down the hallway. Chris followed him as Adam ducked into a room. It was a large room with a giant conference table in the middle that could easily seat twenty. Adam hustled to the back of the room and tapped on part of the wall. A small opening appeared. Gripping the panel with both hands, he slid it farther open, revealing a small hidey-hole hidden in the wall. "You need to get in and stay silent."

"Why?" Chris asked, eyeing the dark space with more than a little skepticism.

"If you want to know what's going to happen, you need to get in there," Adam said.

The low murmur of voices reached them from the open doorway. Chris shot a glance at Adam, who nodded back at him. Chris dove into the space. Adam shut it, blocking out all light.

It was a tight fit. Chris could stand straight, but he only had about four inches on each side of him. *Thank God I'm not claustrophobic.*

There was a small vent near his head that he hadn't noticed from the outside. It allowed him to both see and hear what was happening in the room. Apparently it had been covered over with mesh to hide it.

He had no idea how Adam even knew it was here. From Chris's vantage point, he could see the room well. Adam took position by the door at the front of the room. He stood with his legs shoulder width apart, his arms by his side. As Pearl stepped into the room, she looked up at him. Adam nodded back coolly.

Pearl turned to the people behind her. "Please take your seats. As soon as everyone has arrived, we will begin."

Chris watched as people slowly filtered into the room. He didn't recognize all of them, but he did recognize the uniforms. There were representatives from the Air Force, Navy, Army, Marine Corps, and Coast Guard. He also recognized the second in charge of the FBI. The rest of the suits he wasn't familiar with, but he guessed they probably filled up the rest of the Who's Who of the United States government's hierarchy.

Tilda stepped into the room. Chris was surprised she was upright. She moved with only a slight limp. Tilda walked to the end of the table, using a cane. He'd thought she'd be laid up a lot longer than that. But the bandage on her head had been replaced with a much smaller one.

And there was a lot more color in her cheeks than there had been the last time he'd seen her, although he had a sneaking suspicion that was due to makeup rather than good health.

She took the seat at the end of the table, her back to Chris. A tall, extremely thin man with glasses held out a chair for her. Tilda nodded at him as she took her seat. "Director Harrison."

And that would make him the head of the DNI.

Adam moved so that he was positioned to the right and behind her. Pearl took position behind her on her left.

The Navy representative leaned forward. "I'd like someone to explain to me what exactly is going on. This MAURC order came out of nowhere. We didn't even know it existed until it was issued. And I have a great deal of reticence at simply handing over military control to a body I've never even heard of."

"I'm sure you do. But as I'm sure you're also aware, the order was ratified by President Eisenhower and then President

Kennedy. And it has been in existence since then. We don't get to choose the orders we follow, Admiral. We simply follow them," Tilda said.

"If you could perhaps explain the history of this order, I think it would be easier for the rest of us to understand exactly what is happening here," the representative from the Marine Corps said, her voice measured.

"As soon as everyone is here, I will do exactly that," Tilda replied.

Director Harrison looked around the table with a frown. "Who exactly are we waiting for?"

"Me." Martin Drummond strode into the room.

CHAPTER 76

EDMONDS, WASHINGTON

The wind blew hard outside the Maybach window. The Puget Sound was choppy with white wave crests dotting the surface. Tatiana glanced at her watch, her annoyance growing. They were late. Granted, by only five minutes, but late was late.

Bad enough she had to come to this metropolitan wasteland. She hated Washington State. It was always raining, always gray. She was fifteen miles north of Seattle, but it might as well be a different world.

The warehousing district she found herself in was a blight on the landscape. Concrete and cement as far as the eye could see, and most of it in need of repair. It wasn't an abandoned area, but that did not help the look of desolation surrounding it.

Tatiana owned five of the warehouses. She kept them staffed with security, but they held no goods. The remaining thirteen warehouses in the area were all owned by other businesses, and a large part of the job of her security was keeping an eye on them and making sure they didn't stray anywhere near *her* business.

A Hummer appeared from between two of the warehouses, turning toward her, followed by a large boxy white truck and then a second Hummer. "Finally," she grumbled as she grasped the car handle and stepped out.

A gust of wind slapped up against her, pushing her blonde hair into her face. With an impatient gesture, she shoved it behind her ear. She grimaced as the smell of freshly caught fish reached her nose. She hated being down here. But she needed to be here when her guests arrived.

The Hummer pulled farther ahead, but the white truck came to a halt in front of her. Dietrich climbed down from the driver's seat. The man in the passenger's seat made his way to the back of the truck.

Tatiana strode up to Dietrich. "You're late."

"It could not be avoided. There was heavy wind. I had to force the pilot to land."

Annoyed, Tatiana waved away his words. "I don't want excuses. Where are they?"

Dietrich led the way to the back of the truck. Tatiana followed him, her anticipation growing. For decades, they had searched for the Council's betrayal. When they had first settled this planet, they had agreed that the humans would be modified to contain a mixture of all of their DNA. The Council believed it would keep them safe.

Tatiana smiled. *But we found a way around that.* The small amount of Draco DNA within the human genome was incredibly powerful. It had allowed them to find allies over the years, people interested in furthering their own narcissistic goals, even to the detriment of the community they allegedly served, allowing them to establish a foothold in many lucrative areas, ranging from government to the financial world to the entertainment industry.

So lucrative, in fact, that it had laid the groundwork for the Draco to finally return to their former glory. Attacking the R.I.S.E. base was just the beginning. Now it was time for the next step in their plan.

Dietrich raised the back door of the truck. Inside, the humans were bound and tied together, their eyes closed. Tatiana could see the rise and fall of their chests. These were the two scientists who had helped create the abominations. But they had gone beyond merely replicating the Council's betrayal. Her gaze strayed over the man and the woman. They were both incredibly intelligent. They could prove useful. Her gaze lingered on the male. *And if not, he could prove useful in other ways.*

Tatiana had learned of the first abomination when she was young. It had been destroyed nearly a thousand years ago.

As it should have been.

But then they heard rumblings about a new creation or copy of the original. The humans just couldn't leave well enough alone. At first she planned on killing them. And she still would, at least the older one. After, of course, a complete and thorough physical examination.

The fact that there was a female one opened up all sorts of possibilities. Tatiana wanted to give herself some time to decide exactly what to do with both. After all, she'd already waited hundreds of years for this moment. She could give it another few days while she contemplated the best way to make use of these two specimens.

Dietrich climbed into the back of the truck and then reached back, extending a hand to Tatiana. She grasped it and allowed him to help her into the truck bed.

He nodded to a trunk with air holes cut in it. "There was an additional species with them. We think it is a Maldek. Would you like to see it?"

Tatiana shook her head. It couldn't be a Maldek. They

hadn't been seen since Mars. It was probably one of the abominations the humans had cooked up in their labs. "No. I'm interested in the *other* abominations."

She ignored the humans and the trunk. She made her way to the three protective chambers that held the important subjects.

She stopped at the first one. It looked like a human boy. But it was so much more than that. She ran a hand over the top of the glass with a smile. *And what will you teach us, my young friend?*

Then she moved on to the next two containers. She stood between them, glancing through the glass tops on each of them in turn. On her left was a smaller one with longer hair. It was the young female. To her right was the larger one. From her report, she knew he'd been alive for close to thirty years, yet he was so small. She curled her lip in disgust. Not a drop of Draco DNA to be found within the two creatures.

But they would be useful, especially the female. It would be interesting to see what breeding her would create.

She turned her attention to the larger male. *But you, my friend, will be our greatest prize. You will keep the Council at bay. And you will keep me entertained.*

CHAPTER 77

MAXWELL AIR FORCE BASE, ALABAMA

Chris had disappeared with Adam a few minutes ago. Norah wanted to go with them, but that wasn't in the cards. She was beginning to understand Adam, and she knew whatever he was up to was not something that was out in the open. More people would only increase the likelihood of them getting caught. And she had a feeling this was the only way they were going to get any information.

But she still wanted to *do* something. She felt completely helpless here.

It felt like a hole had opened up in her chest at the idea of Iggy being in trouble. At the idea of him being held by those creatures.

She paced up and down the barracks floor, racking her mind for some angle she could play. She considered and discarded a hundred different ideas, from storming into Tilda's office and demanding answers to hijacking a plane and taking off to find Iggy. The problem with every single idea she came up with was she knew they were doomed to failure. She needed intel. She needed a specific location. Randomly searching would get her nowhere. The Draco could be anywhere.

She stopped. Penny. Penny would have information. She just needed to find out where Penny had been taken.

Sandra stepped out of the latrine at the end of the hall, pulling Norah from her thoughts. Sandra's face was pale, her eyes unfocused.

Norah stopped a few feet away from her. "Hey, how are you doing?"

Sandra sank onto the nearest bunk. "I don't know. I just ... it's hard to wrap my head around everything that's happened."

Norah took a seat on the bunk across from her. "I can understand that. It feels like we've been dropped into this alternate universe, where aliens are real and there are secret government projects."

Sandra gave her a small smile. "Except that's the actual reality."

"Yeah."

They both fell into silence. Norah was replaying meeting Iggy, seeing his little face under that bridge that day and choosing not to raise the alarm. How different her life would be if she had followed the rules and done what she was supposed to do. Iggy in all likelihood would be dead right now, probably by her hand. And she would be the worse for it.

Sandra let out a shaky breath. "I found out I was pregnant with Luke two weeks after I learned Noah was gone. I was so scared. I didn't know how I was going to be able to do any of this on my own. But then when Luke was born, I knew I would do whatever was necessary to make a life for him. We didn't have much. I was always struggling to pay the bills, but every once in a while he would give me this smile, and everything was all right then."

Norah wasn't sure what to say. But apparently she didn't need to say anything, as Sandra continued.

"He was two when I realized that he was a little different from other kids. Nothing major, he just took a little longer to figure toys out than they did. I thought maybe he was just a slow learner. But he was just so sweet. He loved everyone and everything. I thought I'd hit the jackpot. And I had. Even with the Asperger's, or maybe because of it, he's still the sweetest little boy. Now ..." Sandra's eyes filled with tears.

Norah reached across the space between them and gripped her hand. "He's with Maeve and Greg. They'll look out for him like he's one of their own. And Alvie, I know you don't know him, but he's a pretty incredible little man, as is Iggy. They'll all do whatever is in their power to keep Luke safe."

Sandra's tear-filled eyes met Norah's gaze. "You saw those things. They're out of a nightmare. Even though I know Maeve and the others would protect Luke with everything in them, what can they possibly do to keep him safe when all of R.I.S.E. couldn't?"

Norah didn't have an answer for that. And Sandra's words opened a door in Norah's mind to all the possible things that could go wrong. She moved so she was sitting next to Sandra and wrapped her arms around the other woman's shoulder. There was nothing that she could say that would make this better. The hole in her chest opened up wider when she accepted the fact that despite all her hopes and plans, there was nothing she could do either.

Both her and Sandra had been relegated to the wait-and-see category. And staying there was going to kill them both.

CHAPTER 78

At the sight of Martin Drummond, it took all of Chris's discipline and willpower to keep himself from bolting into the room. But he knew the temporary satisfaction of taking a swing at Martin would result in immediate removal of Chris from any chance of helping Maeve. And he simply couldn't risk it.

Instead, he dug his fingernails into his palms so hard that he drew blood, pain flaring up as it dribbled down his fingers.

In the room, Martin took a seat at the other end of the table. Chris narrowed his eyes at the positioning, almost as if Martin was the yin to Tilda's yang.

Tilda gave Martin a cool nod. "Martin."

His response was just as cool. "Tilda. It's about time."

She ignored the comment. Her gaze roamed over the rest of the gathered individuals as she spoke. "As you know, military protocols are put into place so that long-winded explanations are not necessary during crucial times. MAURC is one such protocol."

Her comment did not go over well with the rest of the individuals at the table.

Tilda continued. "However, I will concede that MAURC is a rather unusual protocol."

"Unusual? It's extreme. You cannot subsume the entire U.S. military under one individual's command. Unless that individual is the president. Does he even know what's going on?" The Navy representative demanded.

A woman stood up three down from Martin. "He does."

All heads swiveled toward the woman, and Chris recognized her. He hadn't noticed her in the crowd of others in the room. She was Leslie Caruthers, the chief of staff for the President of the United States.

"And he's okay with this?" the Marine Corps rep asked.

Caruthers's voice was the voice of command. "Dr. Watson is the individual with the largest grasp on the situation and therefore the one most capable of making these decisions. She has his complete support."

"This will be a multi-agency, multi-force initiative," said Tilda. "The packets in front of you detail what will be needed from each of you. Make no mistake, this is the greatest threat that has faced the United States in its history." Tilda paused. "Actually, it's the greatest threat that has faced the *world* in its history."

The individuals at the table began to comb through the directive in front of them. Chris, more than anything, wanted to get a look at that packet, but he supposed he was just going to have to wait until they started to talk.

It didn't take long.

"What the hell is this? Is this some sort of joke?" the representative from the Army looked up with disbelief splashed across his face.

Tilda shook her head. "I assure you it is no joke. The Draco have been on this planet for centuries. They have been hidden and contained for the majority of that time, although we do know that in recent years, they began to expand into the human populations. Some of them can mask themselves as humans, but most are unable to achieve this. If you turn to page twenty-eight, you will see a photo of a Draco in action. It was taken less than fourteen hours ago at the R.I.S.E. base."

An audible gasp went through the individuals at the table. Chris understood the response. His first sight of the Draco had been difficult, and that was even after he'd seen Hank in action.

"What do they want?" the DNI director asked.

"Everything," Tilda said her voice firm. "They want to be in charge of the planet. Their attempts at destroying R.I.S.E. were the first gambit in an all-out assault on the human race. We must strike back before they can respond."

She turned to the Army representative. "We need MOABs. They will be striking the Arctic as soon as we get them into position."

"The Arctic?" The rep asked.

Tilda nodded. "That is where their main base is. It needs to be destroyed."

"If you know where their base is, why haven't they already been destroyed? Why wait?" the Marine Corps rep asked.

"I'm afraid none of you have the correct clearance to be given that answer. But what you do need to know is that we have now been cleared to remove that base. There will also be a second strike on a target within the United States mainland," Tilda said

"You're setting off a MOAB in the United States?" His eyebrows disappearing into his hairline, the Army representative stared at her.

Tilda shook her head. "No. Not a MOAB. We'll be utilizing bunker busters. Once you have reviewed the targets, I want your recommendations for the most effective munitions for the job."

"What level of destruction?" the Army rep asked.

"Complete."

Tilda's answer caused a stir around the table.

"What about civilian casualties?" the Marine Corps rep asked.

"The areas should be relatively isolated, but we cannot rule out casualties. You each have your marching orders. From this point forward, there will be no more questions. There will be orders, and they will be followed. Is that clear?"

Tilda met everyone's gaze at the table, not moving until everyone gave her a nod of acceptance. Finally, she stood. "This meeting is dismissed. We all have work to do."

CHAPTER 79

After Tilda's statement, she left the room, leaving Pearl to handle the details. Chris couldn't see it in her walk, but she must be exhausted. She shouldn't even be out of bed. But man, she was impressive.

The meeting continued without her as each of the representatives conferred with colleagues on the phone, computer, and across the table.

Staying quiet during it was the hardest thing Chris had ever done. He listened as they made plans, arranging for the different branches of the U.S. military and intelligence community to work together.

Drummond was right in the middle of it, providing intel on the Draco and their base in the Arctic as well as information on other locations where they might be.

In fact, Drummond seemed to be the Draco expert.

Chris narrowed his eyes. Had Martin known about the attack in advance? Was that possible? Why would he keep it a secret?

Chris had to hold in a scoff. Of course he kept it a secret.

His job *was* secrets. And Drummond seemed a little too happy about the plan to take out the Draco.

Which never would have happened without the attack on the base.

But would Martin really have let that happen? Was anybody truly that evil, even him?

More disturbing was that no one mentioned the fact that the Draco had taken hostages during their attack. The meeting lasted about an hour before Pearl ordered everyone to get to work and to await Tilda's instructions. Adam stood at the front door, ensuring everyone left. Chris leaned back heavily against the wall. No mention had been made about Maeve and the others. No plans were made to rescue them.

The wall in front of him slid open. Adam stood in the opening and beckoned for Chris to come out. Stepping out, Chris stretched out his limbs as he did so. His whole body felt cramped, and there was an ache in his lower back. "Why did you let me see that?"

"So that you would understand that they won't help your family," Adam said.

"Yeah, their goal is containing the threat. But why would they risk Alvie?" Chris asked.

Even with the sunglasses on, Chris could feel his heavy stare. "Because they have two others."

He felt sick. "They're not interchangeable."

"To the U.S. government they are," Adam said.

"They're not even on the planet," Chris said.

Adam shrugged. "But they exist. That is good enough for now."

Chris sucked in a breath. "And Maeve, Snap, Luke, Iggy, and Greg?"

"Acceptable casualties to eliminate the Draco threat," Adam said, his tone conveying he did not agree with the opinion.

Closing his eyes, Chris knew that Adam was speaking the truth. As far as the U.S. government was concerned, the lives of three humans, two half humans, and one full-blooded alien would mean nothing when compared to the threat the Draco offered.

"We need to get moving," Adam said.

A certainty settled in Chris's chest. He shook his head. "I'm not going back to the barracks. The U.S. government might think they're expendable, but I don't."

A hint of a smile appeared on Adam's face. "I don't either. So let's go get them back."

CHAPTER 80

EDMONDS, WASHINGTON

It was dark. There wasn't even a sliver of light with which to see. Maeve wasn't sure at first if her eyes were even open, the darkness was so complete. She reached up and touched her face, checking to make sure there wasn't a blindfold covering her eyes.

No blindfold, just total darkness. Her body began to shake, the fears from the attack working their way through her. Where was she? What was going on?

She struggled through the murkiness of her memories. She could remember the attack. It had come out of nowhere. And then the Draco had appeared. They looked like walking crocodiles. They were similar to Hank, but the skin wasn't quite as rough as Hank's. The snouts weren't as developed as his either. But they moved just as fast.

She had been with the group. And then they'd been separated. Adam had been there, and then ... She shook her head, trying to wipe away the thoughts of the Draco on the base and the plane.

She swallowed a few times, trying to get moisture into her mouth. "Is anyone here?" Her voice came out in a hoarse whisper, making her wonder how long it had been since she'd used it.

Here.

Her heart plunged. She'd hoped she was alone, as terrifying as that would've been. She didn't want Alvie here too.

Is there anyone else here?

She sensed movement, and then a small hand reached for hers while she felt the presence in her mind.

Oh no. Snap. She reached down and pulled the little gray into her lap. Snap was trembling so hard that Maeve worried that she would break in two.

Somewhere to her left, Greg's voice came out of the darkness. "Yeah, I'm okay, Alvie. I've got Iggy."

A small whimper came from somewhere right in front of her. Maeve didn't recognize the noise. It wasn't Pop or Crackle. The hairs on the back of her neck stood straight up. *Alvie, who else is here?*

Luke.

Oh my God. Maeve scrambled forward, keeping Snap curled to her. On her hands and knees, she reached out, trying to find him in the darkness. "Luke? Luke, it's Maeve. Where are you?"

The only sound was a small cry. He sounded like a wounded animal. She reached out and touched his sneaker. "I'm here, Luke. I'm here."

But his cries didn't diminish. Maeve wasn't sure what to do. She knew he didn't like to be touched. And she worried that doing so would only make it worse. But everything in her screamed that this poor boy needed to be comforted.

Let Iggy. The words appeared in her mind just as she felt a figure brush past her. She gasped, her heart racing. He'd come out of nowhere.

Her eyes had adjusted enough to the dark to vaguely make

out Iggy reaching Luke's side. Iggy stood up, placing his hands on the side of Luke's head. Luke's crying cut off, and he leaned his head into Iggy's.

Greg scrambled over to Maeve and crouched down next to her. "He okay?"

Fear, worry, and anger warred for dominance inside of Maeve. "No, he's not. And none of us will be until we get out of here."

CHAPTER 81

MAXWELL AIR FORCE BASE, ALABAMA

It was a silent ride back to the barracks. Chris had to duck down in the back seat because with so many top government officials here, there was a ton of extra security.

"You can get up now," Adam said as he turned down the lane that led to the barracks. Chris knew it was now or never for answers from the reticent soldier. "Do they know where they're keeping Maeve and the others?"

Adam shook his head. "No. And I don't think that once they do that will protect them."

Chris frowned. "What do you mean?"

"The one thing that we know for certain is that Maeve, Luke, Greg, Alvie, Snap, and Iggy were all taken by the Draco. The U.S. government has just declared war on the Draco. Destroying them is their priority. It's in the R.I.S.E. charter. That when the Draco make the move, they must be destroyed. The Council supports that move as well. The peace with the Draco has only been a stopgap. Everyone has known that, including the Draco."

Chris realized he'd never heard Adam talk this much in the entire time he'd known the man. "So you're saying even if they find out where they're holding Maeve and the others, they won't attempt a rescue?"

"No. They have nothing to gain and everything to lose," Adam said.

Horror crawling over him, Chris stared at Adam even as he knew his words were true. "But Alvie and Snap—"

"They still have Crackle and Pop, or at least still have access to them. Like I said, in the government's mind they're interchangeable."

"You mean in Tilda's," Chris said bitterly.

Adam didn't say anything for a long moment. "No, not in her mind. But she's focused on the greater threat. And the greater threat is the Draco surviving." He pulled to a stop in front of the barracks and stepped out without another word.

Taking a deep breath, Chris tried to hold back his anger. He knew the government made decisions based on cost and benefit. He himself had been in military situations where he'd been sent on missions and taken part in discussions about acceptable casualties. He knew in the final calculation that the loss of five lives against the potential devastation of the human race wouldn't even raise an eyebrow.

But this time, Chris could not go along with that.

Adam strode into the barracks. Chris was right behind him. Norah stood in the middle of the row of bunks, her arms crossed over her chest. Sandra appeared farther down, her face pale as she walked slowly toward them. "Is there any news? Have you found them?"

Adam's voice softened as he spoke. "No, I'm afraid not."

Sandra took the news like a blow. She grabbed on to the nearest bunk and held on, swaying for a moment.

"But you do have information," Norah said her gaze Locke don Adam.

"Yes. Chris and I are going to get the others back. And we could use some help."

Norah frowned. "I thought you said you didn't know where they were?"

"We don't, not yet," Adam said. :But we're not going to be able to get them back on our own when we get the information."

"I'm in," Norah said without hesitation.

Her back straightening, her eyes focused, Sandra nodded as well. "I am too."

Although Chris wanted their help, they couldn't be in the dark about what they were facing. "You have to understand—the U.S. government is not going to help us. They've written them off as acceptable losses. And in all likelihood, they will bomb the location where they are being held whether we are there or not."

Sandra gasped. But Norah just straightened her shoulders. "I *said* I'm in."

Chris gave her a nod.

"Me too. Whatever it takes," Sandra said although there was a slight tremor in her voice.

"Good. Then come with me." Adam strode back toward the door.

Chris kept pace with him. "How are we going to find out where they are?"

"We'll find them. But there's one more person that we need for this team," Adam said.

Chris racked his brain, trying to figure out who exactly that would be. Maybe some of Tilda's special ops guys? "Are you sure we can trust them?"

"We *can't* trust him. But we're going to need him."

CHAPTER 82

Martin commandeered an office in one of the unused administration buildings. He'd brought Stacy along, who was in communication with the rest of his team.

They had finally initiated the MAURC protocol. Personally, he thought they should have done it years ago. The Draco never should've been given the benefit of the doubt. The blight of their existence should have been removed from the planet as soon as it was technologically possible. But it had taken an attack on the R.I.S.E. base to get them to act.

Martin smiled. *Of course, if I'd known it was that easy, I would have leaked the location years ago.*

Martin himself had learned about R.I.S.E. when he'd been hired by the CIA. The U.S. government had created his position as a safety net for R.I.S.E. His priority was to gather as much information as he could on the Draco bases in case R.I.S.E. didn't work. He'd been responsible for overseeing the United States' offensive response in case the Council failed to live up to their bargain or in case the Draco decided to quit playing possum. Hence, the A.L.I.V.E. projects.

A much better use of taxpayer money in Martin's not even slightly humble opinion. R.I.S.E. had always been a foolish endeavor, an act of eternal optimism. Aliens had no compassion for humans. Humans were continually being abducted to be studied. Tagged like animals in the wild.

Because that's all we are to them. Animals. Humans were millions of years behind the Draco technologically. Physically, they were vastly inferior. It was only a matter of time before the Draco rose up.

And where was the Council in all of this? The group of benevolent beings that the United States had been counting on to keep them safe? Well, those benevolent beings were safe, but humanity was about to get royally screwed.

Martin flipped to the file on his laptop. He kept a listing of all Draco holdings. He'd been given the authority to oversee a takedown of each and every one of them. He'd handed over the information that was critical to the R.I.S.E. command structure, except for a few individual sites that he would have his people handle.

He brought up the most recent image he had of Tatiana. He'd officially met her ten years ago. If he was being honest, though, he'd met her closer to forty years ago. Or at least he'd met her representatives.

He narrowed his eyes as he studied the image of her from Edmonds, Washington. No one knew about the warehouses she owned along the Puget Sound, not until Martin had ferreted that information out five years ago.

To the world, Tatiana was the personification of a wealthy, spoiled aristocrat. She had occasionally been described in the media as having a voracious appetite for lovers. But the media had no idea how right they actually were.

He narrowed his eyes at the image. She stood next to Dietrich, her bodyguard. He towered over her. She almost looked frail in comparison. But appearances, in this case, as in many others, were extremely deceiving. Tatiana was the power of those two. And not just physically.

Although the two of them looked to be about the same age, Tatiana was hundreds of years older. One of the little-known facts about the Draco was that they had extended lifespans. Tatiana, as far as Martin could tell, was easily three hundred years old.

And she was the leader of her people. The Draco were a matriarchal race. Rule passed down from queen to queen. But Tatiana had no offspring. A wise move on her part. Because usually a queen was only displaced when she was killed by her daughter.

Apparently they didn't like to wait for natural causes to provide them with the throne.

Martin dashed off a message to Stacy. He knew that's where they would take their captives. Underneath the warehouses was a labyrinth of tunnels that extended beneath the Puget Sound. In fact, within that labyrinth, they had submarine docks that they used to travel back and forth to the Arctic.

He'd sent an agent into the labyrinths once. The man had worn a camera so that Martin was able to see everything. Most of the rooms were pitch black, although the hallways had some dim lighting. The Draco didn't need light. In fact, sunlight was often difficult for them to handle. Their eyes were much more sensitive. The tunnels were dank, dark, and humid.

His agent had only been able to investigate the first two levels before he was killed. But it was enough time for Martin to see the laboratories, the submarine docks, and the holding cells. From the state of the place, it had obviously been there for years. It might even predate the establishment of the United States.

A knock sounded at the door. Martin looked up with a growl. It was probably some military aide asking if he needed any additional resources. "Go away!"

He flipped open to a new file, this one describing the traffic patterns in and around the warehouse. The knock sounded again. Martin pushed back from his desk.

I thought military people were supposed be able to take orders.

He yanked open the door. "I said—"

A fist slammed into his face.

CHAPTER 83

Martin flew back with Chris's first punch. Chris stormed in, following the first cross with a left hook to the ribs and then a right hook to the face. Adam followed him in, saying nothing, simply closing the door behind him.

Martin got his hands up in front of his face as he stumbled back and righted himself. "How dare you—"

Chris threw a kick to his right knee, throwing him off balance before slamming a left cross into his face. Martin flew back once again, this time crashing into his desk. Chris stepped forward to do more damage, when Adam's hand landed on his shoulder. "We need information."

Chris knew he was right. But this was the man who'd caused so much destruction for his family. He was the one who'd *tortured* Alvie. He needed to feel pain.

Now was not the moment for that. That moment, though, would arrive and soon.

If they were going to cause Martin some pain, it had to have a purpose, and that purpose would be getting the information they needed out of him.

Chris grabbed Martin by the lapels and yanked him up. "Where are the Draco holding Maeve and the others?"

Martin glared at him in response. "How would I know?"

Chris threw a hook into his ribs. Martin grimaced, letting out a little puff of air. Chris shook him again. "Where. Are. They?"

"I wouldn't tell you even if I—" Martin's gaze shifted to over Chris's shoulder, and his face paled. "Joseph."

Chris glanced back at Adam, who had his usual non-expression on his face. And then he looked back at Martin. "Tell me where they are."

Some of the cockiness reappeared on Martin's face. "Why don't you ask your friend there?"

Chris slammed Martin back against the desk. "Because I'm asking you. And I'm getting very tired of the lack of answers. Let me make this very clear, either you help us, or you die. If anything happens to Alvie or any of the others, you die. If I don't like the way you look at one of us—"

"Let me guess, I die," Martin said.

"Now you're getting it. So where are they?" Chris demanded.

Martin stood up straighter. "It may surprise you to know that my death is not something that I'm worried about. The Draco must be destroyed. And I won't do anything that will interfere with it."

"But Maeve doesn't need to die. Alvie doesn't need to die. Luke, Greg, Snap, Iggy—they're no threat to anyone," Chris reminded him.

"If they're not human, they're a threat." Martin glared over his shoulder at Adam.

Adam stepped forward. "We know the base is on the West Coast. Bring him. We'll get the information in the air."

Martin scoffed. "I'm not going anywhere with—"

Chris's uppercut stole the rest of his sentence. Martin's

eyelids fluttered as his eyes rolled back into his head before he dropped.

Chris stepped out of the way to make sure the landing wasn't soft. Then he squatted down and rifled through Martin's pockets. He pulled out a phone while Adam grabbed the tablet off the desk. Then Adam reached down, and with very little difficulty, threw Martin over his shoulder. "We should go."

Flicking a glance at the unconscious Martin, Chris nodded. He hoped they didn't run into anyone on their way to the jeep. An unconscious Martin would be difficult to explain.

He opened the door and nearly ran straight into Jasper.

CHAPTER 84

Jasper opened his mouth. Before he could say a word, Chris grabbed him and yanked him into the room.

Mike Bileris was standing just behind him. He stepped into the room quickly and closed the door.

Jasper raised an eyebrow as he caught sight of Martin over Adam's shoulder. "Well, Mike, looks like we missed all the fun."

Tensing, Chris wasn't sure what he was supposed to do now. He couldn't let them raise the alarm. And he definitely couldn't let them take Martin.

His hands up, Jasper eased back a half step. "Hey now, I know that look. We were coming to get the same information you were from Martin."

"Yeah, but I don't think you had the same intention," Chris said.

Placing his hand over his heart, Jasper shook his head. "Now that hurts. It really does. After all we've been through?"

Chris curled his hand into a fist. Mike shook his head. "Cut it out, Jasper. We're not here on R.I.S.E.'s behalf. We want to get Maeve and the others out. We were coming to get the information from Martin so that we could initiate a rescue."

"Why should I believe you?" Chris demanded.

Jasper shrugged. "Hell, I wouldn't. But Alvie is important to R.I.S.E., and the truth is, Mike and I aren't really thrilled at the idea of sacrificing people if it can be avoided. So here we are."

Jasper eyed Martin, who was still obviously unconscious. "Although that looks like it might be a bit of a problem."

"Look, we're on the same side here," Mike said. "None of us wants anything to happen to Maeve or the others. So let's combine forces."

Chris studied the two of them. They worked for Tilda. And right now as far as he was concerned, Tilda was the enemy. Of course, Adam worked for Tilda too, and yet he was trusting him.

Regardless, they couldn't leave Mike and Jasper behind because they'd raise the alarm. And he didn't want to think of the way he would need to silence them.

He glanced over his shoulder at Adam, who gave him a slight nod. Chris took that as acceptance of Jasper and Mike into their little mutiny. "Okay. We've got a car outside."

Jasper smiled. "I see your car and raise you a plane. We've got one waiting on the runway."

Chris raised an eyebrow at that statement.

This time it was Mike who shrugged. "We figured we'd have to do something similar to Martin to get answers, and we wanted to have a quick getaway if needed. The plane's gassed up, we've got clearance, and we're ready to go."

"And most importantly, it has a hold full of weapons." Jasper rubbed his hands together. "So let's get this party started."

Mike rolled his eyes and opened the door, shooting a quick look down the hall before stepping out. Jasper followed him.

Chris exchanged a quick glance with Adam and then stepped out, hoping he could trust these two and that he didn't have to kill them.

Because if they in any way, shape, or form interfered with the rescue of Maeve and the others, that was exactly what he would do.

CHAPTER 85

Sandra felt as if her mind was being split into two. One part forced her to do the everyday things that you're supposed to do: breathe, walk, talk. But the other part was screaming, constantly screaming.

Those things had taken Luke. She couldn't imagine the terror he was feeling right now. Or maybe she could, because underneath her walking and talking and breathing, she felt it down to her bones. Luke being in danger and not being able to do anything about it was destroying her bit by bit each second that passed.

She grabbed an M4 and checked to make sure it was in working order. She grabbed half a dozen magazines and stuffed them into a pack. Norah was on the other side of the room, loading up some heavier artillery. Sandra didn't recognize all of it, but she did recognize the RPG launcher and the armor-piercing rounds.

Instead of it scaring her, it gave her a calming sense of resolution. Getting Luke and the others back was going to be its own kind of war. Those creatures had been close to indestructible. And they were going to need as much heavy firepower as they could manage. She knew there was a good chance that she wouldn't come back. That she would fail in trying to get Luke.

But she would rather die than sit quietly and safely somewhere while he was going through hell. She slammed a magazine into the M4 and chambered a round.

Norah looked up from where she was stringing grenades to a belt. Sandra met her gaze, but the other woman didn't say anything, just gave her a nod and continued her work.

Sandra appreciated that. She wasn't in the mood to have a conversation. She wasn't in the mood to talk about how she was feeling. She was feeling rage. She was feeling grief, and if she opened the door to either of those, she wasn't sure she would be able to close it.

Norah nodded at the stack of crates by the door. "I'll load those up. You got the rest?"

"I got them." Sandra placed the M4 in the crate to her right. Placing the lid over the crate, she picked it up and followed Norah to the waiting jeep. Chris and Adam should have Martin soon, and then they would have a target.

Waiting in the barracks had been sucking at her soul. She thought she'd go crazy if she had to stare at those walls for any longer. Moving, acting, that's what she needed right now.

That and to kill as many Draco as humanly possible.

CHAPTER 86

Between Jasper, Mike, and Adam's credentials, they made it to the airfield without any problem. As promised, a Cessna Citation X sat on the tarmac, fully fueled and ready to go. They wasted no time boarding.

"That is *not* a military jet," Sandra said, eyeing the large plane.

"Nope," Jasper said with a grin. "But it is R.I.S.E. property for when we need to move quickly and in style. The Aerion was destroyed in the attack. Damned shame. That was an incredible plane."

Adam carried Martin, who was still out, over his shoulder. As soon as they were inside, Jasper turned toward the cockpit.

Chris reached out a hand. "No. Adam's flying."

Pausing, Adam raised an eyebrow above his sunglasses.

"You can fly this thing, right?" Chris asked.

Adam nodded.

"I'll get Martin settled. You get us up and running," Chris said.

Adam unceremoniously dropped Martin into the nearest chair and then headed for the cockpit.

Shaking his head ruefully, Jasper gave Chris a baleful look. "Where's the trust, Chris? You're really beginning to hurt my feelings."

Chris ignored the man. On many levels, he really liked Jasper. But the fact was, Jasper was really good at lying. And in this situation, Chris wasn't taking any chances. Adam had taken Chris to that meeting. It's possible he, too, was playing some sort of game, but nothing about the reticent man indicated that he was anything but straightforward. He didn't think lying was in Adam's bag of tricks.

Pulling the zip ties from his pocket, Chris quickly attached Martin's arms to the armrest. He grabbed some zip cords from his other pocket and secured them to the chair. Norah and Sandra had picked them up on their little shopping spree at the base.

Jasper handed him a strip of fabric. Chris looked up at him. Jasper shrugged. "Thought you might want to gag him."

Good idea, Chris thought as he accepted the fabric. He quickly tied it around Martin's mouth. Jasper was right. He didn't want to hear anything from this man except for answers to his questions. The engines rumbled, springing to life.

Chris took a seat. Sandra and Norah entered the cabin and took seats close to the cockpit. Chris studied Sandra. She looked better. She had a little color in her cheeks. Having a plan helped make some of the ache go away. He knew from personal experience.

Jasper sat down across from him. Chris met his gaze unflinching. "So what is your deal, Jasper? Who are you loyal to?"

"Well, who are you loyal to?" Jasper countered.

Chris didn't hesitate. "Maeve and the kids."

"Kids? An interesting choice of words," Jasper mused.

"An *accurate* choice of words," Chris replied. "And you haven't answered me."

As the plane started to move, Jasper stretched his legs out. "I find loyalty to be a strange word. I would say I'm not loyal to any one person. But I am loyal to an ideal."

"And what's that ideal?"

Jasper looked him right in the eyes. "Doing the right thing. It often coincides with the goals of protecting my country. And that works out just fine."

"And saving Maeve and the others? Does that align with the goals of your country?" Chris asked.

Meeting his gaze, Jasper tilted his head. "That's an interesting question. Because you see, before that *was* my focus, protecting my country. But recent events have made me realize that sometimes there's something that has to come above protection of one's country."

"And what's that?" Chris asked.

"Protecting my world," Jasper said simply.

Chris tensed. "So you think we should destroy the Draco."

"Of course. But ... I also wonder about all this that has come about. The Council has known about the Draco for eons. The U.S. government has known about them for a long time as well. But now we are forced into a position where the creation of the Council is in danger by the Draco. Yet the U.S. government is rushing to destroy the Draco, creations be damned." Jasper fell silent.

"And?" Chris prodded.

Jasper shrugged. "And I think that is a mistake. The Draco were banished for their warlike nature. I don't think blindly killing will endear us to the Council. So I think this is a test. A test to see who has more sway on humanity: the forces of good or the forces of evil?"

"So you want to save them," Chris concluded.

Shaking his head, the normally jocular man looked dead serious. "No, I *need* to save them. Because if we don't, it doesn't matter if we wipe out every last Draco. Humanity will be lost."

CHAPTER 87

EDMONDS, WASHINGTON

The dripping was getting to him. Greg wasn't sure what it was that was dripping, but it was a constant drip. *Drip, drip, drip.*

It was making him insane.

He clenched his fists as the drip sounded again. Iggy stirred from where he was playing on top of Luke. Maeve had her eyes closed with Snap curled up in her lap. Alvie was sitting between her and Greg, his head resting on Greg's arm. Luke was sitting on Greg's other side, a few inches separating them so they weren't touching.

Greg had to give the kid credit for not completely losing it. He'd been upset when he'd come to. He'd let out this little tiny mewling sound. Like a rabbit caught in a trap. Iggy had acted instantly. He'd hurried over to Luke and crawled into his lap. Luke had gone still for a moment and then wrapped his arms tightly around Iggy. Iggy made some soft purring noises similar to a cat. Luke closed his eyes, a tear rolling down his cheek.

Greg had felt so helpless. There was nothing he could do for Luke. He couldn't even hug him and offer at least a small amount of connection to help him feel as if he wasn't alone.

Thank God for Iggy.

Drip, drip, drip.

Standing up slowly, his eyes had adjusted to the dark, so he could at least make out where the walls were and where the door was. He stepped away from the wall and moved to the other side of the cell, pacing from one wall to the other but careful to keep his footsteps quiet so as not wake any of the others. If they could sleep through this at least a little bit, that's what he wanted for them. God knew he wished he could sleep. He wished he could disappear into a dreamland and pretend none of this was happening.

But apparently that wasn't for him. How was it possible that this was the place he'd ended up? He was Greg Schorn, for God's sake. Growing up, he was the last picked for any sort of sports team. He'd had braces and glasses starting in high school and still had them when he finished. Acne had been his most faithful friend during his teenage years. And he hadn't even grown to his full height until he was a senior in college.

He was not the type who was supposed to be in the middle of some sort of crazy intergalactic conspiracy. He was the type who was supposed to be an accountant, getting stressed during tax time and more relaxed during the rest of the year.

But Greg had been fascinated by biology since he was young. He'd read every book he could on anatomy and creatures of all sorts. In college, a whole new world had opened to him when he'd started taking biochemistry courses. But never in his wildest dreams did he imagine that one day he would be working on alien hybrid experiments for the U.S. government.

His gaze strayed back to where Maeve sat on the floor. And never could he have imagined that Maeve had grown up with an alien. He'd met Maeve in college. They had lived in the same dorm. Bonded over their love of science. And he'd had a huge crush on her for freshman and sophomore year before he realized that it was never going to happen.

Luckily he was smart enough to recognize that he could either have Maeve as a friend or completely ruin everything by trying to make it more than that. And Maeve's friendship had meant the world to him. She was his best friend.

Even with all of the crazy she had in her life, she'd always made time for him. He couldn't imagine how difficult her life had been, keeping the knowledge of Alvie hidden from everyone she knew. It must've been incredibly hard ... And lonely. But he supposed she had her mother to share Alvie with.

Greg had never been very close with his family. They *were* accountants. They simply did not understand why Greg didn't want to go into the family business. But Greg had known his curiosity was leading him somewhere else. And he also knew that if he spent his life sitting in an office running numbers, it would be the death of him.

He glanced around the cell he currently found himself in. *Of course, if I'd known my life choices would've taken me here, perhaps I would've chosen differently.*

But even as he thought it, he knew that wasn't the case. He was meant to be here. He'd done some good. He'd helped people. And he wouldn't trade it for anything.

Of course, he would be deliriously happy if Adam showed up, kicked in the door, and rescued them all. He looked at the door, holding his breath for a few seconds before releasing it. *Nope.*

Drip, drip, drip.

Greg pulled at his hair, feeling the tension and fear crawl over him. He'd seen what those creatures had done on the base. He had no illusions that he would be able to fight them off in any meaningful way.

Chris would be trying to find them. Of course, being they'd been flown to God knew where, he wasn't sure Chris would have the resources to track them down. Would getting them back even be a priority for R.I.S.E. right now? He knew Chris would move heaven and earth to get his family back, but that will to get them back might not be enough without the resources to find them.

Agaren seemed to be completely focused on Alvie and the triplets. But he'd been missing in action ever since he'd been released from New Mexico, so who knew if he'd be any help?

His gaze roamed over Maeve, Snap, Alvie, Luke, and Iggy. None of them deserved this. They were all so young. Snap and Iggy were only a few years old. It was hard to keep that in mind when you interacted with them, but they were basically toddler aged. He couldn't imagine a human three-year-old being thrown into this life. They deserved to have a childhood, one free from all of this violence.

And Luke, he hadn't had an easy childhood himself. Kids could be cruel. Greg could still remember some of the bullies from his childhood. They *still* made him shiver. And from what Sandra had said, kids were no more understanding these days, especially for a kid on the autism spectrum.

At the same time, Greg had to wonder what the Draco knew about Luke. They had to know about his connection to Sammy. Norah had explained to him about Project Antaeus and Luke's dad. Greg knew there had to be a connection between Sammy and the project, which was why the creature was so protective of him. Anger welled up in Greg. They had treated American soldiers like guinea pigs. They hadn't given any thought to the repercussions for the next generation. Luke was basically collateral damage of a U.S. government experiment run amok. But that experiment had brought all of this misery into Luke and Sandra's life.

They deserved better than this. They deserved a normal life.

But that wasn't in his power. Right now there was a lot that wasn't within his power. He wasn't a religious man. He'd been raised Protestant, and his family had gone to church every weekend, but it never really took. He'd just gone through the motions.

Greg looked up at the ceiling. *I don't know if you exist or not, but if you do, please help us all get out of here. And if you can't do that, please help me find a way to at least keep them safe for as long as I can.*

CHAPTER 88

SOMEWHERE OVER THE UNITED STATES

They didn't have a firm destination in mind, so Adam aimed for the West Coast of the United States. They knew that the Draco base was somewhere in that vicinity, but they had nothing more specific. Martin was still out as Mike stepped back into the fuselage. Chris looked up.

"Adam's setting the autopilot. He said we can get started," Mike said.

Sandra and Norah joined Chris and Jasper. All four of them sat in front of Martin as his eyes blinked open before closing again.

Mike stood one row away from him, leaning against the top of a chair.

Chris grabbed a glass of water and threw its contents into Martin's face. Martin's eyes flung open.

"Ah, Sleeping Beauty awakens," Jasper said.

Martin spluttered, water dripping down his face and onto his shirt. He coughed and then glared at the people surrounding him. "Do you realize what you've just done?"

Jasper snorted. "Yes, and no one's interested in your abduction. They have bigger issues to worry about right now."

Martin narrowed his eyes. "When my people learn—"

Chris cut him off. "No one's interested in your threats. Where did the Draco take Maeve and the others?"

Martin shrugged, trying to look nonchalant in his water-stained silk shirt. "I have no idea. They don't include me in their plans."

Jasper leaned forward. "Oh, I get it. We're going to have to ask the correct series of questions to get an answer. All right, I'll play: What properties do the Draco own on the western seaboard of North America?"

Martin closed his mouth and just stared at the man.

Norah moved closer. "Let me make this clear: You are either helping or you are dead weight. And we do not need dead weight. So start talking."

Martin smirked. "Oh yeah? And what exactly are you going to do?"

Sandra's voice was deadly when she spoke. "I vote for dropping him out the plane door."

Martin's eyes flared. "You wouldn't dare."

Jasper nodded thoughtfully. "Actually, I like that idea. I mean, he won't survive the fall, but the body will be eaten by something in the ocean, or lots of somethings. Maybe it'll eventually catch a current and wash up on some shore somewhere. Of course, depending on the current, that could take months, and even then, none of your prints or DNA are on file, I'm sure. Which means you'll just be another body that washed up on shore, no name, no grave, no one to mourn. Not that anyone would mourn you anyway."

Martin's jaw clenched, the only indication that he was bothered by the scenario Jasper described.

"Why are you protecting them? You know what they are," Chris said.

"Yes, I know what they are. And I know they all deserve to die. And if you go storming in there, you'll tip them off to what's coming. They'll escape, and then this little adventure continues," Martin said through gritted teeth.

"Not a single one of them is getting out of there," Chris said.

Martin laughed. "You have no idea what you're going up against. Didn't you learn anything? The Draco have two weaknesses: their eyes and the back of their mouth. That's it. Their skin is the equivalent of body armor. You think this little ragtag group is going to be able to put a dent in their forces? Please. You'll be their evening snack."

Adam stepped out of the cockpit. "We don't need him. Penny broke through his files. She has the base. It's in Washington State. A place called Edmonds."

Venom dripped off Martin's words as his eyes narrowed to slits. "Hello, Joseph."

With a frown, Chris looked between Martin and Adam, not sure what that Joseph thing was about. But Martin kept making these little jabs at Adam. And Jasper had a guilty look on his face.

Norah looked between Adam and Martin. "What's going on?"

Turning his head, Martin speared each of them before he spoke. "Oh, you want to know about the Draco? Why don't you ask Joseph? I mean, *Adam*, about them. After all, he is one."

CHAPTER 89

EDMONDS, WASHINGTON

Although Maeve's eyes had grown used to the dark, there was still precious little to be seen. She and Greg had searched their cell. They'd walked its entirety. It was ten by twelve feet. There was no one else in there with them except for Alvie, Snap, Iggy, and Luke. The walls were made of rock and were damp. In fact, the whole area had a damp, humid feel to it.

Maeve knew that all of them would get sick if they spent too long in here, especially Alvie and Snap. But she had no idea how they were going to get out. There was a drain in the floor, but it was only a few inches across. She didn't like to think of what it had been installed for. The door itself was steel. They wouldn't be able to get through that either.

And the rock walls were rough, almost unfinished. Without a jackhammer, they wouldn't even be able to make a dent in them. No, they weren't getting out of this room until someone let them out.

There was a small window at the top of the door with four slats across, its metal bars reminding her of an old-fashioned jail-cell door. It allowed them to hear what was happening in the hall. But other than the drip of water, it was silent.

No one had come by. In fact, there hadn't been another sound outside of the door in the hours they'd been there.

Now the five of them sat close together in the corner opposite the door. Alvie sat on one side of Luke while Iggy sat in Luke's lap, with Snap on his other side. Apparently he didn't mind any of them touching him. Maeve could just make out the boy's face. He was terrified. It was a familiar emotion. But she couldn't think of a single comforting thing to say. Because everything that came to mind was a lie.

Everything will be all right.
There's nothing to worry about.
Help is on the way.

It was that last one that she hoped there was a chance was true. Chris was no doubt searching for them. But how would he even know where to start?

And besides, the Draco had proven to be an insidious enemy. They had planned to take over the R.I.S.E. base for decades. And they had done so with brutal efficiency. She had no doubt that they had planned this particular hiding space just as efficiently. So what chance did any of them have of being found?

Greg whispered over to her. "They're going to find us, right? I mean, they have to, right?"

Aware of the other ears listening in, Maeve kept her voice equally low. "Of course. It's just a matter of time."

Footsteps echoed down the hall, heading toward them. Maeve tensed, shooting a look at Greg before the two of them shot to their feet, placing themselves between the door and the kids. Maeve knew it was a futile gesture. The Draco were so much more physically enhanced than either she or Greg. And between them, Maeve and Greg had zero training and weapons. But Maeve couldn't simply allow the kids to be hurt without a fight.

The lock on the door turned, and the steel door was pushed in. A woman stepped through. In the dim light, all Maeve could really make out was that she had long hair that she thought might be blonde. She was slim and held herself with confidence. A tall, hulking man stood behind her like a bodyguard. The thought of that made her laugh. Like a Draco needed a bodyguard against them.

For just a split second, she thought that maybe someone had come to rescue them. But then she saw the Draco guards behind the two humans. And it was clear that these two, although they appeared human, were definitely not on their side.

"Dr. Leander, a pleasure to finally meet you. And Dr. Schorn, your work has been most illuminating," the woman said.

Neither Maeve nor Greg said anything. But she felt Alvie walk up behind her. He took her hand, standing in between her and Greg. Iggy let out a low growl. A small light in the ceiling flickered on. Maeve blinked, and it took her eyes a few seconds to adjust, even though the light wasn't that bright.

The woman stepped to the side, peering behind Maeve and Greg. "It *is* a Maldek. When I heard the reports, I thought they had to be mistaken. Amazing. I thought they were all extinct. Oh, won't you be a perfect little toy."

Iggy's growl got deeper. The hair on the back of Maeve's neck stood up. "Iggy, no."

She'd seen Iggy fight. She knew what he was capable of. But she'd also seen the Draco fight. And they were outnumbered.

Iggy's growls quieted. Alvie squeezed her hand lightly, and Maeve knew he'd communicated with Iggy as well.

The blonde woman raised an eyebrow. "Interesting. Now, where are my manners? I am Tatiana Brecknoff, the leader of the Draco. Technically I am the queen, but that seems such an old-fashioned phrase these days, doesn't it?"

"What do you want with us?" Greg asked.

Her giant shadow followed her as Tatiana took another step forward. "What an excellent question, Dr. Schorn." She reached out a long fingernail toward him. He reared back. She smiled in response, taking a step away from him, reminding Maeve of a cat playing with its food.

Clasping her hands in front of her, Tatiana smiled at both Greg and Maeve before focusing her attention on Alvie in between them. Maeve shifted, pulling Alvie behind her.

The woman smiled even wider. "Why, I have multiple uses for each of you. You and Dr. Leander have made strides in the scientific world that will be of great use to us. And of course, your connection to the Orion, the Maldek, and the hybrid will be of great use as well."

Maeve started at the term Orion, having to keep herself from turning to look at Luke. "Orion?"

Tatiana let out a small trill of laughter. "Oh, there is so much for you to learn, and so much for you to teach us. I believe this is the beginning of a beautiful relationship."

Her heart pounding, Maeve swallowed. Tatiana sounded like she had quite a few plans for them. On the one hand, that was good, because the longer they stayed alive, the longer it gave their people to find them. But on the other hand, the idea of Tatiana making plans that included them made her grow cold. She couldn't help but think of how the creatures were treated by the humans back at Area 51. And she had a horrible feeling that now they were the ones who were going to be the specimens.

R.I.S.E.

"But before all of that, you five will play a very important role." Tatiana went silent, looking at them expectantly.

"What role?" Greg finally asked.

Tatiana smiled brightly. "Bait."

CHAPTER 90

SOMEWHERE OVER THE WESTERN HALF OF THE UNITED STATES

No one said a word. The fuselage was dead silent. Chris studied Adam, thinking of everything he'd seen the man do. He'd taken on two Hanks by himself. He always wore those sunglasses as if the light bothered him. And he had an almost preternatural sense for danger.

Chris stood up, his hand resting on the Glock at his belt. "Adam?"

"Well, enough of this nonsense." Jasper slammed his fist into Martin's chin. Martin's eyes rolled back in his head, and it dropped to the side as he went unconscious again.

Norah had her P90 in her hand, aimed at Jasper. Sandra had hers aimed at Mike.

"What the hell is going on?" Sandra demanded.

"Adam, is it true? Are you a Draco?" Chris asked.

Adam nodded slowly. "Yes."

Chris's mouth fell open, and he wasn't sure what to do. "I don't understand. You helped us. You saved Alvie and Greg."

Jasper put up his hands. "Okay. Let's have everybody take a step back and calm down for just a minute. Maybe we could all lower those weapons?"

No one dropped their weapons.

Jasper sighed. "Okay, let's everybody keep their weapons right where they are. But let's all try to take a calming breath, and we can talk this out."

Chris looked at Jasper. "You knew. In New Mexico, you said not to worry about Adam when he was down there fighting the Hanks. You said he could handle himself."

"Yes, I know," Jasper said. "I've known for decades. I met Adam when I was twenty-one years old and had just enlisted in the Navy. We had both been sent overseas. He saved my life. In fact, he's saved my life dozens of times over the years. And not to toot my own horn, but I saved his a least twice."

Adam tilted his head, looking at Jasper.

Jasper shrugged. "Okay, once. So why don't we—"

Chris cut Jasper off. "No. I want to hear it from Adam."

Adam hesitated for a moment, and Chris wondered what was going through his mind. But finally, he nodded and took a seat. "Okay."

CHAPTER 91

EDMONDS, WASHINGTON

The Draco guards led them from the cell after Tatiana's pronouncement. There had been an additional six guards waiting in the hallway. The sight of them was terrifying. She'd seen them at the Hy-Brasil base, but she hadn't had a chance to see them up close and personal like this. Their skin was dark green, and it looked like rough alligator skin. Each stood at least six feet tall, although some were closer to seven.

Their arms and legs were strong and humanoid, but their feet were long, flat, and wide. They wore no shoes but had sharp, rounded nails at the end of each foot. And instead of hands, they had three talons on the end of each arm.

Their faces were more similar to humans, at least compared to the Kecksburg-AG2s. Their chins were more rounded in their skulls, more bulbous. But their noses were flat rather than extended. Their mouths were about the size of humans, although they had sharper teeth. Their eyes were the same size as humans, although now that Maeve knew they had them, she could see their second set of eyelids and the unusual shape to their pupils. They resembled lizard eyes more than human eyes.

But Tatiana and her bodyguard looked human. They each had a normal skin tone, which was smooth. They had fingers and a normal musculature. And they had hair. The rest of the Draco did not.

Tatiana glanced back at Maeve as they headed through the hallways. "You're wondering how we are all the same species?"

Maeve started, not sure if the Draco could read their minds. If they could, that opened a whole new realm of horrible. "How did you know that?"

The terrifying woman's laughter filled the hallway. "You two are scientists. You are perpetually curious, are you not?"

She was right. And Maeve felt better.

"So how are you the same species? Your physical appearance is radically different," Greg asked.

"We are of royal blood. It allows us to be more adaptable to our surroundings. When we first arrived, we noticed that those of royal blood started to change. Our offspring began to show some characteristics of the native population. Of course, at first those offspring were simply killed. But it did not solve the problem. As a result, we allowed one child to live and monitored it. There is nothing different about the child except for how it looked. It could not pass for human, but it was close. In that case, the child was simply the same skin tone as the humans, although everything else remained perfectly Draco."

Maeve pictured an essentially pink Draco. It was not a nice image.

Tatiana continued. "In successive generations, we experimented, and the adaptations increased. Until finally, we appeared human. There is no way to distinguish between

Draco royalty and humans. This allowed us to interact with your society."

That was why it had taken them so long to retaliate against the humans. It wasn't because they were patient. It wasn't because they were waiting for the perfect time. It was because they had to wait until their disguises were in place.

"How long has that been?" Maeve asked.

Tatiana shrugged. "I am five hundred years old, give or take a few decades. I was one of the first fully human-looking Draco. It took longer than those with less royal blood to adapt, so I had to bide my time. But finally, everything fell into place. And now we are ready."

Maeve wanted to ask what they were ready for. But at the same time, she didn't want to know.

Greg, however, had no such reservations. "Ready for what?" He asked.

Tatiana smiled, a pure predatory smile. "Ready to take over."

CHAPTER 92

SOMEWHERE OVER THE WESTERN HALF OF THE UNITED STATES

Adam sat facing the back of the plane. Chris could read nothing in the man's face. But then, he'd never been able to read anything in the man's expression. Emotions just simply didn't cross his face often.

But he *had* seen Adam show emotions. He'd been kind to the triplets and Alvie. He'd connected with Penny in a way that none of the other adults had managed to.

Chris studied him now, not looking for emotions but looking for any telltale sign that gave away that he was a separate species. His hair was extremely blonde but not out of the realm of humanity. He had those chiseled cheeks that came from a body with very little fat, but again, that looked human too. The only thing that really set him apart, which came off more as a quirk than anything else, were the sunglasses.

"Take off your glasses," Chris said.

Adam paused for a moment, then reached up and removed them. His eyes were a blinding blue, startling in their clarity.

He blinked, and for just a split second, the pupils shifted, elongating.

Gasping, Norah took a step back. "Oh my God. How have you passed for human?"

But Chris knew it had been relatively easy. None of them had suspected who or what he was. And they'd spent hours with the man.

Even as Chris acknowledged that, his mind still rebelled at the thought of Adam as a Draco. "I don't understand. You helped us."

Adam nodded. "Yes. And I intend to continue helping you."

"But the Draco don't do that, do they?" Norah asked, her gaze shifting to each of the people around her.

"Why don't we just let Adam tell his story?" Jasper suggested.

Everyone's attention returned to Adam. Without the glasses, Chris could see emotion on the man's face. "I am one of the first human-looking Draco. There were two of us, myself and my sister. After generations of experiments and mixing of species, they finally created a Draco who could pass for human, all except for our eyes." Adam fell silent.

Walking over, Jasper patted him on the shoulder and said, "But something went wrong in this case. Twins were born, both looked human. They had been created by merging human DNA with Draco DNA. But they did not receive equal shares of each. The other twin looked human but was full Draco. Adam here also looked human but also has human emotions, even though his anatomy was that of a Draco."

Adam continued the tale. "They didn't detect the flaw until I was two. By the time I was four, they knew I was different. And the Draco don't like different."

"What did they do?" Norah asked.

"A test," Adam said softly. "To see which of the twins was more Draco. A fight to the death."

"When you were only four?" Sandra asked, aghast, anger clouding her words.

Although Adam shrugged, the tight set of his jaw gave away his anger. "The Draco do not coddle their young. Once they can walk, they are expected to fend for themselves in many ways."

"You lost the fight?" Chris asked.

Adam shook his head. "No. I beat my sister, but I refused to kill her. So the Draco hierarchy tried to kill me. I don't remember much. There was a water source near our base. Somehow I ended up in the water and was pulled away by the current. After the beating I took, I believe they thought I was dead."

"How did you survive, then?" Norah asked.

A small smile crept across Adam's face. "A family found me. They took me into their home. They raised me as their son, their brother. They showed me human kindness. They were good people."

"Where was this?" Norah asked.

"It was in the country that is currently called Norway," Adam said.

Chris frowned. Currently called? It was a strange choice of words. Unless … "Adam, how old are you?"

Adam hesitated, and Chris's body tensed. If he was reticent about answering that question, then Chris knew it was not something any of them wanted to hear.

"The Draco reach maturity at the age of twenty. And then we age incredibly slowly from that point on. I was born over 500 years ago."

Norah grabbed onto the back of a chair. "The Draco live for hundreds of years?"

"Not all of them. Most have a lifespan similar to humans,

although slightly longer. The soldiers that you have seen usually live no more than 100 to 130 years," Adam said.

"But the human ones live longer," Sandra said.

Adam nodded.

"Why is that? Human DNA can't possibly extend their lifespan," Chris said. He'd learned enough from Maeve about DNA to know at least that much.

"No. In fact, the worry was that the human DNA would shorten the lifespan," Adam said.

"Tell them about the other twins," Jasper said.

"*Other* twins?" Norah asked.

His voice grim, Jasper said, "A few children have been found over the years, in a similar state to Adam when he was found. None of them survived their injuries," Jasper said.

"They were Draco?" Norah asked.

Adam nodded, his jaw tight. "That's when we realized that twins were the only way that you could make a full Draco who looked human. If it was a single birth, the hybrid had too much human in them. But with twins, the human seems to vest in one twin while the other is left pure Draco."

"But why would that work? At least for Adam. He was a fraternal twin, not identical. Male and female are always fraternal," Norah said.

"Actually," Mike said, "that's not always the case. We've learned that male and female twins can be semi-identical. They are created from the same egg, but by different sperm. It's incredibly rare. There are only two documented cases. But we believe the egg is the critical factor in determining the breakdown of the human versus Draco genetics. It's pretty cool."

"So you're a bit of a medical unicorn," Norah said.

Adam shrugged. "I suppose so."

"But what makes them different? Why do they live longer?" Sandra asked.

Jasper cleared his throat. "The human-looking ones all have royal blood."

"You're royalty?" Norah asked.

Adam hesitated. "Yes. But I never would have ruled. Only the women in my family rule."

Chris stared at him, his words niggling in the back of his mind. "So your sister, your twin …"

His gaze meeting Chris's, Adam nodded. "Yes, she is the queen. She rules them all."

CHAPTER 93

EDMONDS, WASHINGTON

Maeve and the others were led through the underground halls and into a stairwell. As they rose, the walls became less damp and then smoother.

We must be going to the surface. Finally one of the Draco guards pulled open a door. Tatiana strode through. After a moment's hesitation, Maeve stepped through as well.

Bright sunlight hit her face, causing her to blink. It had never felt so good to see sun. Ahead of her, Tatiana put on sunglasses, even though they were not outside. Just like Adam. She started at the thought and took a longer look at Tatiana. Her and Adam did bear a striking resemblance to one another.

They were in some sort of small building. The rectangular room they were led to was about twenty by forty feet and had long windows along each side, which were open. A breeze blew through, bringing with it the smell of seawater and fish. A seagull squawked somewhere overhead. *We're on a coast.*

She looked longingly at the windows, but she knew escape was not an option.

Tatiana gestured to the middle of the room where there were couches and chairs set up. On a table in between them was a water pitcher. A bowl of fruit had been placed there as well. "Make yourselves comfortable. You may be here for a while."

Maeve exchanged a glance with Greg and then escorted the group over to the middle of the room. She didn't understand why Tatiana had brought them here. She had said that they were going to be bait, but they were inside. She scanned the walls for some sort of camera, but there didn't appear to be one. And the windows were up high on the wall, so no one would be able to look in and see them unless they were ten feet tall.

Maybe Tatiana had told someone where they were. But why then not keep them down in the dungeon where it would be harder to get to them? None of this made any sense. But she didn't want to ask Tatiana. Being out of the damp cell was a small blessing, and she wasn't going to do anything that might get them thrown back in there.

So she took a seat on the couch and poured glasses of water for everyone. She exchanged a worried glance with Greg as she handed him a glass. Then she sat back, waiting to see if anyone would take the bait.

CHAPTER 94

SOMEWHERE OVER THE WESTERN HALF OF THE UNITED STATES

The plane was quiet. Martin was still out cold. Jasper apparently packed a pretty good punch. According to the files that Penny had managed to find on Martin's computer, the Draco owned a series of warehouses on the edge of the state of Washington. But according to Martin's notes, any prisoners would be held in the tunnels underneath the warehouses.

Norah shivered at the thought. Apparently the Draco had difficulty with bright light, so they tried to stay in darker areas, at least the Draco that did not look human. Adam was sensitive to sun as well, but he seemed to be fine with sunglasses.

Adam had disappeared back into the cockpit after sharing his story. Jasper had explained how Adam had saved a young Wernher von Braun's life, and von Braun had kept him with him from that point on. He also told stories of Adam's other heroic deeds, trying to drive the point home that Adam was on their side.

Norah didn't need as much convincing as the others. She'd been as shocked as they were that Adam was a Draco, but at the same time, she'd known there was something different about him. She'd expected it to be more of a super soldier kind of thing than a renegade alien, but unlike Sandra, who stared at him with suspicious eyes, Norah knew Adam was on their side. Even before the story about his family—if you could call them that—she'd known that he would do whatever was necessary to protect Iggy. To protect the triplets and Alvie.

There was something almost old-fashioned in his loyalty.

She supposed the same was true for the Draco. They had unbending loyalty to their cause. She pictured one of the Draco leaping and landing on a soldier at the R.I.S.E. base. Norah hadn't even been able to raise her weapon in time before he'd ripped out the man's throat. And then he'd looked at her and smiled. She shivered, remembering that smile.

She'd heard about the belief people had that lizard people existed. She knew that polls had been done, and about four percent of the population believed that lizard people controlled the government. She thought they were crazy. Now she realized that they were just premature in their thinking. They didn't control the government yet, but they were aiming to.

Jasper appeared in the aisle. He pointed at the seat next to her. "Do you mind?"

"I guess not."

As he took a seat, she studied the man, trying to figure out what his angle was. She understood Sandra's, Chris's, even Adam's. But Jasper was a hard read.

"How you doing?" Jasper asked.

Norah just shrugged and looked out the window.

Jasper wasn't deterred. "I have to say, I thought it was pretty amazing how you managed to protect that Maldek. And the way he's bonded to you, I won't lie, I'm a little jealous. That guy loves you."

Grief welled up in Norah, and she took a shaky breath, trying to clamp down the emotions. She couldn't let the dam burst now.

With a wince, Jasper seemed to recognize her precarious position. "Sorry. Just thought you should know I think it's a good thing you did, protecting him."

Yeah, but not good enough, Nora thought.

Jasper settled back in his seat. "You know, there have been rumors about lizard people for eons. According to theosophists, they actually existed in the ancient times of Lemuria and Atlantis. They were called Dragon men and had an advanced civilization on the continent of Lemuria. Others, of course, speak of lizard people in UFOs who are violent and destructive. It seems to be a mixed bag. Do you know there was even an attempt in the twentieth century to excavate down to the lizard people's warren of tunnels?"

Norah looked over and raised an eyebrow.

"It was back in the 1930s," Jasper said with a smile. "A man by the name of George Warren Shufelt was convinced that lizard people were living underneath Los Angeles. Now, you have to remember that this was right after World War I and right before World War II, not to mention the Great Depression. The U.S. was in an unusual place.

"Anyway, he got all the correct permits and everything else and started to dig a tunnel right underneath Los Angeles. He believed the lizard people were linked to the Mayans and had a magical chemical that could burn through rock easily to create these tunnels. And of course, Shufelt believed there was gold in the tunnels." Jasper grinned.

Although interesting, Norah wasn't sure why he was telling her this. But at least it was distracting.

Jasper continued. "So Shufelt, in 1933, gets permission to

dig based in part on an old sheepskin map he had that purported to show where these tunnels are. Shufelt made it 250 feet down before the project was abandoned."

"So he never found anything?" Norah asked.

"Nope. Not a thing. But the interesting thing is if he had dug just a few feet to the left or a few feet to the right, he would have run into the tunnels. He dug a perfect hole right in the middle of them," Jasper said.

Norah frowned. "How's that possible?"

"I looked into that. There were reports of a very attractive blonde woman who helped him figure out where to dig. She had light, almost white-blonde hair, long."

Earlier, Jasper had explained about Tatiana Brecknoff, the leader or queen of the Draco. All the information on her had been on Martin's computer, so Norah knew where he was going. "You think it was Tatiana."

He nodded. "I think she's been manipulating things behind the scenes for decades. Setting herself up to take over one day."

"To take over what?" Norah asked.

"Everything."

Norah looked up as the cockpit door opened. Adam stepped out. He hesitated for a moment, noting Chris and Sandra sleeping, and made his way to Jasper and Norah, kneeling down in the aisle. "I received word from Penny. The strike has been green lit. They are going to take out the bunker in Edmonds."

"How long?" Jasper asked.

"Three hours."

Norah frowned. "When do we land?"

Adam paused for a moment. "Two hours."

Oh crap.

CHAPTER 95

EDMONDS, WASHINGTON

It had been two hours. Eight Draco guards were arranged along the perimeter of the room. None of them came close to where Maeve and the others sat in the center of the room. A breeze blew through the windows, for which Maeve was grateful. It made her feel free, even though she was so far from that it was laughable.

The Draco completely ignored them. The only time they paid attention to them was if they stepped beyond the boundaries of the sitting area.

So Maeve made sure no one did. As time wore on, everyone fell asleep except for Maeve and Greg.

Greg moved over next to her, keeping his voice low. "I don't get it. What are they waiting for? How exactly are we bait? I mean, if they're putting out some sort of call for ransom, there's no need to move us here."

Maeve just shook her head. She didn't understand it either. There was no reason to bring them to the surface. She glanced up at the windows. It seemed odd that they had left them all open. The fresh air made her feel as if there was a chance maybe she might get out of this, but she doubted they were giving them fresh air just so that they had a sense of hope.

"Why do you think they left those open?" Maeve nodded toward the windows.

"I don't know. Maybe they're stuck," Greg said.

"Really? All the resources the Draco have, and you think they left windows open because they couldn't figure out how to close them?" Maeve asked.

Greg grinned. "Doubtful, but it would be nice if they were that stupid, wouldn't it?"

She couldn't help but smile back. "Yeah, that would be nice."

The breeze once again ruffled her hair. She frowned as the wind tugged on the kids' clothes. She glanced up from window to window on either side of the building. "Scents."

"What's that?" Greg asked.

She turned slowly, her mind racing. "We've been thinking about this wrong. We keep thinking that this is aimed at humans. And it makes no sense for them to use us as bait this way for humans. But what if it's not humans they're trying to attract? What if it's one of the creatures from Area 51?"

Greg's mouth fell open. "No, not Hank or, God, one of the Blue Boys."

The shadow of a bird drifted across the window before disappearing quickly. Maeve shook her head, her eyes locked on the window where the shadow had been before focusing on Luke. "No, I don't think it's either of those that the Draco are trying to attract."

CHAPTER 96

Gray clouds greeted them as they touched down at a small airport outside of Edmonds. Chris stepped outside as a strong gust blew, bringing a crisp shot of air. He glanced toward the horizon. Darker gray clouds were moving in beyond the light gray, and they were moving fast. A storm would hit in another hour or two if they were lucky. *Just as the bomb hits.*

Chris felt like his skin had electricity running over it. He'd felt that way ever since he'd been informed about the countdown. They had a little under an hour to get to Edmonds, get their people out, and get far enough away to avoid getting caught in the blast. Chris didn't think it was going to be enough time. No one thought it would be enough time, but no one said so out loud.

Besides the news of the countdown, the flight had been uneventful. But prior to landing, they'd had to take care of one small problem: Martin. They couldn't bring him with them because they couldn't trust him. And they couldn't leave him behind for the same reason. Which left two options: killing him or figuring out a way to make sure he couldn't interfere.

They came up with a compromise, based on Sandra's earlier threat: They shoved him out the plane with a parachute. They'd flown out over the Pacific, twenty miles from shore. He would probably survive. And if he didn't, well, no one was going to lose sleep over it.

Chris hustled down the stairs and made his way to the cargo hold. Everyone pitched in, unloading the crates into the back of the SUVs Jasper had arranged for them. One was an old Durango and the other was a Land Cruiser. Both had seen better days.

"These things run, right?" Norah asked as she pushed a crate farther into the SUV.

"Don't let their appearance fool you. They have been tried and tested." Jasper pushed another crate into the back.

Norah gave the rusted bumper a disbelieving look. "Uh-huh."

Chris, however, appreciated the disheveled appearance of both SUVs. It would help them blend in better than some brand-new, top-of-the-line automobiles.

And when Chris hopped behind the wheel and turned the engine, it purred like a racecar. He glanced over at Jasper in the passenger seat.

"Told ya." Jasper grinned.

"Yes, you're wonderful," Mike grumbled from the back seat.

Chris looked past Jasper at Norah, who was at the wheel of the other SUV. Adam was riding shotgun, while Sandra was in the back. Chris was a little concerned about Sandra. Adam's revelation had shaken all of them, but Sandra kept watching him. Chris hoped it didn't cause any problems

A few minutes later, they were on Highway 99 South, heading toward Edmonds. The wind was pushing hard, and occasionally Chris would have to correct to make up for the gusts that seemed to be trying to shove them off the road. It was late in the afternoon. People trying to get home early from work were already on the road. But as they exited the highway onto 196th Street, the traffic eased, and especially once they neared the business district, where the warehouses were located.

Five miles from their destination, they pulled over into the parking lot of a truck stop. It was a ten-minute drive, probably less, to the warehouse from here. Now was where things got dicey. They would need to move quickly. None of them had any doubts that the Draco would have security in place and eyes on the waterfront and the building surrounding them. They needed to go in hard and fast.

Chris pulled up the map of the area on his tablet. He quickly shuffled through the exterior shots to bring up the layout of the labyrinth of tunnels that Penny had forwarded them. She'd gotten them from Martin's files. Apparently Martin had sent one of his agents in on a suicide mission. Martin's people had then plotted out the tunnels based on the doomed agent's recordings.

We should have shoved him out of the plane without a parachute, Chris thought before he pointed to the entrance underneath the middle warehouse. "Okay. There's only one entrance from here. Some of the other tunnels branch off, eventually leading to city streets. Those connect with the sewers."

Norah leaned forward. "Why are we going through those?"

"There's no direct access to the tunnels, which is where Penny believes our people will be kept. It would take too long to get to them, and by then the Draco could make their escape," Chris explained.

"I've already set up blocks for each of those entrances," Jasper said.

"What kind of blocks?" Sandra asked.

"I paid some of my contacts to park right on top of them. They won't be getting those entrances open anytime soon. My people will stay there until we've given them the all-clear," Jasper said.

"So how are we getting in?" Sandra asked.

"We have to assume that they're going to have armed guards on duty. We're not going to slowly take out the guards. We don't have time for that, and even if we did, it increases the likelihood that they'll know we're there," Chris said.

"So we're sneaking in?" Norah asked.

Chris shook his head. "No. Stealth isn't an option. We're going in and they're going to know that we're there, which means we need to move. You see anything move, you blast it. There is no time for second-guessing. Our people are in there, and we are going to get them out. Jasper and Mike, secure the perimeter. The rest of us will be going on the rescue."

Norah met Chris's eyes and flicked a glance at Jasper and Mike. He knew she didn't trust them, but at the same time no one else would be willing to stay up on the surface when their loved ones were below. Adam would probably agree, but Chris wanted him down below. If he had to choose only one person to take in with him, no offense to anyone else, but it would be Adam, Draco or not. Their chances of successfully getting everyone out greatly increased with the man's presence.

Chris went over the details for another few minutes until finally he stopped and looked at everyone. "Any questions?"

Everyone shook their heads. Chris picked up the tablet, shutting it off. "Then let's suit up. It's time to get to work."

CHAPTER 97

The waiting was growing intolerable. Maeve wanted to pace around and stretch out her legs and her arms. But each time she moved, she felt the Draco's eyes slide over her. She felt like a mouse in a cage while the snake slithered around outside, watching.

The Draco seemed to be growing more uncomfortable. Maeve noticed that they stuck to the darkest parts of the room, moving when the sun shifted.

They really didn't like the light. It was a small weakness, but it made her feel better to note it.

Luke, Alvie, and Snap all opened their eyes at the same time, jolting on the couch. Maeve frowned. Something was wrong. A shadow wafted across the windows.

Maeve looked up, wondering if it was another bird.

Not a bird. Sammy, Alvie told her silently.

Maeve had to swallow her gasp. Sammy. She was careful not to look at Alvie. *Are you sure?*

Yes.

Why is he here?

To set us free.

Greg looked around, and then his mouth fell open. Alvie must have clued him in. Reaching over, he rubbed Iggy's back, who was still sleeping in Luke's lap. Iggy opened his eyes lazily and then stretched. He caught sight of Greg and gave him a small grin before his smile disappeared as he took in their surroundings.

The shadow passed over the windows up above. Iggy hopped on the back of the couch. His movement stirred the Draco into action, and they were now staring up as well.

Keeping his voice extremely low, Greg leaned closer to Maeve. "What do we do?"

Maeve shook her head. She had no idea. She didn't like the idea of being used for bait. But she couldn't think of any way to warn Sammy without endangering the rest of them.

Apparently Iggy didn't share the same quandary. "Ig! Ig! Ig!"

His cries rang out through the warehouse. One of the Draco near them let out a snarl. Greg grabbed Iggy and pulled him into his chest. "Shh, shh."

Iggy wants to help. He doesn't want the Sentinel to be hurt.

Taking Alvie's hand, Maeve squeezed it. Snap crawled over Alvie and into Maeve's lap. Maeve rubbed her back, feeling the small tremors run through her. Once again, she felt helpless. Helpless to help those with her and helpless to help the creature coming to try and save them.

Maeve looked at the doors and the windows, trying to figure out where Sammy would enter. Or if he even would. Maybe he would just stay outside until an opportunity presented itself.

A slight spraying of paint chips from the ceiling was all the warning they had. Sammy crashed through the roof of the warehouse, dropping to the floor.

CHAPTER 98

Sammy landed next to the couch, his wings curled around him. Up close, he was even more intimidating than from a distance. His wings looked sharp and impenetrable. His skin was a dark maroon color. His shoulders were easily four feet across, not including his wingspan.

He looked up, his gaze sliding over all of them on the couch before he looked to the creatures lining the room. He opened his wings to a full twelve-foot wingspan as he stood and let out a bellow that shook the windows. Maeve covered her ears at the pressure of that scream.

The Draco cowered against the walls at the sound. But they didn't stay down long before they attacked. She grabbed Alvie and Snap, pulling them to the floor and covering them. Greg did the same to Luke. He reached for Iggy, but Iggy bounded out of his grasp, flinging himself at one of the Draco sneaking up behind Sammy.

Iggy plunged one of his talons into the creature's knee, and it let out a bloodcurdling scream. He used that talon as a lever to swing himself up, plunging the second talon into the creature's groin before climbing up its chest and plunging both into its eyes.

Three Draco jumped on Sammy at the same time. Sammy's wings spread out, flinging them away. One crashed into the couch, shoving it toward Maeve and Greg.

Greg grabbed Luke around the waist, still staying over him. "We need to move."

Maeve didn't need to be told twice. She hauled Snap into her arms and grabbed Alvie. Alvie pulled away, sprinting toward Sammy.

"Alvie, no!" Maeve yelled.

Ignoring her, he leapt off the back of the couch, his foot slamming into the cheek of one of the Draco, who had his arm extended, ready to slash at Sammy's back. The Draco wobbled, stumbling to the side as Alvie fell to the ground and rolled to his feet.

Alvie dove to the ground as Sammy whirled around, his wings coming within inches of Alvie's head before the talons on the edge of his wings plunged into the Draco. With a vicious yank, Sammy yanked the talons out. Blood pooled on the floor as the Draco dropped to his knees before collapsing face first on the ground.

A group of six more Draco, Tatiana, and her bodyguard behind them rushed into the room. Each of the Draco held one of their Tasers. They each released the prongs. Two missed, but one came incredibly close to Alvie.

The other four sets slammed into Sammy. Electricity rolled over his skin as he arched his back with a scream.

The group of six aimed six additional sets of prongs into the now kneeling Sammy. He swiped out with his wings, but they were too far away. He struggled to get to his feet, but it was no use. He dropped to the ground.

Alvie! Come back. You can't help him now.

Alvie looked at Maeve and then hurried toward Sammy,

crawling in front of him and spreading his arms wide, as if to protect him.

Maeve shoved Snap into Greg's arms. She sprinted across the room as the Draco approached. They had their Tasers out, aimed at Alvie. Maeve dove, wrapping Alvie in her arms and rolling him away. A Taser just missed her thigh.

She hugged him to her as he trembled. Or maybe she was the one trembling. She couldn't really tell. Alvie struggled to get back to Sammy.

No, Alvie. Now's not the time. We can't fight like this. There's too many of them. You'll only get killed. We need to wait, Alvie. We need to wait.

Alvie looked up at her, hope dimming in his eyes. She kissed his forehead as the Draco approached Sammy, who was barely moving. "I'm sorry," she whispered.

Iggy slammed into one of the Draco that moved near him. His hit sent the Draco flying.

"Bring that thing down!" Tatiana ordered. The Draco reloaded, shooting at Iggy as he bounced along the floor, practically running up the wall before grabbing onto the rafters up ahead. Iggy flipped himself over so he was standing on the rafters, peering down at them.

Maeve looked at the Draco as they snarled up at Iggy. They were going to kill him. "Go, Iggy! Run!"

He took one last look as bolts of electricity jolted up toward him. Then he scrambled across the rafter and disappeared through the window. Maeve smiled, watching him go. At least one of them would be free.

The click of heels moved quickly toward her. Tatiana glared, her mouth a thin line. "You think you're so brave, encouraging him to escape. But you'll pay for that." She backhanded Maeve across the face.

The force of the blow flung Maeve to the ground, the whole side of her face on fire.

"Maeve!" Greg struggled to get to her.

Tatiana pointed a long finger at him. "Don't."

She walked to Maeve, grabbed her by the back of her hair, and yanked her to her feet. Tears sprang to Maeve's eyes. "Time to earn your keep, doctor."

She shoved Maeve into the waiting arms of one of the guards. The guard looked down at her, showing its teeth in the facsimile of a smile. Saliva dripped onto Maeve's face, and she turned her head, catching Greg's gaze. The look of terror on his face said everything that needed to be said.

We're dead.

CHAPTER 99

The talons from one of the guards that grabbed Maeve cut into her arms. She swallowed down the cry, not wanting to worry any of the others. But Greg looked at her in alarm. She shook her head, not wanting him to say anything.

The Draco hustled them out of the room and down the stairs. Tatiana led the way after ordering the six that had taken down Sammy to bind him before bringing him down to the tunnels.

Maeve couldn't be sure, but she thought they were bringing them to a different part of the tunnels than where they had been before. The Draco yanked her forward as they reached the second level. Greg was being pulled unceremoniously behind her.

Alvie let out a little cry. Maeve struggled to look behind her. Alvie, Snap, and Luke were being led farther down the stairs to another level. "Where are you taking them?"

"That's of no concern to you. In fact, they are of no concern to you. Not anymore." Tatiana led them down the hall as Alvie's voice faded.

I love you, Alvie. I love you, Snap. I'll find you. I'll find you.

Tatiana stopped halfway down the hall and turned into a room, flicking on lights as she entered. The Draco holding Maeve shoved her in. She crashed to the ground, her knees and palms hitting the rock floor painfully. Greg was tossed to the ground next to her.

The room looked like it had been hewn straight out of the rock face. The floor was relatively flat, but the walls still had sharp, uneven edges. Bright fluorescent lights had been stretched across the rectangular space. Lab equipment had been lined up on long steel tables.

Maeve looked in disbelief at the centrifuge and genetic sequencing equipment. It was such a contrast with the primitive nature of the room.

Twirling her arms out wide, Tatiana said, "How do you like your new lab? This is where you will be conducting your research on that thing upstairs."

Getting to her feet, Maeve wiped her palms on the side of her jeans. "I'm not doing anything until I know Alvie, Snap, and Luke are safe."

"Oh, really?" Tatiana waved a hand toward her. One of the Draco stormed over to her. Maeve backed up, but there was nowhere to go as she crashed into one of the tables. The Draco picked her up by the throat. Her feet dangled in the air. The Draco began to squeeze her neck slowly.

"Let her go!" Greg yanked on the Draco's arm but to no avail. A second one grabbed Greg, pushing him up against the wall with a thud that left him looking dazed. That Draco's hand circled around his throat as well.

Maeve scrambled, her feet finding no purchase. She grabbed the Draco's hand, trying to pull it from her neck, but it was as if the hand was made of iron. She couldn't get it to budge, not even an inch. Spots began to appear before her eyes.

Tatiana walked in between the two of them. "You two seem to be under the mistaken impression that you have some sort of rights or power here. You do not. You will do what I say. You will do it when I say so. If you fail to, you are of no use to me. Your young ones will be safe so long as you follow my commands." Tatiana took a step back. The Draco released Maeve and Greg.

Falling to the floor, Maeve gasped for breath. Greg crumpled to the floor next to her. Blood dripped down the back of his head.

Tatiana smiled. "Now, I will give you some time to familiarize yourself with the lab. And then you can get to work."

CHAPTER 100

The warehouse district was quiet. Norah made the left turn, following Chris. She was amped up, her blood thrumming. She hadn't felt like this since her military days, before going on a mission. She'd always feel that mixture of fear and excitement, both warring to take over.

But this wasn't any other mission. The time the military had sent her on missions, she had focused on the job at hand. There was no personal stake involved beyond her own life and that of her fellow soldiers. But here the stakes couldn't get more personal. Everyone going into this thing had a personal stake.

And if Agaren's warning was right, the stakes were never higher. The whole world would pay the price if they did not succeed.

But no pressure.

Norah took a breath, trying to calm her racing heart. To her left was a large white truck pulled up to a loading dock. Two people in white overalls were pushing dollies loaded with boxes into it. Apparently this really was a working business area and not just a front.

Norah knew they couldn't warn these people without tipping off the Draco, but she worried what would happen when the time came to destroy the Draco's location. Would R.I.S.E. actually warn the people in the surrounding area? Was there a way to do it without letting the Draco know?

Here they were, racing to save the people they loved, but someone loved these people, people who were just going about their everyday lives. Shouldn't they warn them and give them a chance as well?

That was the one part of the military that Norah had hated, the calculation. How much collateral damage was too much? Was the life of two soldiers worth more than the life of three civilians? Was taking a particular location back worth the cost in blood and lives?

As a soldier, she'd let other people make those decisions. She'd been *required* to. This mission was the second time in her life she'd gone against orders. First had been when she'd refused to kill Iggy. She'd let him go free. And while that had opened a Pandora's box of problems, she did not regret it. Meeting Iggy was bar none the greatest moment of her life.

Now, R.I.S.E. had ordered all of them to stand down, to essentially wait. And R.I.S.E. currently controlled all aspects of the military. They *were* the authority. But Norah along with everyone else was ignoring their orders. They were going to get their people out or die trying.

Norah just hoped it wasn't the latter.

Sandra sat quietly in the back of the SUV, her gaze shifting from window to window as she took in all the activity around them, or lack thereof. Norah wondered what she was thinking. None of this was easy for Norah, but for Sandra, she'd been thrown in the deep end. The existence of aliens had been thrown in her face at the same time as she was on a desperate journey to save her son. And now that son was in jeopardy from a whole new group of aliens more frightening than any

Norah had ever seen. Sandra was made of incredibly tough stuff to still be moving forward.

Or maybe it was just an example of how much a mother would do to save her child.

"What's that?" Jasper leaned forward from the passenger seat, peering up through the windshield.

Norah followed his gaze. "What?"

Frowning, Jasper continued his scanning of the rooftops. "I could've sworn I saw something up there, along the roof." He grabbed the radio and clicked on the mic. "Guys, you need to keep an eye out. I think there might be something or someone up on the rooftop."

"Where?" Mike asked over the radio.

"East side. I can't be sure, but I could have sworn I saw movement. Just stay vigilant," Jasper warned.

"Roger," Mike replied.

Norah shifted her gaze from the street in front of her to the rooftop above. Jasper didn't seem the type to spook easily. Although Norah supposed it could be something as simple as a pigeon.

The car was tense as all three occupants shifted their gaze, trying to figure out what it was that Jasper had seen. No one spoke for a few minutes, and finally Jasper sat back. "Maybe I was wrong. But I could've sworn—"

A thump sounded from the roof of the SUV. Norah slammed on the brakes. Something rolled toward the front. Each of them had their weapon in their hand a second before a small green face peeked over the windshield.

Scrambling from the car, Norah practically fell in her haste. Iggy leapt from the roof and into her arms, his whole body shaking. Norah held him tight, crooning to him and feeling relief crashed through her. "I've got you. I've got you."

CHAPTER 101

Everyone was happy to see Iggy. And not just for Iggy's sake. The fact that he was here meant that Penny's information was correct. The rest of the group had to be nearby.

Of course, Iggy couldn't actually tell them anything about where they were being held.

"Ig, ig, ig." Iggy leaned forward on the hood of Norah's SUV, as if trying to convey something. But Chris would be damned if any of them could figure out what it was.

Norah explained to Iggy the plan, showing him on the map where they were going. Iggy nodded his head quickly multiple times, jumping up and down on the roof. "Ig! Ig!"

Chris looked at the strange little guy and couldn't believe he was about to question him. "Is Maeve there?"

Iggy nodded. Chris ran through everyone else who they believed the Draco had taken. Iggy nodded for each of the names. Sandra gave a little small gasp when he nodded at Luke's name, her hand flying to her mouth.

She took a step back and then walked to the back of the SUV, taking a seat on the bumper. Chris looked at each person in the group. "Okay. That's as good a confirmation as we're going to get. So everyone be prepared and keep an eye out. Let's get going."

"Ig!" Iggy thumped on the hood of the car.

Stopping, Chris tilted his head toward him.

"Ig, ig, ig, ig, ig."

"I'm sorry, Iggy. I don't understand," Chris said shaking his hand.

Iggy stood straight and held out his arms and then swayed from side to side, like he was flying. Sandra, who'd returned to the group, looked shocked. "Sammy? Is Sammy there?"

A smile on his face, Iggy nodded

"Is he helping the Draco?" Jasper asked.

Iggy let out a snarl.

Jasper put his hands up. "Okay, I guess he's not helping the Draco. Is he helping our people?"

Iggy hesitated. "Ig?"

Chris looked around the group. No one seemed to understand what that meant.

Norah leaned forward. "Did he try to help?"

Iggy nodded, and then Iggy's face drooped.

"Is he hurt?" Norah asked.

Iggy nodded again.

Norah looked at Chris. "Looks like there might be one extra hostage."

CHAPTER 102

MAXWELL AIR FORCE BASE, ALABAMA

The hangar was a buzz of activity. R.I.S.E. had taken over one of the hangars to use as their base of operations and command center. Tilda nodded at the attaché from the National Security Agency as she made her way to the office at the back of the hangar, leaning heavily on the cane Pearl had found for her. But she made sure to keep her shoulders straight and her eyes wide.

And she also made sure there was no sign of the pain that was roaring through her body. The doctors had offered her heavy painkillers, but she couldn't take them. If she did, her thinking would be muddled, and she could not risk that. Ibuprofen was as strong a painkiller as she was on, and she was downing them by the handfuls.

The bombing raids were set to go in twenty minutes. She needed to get to the office and get some quiet for just a minute. The gravity of the situation wasn't lost on her. There were scientists up in the Arctic who would most likely lose their lives, not to mention the wildlife. They were going to try to keep the casualties to a minimum. The bombs were bunker busters, so they should be able to go underground and set off there. But casualties were unavoidable.

The bigger problem was going to be the bomb in Edmonds. She had people on standby to empty out the warehouses nearby, but they couldn't do it until the very last second. Luckily it was toward the end of the day, and hopefully most people would already have headed home. At night, the warehouse district was quiet. But once again, she couldn't guarantee that there wouldn't be casualties.

Pearl was sitting behind the desk and quickly got up as Tilda stepped into the room. She walked past Tilda and closed the door. With a quick glance outside, Pearl closed the Venetian blinds. Tilda all but fell onto the couch by the windows. "God, I feel awful."

Pearl sat down carefully next to her. "Can I do anything? Can I get you anything?"

Tilda shook her head and then gritted her teeth against the motion. Her head felt like it had been cleaved in two. She didn't really remember much about getting injured. Her security detail had met her at the apartment. She'd been on the phone with her top aides arranging for emergency evacuations.

They'd only been in the apartment for a few minutes, but by the time they had left the building, all hell had already broken loose. The Draco had overrun the base. Even for Tilda, the sight of them had been a shock. She had read reports on them over the years and seen grainy pictures, but seeing them in the flesh was a whole new ballgame.

Her security detail had fallen in around her, hustling her through the streets. Tilda had ordered them to stop when three of her soldiers had been attacked by Draco. Two had peeled off to go to the aid of the soldiers while the others insisted on getting Tilda to the safe zone.

But then a Draco had appeared on top of a jeep, letting out a roar. Her security detail had opened fire, but the bullets had done nothing to stop the creature. He leapt at them. His first swipe had all but decapitated the leader of her security. His next move flung the other security guards around like they were toys.

Then the jeep the creature had been standing on had exploded. Tilda had been thrown clear and knocked unconscious. All she remembered was looking up and seeing parts of the Draco before everything went black.

But the building near her had been demolished in the blast and crumbled around her.

She'd been told that Adam had found her. She wasn't surprised by that at all. She knew he would always find her.

"Is the room clean?" Tilda asked quietly, partly to avoid any recording devices and partly because any louder made her head ache.

Pearl nodded. "I had the room swept. There were two recording devices, both CIA issue."

Martin, you bastard. "Have you heard from Adam?"

"No. But they should have arrived by now," Pearl said.

Tilda knew that giving Adam the okay for the mission was dangerous. Dangerous for Adam and all the people that were with him if they failed. And dangerous for Tilda if anyone ever learned that she had okayed it. Which was why she'd had to make it appear that she was against it.

The next few hours would change the course of the world. If they were successful in their bombing campaign, they would wipe out the Draco, and they would hopefully be able to keep the world from knowing that they ever existed. But if they failed, then the world would be overrun within a matter of months.

And if R.I.S.E. had been unable to stop a group of Draco on their base, the rest of the world didn't stand a chance.

Tilda wanted to reroute some satellites to get herself a view of the warehouse in Edmonds, but that could be problematic. She couldn't go through the normal channels. "Is she back there?"

"Yes."

Tilda steeled herself and then stood up, holding on to the edge of the couch for a moment as the room swam. Pearl jumped to her feet. "Hold on. Hold on."

She ran to the back of the office and grabbed a wheelchair that had been hidden next to a large office cabinet. She hurried it over to Tilda. "I know you probably won't like this, but I thought—"

With a grimace, Tilda grabbed onto the arms of the wheelchair and slowly lowered herself in. "You are an angel. But let's make sure no one sees me in this thing, okay?"

Positioning herself behind Tilda, Pearl quickly wheeled her to the back of the room. There was an unmarked door back there. It was normally used as a supply closet, but Tilda had commandeered it for a different reason.

Pearl scooted around the side of Tilda's wheelchair and pushed the door open before wheeling Tilda inside. Penny didn't even look up from within her nest of computer towers and monitors. Pearl wheeled Tilda around the monitors to the open area at the back.

Tilda cleared her throat. "Penny, do you have eyes on our people in Edmonds?"

One of the monitors on the second row flashed to the scene. On screen were two warehouses sitting on a waterfront. There was nothing moving.

"Has anything happened?" Tilda asked.

"The angel went in. He didn't come out. Iggy did." Penny didn't look up from her keyboard as she spoke.

"What about our people? Are they on site?" Tilda asked.

The monitor flickered again. This time it displayed two

SUVs driving in between warehouses that looked similar to the one on the first screen.

Heart racing, Tilda took a small step forward, wincing as pain lanced through her. "How long until they arrive?"

"Two minutes."

CHAPTER 103

The warehouses whipped by. Chris pressed down on the accelerator. He didn't know what they were going to face in there, but he did know they didn't have much time. The clock on the dashboard glowed, illuminating the fact that they only had fifteen minutes to get in, get their people, and get a safe distance from the bombing.

Sweat beaded along his back as he crushed the accelerator down a little harder, only partly because of the deadline. They didn't know the numbers they would face, but they did know the type of opponent they would be going up against. Each of them had special suits lined with Kevlar. Jasper had dug them up somewhere.

And more importantly, each one had lights on their shoulders that simulated daylight. They were hoping that would give them at least a slight edge if it came down to hand-to-hand.

They were as prepared as they were going to be. And even if they hadn't been, Chris would still be going in. Sandra would still be going in. Even Norah, while Iggy was back with her, was committed to getting everyone back.

He flicked a gaze at his rearview mirror. Norah shifted, coming around his side. They raced side by side toward the warehouse. Penny had indicated which one Sammy had crashed into.

Chris shut off all emotions. He needed to focus on what needed to be done. Gripping the steering wheel, he took calming breaths, trying to slow his heart rate, and in his head he imagined the steps that would happen as soon as he stopped the car.

Seconds later, he was slamming on the brakes. Adam bolted from the car before he was even fully stopped. Two human-looking Draco stepped out from the building. Adam shot each of them. Large gaping holes appeared in their chests. Chris nodded. Good. The hollow points worked. At least they had that in their favor. Sandra was out of the car almost as quickly as Adam and followed him into the warehouse.

Jasper and Mike split up, each going around the side of the building to make sure there were no surprises around back. Chris went through the door, with Norah right behind him. He took in the scene at a glance.

Sammy lay on the ground, straps holding down his arms and legs. Adam fought two Draco hand-to-hand. And he was winning.

Sandra took cover behind a couch and took aim at the Draco that lined the room. Anyone who got close was mowed down. She flicked a glance at Norah and Chris. "They're coming from that door there. That's where we need to go."

As if to prove her point, two more Draco appeared through the doorway. Chris took down one while Norah took down the second. They sprinted across the room, jumping over the two fallen Draco, each taking a side of the doorway.

Chris peered in. "Clear."

He flicked on the lights on his shoulders. Norah did the same, illuminating the dark space in front of them. There was a set of stairs leading down. Iggy swung in through the doorway and started down the stairs. Chris followed him with Norah at his back.

Iggy led them three levels down. He stopped at the landing, glancing back at them before hurrying through the darkened doorway. Chris took a breath, pausing for just a second before he followed.

CHAPTER 104

Maeve's throat still ached. The cut on the back of Greg's head was luckily superficial. But head wounds tended to bleed a lot, so the back of his shirt was now discolored with blood. Maeve had held pressure to the cut until it stopped bleeding, but there was no way to bandage it without shaving part of his head, and Greg had put his foot down on that.

Now the two of them were exploring the lab, looking at all the equipment. There were two Draco just outside the open door. Maeve wasn't sure if they could understand her and Greg or not, but they kept their voices low just in case.

"This is all top-of-the-line equipment," Maeve said with awe. The genetic sequencer alone was making her knees weak. It had taken her two years of requisitioning to get her own at the lab, and this one had a lot more bells and whistles than hers did.

Flipping open the lid of the centrifuge, Greg peered in before closing it. "I don't get it. Why do they need us? I mean, they have to be technologically advanced, right?"

"I'm guessing they're aware of our unique areas of knowledge. We do specialize in rather unusual biological specimens," Maeve said

Greg nodded, conceding the point. "I suppose that's true."

After a glance toward the door, Maeve lowered her voice even more. "Do you think the kids are all right?"

"I don't think they want to hurt them if that's what you mean," Greg said.

"But you do think they want them for a purpose," she said.

Frowning, Greg nodded slowly. "Yeah. I get them wanting Snap and Alvie, but I still don't understand Luke. What could they possibly want with him?"

Thinking of what she knew of the young boy, Maeve said, "It has to be his connection to Sammy. That's the only thing I can think of."

Turning to her, Greg's frown only deepened. "I don't really get that. I mean, how does Sammy fit into all of this?"

Maeve nodded at all the equipment. "I'm guessing we're going to be in charge of figuring that out in the not-too-distant future."

A crash and a thud sounded from the ceiling. Dust and dirt broke free of the rock ceiling above them and trickled down to one of the lab tables. Maeve looked up in surprise. "What on Earth was that?"

The two Draco by the door yanked the door closed with a slam before running away. Greg looked at Maeve with a grin. "I'm really hoping that's the cavalry."

Then Greg pointed to the door. "Maeve, look." It was slightly ajar.

The lock on the door hadn't caught. Maeve couldn't believe it, but she wasn't going to look a gift horse in the mouth. Greg was of the same mind. The two of them perched next to the door and then slowly opened it, peering into the hall. It was empty.

"Hold on a sec." Maeve grabbed Greg's arm as he started

out of the room. She shut off the lights in the lab and gave them a few seconds for their eyes to adjust to the dark. The hallway was much darker. She wanted to give their eyes a chance so that they would be able to see.

"Okay, let's go." Maeve led the way down the hall, heading back toward the stairwell. A sane person would take the stairs and head up to the surface and ask for help. But there was no chance Maeve was leaving Alvie, Snap, and Luke down there. She turned to Greg. "I'm going for the kids. Do you want to—"

Greg cut her off before she could even finish the sentence. "If you think I am letting you face them alone or that I'm leaving those kids behind while I run to safety, then you don't know me well at all."

She squeezed his hand in gratitude. She was about to step into the stairwell when the sound of pounding feet reached her. She reared back, keeping the door propped open a little so she could see.

Four Draco sprinted up the stairs. Maeve held her breath, knowing that even if they tried to reach the lab, they'd never make it in time, but the Draco didn't stop. They headed to the upper levels.

Greg gave her a nervous smile. "Well, I guess it's now or never."

She opened the door and quickly ran down the stairs. She peered into the hallway on the next level, but pounding feet forced her into the hallway without getting much of a look. Greg slipped in the door behind her. It had just closed shut behind him when two more Draco sprinted up from the stairs and continued on to the surface levels.

"It looks like all the excitement is happening upstairs," Greg whispered.

Maeve recognized the level they were on. It was where the cells had been. She hurried down the hall. Part of her thought that she should move slowly, but at the same time there were no places to hide. If they were seen, that would be the end of it. So speed was their friend right now.

She sprinted down the hall and then turned to the left before coming to an intersection. She started to go right, but Greg shook his head, grabbing her arm. "It's straight."

"Are you sure?" She asked.

Greg pointed to a rock face sticking out from the wall. "I'm sure. That nose looks like my uncle Ralph's. I noticed it when we were led upstairs."

Not one to doubt Uncle Ralph's nose, Maeve sprinted forward. At the next intersection, she turned right. And the whole time she was running, she tried to reach out to Alvie. *Alvie? Alvie, where are you?*

There was no answer until they crossed the next intersection.

Here. We're here.

Maeve focused on the sense of him and hurried down the hall. *Are there any guards near you?*

No. They all left.

Which made sense. The kids wouldn't be able to get out of the cell. Maeve wasn't even sure how she and Greg would get them out of it, but that was a problem once they got there.

She rounded the corner, and at the end of the hall she could see the cell they'd been held in earlier. She sprinted forward and looked in the small window. Alvie stood right at the door, looking up at her with Snap in his arms. Luke was on his other side, his whole body vibrating with fear.

"We're here. We're here," Maeve said.

Greg nudged Maeve aside. "Let me get the lock."

He pulled a small container from his pocket. "Guys? I need you all to get to the far end of the cell, okay? Get away from the door."

Greg gave them a few seconds and then sprayed the door handle with the liquid. Then he stood up and squirted the locking mechanism above the handle. Slowly the metal began to disintegrate.

Greg grinned. "Highly concentrated hydrochloric acid. Like I said, that lab was fully stocked."

As soon as the handle was gone, Greg kicked in the door. It flew back against the wall with a resounding thud. Maeve rushed past him to the other side of the room and dropped to her knees, pulling Alvie and Snap into her arms. She peered up at Luke, who was rocking back and forth in place.

She wasn't sure what to do to comfort him. Alvie reached out and took Luke's hand. He stared up at him for a long moment before Luke's trembling lessened.

"Okay, this is very sweet, but we really need to go." Greg shifted from foot to foot by the door.

Maeve stood with Snap in her arms. "Alvie, can you hold Luke's hand?"

Yes.

"Stay close to us," Maeve ordered. "Greg, it looks like you're in the lead."

Greg winced. "Great, that's just great."

He glanced out the door and then quickly headed back the way they had come. Maeve, with Snap cuddled to her chest, hurried after him. Each time they reached an intersection, Maeve tensed, but they didn't see anyone. The place seemed abandoned. She strained to hear any noises, but there was nothing.

By the time they reached the third intersection, she was thinking that maybe they might at least be able to get to the surface without any problems. "Okay," she whispered to Greg, "let's head to the upper levels. If there's anybody that's coming down the stairs going up them, we'll duck into one of the levels that we passed, okay?"

"Sounds like a plan," Greg said, a tremor in his voice.

They passed the last turn before turning into the hallway that led to the stairwell.

"There you are, doctors. We've been looking everywhere for you." Tatiana stood at the end of the hall, four Draco fanned out behind her.

CHAPTER 105

Chris flattened himself against the wall next to the door on the third floor. He peeked inside, his heart rate spiking when he caught sight of the four Draco at the end of the hall.

But then his heart lifted at the presence he felt in his mind. *Chris?*

I'm here, Alvie. I'm here. He ducked his head back into the doorway and looked at Norah. "They're here," he whispered. "Four Draco."

Norah nodded and then stepped through the doorway, dropping to a knee and lining up her shot. Iggy burst through the door before Chris or Norah could say a word.

Iggy was almost at the Draco. "Iggy, down!" Norah yelled.

Iggy dropped to the floor, lying flat. Greg threw himself over Luke and Alvie, pushing them to the ground. Norah took out the Draco on the far left. Chris dropped to a knee next to her and took out the one on the far right.

Then there were two. And the blonde woman that Chris hadn't seen before. She'd been hidden by the towering Draco.

The two Draco sprinted down the hallway toward them.

Iggy burst from the floor, his talons extended. They plunged into the chest of the Draco on the left. Then Iggy dragged his talons down, eviscerating the creature. It screamed out in pain.

Iggy flipped backward, landing on the creature's shoulders before plunging his talons into the creature's neck.

At the same time, Chris and Norah aimed at the other Draco, dropping him with two shots to the chest.

"Run!" Maeve yelled. Greg picked up Luke and sprinted with him down the hall. Snap leapt from Maeve's arms, running behind them as Alvie took her hand.

Maeve took off as well, but the blonde woman darted in front of her. She grabbed her by the throat, holding her up high. "Not so fast, Dr. Leander."

CHAPTER 106

Alvie, Snap, and Greg, along with a screaming Luke, sprinted down the hall toward Norah and Chris. Norah kept one eye on them, but her focus was on Tatiana at the end of the hall. The woman held Maeve up by the neck, keeping Maeve between her and Norah. "Do you have a shot?"

"No," Chris growled.

Dammit. Norah wasn't sure what to do. She had no shot. The bomb would be coming in at any moment. They needed to get out of here. But at the same time, everything in her rebelled at the idea of leaving Maeve behind. And she knew for a fact that Chris would not leave her.

Adam bolted into the hallway and sprinted past her. "Ricochet."

"What did he—" Chris started to ask.

Norah tucked the handle of the rifle tighter to her shoulder and pulled the trigger, aiming at the rocks to the left of where Maeve and Tatiana stood. She prayed that her aim was true.

The shot careened off the rock wall and angled for Tatiana and Maeve. Tatiana let out a yell, diving to her left. But she loosened her grip on Maeve slightly. Maeve yanked herself from Tatiana's grasp, falling heavily on the floor.

Tatiana lurched forward, reaching for her, but Adam dove over Maeve, slamming his shoulder into Tatiana's face.

"Maeve, run!" Chris yelled.

She wasted no time sprinting toward them. The others had already reached them, and Chris had them tucked in behind him.

"Get them out of here," Norah ordered.

"What about you?" Chris asked.

"I'm going to make sure Adam gets out," Norah said.

"Ig."

A small smile crossed Norah's face. "Correction, we're going to make sure Adam gets out."

Maeve reached them, her face red.

Norah turned her attention back to the fight at the end of the hall. "Go! Now!"

CHAPTER 107

It was a mad dash up the stairs. Maeve's thighs screamed in protest as she vaulted up them, but she didn't dare slow. Images of the Draco coming up quickly behind them helped keep her moving. It wasn't until they were about to step onto the first level that she realized that Norah and Adam weren't with them.

Maeve grabbed Chris's shoulder. "Wait. We're not all here."

He looked into her eyes. "We need to go, Maeve. They'll be right up."

Maeve wasn't sure she believed him, but the scream from the other side of the door told her that whatever fight was happening downstairs, there was still one going on upstairs as well.

At the side of the door, Greg held on to Luke, who was screaming. Alvie and Snap were huddled on the other side of the door. Chris ushered them back. He pulled his rifle into his shoulder and let off three quick bursts.

"Everybody needs to stay low and head for the exit. We're going to— Oh shit! Everybody down!" Chris threw himself over Alvie and Snap. Greg pulled Luke farther from the doorway and threw himself over him as well. Maeve dove to the ground as an explosion sounded from the other room.

Everything was quiet. Dust and debris filled the air. Alvie crawled up to her side as she made her way to the edge of the doorway and peered in. Maeve's breath came out in pants as she hugged Alvie to her.

Sammy lay on the other side of the room, the Draco ten feet away from him. He was crumpled to the ground, his neck at an unnatural angle. From here, Maeve had a perfect view of Sammy's back. His spine was a series of ridges that she could count. His back moved forward and back with his breaths, but they were labored, uncomfortable to watch.

Alvie broke away from her and sprinted across the room with a cry. He circled Sammy and then fell to his knees in front of him. Greg stood up slowly. "Are you sure that's safe?"

"No, but Alvie is." Maeve hurried after Alvie, slowing as she approached Sammy.

He was even more fearsome looking close up. His wings had a leathery appearance up close, which made them look tough and invulnerable. And they had been. The Draco had been unable to cause any rips that she could see.

She slowly moved around toward his front, careful to keep out of striking distance. She knew that Sammy was protective of Alvie and Luke. But she wasn't sure how wary he would be of her. And besides, when people were injured, when animals were injured, they tended to lash out.

She rounded his head. Alvie was kneeling on the ground next to him, his hands on Sammy's face. "Alvie."

Alvie looked up, tears streaming down his cheeks. *Help him. Help the Sentinel.*

The Sentinel. It was an apt title for him. Her eyes scanned Sammy's body. She sucked in a breath as she saw the gaping wound in his abdomen. His wings might be invulnerable, but apparently his skin wasn't. She hurried forward, just then noticing that Greg had followed her over.

"I need your sweatshirt," she said.

Greg slipped it off without comment, handing it to her as she knelt down. She shot a quick glance at Sammy, surprised to see his eyes open and focused on her. In shock, she realized his eyes were a bronze color.

She swallowed down her fear. "I have to stop the bleeding. This may hurt a little bit."

He gave the smallest of nods.

Taking a breath, Maeve pressed the sweatshirt to the wound, trying to staunch some of the bleeding. It quickly became clear that rudimentary first aid wasn't going to cut it. Chris appeared from the side of Sammy, his face a mixture of joy seeing Maeve and Alvie and concern at what they were doing. Maeve wanted to run into his arms and hug him and tell him how much she loved him. But she couldn't stop the pressure on Sammy's wounds.

She looked up at Chris. "We need to move him. We need to get him somewhere where there's medical supplies."

Jasper appeared next to Chris. "Let's get him to the plane. There's a special compartment in the cargo hold set up for just this kind of occasion." Jasper glanced at his watch. "And we need to make it quick."

CHAPTER 108

Norah's whole body was soaked with sweat. She stared in wild-eyed fascination at the fight at the end of the hall. Adam swiped out at Tatiana, his hand connecting with her cheek. She let out a yell as she threw a fake at his face before landing a rib-breaking hit to his side.

"Ig!" Iggy yanked on Norah's back, pulling her to the doorway.

Heavy footsteps sounded from the lower levels. Norah tucked herself into the side of the doorway and prayed there weren't many. Two Draco appeared. Using the doorway as leverage, Iggy flung himself at the first one, his talons aiming for its throat. But the creature saw him coming and ducked out of the way at the last second. Iggy went flying over him, hitting the ground, landing in a roll. He whirled around, showing his teeth.

Both Draco turned toward him. Dammit. Norah had no shot and she'd already gone through all her armor-piercing bullets. There was absolutely nothing that could take them down from the back. The Draco let out a bone-chilling scream before they leapt down the stairs toward Iggy.

Norah slid her baton from its holder. With the snap of her wrist it extended to its full length and snapped into place.

God help me. She sprang down the steps. She slammed the baton into the back of the Draco's lower back before stomping on the back of its knees. The creature wobbled, his shoulders lurching back. She grabbed it by the shoulders and yanked it to the ground, pulling her M4 around and letting loose before it could regain its feet. The first two shots missed the eyes but the third was a winner. The creature's head fell back. Norah stepped forward and quickly put a bullet in the other eye as well, figuring there was no sense in taking chances.

Iggy had taken his guy down as well. Blood poured from the creature's neck. Norah walked up and put another bullet into its eye. Then she hurried back up the stairs.

At the end of the hall, Adam was on the ground. Tatiana straddled him, her fist pounding away at his face.

Norah didn't think, she just acted. She sprinted down the hall toward them. Iggy galloped after her.

"Hey!" Norah yelled.

Tatiana paused for a second. Norah took her shot, and Tatiana ducked. But that was all Adam needed. He bucked her off of him with such force that she crashed into the rock wall. He grabbed her by the front of her face and slammed it into the rock wall three more times. She crumbled to the ground.

Jasper's voice burst through Norah's earpiece. "Norah? Norah, where are you? This place is going to go! You need to get to the surface now!"

Adam reached for Tatiana again.

"Adam, we need to go!" Adam looked down at Tatiana one more time and then turned toward Norah. His knees buckled, and he staggered, grabbing on to the wall.

Norah sprinted toward him and threw his arm over her shoulders. She hurried him down the hall. Iggy bounced up and down in front of them, his agitation clear.

"Go, Iggy! Get upstairs!" Norah yelled.

But Iggy would only go a few feet in front of them.

A figure burst through the stairwell door when Norah was only six feet away. She aimed her weapon at the intruder.

Mike dove to the side, his hands over his head. "Good guy!" He yelled.

Norah lowered her weapon. "Next time give me a heads-up that you're coming."

"Noted," Mike said as he pulled Adam's other arm over his shoulder. "How the hell did this happen?"

"Sibling rivalry." Norah glanced over her shoulder. Draco littered the hallway ... all except one. Tatiana was missing.

CHAPTER 109

They were in a rush, but they had a big problem: Sammy's size. He wouldn't fit in either of the SUVs, not with his wings. So they commandeered the white truck sitting outside the warehouse.

The second problem was getting him into it. He wasn't exactly light, and he was struggling to walk. Jasper and Maeve took one arm while Greg and Chris took the other, and they slowly walked him toward the door.

"Man, we could really use Adam and some of that extra strength right now," Greg said, his face red from exertion.

Chris grunted in response.

"Where is he?" Jasper asked.

"Behind you," Maeve said as she helped guide Sammy to the ramp.

Chris glanced over his shoulder as Adam walked out of the building, Norah and Mike supporting him. Blood soaked his shirt. "Damn."

Alvie sprinted over to him.

"Alvie, is he okay?" Maeve asked.

Hurt. Hurt bad.

Sandra hurried over to the other SUV and opened the back door, flattening out the seats so Adam would be able to lie down.

They got Sammy into the truck bed and as gently as they could, lowered him.

As soon as he was down, Jasper scooped up Snap and hopped out and leaped into the driver's seat. "Haul ass, people!"

Greg jumped from the truck bed and sprinted across the open space toward Adam.

Maeve sank down next to Sammy, rummaging through the first-aid kit from one of the SUVs. "I'm staying with him." She looked up at Chris.

Chris tossed his keys to Mike. "Go."

Mike wasted no time leaping from the back of the truck. He climbed into the other SUV with Sandra and Luke. Norah already had her SUV moving, with Alvie and Greg in the back with Adam, Iggy riding shotgun.

Chris stumbled as Jasper got them moving. He moved to the end of the truck and pulled down the door. He didn't need any of them being flung out the back.

He crouched down next to Maeve so the lights from his suit would let her see what was going on.

Maeve was applying bandages to Sammy, but he was bleeding out. She didn't look up as she spoke. "What's the hurry?"

"There's an attack planned on the Draco sites, including this one," Chris said.

"An attack?" Maeve asked, focusing on stopping Sammy's bleeding as fast as she could manage.

"The U.S. government is going to bomb them out of existence," Chris said.

Her hands stilled for a moment as she stared up at him. Hands shaking, she returned to her ministrations. "How much time do we have?"

Chris checked his watch. "Five minutes."

CHAPTER 110

RAF BENTWATERS, UNITED KINGDOM

All air traffic in the western half of the United States had ground to a halt. Flights that were supposed to take off within an hour of the planned detonation were delayed, citing weather. Law enforcement agencies across the nation as well as the National Guard had been put on notice, although few details were provided. They couldn't chance anyone learning about the bombing until it had been completed. Any hint and the Draco could slip from their net.

Tilda looked up from her desk as DNI Director Harrison stepped into the room. "William."

William closed the door behind him before moving to the desk. "We may have a problem."

"What?" Tilda said.

"No one's seen Martin Drummond in hours."

Her mind racing, Tilda sat back. Drummond had provided them with the intel on the Draco. He'd had the information for years, she had no doubt. But he'd dribbled it out. And if he was missing, it was entirely possible that he'd kept a few nuggets of information for himself.

Dammit, Martin. What the hell are you up to?

William knew Martin as well as she did. He knew he was always playing an angle. That there was always another card up that man's sleeves. But she'd be damned if she could figure out what the hell the card was this time.

"Should we postpone?" he asked.

She shook her head. "No. The longer we wait, the better chance the Draco will be warned. We move ahead."

"Very well. Would you like some company?" William asked.

"No, I think this is better done on my own."

He inclined his head and then stepped from the room. Pearl appeared from the computer room at the back of the office.

Tilda glanced over at her, raising her eyebrows.

"Three minutes," Pearl said quietly.

A shiver tried to roll up Tilda's spine but she wouldn't let it. "Any word?"

Pearl shook her head. And there were no longer any satellite feeds of the area. Tilda had instructed Penny to divert all satellites so there was no image of the bombing that could make it to the media. The explosion would be explained as a gas leak and nothing more.

Tilda's hands shook, and she clasped them in her lap. Adam had promised he would get them out in time. He had promised he would get himself out in time, and he'd never broken a promise to her.

Be safe, Adam. Please be safe.

CHAPTER 111

EDMONDS, WASHINGTON

The SUV jerked to the left. Greg fell forward, managing to catch himself on the other side of the car before he fell on top of Adam. He pushed himself back. "Give a guy a little warning, would you?"

"We're in a bit of a hurry," Norah said, her voice tight.

Greg unrolled the tape, ripping it with his teeth. He placed it on the side of the gauze he'd placed on Adam's wounds. Adam lay with his eyes closed, his breathing even. He hadn't made a sound or even a twitch since he'd been laid inside the SUV.

He had this weird feeling he was meditating. That he'd somehow put himself into a trance. He glanced through the rear windshield. "Are the Draco following us?"

"No." Norah paused. "They're going to bomb the Draco holdout. It should be any minute now."

Greg's gaze shot to the sky. Sure enough, the unmistakable sight of a missile heading toward the coast appeared over the water. "Oh my God."

The missile hit, and for a second it seemed like there was no explosion. Then light burst out from the point of impact. Greg shielded his eyes, turning away. A large mushroom cloud blew up over the site. Wind raced along the ground, followed by fire.

"Faster, Norah, faster!" Greg yelled.

"I'm going as fast as I can!" She yelled back.

The wind reached the SUV, first pushing it along the ground and lifting up the back wheels for a split second. And then the fire kissed the back bumper. Greg held his breath, praying for everything he was worth until the fire receded. Then he was issuing a new prayer as the car was bombarded with debris.

Norah had to jolt the wheel from side to side to avoid the larger pieces crashed into the road ahead of them. Greg let out a yelp as a fishing boat, an actual fishing boat, flew overhead and landed to their left.

"Did you see that?" Greg demanded.

"Saw it." Norah swerved around a large piece of concrete. Other cars pulled off to the side of the road. Two cars crashed into one another, their attention no doubt on the fireball by the coast.

Ahead, Greg saw the vehicles of the other members of their group getting pelted as well. The back windshield shattered as a metal pole crashed through. Greg let out a yell as Adam's hand slammed into Greg's chest, flinging him against the side of the car. The metal impaled the seat right next to Adam's head. If Adam hadn't moved him, it would have gone right through Greg's chest.

"Thank you," Greg whispered, his heart racing.

Adam merely nodded, his hand dropping back to his side.

Norah looked up and through the windshield. "I think that was the worst of it. I think we're in the clear."

His gaze falling on the white truck that held Sammy, Greg let out a breath. *God, I hope so.*

CHAPTER 112

The ride back to the airport was hair-raising. Maeve wasn't sure what was going on outside the truck, but it sounded like they were under assault.

"Is that the Draco?" she asked.

Chris shook his head. "No. The United States government just bombed the warehouse."

Maeve's hands stilled. "They were cutting it kind of close, weren't they?"

Chris met her gaze and then looked away.

But that small glance was enough for her to see the truth in his eyes. She sucked in a breath. "They had no intention of saving us."

Shaking his head, Chris reached out and then squeezed her hand. "Good thing the rest of us don't listen to bad plans."

Although Maeve nodded she felt a little lightheaded. The U.S. had okayed their deaths. She, Alvie, Snap, Iggy, Greg and Luke—they were acceptable losses.

"Maeve?"

She shook her head. She'd deal with that later. Right now she needed to focus on Sammy. "I'm okay."

There was a medical kit in Jasper's SUV, but they quickly worked their way through all the bandages provided. Maeve was worried about the amount of blood Sammy was losing. She wasn't sure how she was going to replenish it.

As the pulled onto the airfield and slowed, Maeve's mind raced. It wasn't like she could do a transfusion. She couldn't risk giving the wrong blood type. His blood was red. It *looked* like human blood, but she knew looks could be deceiving.

The truck stopped and Greg jumped in as soon as the door was opened. "How is he?"

"Not good."

"Adam?" Maeve asked.

"He'll be fine. Sore, but fine."

Mike was already running for and opening the cargo doors at the back of the plane, where Maeve guessed the medical unit was.

"We're going to back right up to the plane. It'll make it easier to transfer him," Chris said.

Maeve nodded. Getting Sammy into the truck had been difficult. His weight and size had made it awkward. She didn't think getting him into the plane would be any easier.

Walking behind the truck, Chris waved to direct Jasper, who was driving toward the hold. Maeve kept the pressure on the wound, her mind already running through what needed to be done.

Kneeling down next to her, Greg spoke softly. "He's going to need blood," Greg said softly.

"I know. But I don't know where we can get it from."

From Luke.

Maeve tore her gaze from Sammy to stare at Snap, who'd crawled up through the open door, Now she sat next to Sammy's head, running her hand gently over his forehead.

"What?" Maeve asked.

Snap looked over at her. *Sammy says Luke has the same blood.*

"What's going on?" Greg asked looking between the two of them.

"I'm not sure."

Maeve stared at Sammy, who looked back at her.

It is close. It will work. She started realizing that thought hadn't come from Snap.

Mouth falling open, she stared at the large being before she turned to Greg. "Sammy said that he and Luke have the same blood."

Greg looked shell-shocked. "Really?"

"That's what he says," Maeve replied.

She did not understand his connection to Luke. But she did know there was one. If Luke was somehow genetically related, that would explain how Sammy was able to find him. There were reports of creatures being able to find their pack from miles away. Perhaps Sammy had some of that same ability.

Maeve looked at Greg. "What do you think?"

"I think we don't have a lot of options. I'll go speak with Sandra."

He patted Maeve on the shoulder before climbing from the truck bed. It had pulled to a stop only a few feet away from the cargo hold. Chris, Jasper, Mike, Norah, even Adam, all stood waiting to help transfer Sammy to the cargo hold.

Maeve took a deep breath and sent up a prayer. *God, or whoever's listening, please help us save him.*

CHAPTER 113

Greg found Sandra and Luke sitting in the middle row of one of the SUVs. Sandra had her arms around her son and was rocking with him. Luke clutched Sandra's arms, still looking terrified.

Man, that poor kid. Greg knew how terrifying these situations were. As a grown adult, they were difficult to say the least. But for a sensitive kid? It must've been absolutely traumatizing.

Luke would never be the same again. Neither would Sandra. But Greg hoped that one day he could get past this. He'd never forget. Greg had never forgotten.

But Greg liked to think that he'd grown stronger from it. Not just physically but mentally. He knew now that there were things that went bump in the night. He knew now that faced with death, he would still try to save those he cared about. He knew himself better.

He wasn't sure, though, if life-threatening situations worked the same for kids. Did they come out the other side stronger? Or because they were still growing and maturing, did it set them back or maybe even push them off the course to complete maturity?

And for a kid like Luke, would it be even more difficult to come back? Luke was an extremely trusting kid. He saw the world in a way that Greg wished more people did. But it also led to pain in his young life. Greg had overheard Sandra telling Norah about the kids at school. Maybe in some weird sort of way, that bullying had helped prepare him for this situation.

But those were thoughts for another day. The car door was open. Greg walked up to it, placing his hand on top of the frame. He kept his voice low. "How's he doing?"

Sandra shrugged. "I ... I'm not sure."

Luke caught his glance for just a second before looking away. "Hey, buddy. You did really great down there."

"Sammy?" Luke didn't look at Greg while he asked the question.

"Actually, that's what I'm here to talk to you about." Greg paused. He didn't want to blurt out the request in front of Luke because he wanted to give Sandra the option to say no. But he also didn't see how he was going to be able to get Sandra away from Luke. And time was of the essence. "Um, we have a little issue that we were hoping we might be able to get Luke's help on."

"Now?" Sandra asked.

Greg nodded. "Most definitely now. Sammy's hurt. Maeve and I think we can repair the damage. But we need a, um, well, a blood donor."

Sandra stared at him, and he could tell she didn't understand what he was saying.

Probably because I haven't said it. Greg took a breath. "Okay. Here goes: According to Sammy, Luke is related to him and therefore can donate blood to him."

Sandra continued to stare at him before she shook her head. "No, no. He's already been through too much. We can't—"

Luke interrupted her. "He saved us, more than once, Mom. It's our turn to save him."

Out of the mouth of babes, Greg thought.

Sandra looked down at Luke and hugged him tight. "Are you sure? They'd have to put a needle into your skin. I know you don't like that."

"I'm sure. I want to help." Luke nodded, looking more confident.

Watching her son for a long moment, Sandra finally looked back at Greg with a shrug. "Okay, I guess we're in."

Greg smiled. *And now I guess that means that Sammy has a real shot.*

CHAPTER 114

Getting Sammy into the plane had proved to be a tricky endeavor. But after quite a bit of maneuvering and some cursing, they managed it. They'd had to push two stretchers together in order to compensate for his wings.

With shaking hands, Maeve transfused Luke's blood into Sammy. She held her breath, her eyes shifting between the monitors and Sammy's face, looking for any sign that he was rejecting the blood. But if anything, his vitals improved. After fifteen minutes, he stabilized and seemed to fall into a deep sleep.

Maeve sank to the floor at the edge of the medical unit. Greg collapsed next to her. "I can't believe that worked."

"I wonder *why* that worked," Maeve said.

With a tired grin, Greg patted her thigh. "Let's save that little medical mystery for another day. I'm tired."

She gave a shaky laugh. "Yeah, me too."

"I'll take the first shift. Go see your gang," he said.

Grateful, Maeve got to her feet. "I'll send someone down here to keep you company, okay?"

Leaning back, Greg closed his eyes. "Sounds good. They can also keep me awake, because I'm pretty sure I'm going to fall asleep."

With effort, Maeve pushed herself to her feet. She made her way over to the stretchers and checked the monitors one last time. He looked like he was doing well. But they knew nothing about his physiology. They were basing the readings solely on what would be good for a human of his size.

Her gaze drifted over to him, wondering where he'd come from. But soon her scientific thoughts drifted away, and only her grateful ones remained. She spoke low, knowing he was in a deep sleep and probably couldn't hear her, but she still felt it needed to be said. "Thank you. Thank you for saving Luke. Thank you for saving my family. Thank you for looking out for all of us. I don't know where you came from or why you've become our guardian angel, but I am very grateful that you are."

Reaching out, Maeve squeezed his hand, and for just a split second, she could've sworn he squeezed hers in return. She made her way out of the medical unit and up the narrow staircase to where everyone else was.

Adam and Jasper stood at the top of the staircase, waiting for her.

"How is he?" Jasper asked.

Running a hand through her hair, Maeve said with more than a little disbelief, "I think he's going to be all right. The blood from Luke seems to have done the trick. I can't explain why, but we got lucky."

Nodding, Adam turned to head down the stairs, but Maeve put out an arm, blocking him. "Wait."

Adam looked up at her.

"Will he be safe at R.I.S.E.?" she asked.

Shifting his gaze down the stairs and then back at her, Adam said, "I'm not sure."

While Maeve appreciated the honesty, the answer was not the one she wanted. "The U.S. government just okayed the death of half the people on this plane. Will *we* be safe at R.I.S.E.?"

Jasper shook his head. "R.I.S.E. has just been exposed to every branch of the U.S. military. That information is supposed to stay secret. But no one knows if that will be the case. Human error or greed is always unpredictable. No one knows what will happen to R.I.S.E. in the weeks to come. But what I can say for sure is that there will be government oversight. No agency likes to think that someone else is getting all the toys. Someone is going to make problems for us."

"And my family? Can you guarantee their safety if we go back?" Maeve asked.

Jasper opened his mouth to answer, but Adam beat him to it. "No."

Maeve sucked in a breath. "We can't go back there, then. I won't put them at the mercy of the U.S. government. I've seen that mercy up close and personal. I will make some calls. I will find somewhere for us to hole up until we can figure out our next moves."

"That's not necessary. I know a place," Adam said softly.

Maeve stared at him. She'd been told about Adam's Draco nature. She didn't care about that. It was the human component of his nature that she worried about. "What about Tilda?" She asked softly.

"She'll understand. Protecting all of you, she knows how important that is," he answered.

"Didn't she okay that missile that almost wiped us all out?" asked Maeve.

Jasper cleared his throat. "Tilda wasn't sure if she could trust all her people after Ethan's betrayal. She okayed this mission. She provided the plane, the weapons, the resources, everything. She just couldn't let anyone know."

"Will you tell her where we're going?" Maeve asked.

Adam nodded. "Yes. But in a way that no one else would be able to understand. And she would never tell. But I need to tell her I'm alive. I owe her that. I owe her everything."

Maeve understood that level of commitment. And she prayed that Adam's faith in Tilda was well deserved. "All right. I'm trusting you. We're all trusting you."

Even with his dark glasses, Maeve could feel the intensity of his gaze. "I won't let you down. And neither will she."

CHAPTER 115

RAF BENTWATERS, UNITED KINGDOM

Outside the office, the hangar had emptied out. Even Penny had left her little nest, her mother coming to take her and force her to sleep. Tilda sat at the desk, reading through reports.

The bombing in the Arctic had gone off without a hitch. The team she'd sent reported back that the facility had been completely destroyed. All of the tunnels leading in and out of it had collapsed. They were in the process of going through the wreckage. If there were any Draco alive and if they put up any sort of resistance, a second bombing would immediately commence.

Her people knew the stakes. They knew what they had signed up for. But it still didn't make it easier to sign off on the order.

The bombing in Edmonds was more difficult. The governor of Washington had declared a state of emergency. Tilda's people had taken over the site under the guise of the Department of Homeland Security. No one outside of her people would be allowed access.

Over three dozen people had been taken to the hospital. So far, two deaths had been reported.

And there was no word from Adam's team.

Tilda couldn't remember ever being so tired. Everything ached, even though she'd given in and taken the stronger painkillers. Right now, she wanted more of them. But what she wanted even more than that was to see Adam's face.

She didn't know when she would see him again.

Or *if* she would.

She didn't know if his team had succeeded or if they were some of the bodies that would be pulled out of the wreckage in the days to come. She glanced at the small nondescript cell phone sitting in the middle of her desk. It remained annoyingly silent.

There was similarly no word from Agaren. Tilda had no doubt Pop and Crackle were safe. And as much as it would kill Maeve and Chris, it was perhaps safest for them to remain with Agaren for at least a short time. R.I.S.E. was about to change. And Tilda wasn't sure how much longer she would be able to protect them.

Martin was also still AWOL. But Tilda knew he would show up eventually, like a bad penny. The fact that he'd disappeared at the same time the rescue mission took off gave her a good idea of where he might have gone.

Or been taken. But Martin was not going to occupy her thoughts. Besides the trouble he could cause, he was not on her list of concerns.

Across the office, Pearl had fallen asleep on the couch. Tilda didn't want to wake her. There were still a few more reports she needed to go through, a few more phone calls she needed to return. She yawned, one big enough to swallow her jaw. She lowered her head to the desk, laying it on her hands. Five minutes. She'd give herself five minutes, and then she'd get back to work.

A buzzing worked its way into Tilda's consciousness. She knew she should recognize the sound, but she was struggling through the exhaustion. Then her eyes flew open. She scrambled for the phone and flipped it open. She read the message, her heart lifting.

We are fine. All accounted for. Need to go quiet. Going home.
Tilda closed the phone, a smile on her face.

Pearl sat up from the couch, rubbing her eyes. "Is everything all right? Any word from Adam?"

Clasping the phone in her hand, Tilda shook her head. "No, nothing yet."

NEXT IN THE A.L.I.V.E. SERIES

www.vinci-books.com/save

Martin Drummond will stop at nothing to find Maeve Leander and her family. But the threat Martin offers pales in comparison to the world ending cataclysm that is now on the horizon . . .

Turn the page for a free preview.

S.A.V.E. - PREVIEW

CHAPTER 1

Off the coast of Seattle, Washington

The rain beat a steady rhythm against the roof of the wheelhouse of the *Destiny*, a seventy-foot rusted blue crabber off the coast of Washington state.

Martin sat in the corner of the wheelhouse, a heavy gray blanket draped over his shoulders. He wrinkled his nose as yet again the smell of fish invaded his nostrils. He'd made the mistake earlier of trying to cover his nose with his hand, but it had only made the smell stronger.

He held out a hand with disgust. His hands were still wrinkled. He'd spent a full day in the water after Garrigan and his cohorts had dumped him out of the plane.

A plane.

From the water, he'd seen the explosion as the bomb hit the factory in Edmonds. The blast had set off a small tsunami, which had shoved him farther out to sea. It was pure dumb luck that the crabber had found him. He'd managed to pull himself up onto a buoy but only after he'd spent hours floating. Then he'd spent a cold, miserable night clinging to life on the rusted metal.

The door to the wheelhouse opened. It brought with it a gust of cool air and a spray of rain and seawater. A rough man with a black stocking cap on his head, waders, and a thick raincoat stepped into the room. Captain Ernesto Flavigo gave him a bright smile. "Ah, you're still awake. I thought perhaps you might have gone below to catch some shut-eye."

Martin shook his head. "No. Have you had any luck?"

Ernesto nodded his head as he walked to the coffee machine and poured himself a cup. Martin held his tongue with barely concealed anger as Ernesto took a long sip. He let out a deep, contented sigh. "Yes. I've reached the Coast Guard. I told them about finding you. It appears quite a few people have been lost at sea after the events in Edmonds. The Coast Guard has been run ragged. They don't have enough people for the demand."

Martin didn't give a damn about the Coast Guard and its staff shortages. "When will we be back on shore?"

The man shrugged. "Another two hours at most. But the seas are getting choppy, so you may want to go below. It will be safer."

Martin reined in his growl. On one level, he knew the man was just trying to be polite to his unexpected guest. He and his crew of four had plucked him from the sea two hours earlier. They'd been far off the coast and had been shocked to find him on the buoy. But they'd done their best to make him comfortable. They'd given him a change of clothes and plied him with food and hot drinks to help warm him up.

But they were slow men. Slow-moving and slow-thinking. They were also stubborn. He could see that in the set of their shoulders and the cadence of their talk. Pushing them would only make them grow suspicious. He was lucky they believed his "I fell off a boat" story.

Besides, he had no leverage here. There was nothing to hold over the man's head, at least not yet. So he bit his tongue. "I'm sure I'll be fine. What about your SAT phone?"

The weather had made the SAT phone unusable. Either that or the missile strike in Edmonds had wiped out communication lines. He still couldn't believe that Tilda had gone through with it. He hadn't thought she had the spine for it.

She'd shown him, hadn't she?

Of course, he also hadn't thought Chris Garrigan and Adam Watson would kidnap him. He hadn't read their desperation correctly.

Martin didn't understand that kind of response, at least not when it was linked around the well-being of another living creature. He wasn't sure what he would do if someone took his daughter. Oh, he'd send people after her and make sure those who dared to harm what was his were destroyed. But he would not be in the state that Chris Garrigan had been in. The man had been beside himself.

As had Norah Tidwell. Nothing in her file indicated that she would become so attached to the Maldek. She'd been just as desperate to get him back.

They were probably all dead in the blast now. He smiled. At least one good thing had come out of this. That and the decimation of the Draco. That scourge should have been wiped from the planet years ago. And if Martin had been in charge, they would have.

He knew that not all of the Draco had been destroyed. There would be pockets of Draco across the globe that escaped the attack. The United States had underestimated the defenses at the Antarctica base as well. That base went extremely deep. Even with a MOAB, they would not be able to reach the farthest depths of the Draco stronghold. Some would survive.

And like cockroaches, they would eventually crawl from the rubble.

But the attacks would set them back on their heels. It could be decades, if not longer, before they reemerged.

"Is the SAT phone working?" Martin asked.

"Yes, yes. Do you want to make a call?" Ernesto pulled the phone from his inside jacket pocket.

Martin had to keep himself from snatching the phone from Ernesto's hand. Of course he wanted to make a call. He'd been asking to make a call for the last two hours. Ernesto had assured him that eventually the SAT phone would work. But he seemed in no hurry to make sure that it did.

Martin took the phone and headed for the door.

"Are you sure you want to go out there? The storm is getting worse."

The storm is just beginning, Martin thought but said nothing.

"Hold on a second." Ernesto slipped the rain slicker off of his shoulders and handed it to Martin. "At least take this. It'll keep most of the rain off of you."

Martin nodded his thanks as he slipped the jacket on. It was still warm from Ernesto. Martin was surprised at the amount of comfort he received from that warmth.

Rain slapped him in the face as he stepped outside. He gripped the railing as he made his way to the stairs and down to the main deck. Two of the crewmen were walking along the aft deck, so Martin headed to the foredeck. Dozens of crates lined the deck, most of them empty. A few crabs stuck in traps eyed him as he walked past. He stepped to the back of the boat. Leaning against the wet railing, he dialed.

Stacy Mal, his assistant, answered the phone quickly. "Who is this? How did you get this number?"

"I *gave* you this number," Martin said with a growl.

"Mr. Drummond. My God. Where have you been? I've had

people searching everywhere for you, but we've had no luck at all."

"That's because someone tossed me out of a plane." He swallowed down his anger. "What's the status of MAURC?"

The worry and concern disappeared from Stacy's voice as she immediately slipped back into assistant mode. "It's been rescinded. The facilities at both Edmonds and Antarctica were bombed as scheduled. Satellite imagery indicated that there was no movement at either site. With the threat removed, there was no longer a need for MAURC."

Martin grunted. Well, at least Matilda no longer had all the might of the U.S. military at her fingertips. "Has Watson crawled back into her hole?"

"Um, not exactly," Stacy said.

"*What* does that mean?" Martin demanded.

"R.I.S.E. is acknowledged by all branches of the U.S. military now. They have an official seat at the table."

Martin gritted his teeth. "What about Garrigan and the others?"

"The sat photos indicate that they were able to escape the site at Edmonds moments before the blast. They are believed to still be alive, although no one has been able to find them after they left the airfield in Seattle. Satellites were misbehaving for a while after the blast," Stacy added.

Exhaustion weighing him down, Martin nodded. Why couldn't they all just die the way they were supposed to?

"And there was one additional, unexpected passenger with the Garrigan crew," Stacy said.

Martin frowned. Who could they have possibly taken with them? A Draco? Why would they take one? To experiment on? To find its weaknesses? But why bother when they already had Adam? "Who?" He asked.

"Sammy."

Martin stilled, his whole body locked in place as fear extended to every single cell in his body. *"What?"*

Stacy's voice came out in a rush. "Apparently the Draco had taken him hostage. The Garrigan crew retrieved him. He looked like he was injured. He was loaded onto the plane with the rest of them and was with them when they took off."

Martin took a deep calming breath. This was too much. Sammy never should've escaped Area 51. He was the one creature that was supposed to have stayed locked away. Martin would've been happier if the Draco had taken him and kept him. At least then he'd know that the creature would be tortured for years to come. But once again, Leander and her people had ruined that possibility.

"I need you to find Maeve Leander and the others. There must be some trace of them," Martin ordered.

"I have everybody working on it already," Stacy said quickly. "It's only a matter of time."

Martin ignored the empty platitudes. "Send a chopper to my location. I expect it within the hour."

"Yes, sir." Stacy paused before she blurted, "We all thought you were dead, sir."

"Get to work." Martin disconnected the call. He stared out at the choppy water. Leander and the hybrid were alive. And they now had Sammy with them.

We all thought you were dead.

Gripping the railing, he stared out at the water, just able to make out the coast in the distance. No, he wasn't dead. And that was their mistake. That small burst of compassion would be their undoing.

The rain picked up its pace, lashing at him. *But I won't make that mistake. Compassion has never been an issue with me.*

CHAPTER 2

Halifax, Canada

Dr. Maeve Leander was tired. Her group of ten had traveled through Canada, mostly by car, for the last seven days. They'd tried to travel mainly at night, switching out drivers in their two-car caravan. The problem had been with Sammy. They couldn't risk anyone checking the back of the truck and seeing him, so they'd traveled at the speed limit.

Today, they'd finally made it to the eastern coast of Canada. There, Jasper had a connection that provided them with the plane for the next leg of the journey. Maeve had been sleeping before they'd arrived at the coast, so she was one of the only ones who was wide awake as the plane took off. Everyone else fell asleep almost immediately after they were in the air. The tension of the trip seemed to drain the energy from all of them.

Maeve walked to the back of the plane where Sammy lay. He was laid out in the cargo hold. At seven feet tall, with a ten-foot wingspan, it was the only place where he could lie comfortably.

He appeared to be sleeping on the stacks of blankets they'd piled up to make a nest.

She moved forward quietly. Crouching down, she pressed two fingers against the side of his throat. His pulse pounded away beneath her touch, speeding along at a faster pace than that of humans. But from what her and Greg could tell, this was his normal rate.

He was sedated to try and keep him from tearing at his bandages. They still weren't sure how exactly to talk to him. He didn't communicate with any of them in any discernible way, although Maeve was pretty sure that he understood them.

Sammy's eyes flickered open, and dark slits watched her.

She gave him what she hoped was a reassuring smile. "Looks good. You're healing nicely. Those bandages will be off in another week or so."

He watched for another long moment before he closed his eyes. Maeve let out a breath she hadn't realized she'd been holding. She wasn't sure what the situation with Sammy was. Alvie trusted him. Luke, Iggy, and Snap did as well. But they were all essentially children. She wasn't sure how much stock she should put in their views.

But as Greg pointed out, children were always the best judges of character.

Back in the cabin, everyone was sprawled out. The blanket over Norah and Iggy had fallen to the ground. Maeve picked it up and tucked it back around them. Iggy opened his eyes and gave a big yawn. His pointed ears wiggled with the motion. "Ig." He closed his eyes again with a sigh.

Maeve smiled at the little Maldek. It was hard not to love him. Norah and Iggy had a bond that was incredibly strong. And absolutely amazing, especially being Norah was a former D.E.A.D. agent.

Falling under the Department of Defense, the D.E.A.D. had been created in the aftermath of the meltdown of the A.L.I.V.E. cases at Area 51. Their mandate was to track down all the A.L.I.V.E. escapees from Area 51, and according to Norah, kill them. But when it came to Iggy, she couldn't pull the trigger, which was what led her to Maeve and the rest of them. And which was also what put her life on the line and her on the run. But Maeve knew if given the same choice again, she wouldn't change a thing.

Just like Maeve wouldn't.

Maeve continued up to the cabin. Chris was two rows up from Norah with Alvie and Snap snuggled into his sides, one hand resting protectively on each of them.

She was happy to see him sleeping. It had been a rare thing

for him this last week. She knew he felt guilty for what had happened to Crackle and Pop. She'd told him over and over again it wasn't his fault. But he couldn't seem to accept it. Now he was hypervigilant when it came to Snap and Alvie.

The last two of their group in the cabin were Jasper Jenkins and Mike Bileris, both R.I.S.E. operatives. Jasper and Mike had risked everything to save Maeve, Greg, Alvie, Snap, and Luke in Washington. And without them and their resourcefulness, Maeve knew they wouldn't have made it this far.

Greg was in the next row, an arm thrown over his head. Sandra and Luke Gillibrand had taken the last two rows and were each sprawled out. Maeve hoped they were all getting a good night's sleep. God knew, they all needed one.

Jasper and Mike sat near the front, engrossed in a chess game. They didn't look up as Maeve passed by. She stepped into the cockpit and closed the door quietly behind her.

Adam Watson glanced over his shoulder at her before turning his attention back to the controls. She didn't let his silence deter her. She'd gotten used to Adam's quietness. He wasn't unfriendly. He just quite simply didn't talk unless he viewed it as necessary.

She took a seat in the copilot's chair, careful not to touch anything. "How are you feeling? Are you tired? Should I get you a coffee?"

Shaking his head, Adam adjusted a dial on the control panel. "No. I'm fine. Thank you. Is everyone sleeping?"

"All but Jasper and Mike. They're playing chess again," Maeve said.

Adam made no response, and Maeve felt no need to fill the silence. She just sat with him as she watched the clouds fly by. When she was a kid, she had never once been on a plane, despite essentially living on Wright-Patterson Air Force Base. With her mom and Alvie, vacations simply weren't an option. She and her mother never left Wright-Pat.

But over the last couple of years, she'd been rushed in and out of planes across the country. And now she was rushing across the globe.

And that was by far the least unusual change the last few years had brought her.

She glanced over the control panel, not knowing what any of the instruments indicated. The only one that was even slightly familiar was the compass. They were heading west.

"Do we have a specific destination in mind, or are we just hoping for the best?" She asked.

Adam glanced at her from the corner of his eye. She could tell he was deciding whether or not to trust her with the truth. Sharing secrets was not something Adam did easily, and Maeve wasn't going to push him. Adam was a Draco, yet he had proven his loyalty to the rest of them time and time again. Maeve had lost count of how many times he had saved people's lives. And if he thought keeping their destination secret was the best plan, then she was okay with it too.

"We're going to my home," he said softly.

Surprise flashed through Maeve. She knew that Adam had been alive for hundreds of years, so "home" could have a variety of interpretations for him. "What does that mean?"

A rare smile crossed Adam's face. "You've heard the story of my time with the Draco?"

She hadn't been on the plane when Adam's nature had been revealed to the rest of the group. Chris had explained it to her shortly after their rescue from Edmonds. Maeve had never discussed it directly with Adam, though.

"You were born among the Draco. And you and your sister fought. You refused to kill her, and so they thought that you did not have a cold enough heart to be the leader of the Draco."

There was no emotion in Adam's voice when he spoke.

"Yes, that's true. I was beaten. I was chased. I threw myself into a river as a last desperate attempt to escape."

It was so hard to imagine. "How old were you?"

"About four or five."

Gasping as the picture of a small blond child running desperately in the dark to escape monsters trying to harm him popped into her mind. "That must've been awful."

"It was. But it was also the best thing that ever happened to me. The current took me out to sea. Days later, I landed on the northeastern coast of Norway. My family had been out fishing. It was their annual trip to the coast. They found me and took me with them to their home. I lived with them in the mountains of Norway in the area now known as Geiranger."

He smiled. "It's beautiful country. Rolling hills with the houses hidden amongst them. You can go for days without seeing anyone."

"It sounds beautiful," she said.

"It is. And no one knows about it," Adam assured her.

"Not even Tilda?" She asked.

Adam's mouth flatlined for the barest of seconds before he nodded. "She knows. But she would never reveal it. She would go to her death before she would."

That was one of the most interesting things about him. He was, in many ways, an incredibly old-fashioned man in his sense of duty, loyalty, and love. She supposed that was an accurate assessment, being he wasn't from this time.

"What about other members of your family? They must know about the house."

She felt the sadness before he spoke. "No," he said softly. "The last of them passed away in the early twentieth century. It was a plane crash. There are no more of my family left."

Picturing Tilda, Maeve spoke quietly. "There's one."

With a quick look at her, Adam nodded. "Yes I suppose there is."

"Is there any way for them to tie the house to you?" She asked.

He shook his head again. "No. It's under my Norwegian name. I've created a false trail of descendants for ownership. The house passed from one generation to the next. No one knows that name anymore. There'd be no reason for them to go looking for it. And it is extremely off grid."

Suddenly feeling exhausted, Maeve settled into her seat a little more tightly, "That sounds perfect right now," she said her eyes closing.

"It's okay, Maeve. We're safe for now. Get some sleep. I won't let anything happen to you. Any of you," Adam said.

Too tired to reply, Maeve nodded. But she believed with all of her heart that he spoke the truth.

CHAPTER 3

Geiranger, Norway
One week later

Maeve stepped out of the converted barn and closed the door softly. Sammy was resting. His injury was healing fast. She knew that he wouldn't stay there much longer, maybe another day or two at most. She could feel his need to get away. She wasn't sure if it was because that was ingrained in him or because he just needed to get away from them.

She hoped it was just part of his nature.

She had to admit, she was fascinated by him. His skin was a light maroon, but she'd noticed that it had lightened considerably since he'd been in their care. She and Greg hypothesized that the color might be a reaction to the sun. And when the sun was removed from the equation, it became less vibrant, more human. The human aspect of the creature was hard to miss. His facial features were definitely human, especially his amber eyes.

In the week that he'd been with them, though, he hadn't said a word. She wasn't even sure if vocalization was part of his communication process. It was entirely possible that he did not speak because no one had ever spoken with him during those critical years speech can develop. Humans who were not spoken to as young children never developed the capability for speech either.

And Maeve had no doubt that he was yet another hybrid from Area 51. He seemed older than the other releasees, but maybe that was just part of his intelligence shining through and making him seem more mature, more intelligent than the other creatures she'd seen.

A light wind ruffled her hair. She wrapped the heavy blue-and-white sweater around her. The air had gotten much cooler, even in the bright sunlight. She knew winter wasn't far off. They were at Adam's family home in Norway. Maeve hadn't known what to expect when Adam said that they were heading to his home. She'd pictured an ancient, decrepit cabin.

She was pleasantly surprised to find an incredibly updated home on a high hill. They were 500, maybe 600, feet above sea level in an incredibly remote location that required ATVs to reach.

Adam told her he and Tilda had been coming here for a few years, setting the place up in case they needed it as a hideout. No one else in R.I.S.E. knew about it.

Electricity was provided via solar panels on the roof and more solar panels that lined a field half a mile away. Heat was provided by geothermal springs. A well and a rainwater containment system met all of their water needs. They were completely off the grid. It had sounded incredibly rustic when Adam had described it. Maeve had held her breath when they finally came around the bend on the ATVs, not sure what to expect.

And her mind had been blown, but in the best of possible ways. The cabin was two stories tall and made of stucco and wood. The doorways and windows were framed by hewn logs, and inside, all the doorways were made from rounded trees entwined together into an arch. The floor-to-ceiling windows inside offered a breathtaking view of the fjord. It was like living in a fairytale where everything was lush and green.

But most important, there were no other people anywhere around. In the week that they had been there, they hadn't seen another soul. With a population of two hundred, Adam had been right about how isolated Geiranger was. But that would only last for another few months. In the spring, the tourists would arrive. Nearly a million people would visit this part of the world between May and September. But that problem was a few months off.

Now Maeve stared out at the fjord with her arms wrapped around herself and breathed in deep. She could get used to this.

She felt his presence before she saw him. She glanced over her shoulder as Alvie walked toward her. Only three and a half feet tall, with a large wide face that came to a point at his chin and gray skin tone, Alvie would never be mistaken for a human, even though he was part human. But most people wouldn't look beyond the abnormally shaped head and the disproportionately large dark eyes. If they did, they would see a soul that was incredibly kind and incredibly generous. He was the type of human they should all strive to be.

Maeve held out a hand. Alvie gently grasped it with his long thin fingers with their bony knobs. Love wafted through her. Alvie communicated through emotions. He always had. The two of them had grown up together, and Maeve hadn't really known any other way of living, not until she was much older. So she'd accepted Alvie from the moment she'd met him. And that bond had only grown stronger over the years.

But even without that bond, she would be able to tell that something was wrong. And she didn't have to ask what it was.

"We'll find a way to get them back," she promised.

Alvie looked up into her face, searching not just her facial expressions but her mind, to see if she was telling the truth or just trying to make him feel better.

Crackle and Pop had been seriously injured in the attack on the R.I.S.E. base. Agaren had taken them to the Council's base located on the moon. Chris had made the heartbreaking decision to allow them to go. It had been the only way to save their lives. In the weeks since then, they hadn't heard from Agaren.

But Maeve had to believe that Crackle and Pop were alive and well. She did not know the tall alien well. But for some reason, she did trust him. He would not take Pop and Crackle unless he truly believed he could save their lives. And she was holding on to that.

But their recovery was not Maeve's only concern. Even if the Council was able to save Pop and Crackle, would they consider it a priority to return them to Maeve and the others? Would they take the time they had with two of the triplets to examine them or even just hold on to them for a while until they felt they'd learned enough before they returned them?

The lifespan of the Council could be hundreds of years. For them, years would be no time at all. Whereas for the triplets, each hour would feel like a day, each day a week, each week a year. Maeve missed them so much her heart ached. And she knew that her pain was nothing compared to Snap's.

Snap, the remaining member of the triplets, was struggling at going from being part of the trio to standing on her own two feet. Her entire short life, she'd had Pop and Crackle by her side. Spending these last two weeks without them had been killing her. She'd become more listless and despondent. They'd all tried to get her to feel better, but nothing really worked. The only one who seemed to be able to get through to her was Sammy.

Snap spent a great deal of her time with Sammy and Iggy. She took comfort in the presence of both of them. And Maeve was just thankful that the two of them were around.

A picture of the moon drifted into Maeve's mind. She squeezed Alvie's hand and nodded. "Yes, there's a full moon tonight. We'll stay outside and watch it, okay?"

Alvie leaned into her with a sigh. Maeve wrapped her arms around him, wishing there was more that she could do to comfort him. Truth be told, she wished there was more she could do to comfort herself. But for now, watching the full moon was as close to Pop and Crackle as they were going to get.

Maeve looked up at the sky. *I'll get you back. Somehow I'll get you back.*

FACT OR FICTION

The creation of *R.I.S.E.* was created with that aid of numerous facts that I have come across in my readings. When I write these types of books, I tend to read a ridiculous amount before I even start writing. All the facts found within *R.I.S.E.* are taken from multiple sources.

Below I discuss some of the facts used in the development of *R.I.S.E* and when possible provide one link to at least get you started if you are looking for more information.

Now on to the facts!

Lizard People. I have mentioned the lizard people in other books. It is true that four percent of the population did report believing that the U.S. government is controlled by lizard people. It is perhaps safe to say that some of those answers were made in jest. However, when it comes to alien abductions, the story is less easily explained.

Well known within the UFO literature is the image of abductions at the hands of little grey men. However, there are numerous reports of a second group abducting humans: beings with lizard heads but human shaped bodies. While the greys are reported to be cold and clinical, the reports of the lizard people are filled with menace and a focus on creating a hybrid between the human race and their own.

It all sounds insane, right? Well, it gets stranger. The story about the search for lizard people under Los Angeles is actually true.

In 1933, George Warren Shufelt attempt to excavate a rumored city of the lizard people built some 5,000 years earlier. It was not a lofty archaeological endeavor on Shufelt's part. He was interested in the gold rumored to be found amongst the tunnels. Alas, he ran out of money before he found anything.

Semi-Identical Twins. Semi- identical twins are actually a relatively new classification of twins. Fraternal twins share 50 percent of their genes. Identical twins share 100 percent. Semi-identical share between 50 and 100 percent. In semi-identical twins, one egg is fertilized by two sperm. Three sets of chromosomes are then split amongst two twins. There have only been two documented cases.

A Hollow Moon. Is the moon hollow? The questions seems right up there with whether or not the moon is made of cheese. Yet, there is some evidence to suggest that at least part of the moon is hollow. During the Apollo 13 mission, the spent Intrepid was dropped back to the moon. Unexpectedly, when it impacted a huge gong sounded and the moon continued to vibrate like a bell for over an hour.

Follow up crashes of lunar modules from Apollo 13 and 14 revealed the same phenomena, the moon sometimes vibrating for three hours! The results were decidedly unpredicted. And many have come to the conclusion that at least some parts of the moon must be hollow to result in such a phenomena.

Secret Space Agency. There have been rumors about a secret space agency for decades. I have no knowledge of a secondary space program and the creation of one for *R.I.S.E.* was simply an extrapolation from these conspiracy theories.

Wernher Von Braun. The information on Wernher Von

FACT OR FICTION

Braun is accurate to the best of my ability, with one exception: he did not create a secondary space program. He was however the mastermind behind NASA, the US rocket program and the mission to reach the moon. In addition, he created films with Disney and spoke about manned trips to Mars. He also had a good rapport with JFK and did have a dinner scheduled with him which never took place due to JFK's assassination.

Space Angels. Back in 1984, Russian cosmonauts reported a strange orange mist engulfing their space station. When they looked outside, they saw seven eighty-foot tall winged humanoid creatures with what they described as peaceful expressions on their faces. The winged beings stayed outside the craft for ten minutes before disappearing.

Days later, more cosmonauts joined the crew. And once again, an orange mist covered the ship. This time, six cosmonauts saw the enormous 'space angels.' In some reporting, the cosmonauts speak of a telepathic connection with the angels who warned about the violent nature of humanity, and the need for Earth's inhabitants to turn to a more peaceful existence. In others, there is no report of any contact beyond a feeling of peace and tranquility experienced by the cosmonauts.

Britain's Roswell. The Rendelsham Forest Incident is in many many ways Britain's Roswell. The UFO was allegedly tracked by radar and Kensington did report seeing a craft with strange symbols on it. He also reported receiving a series of zeros and ones in his mind when he touched the craft. There are also many who doubt it ever happened. Like Roswell, the truth will never probably be known.

Thank you again for reading *R.I.S.E.* I hope you enjoyed reading it as much as I enjoyed writing it. The next book in the series is called S.A.V.E.

With great appreciation,

R.D.

ABOUT THE AUTHOR

Author, Criminologist, Terrorism Expert, Jeet Kune Do Black Sash, Runner, Dog Lover.

Amazon best-selling author R.D. Brady writes supernatural and science fiction thrillers. Her thrillers include ancient mysteries, unusual facts, non-stop action, and fierce women with heart.

Prior to beginning her writing career, RD Brady was a criminologist who specialized in life-course criminology and international terrorism. She's lectured and written numerous academic articles on the genetic influence on criminal behavior, factors that influence terrorist ideology, and delinquent behavior formation.

After visiting counter-terrorism units in Israel, RD returned home with a sabbatical in front of her and decided to write that book she'd been thinking about. Four years later she left academia with the publication of her first book, *The Belial Stone*, and hasn't looked back.